COP OUT

R.W. Jones lived in Kenya for nineteen years working as an educationalist. Now, after a short spell in Britain, he lives and works in the Leeward Islands. A Welshman with the usual Welsh passions (beer and rugby football), he has played rugby for Aberystwyth University and Kenya and is an active referee. He is married, and he and his wife have three children.

D0595660

by the same author

SAVING GRACE

COP OUT

R. W. Jones

FONTANA/Collins

First published in Great Britain by
Michael Joseph Ltd 1987
First published in Fontana Paperbacks 1988

Copyright © R.W. Jones 1987

Printed and bound in Great Britain
by William Collins Sons & Co, Ltd, Glasgow

CONDITIONS OF SALE
This book is sold subject to the condition
that it shall not, by way of trade or otherwise,
be lent, re-sold, hired out or otherwise circulated
without the publisher's prior consent in any form of
binding or cover other than that in which it is
published and without a similar condition
including this condition being imposed
on the subsequent purchaser

For Graham and Sue,
in acknowledgement of an
unrepayable debt.

PROLOGUE

THE MAN shifted, a tense shadow in the waiting dimness. Edgy, before the act, however many times he'd rehearsed. Weak light and a grim location: anything might happen. Easy, son. She's on cue, be here any second, you've seen her often enough. Too often. The stench sickened him; stale fry-ups, ripe garbage, and old bold tomcat.

Begloved and clumsy with it, he hauled the helmet on. Not your actual balaclava, more a black bag with holes for the eyes and mouth; nightgear. Scratchy wool and a familiar whiff of his own sweat soothed him. He was faceless now, cold eyes and bared teeth glinting. He had seen the effect mirrored in other faces: gibbering horror. The knowledge lent him comfort. Calmly, looking the part, he picked his way soft-soled and sure-footed to the head of the alley, where she would come.

A clatter of high heels woke the hunter in him. She hurried past, blonde and white-coated, gazing straight ahead. He followed like a faithful, menacing hound. The silence throbbed. There was artifice here; the lonely bright glamour, the lilting walk of the actress, and the whole damn world holding its breath. Yet he was committed, pledged to the script, getting his moves just right. The scene was playing; no way back.

She passed out of brilliance towards a pre-ordained spot. Her coat was a target, her hair a beacon. No trouble, after all. He walked taller, stretching his stride. She would hear, and that was all right, too. Made for a better pay-off. He watched her falter and glance back. Perfect.

Then, for no reason, it was coming apart. She turned much too quickly, saw him far too soon. An unnatural, almost casual response, not nearly enough terror. He lunged forward anyway, letting the blade flare in failing light; mauling her, dragging her onward, screaming the words into her face.

'Cut!'

A sound short and distant, laden with weariness. The girl broke free, furious. 'Here, that hurts!'

He mumbled an insincere apology. Lights blazed, one of the camera crew complained bitterly. The director approached, frustration in a sheepskin coat. 'C'mon, girl, give us a bit of impact. It's the Ripper you got there, not Rhett bloody Butler! Fifteen minutes, right?' He stomped away, trading insults with the technicians.

The girl glanced up in appeal. 'Gives me the willies, that mask. Sorry.'

He shrugged. No point in making things worse. She touched his arm, anxious and vulnerable.

'Rhett bloody *who*?'

'Butler. Before our time. Forget it.'

She flashed him a grateful smile and went off to repair her make-up.

Sipping coffee, struggling to rebuild the mood, he stared morosely at the clapperboard. For take five, read take six. The titles stood out sharply – *Crimewatch UK*.

He strolled towards the grizzled figure in a trenchcoat who hovered behind one of the arc-lamps; a technician, probably.

'*Christ*, it's chilly!' he grumbled. 'I hate outdoor takes in winter, 'specially with a finicky director.'

'My fault, I'm afraid, sir. The Force demands accuracy.'

'You're police?'

'Retired. Professional adviser, they say. Beefs up the pension, know what I mean?'

'Done a bit of nightwork yourself, then.'

'Not half!' The actor swigged more tepid coffee, only mildly interested. 'Accuracy's important, is it?'

'Vital. Every viewer's a potential witness; we're out to jog their memories. Surprising what'll do it, too. The flutter of a coat, a frightened face in the lamplight, footfalls down a lonely

2

alley. That's why we make the reconstruction as real as we can – and insist on your actual location.'

'You mean it happened *here*?'

'Near enough, sir.' The old man's breath plumed like silver smoke in the dazzling beam. The actor shuddered, not just from the cold.

'Good God, he could be watching us right now!'

'You never know, with nutters.' A low and curiously menacing chuckle. 'He'd have a nasty turn, seeing you like that.'

The actor reached up, touching the wool of the balaclava and forcing a tight smile. Behind him, the director was bawling for action again. 'Keeps the ears warm, anyhow.'

'Calm the girl down, I would,' called the ex-policeman. 'Then we can sleep safe in our beds!'

It's all right for you, mate, the actor thought. *She's* about to be raped, and for the sixth time tonight.

CHAPTER ONE

'RIGHT OLD knees-up, was it, after I'd gone?'

A flat Thursday at the nick, smalltalk and typewriters. Feeling distinctly second-hand himself, Evans fixed the speaker with a jaundiced eye. On the nest all night, Beddoes, and still bright as ninepence. Duw, the resilience of youth.

''Ome before you, boyo. How d'you manage it, I wonder?'

'No sweat. Early to bed, early to rise.' An authentic Beddoes leer, brimming with innuendo.

'Stayed over, didn't I. Does a fair breakfast, that Gloria. Clever with 'er 'ands.'

'So that's how you keep it up.'

'Better to wear out than rust, mate. Tell us about the party.'

Nothing to tell, really. A farewell for Superintendent Smythe, a chance to suss out the replacement. Speeches mostly boring, the Brass scratching each other's backs in public. Packet soup, roast and two veg, insipid trifle and cheap wine. Cocktails and coptalk, not a decent pint in sight. Some knees-up. Evans had eaten unwisely and mixed his drinks; he had to take it out on someone.

'Want to walk soft, you do. Your absence was remarked.'

'Leave it out, uncle! 'Oo cares about the errand boy?'

'Smythe does. "Regards to Sergeant Beddoes," he says. "Found something better to do, no doubt!"'

'Got that much right, then.'

'A good Super, Smythe. He'll be missed.'

Beddoes made violin gestures. 'You'll 'ave me in tears in a minute. 'Ow's the new guy?'

In private and on home ground, Evans spoke his mind:

first impressions. 'Talks nice. Educated, see; a college boy.'

Beddoes caught the tone at once. 'Since when was that an offence? Could use a bit of intellect round 'ere.'

'Speak for yourself, you. Too smooth for my taste. Burt Reynolds, supersleuth.'

''Andsome feller, all right.'

Evans lapsed into Valleys dialect. 'Trims the moustache daily, 'aircut regular. Image-conscious, then.' He paused, considering. 'Let's not be hasty. Could be more to him.'

'Oh yeah? Like what?'

'Only speaker worth listening to, fair play. All the accents: Billy Connolly, Ian Paisley, does 'em a treat. Falling about, we were.'

A sarcastic nod from Beddoes. 'A PR man, that's nice. Always fancied me pitcher in the papers.'

'Playboy of the month, is it? Like a bit of quiet, I do. Publicity's for pop stars.'

Steadying, Beddoes broached the vital issue. 'Question is, what sort of *copper* is he?'

'Aye well, we'll find out; tomorrow. We've been granted audience.'

'What, all of us?'

'Inspectors and above, mind. Errand boys is off.'

'My diamonds, Richard. The only thing I asked. And you *forgot*?'

Richard Wilson was shaving; the tricky inside curve of his moustache. He closed his mouth firmly, avoiding soap and confrontation.

'You did it deliberately. You don't *want* me to wear them.'

The accusation carried clearly from the bedroom and he ignored it, slicing careful furrows through the foam.

'Your silly pride; all because *Daddy* bought them. Really!'

Born to wealth and privilege, Gina saw no virtue in unnecessary sacrifice. From the beginning she'd warned, 'Policeman's wife I may be, but we don't have to live like pigs.' The choice of words disturbed him; her mother too had a cruel tongue. Under extreme duress, he'd accepted the house as a wedding present. Next came her 'little runabout' – brand new, of course – and, most recently, the diamonds. His protests were blandly dismissed. 'Nonsense, old boy. Our only daughter. You don't begrudge us, surely?'

Hardly. But it went against his instincts, both personal and professional. In his world, bought men were beneath contempt, and living beyond one's means attracted automatic suspicion.

Distracted, he lost concentration and nicked his chin. 'Blast!'

'I don't see what *you've* got to swear about!'

'Cut myself.'

'Oh *marvellous*! A fine start – me dowdy and you plastered!'

He rooted among her perfumes for the styptic pencil. 'I've said I'm sorry,' he muttered, wincing at the small pain. 'The bank was closed.'

'You should've sent a uniform. What could be safer?'

Correct jargon, but she made it thoroughly demeaning.

'They're not actually messengers, darling.'

This mild sally, and the respite it created, cheered him immensely. He made free with the aftershave, surveying himself critically. He counted good looks an asset, freely granted and assiduously preserved. It was, he reckoned, his only vanity. Time for gallantry.

'You couldn't look dowdy if you tried. Your escort's no slouch, either.'

He opened the door, venturing a snatch of song. 'We'll be the finest couple in the Ea-ster Per-rade! Look, no blood.'

But she wasn't mollified, merely resting between rounds.

'For goodness sake! Harry's buying, it's bound to be somewhere chic.'

'Fair enough. A proper celebration.'

She seized the opening gladly. 'I should think so after Wednesday's fiasco. Stodgy policemen, dull little wives, and the *food*! Party, indeed; more like an ordeal!'

'Call of duty, darling.'

'The last, I hope. You've got your promotion. Now you can please yourself.'

Sometimes she seemed startlingly naive; as if all coppers were supermen in Savile Row suits, hobnobbing with the mighty. For minutes they moved in silence, passing one another between wardrobes, as reserved as strangers on the Tube.

Struggling with cufflinks, he tried a conciliatory tone. 'You won't suffer shoptalk tonight; Clare will see to that.'

'Touting all the gossip from darkest Sussex. We *are* honoured.'

'Miaow.'

'Come, Richard. You don't have exclusive claims on scandal. *Everyone* knows about Harry and Clare.'

'Really?'

Suddenly Gina was enjoying herself, alight with pleasurable malice. 'Harry's city-wise: wheeling, dealing and fornication. Clare manages the country seat: hunting and agriculture. Division of labour. Occasionally, their paths cross: in due course, the dynasty will prosper.'

Aware of this arrangement, Richard had demanded Clare's presence. These days, his public contacts had to be respectable; even the rich and powerful ones.

Her pique temporarily forgotten, Gina developed the theme. 'My grandfather set no store by love. Glands and moonshine, he called it. Marriage, he believed, was an important commercial transaction between *parents*. You'd be surprised how often it happens; and works. Take the Mortimers. Harry prefers younger women: so does Clare. The perfect match.'

He hadn't known *that*. Intrigued, he asked, 'So how does the dynasty prosper?'

At last a genuine smile, warm and dazzling. 'When the time comes, Clare will grit her teeth and think of England. It shouldn't take long, Harry gets plenty of practice. Issue springs forth, the families rejoice and everyone back to their own beds. Don't look so pained, darling. That's what made Britain great.'

She was sending him up, mocking his middle-class morality; but gently. This is what she missed most of all, he realised. *People* were her consuming passion; people of her own ilk. For the first time, he understood the full extent of her sacrifice, and it couldn't be measured in material terms. A moment of unique insight and rare tenderness.

In cocktail gear and warpaint, she looked cool, fair and slender; an aloof English rose. Naked and in private, she was full-bodied and wholly unselfconscious, with an earthy sexuality which surprised and delighted him.

She caught his eye and smiled lazily. 'Now, Richard, we're late already. Be good.'

'I always am.'

He settled for one yielding, open-mouthed kiss which left him weak-kneed and semi-erect. After eight years of marriage, she still had that power. He pulled himself together, quite unreasonably happy. 'Right. Let's go and do the town.'

Mid-morning coffee in the common room, a brief truce between academic skirmishes. Sara Holroyd was hearing, in private amusement, of not-so-secret undergraduate affairs.

'Rodney was hopeless, Saturday. Twelve pints and an hour of slurred apologies.'

Jenny Price speaking; slim, dark and intense, the *femme fatale* of fourth-year languages. Rodney, a rugger hero, was renowned for generous proportions and erratic performance.

'Boredom and masculine inadequacy,' continued Jenny, apeing a despised lecturer, 'no wonder the place is crawling with lesies.'

'Ditch him, Jen. There's a gorgeous fresher in drams, simply exploding with virginity.' An aspiring actress, Fran Moore frequently baited Jenny, her only serious rival in the campus glamour stakes. Two of the lesser lights weighed in, tales of moonlit fumbling and improbable bodily contortions.

Sara let it wash over her. Had she remembered her Pill this morning? He would call today, the familiar pleas and the usual convoluted directions. She'd been sleeping with him for over a year, a married man with a comfortable income and rather beautiful hands. Nothing permanent, naturally. A steady relationship which lifted her lifestyle above the breadline, and gave her something to look forward to at weekends.

At fifteen, she'd watched the dying convulsions of her parents' marriage; the trauma almost cost her her 'O' levels. Colder and harder at seventeen, she sat down and mapped out the future. A degree in modern languages, another year to get secretarial qualifications, and the world would be her oyster. She was well on course, near the top of her year and free of commitments. In this company, she felt sophisticated and very mature.

Rebuffed by Jenny, Fran was stalking new quarry. 'Why so quiet, Sara? Nothing to report?'

'You know me, sweetie. Busy with the books.'

Fran sniffed, haughty and disbelieving. 'Hiding your light. That lovely hair, the fragile, vulnerable look. They'd fall over for you, at the hop.'

'They fall over anyway, at the hop.'

A neat touch, winning sympathetic laughter; but Fran was not so easily diverted. 'You're putting us on, darling. Bright eyes and a bushy tail; who's the lucky man?'

'No one you know.' Nor ever will, she thought. Charles would remain private until *she* decided otherwise; and that would be for some time yet.

And as Fran turned away, thwarted, Sara savoured the warmth of inner contentment. Nice to know where you're going, nice to be in control ...

Nine and very full of herself, Philippa Elliot – Pippa to friends – was feeling just a wee bit naughty. Sunday morning, warm, sunny, and only the early starlings for company. She'd collected the paper, exactly as Daddy asked. The change rested safely in her Strawberry Shortcake purse. 'Come straight back,' Mummy had said, and she meant to, really she did. But the empty playground was so tempting; they wouldn't miss her for five minutes, surely.

She noticed him almost at once; he seemed to come from nowhere. A big, silent man, leaning on the gate, watching her. An audience. She began to show off, flinging her legs up high, squealing with delight. To finish, the special trick she'd just perfected. As the swing reached the top of its arc, she slid clear and landed lightly, skirt billowing. That spoilt it. The purse flew out and she had to bend for the scattered coins. Bother! She shoved the paper under her arm and marched crossly to the gate.

'Hello,' he said. 'What's your name?' A rich, deep voice, merry dark eyes and an easy grin.

Even so, she answered briskly, 'I'm Philippa Elliot and Mummy says I shouldn't talk to strangers.'

The grin broadened. He opened the gate, bowing as she'd seen it done in old movies. It was funny, really. She couldn't hide her smile.

He strolled along beside her. 'Quite right, too. But I'm not strange, I'd like to be your friend. May I call you Pippa?' He was very polite; Mummy would say he was 'charming'. But she strode out across the park swinging the paper importantly.

'I've been for Daddy's *Telegraph*,' she said, proud of the new word.

'Daddy's a lucky man. Would you care for a bon-bon?' He stopped as he spoke, offering a paper bag. Blue and gold wrappers, toffee eclairs; yummy. Briefly, politeness warred with prudence. He seemed a nice man, she could see the main road from here, and she did love toffee eclairs.

'Well, thank you.'

'Close your eyes and open your mouth.'

She'd done this before, humouring grown-ups. She shrugged and obeyed, hearing the rustle of paper, tasting the milky smoothness, feeling his hand, warm and strong and gentle on her neck. She took a wary half-step backwards, munching cautiously. 'Mm. Lovely.'

'I have plenty more. Do you like games, Pippa?'

'Wha' sor' of games?'

His face changed, kind of sad and distant. 'Children's games. The sort you can't play, when you're older.'

His voice had gone thick and blurry. She edged a little further away, and he followed eagerly.

'I know a very good one. It's called "Ticklebum".'

The name intrigued her. It sounded funny and naughty at the same time. 'How d'you play tha'?'

'Easily. Just how it sounds.'

Pippa stopped and looked straight up at him. The toffee was finished; she could talk clearly again. Firmly, she said, 'That's a bath game. You can't play it outdoors.'

He nodded quickly. 'But, of course! We would go some-where quieter.' He held the sweets invitingly.

Pippa thought carefully. There was something odd here. Adults didn't *bother* about games like this. His eyes looked strange, he was staring right through her. Around them, the park was hushed and completely deserted; the birds had stopped singing. She felt lonely and afraid. She didn't want to play, and he was going to make her.

The idea came suddenly; she tried to say it calmly. 'I live in that house.' She pointed at random. ''Spect Daddy's watching us.' She took a quick breath for the big lie. 'He's a policeman.'

It was like seeing someone wake up. He blinked, stopped, pushed the toffees into a pocket. And stood his ground, waving, as she walked on. 'Another day, perhaps. Goodbye, Pippa.'

She hurried home, meaning to explain straight away, but they didn't seem to notice her anxiety. Mummy looked flushed and very pretty, and Daddy made a silly joke about loving his big girls. She *would* tell them about Ticklebum, Pippa promised herself; tomorrow.

CHAPTER TWO

IT BEGAN, they would later agree, with a bizarre phone call via
Warner, the desk sergeant. Beddoes was alone at the time,
minding the store while the new superintendent held court
upstairs.

'Mornin', Roy. Evans in?'

Confined and fretful, Beddoes reacted tartly. 'Inspector
Evans to you, mate.'

'Oho. Touchy this mornin'. I'll start again then. Might I
beseech a moment of the Inspector's precious time?'

''E's up the mountain. Back soon, bearing wisdom writ in
stone.'

'Yer wot?'

'Wilson's first sermon today. Don't they tell you anything?'

'Mm. Awkward.'

'What's up, won't the 'elp do?'

A thoughtful pause. Warner was thorough but slow.
'Dunno, Roy, it's dodgy. There's this nun on the line, gotta
sex problem . . .'

'Give over, Jack! What kind of mug d'you take me for?'

Suddenly, Warner was on his dignity, very shirty indeed.
'Less of the sauce, *sergeant*. Doing a favour, wasn't I, but if
that's the attitude I'll pass it straight on to . . .'

''Old on, 'old on. What favour?'

'Standin' orders, sonny, *Smythe's* orders. Give Evans a
breather, 'e says. Keep 'im off the sensitive stuff, let 'im earn a
few easy 'ousemarks. Didn't know *that*, did you, smartarse?'

Beddoes' turn to pause, as the implications of this sunk in.
The procession of low-key cases, tarts and touts and pick-

pockets; the growing sense of boredom and futility. No wonder they'd had a humdrum year: no wonder Warner was breathing heavy.

'Listen, I'm grovelling. Sorry I spoke, OK? So what's with the nun?'

Warner sounded somewhat appeased, and more than a little perplexed. 'The vapours, probably; you know, aah, men. She won't say, not to me, anyhow. Wants Inspector Evans, asked for 'im by name. Look, Roy, Smythe's gone, the new man's not *witting*. What the 'ell, I thought. Give the lads a break.'

'Good of you, uncle, I'll tell 'im. Put 'er on, then.'

Still Warner hesitated. 'We-ee-ll ... take it easy. Don't you move a muscle till Evans gets back. And Roy ...'

'Yeah?'

'Keep me out of it.'

'Sorry, 'oo's speaking? Didn't catch the name.'

Warner's approving laughter faded. A click, a buzz; then a soft and lovely Irish brogue. 'Would that be the Inspector, finally?'

'In conference, I'm afraid. Can I help? Beddoes, Sergeant. I'm 'is oppo.'

'Are you now. And what kind of animal might that be?'

Silently damning his own lapse, Beddoes adopted a more public manner. 'His assistant.'

'And another sergeant, to boot. I don't know; it's awfully young you're sounding. Do you have experience in these affairs?'

Couldn't say, yet. Better reassure her, though. 'Sure. Don't worry about that, er ...'

What do you call a nun with a sex problem? he wondered feverishly: Mother? Madam? Christ, not madam! She seemed to grasp his difficulty, coming crisply to the rescue.

'Sister Hyacinth speaking, Head of the Convent School. You'll surely know of us; everyone does.' The pride in her voice gave way to anxiety. 'There's a man about the place these past few days. A tormented soul, no doubt, and may the Dear pity him. You'll maybe think me an ould woman, but he's putting us in fear for the girls.'

14

Beddoes opened a notebook, nodding to himself. Warner had it right; a touch of the overprotectives.

'OK, sister, what's he done? Dates, times and places, please.'

'*Done*, sergeant? Would I be sitting bletherin' had he done anything at all? He's just *here*, don't you see, watching. So silent, so still, so ... *intent*.'

Beddoes sighed softly. A peeper, then, and a pig to nail in court. 'We'll need details and a description. I'll send a uniform round.'

Her exasperation came seething down the line. 'You'll do no such thing! The wee hint of a uniform will see him away. Heavens, man, do you not understand? It's *here*, he is; sure, can't I see him with my own eyes? Listen, I'm wanting the Inspector, alone and inconspicuous. And *now*, sergeant.'

He was acutely conscious of her authority; and the weight of his own dilemma. Don't move a muscle, Warner had advised – where in God's name was Evans?

'Twenty minutes, sister,' he promised. 'I'll have someone there, plain clothes and low profile. Can you hold him till then?'

A low-pitched chuckle, surprisingly earthy. 'As it happens, arrangements have been made. Riveted he'll be, and for a while yet. Don't let that delay you, though.'

It didn't. He sweated on Evans for ten more minutes. Then, surrendering to impulse and opportunity, he scribbled a terse note and left. Like Warner said, give the lads a break.

Winter's coming, Evans realised, reading the skyline outside. A glint of steel in the blue, scudding clouds, and a wind with fangs. Tough on the uniforms, mind; back to terrace warfare already.

Plenty of hot air in the Super's den, though. Wilson, briefing the inspectors, high-falutin stuff and not a smile in sight. Well, what d'you expect first thing Friday: cabaret?

'We're afflicted with tunnel vision,' Wilson was saying. 'Locate the clues, follow the spoor, apprehend the offender. It's a sterile tradition – we need a fresh approach. In university circles, it's called holism.' He paused, eyebrows aloft, for the obvious question. Nobody obliged. Seasoned coppers, these, men who knew how to wait. Apparently unperturbed, Wilson offered enlightenment. 'It means consider the whole picture, see things in context, think yourselves into the criminal mind. Once you understand the villain, you can predict how and where he will strike.'

Duw, there's novel, Evans thought. Been doing it for years.

Very natty, the Superintendent, mind, in his black leather jacket. Not one you'd get from Marks, either: a tailored Italian job. The Force of the future – and Wilson took up the unspoken cue. 'We have to move with the times.' A touch of theatre, a practised flourish of the hand. 'Hence the changes you will no doubt have noticed.'

Evans had noticed, all right. Used to be Smythe's preserve, this, subtly reflecting the character of the man. Now it was a shrine to the great god hi-tech, alien and aloof. Grey metal, black plastic and smoky perspex; no one lived here anymore.

'Faultless information is the key to successful prosecution,' Wilson declared, as heads dipped in homage. 'And modern technology removes the drudgery. This monitor' – another deft gesture – 'is on line to Central Records. Their data bank is at our disposal night and day.' They craned forward in unison, gawping at the blank screen. Aye, watch the birdie, lads. Ask nicely and it'll sing 'Cwm Rhondda'. 'So, armed with holism and instant access, we are able not only to contain crime but actually to prevent it.'

Amazing, really; stood up there like some TV soap ham playing top cop, the hard men eating out of his hand. And who was he? A college boy with a mission. Dangerous mixture, that, youth and fervour. Surreptitiously, Evans scanned the room for fellow sceptics; in vain. Fat Marchant from Traffic seemed comatose. Wainwright of Narcotics toyed longingly with a cold pipe. You'll have to wait, boyo. Smoking can damage your health: sir says. Come back, Smythe, all is forgiven.

In full command, Wilson sailed regally on. 'I'll be relying on you for initiative, local knowledge and individuality – qualities I'm confident you possess in full measure. In return, I expect dedication, commitment and total loyalty.'

Puff and a pep-talk, transparent as gin; and as potent, judging from their expressions. He wasn't finished yet, either.

'I propose to make this room the nerve centre of the Manor. There will be regular meetings, Mondays at ten. Updates on all live case files, enough copies to go round. Everyone in the picture, left and right hands properly co-ordinated. No loopholes, no duplication and no private enterprise. Any questions?'

No takers; the challenge hung, unanswered. 'Come along,' Wilson urged. 'This is your chance to clear the air.'

Say nothing, Evans counselled himself. Doesn't care for dissent, he's just told you. But *someone* had to say it. Reluctantly he mumbled, 'One small point, sir.'

Wilson's gaze hardened, but his response was elaborately courteous. 'Ah, Inspector Evans. What's on your mind?'

A gentle Valleys tone, to soothe the sting. 'Only wondering, mind, with all this co-ordination and communication. I mean, when do we get to nick Chummy?'

Didn't fancy it a bit, anyone could tell. Smart sidestep though, passed it off lovely. A wide grin, a dismissive shrug. 'We're going to get on famously, inspector – I *do* appreciate the lighter touch. Meanwhile, let's work out the details, shall we?' And for half an hour they did that, civil as you please. It all sounded very logical and convincing.

As the meeting broke up and the others trooped out, Wilson drifted casually past. 'Don't rush off, Evans. I'd like a private word. Make yourself comfortable.'

He closed the door and sauntered to the picture window: the window from which, on a clear day, you could see across town to the bend in the river. Parked at the desk, Evans saw only sky. It still looked wintry.

At last, the altered setting took on familiarity. In his day, Smythe, too, had favoured window-gazing. Course he did, stupid; didn't have to bollock you to your face.

'Not so long ago,' Wilson began, 'Grace Yardley killed a man in cold blood – in full view of the TV cameras. And *you* took her part.'

'He was a nutter,' protested Evans. 'He raped and murdered her daughter!'

'Your conduct ill became a senior police officer, even so.'

'I was with her through it all. From the day the kid went missing, while we were hunting Chummy, until the judge delivered the verdict. I *knew* her, see. What she suffered and what she did. Something special, Grace was.'

'Indeed. So special that you attempted to suppress vital evidence during her trial.'

'Oh aye? Who says?'

Wilson shrugged the challenge away. Quietly, he said, 'The truth came out, anyway. After *that* fiasco, I didn't expect gratuitous advice from *you*.'

'Clear the air, is it?' Evans said, equally soft. 'Right then. Looked out for Grace, I did: anyone would. Upset the brass, I grant you, and the media had an orgy. But there was no blemish on the record, not even an enquiry. Been listening to talkers, you have.'

'I've been listening to you! What you said, and the way you said it. You were out of line, Evans; some would call it insubordination.'

Stand for that, boyo, you'll be fetching his slippers next week. 'Spoke my mind, is all. Needed saying, too. Meetings and machines are fine, in their time and place. Policework's about people.'

Wilson sounded coldly furious. 'When I want a lecture from you, I'll ask! I was intending to give you a clean sheet, despite the warnings. It seems I must think again.'

'Take it to the Commissioner, shall we? You pre-judged the issue, just looking for an excuse. What else did he say, while we're about it? I've a right to know, mind.'

Making his way back to the desk, Wilson looked somewhat less assured. '*He*, inspector?'

'No need for games: Smythe, who else?'

Bitterly, he thought, here's me singing his praises, and the bastard shops me. Warnings, indeed!

Wilson's reaction was odd; part surprise, part relief. 'Superintendent Smythe gave you an excellent reference – making a creditable comeback, I think he said.'

Briefly, they confronted totally separate confusions; and a basic shift in balance. Evans sensed it then: a bedrock decency in the new man which might prove both a formidable strength and a crippling weakness.

Almost grudgingly, Wilson admitted, 'There's no real evidence, it's true. You're entitled to the benefit of the doubt. But you haven't made it easy.'

'It never is, sir.'

A silence descended, neither friendly nor hostile; a truce. 'Very well, Evans, a conditional discharge. For the moment, at least, the record stays clear. Now get out there and do the job.' About as much as he could hope for, in the circumstances; round one even.

As he made his way downstairs, memory stirred and the penny dropped. A bleak day on the Yardley case, a clash of wills, a rasping Scottish burr. Scores to settle, a man of proud and vengeful caste. Ten to one Superintendent McKay of Central had laid the poison; and Wilson had been about to swallow it whole. Aye, he reflected grimly, nice to have friends, but safer to know your enemies.

Despite the good sister's boast, convent locations weren't exactly Beddoes' forte. Resorting to the map, he found an oblong oasis in stockbroker country, extending to the main commuter line and bounded by a suburban ringroad. A mid-morning lull and a sequence of friendly lights saw him across town with time to spare.

He turned between wrought-iron gates down an avenue of beech and rhododendrons. Behind the greenery, pale sunlight flickered on chain-link fencing. Not an oasis, then: an enclosure. Within, seclusion, scholarship and birdsong; outside, the sinful city. O Lord, spare these our daughters commerce and intercourse: preserve them from real life.

The gravelled driveway veered right and opened out. The main buildings straddled a slight rise, monuments to well-heeled piety; mellow sandstone mantled in ivy, and a sentinel saint. Had to be Francis, Beddoes reckoned, what with Bambi in his lap and birdshit on his shoulders. Keep your head, my son, no need to get overawed.

She came down the broad steps to greet him, sprightly as a penguin in her pied habit. Late fifties, probably, but it was

19

hard to say. One of those smooth, ageless faces, only a wisp of grey beneath the snowy wimple to go on. Over half-moon spectacles her gaze was sharp and blue, and she frowned when he gave his name.

'The Inspector too grand for the likes of us, is he? No matter, 'tis a blessed relief you're here. Come along in with you.'

She set a brisk pace through corridors of colour muted by the stained glass. Far off, a violin sounded, pure and sombre. 'Sister Amanda,' she announced without turning. 'The resident virtuoso.' Only the clack of her sensible heels disturbed the quiet: an atmosphere of dedication – and wealth. A recent spate of larceny and vandalism had trailed Beddoes round the local comprehensives: punk pupils, disgruntled staff, graffiti and decay. This was a different planet.

She led him to an office littered with silver trophies and sacred pictures. There, from the high bay window, she showed him her domain. 'To your right, the new blocks, laboratories and such, indoor pool and library. Beyond, the Young Farmers' allotment. Goes all the way to the trains, which you'll not see for the poplars.' A line of slim trees nodding to the wind. 'Out front, fields for lacrosse and hockey, the runners' track and the netball.' Her tone hardened. 'And over there, our very own eyesore.' Following her outstretched hand, he saw where the lofty yew hedge had been summarily uprooted and chain-link stood bold and naked.

'The Council,' she said disgustedly, 'widening the road, in the public interest. Ten yards of our ground, and exposure to prying eyes. Compulsory purchase, they say: 'tis little better than theft.'

The gap was unsightly, but innocent enough. Outside, a deserted street, a solitary bus shelter, and in the distance a shadowed arch where the road burrowed through the embankment.

'You'll be wondering what the fuss is about,' Sister Hyacinth said, reading his mind. 'And you'll be needing this.' From the folds of her habit, she conjured a battered brass telescope. 'I found it in Physics; it's a fine old instrument. Go on, now, try it.'

20

They're 'avin' me on, Beddoes thought, she and Warner both. Punchline's due any minute. Yet her expression remained open and eager; she seemed quite unaware of the incongruity.

Cautiously, he asked, 'Er – what am I supposed to be looking at?'

'Why, the netball, of course!'

Far away, white-clad figures cavorted on the grass. The netball, of course. Going senile, poor old cow; best humour her.

The metal felt smooth and weighty in his hands; it took an age to focus. Then, leaping cleanly from the blur, an image of startling beauty. Framed in a billow of dark hair, the face of an angel, bright with the fierce pleasure of the game. She set herself to shoot, the ball held high, and Beddoes caught his breath. Sunlight through thin cotton revealed every detail of her lithe young body. From her post at his elbow, Hyacinth spoke, very matter-of-fact. 'That'll be Jenny Saunders you're watching. You wanted your man detained; can you think of a better way?'

Caught in the act, no better than a peeper himself, Beddoes prepared to vent his guilt in defensive anger. Once more, she anticipated him, holding up a placatory hand. 'Just wait; calm yourself. 'Tis only a truth I'm showing you.' She looked sad but serene, and somehow older. 'They become women too soon these days. Away to the marriage bed and the holy joys of procreation. Sure and don't we prepare them for that, too? It's naïve you'd be, sergeant, to think us unworldly.'

Wrong-footed yet again, Beddoes managed no more than a graceless nod.

'Till then, though,' she continued evenly, 'we have a duty; it's why you're here. Now, if you'll train that thing on the shelter, you'll see the cause of our worry.'

The bus shelter, he realised, offered a grandstand seat for netball spectators. Sister Hyacinth's planning had been shrewd and thorough; anything but senile. Eventually, struggling with the unwieldy spyglass, he made some sense of the picture. Protruding from the roadside corner of the shelter, a pair of grubby trainers. Above them, navy tracksuit bottoms with one zip adrift.

'That's Chummy?' he murmured. 'He of the scruffy feet?'

'I wouldn't know the name: the feet are unmistakable. It's him, all right.'

The moment of shared whimsy steadied him: an issue he could deal with, at last. He gave her the rational view, innocent until proved otherwise.

'He's outside the grounds, harmless enough. No law against waiting for a number forty-nine.'

Her glance was cold and scathing. 'For three hours? I beg to differ. Look, the sisters won't go near when he prowls the fence, and neither will I force them. We've no man at all, don't you see, no one to challenge him.'

Keeping the long-range vigil, Beddoes asked, 'Anyone had a good look at him?'

'Ah, he's a clever divil, there's no approaching him. At the first sign, it's into the shelter. When there's people about, he fades away altogether.' Finally, she was at the heart of it, genuinely dismayed. 'That's the real bother, now. He knows we've seen him, and yet he stays. It's not *normal*, sergeant; where's the sense?'

And suddenly, from a tranquil vantage point on a sunlit morning, Beddoes felt it, too; something strange and dark and menacing.

'How can I get close without being rumbled?'

Concisely, she told him, and added a stern caution. 'You take care, now. He's a powerful thick-set feller.'

Out on the still-sleepy suburban pavement, Beddoes' doubts returned. Some jobless Mick, probably, drawn to this enclave of faith and risking a cheap ogle; a fine juicy sin for the Padre, Sunday. So much for Warner's favour – hardly worth filling the charge sheet.

At the crown of the long bend where the hedge gave out, he paused for a quick recce. A furlong to go and no more cover. Dimly, through the frosted glass of the shelter, he glimpsed a hunched and motionless silhouette. The 'name and address, please' touch would do it, he decided. Always moved 'em on smartish, that did. He started forward, best beatman's pace, deliberate but purposeful.

Chummy came out at once, stretching casually. Been

22

watching, then. Knows an official walk when he sees one. Given a single, swift, over-the-shoulder glance, Beddoes fed the impression into his memory: heavy build, dark unruly hair, a hint of Celtic sallowness. Conscious of the risk, he shouted, 'Oi, you! 'Ang about!'

An offer which set Chummy on his way. Good mover, too, despite his bulk; the rhythmic lope of the natural athlete. He *was* a clever devil. The age of the jogger – so who looks twice at a running man in tracksuit and trainers? Which meant he'd planned it, after all, and there were questions to be answered. Much too late, Beddoes gave chase.

He'd done no running since school, saving himself for horizontal exertions. Stubbornness alone kept him going; Chummy might always break a leg. He pounded downhill towards the railway bridge, flame in his lungs and an incipient stitch raking his belly. Into sudden blackness, eyes still narrowed from the sun and blind as a mole. Never saw it coming, upright one moment and tumbling the next. Cobbles pummelling his ribs, bump scrape and slither, and his head crashing into the kerb.

A timewarp. A straitjacket of pain, a mocking laugh, a vague bulky figure drifting away. Rockabye baby and Christ me skull's cracked; someone whimpering and a wicked reek of drains.

Nausea brought him back, an irresistible need to roll over and throw up. This accomplished, he followed his instinct into daylight and slumped to the pavement. Dully, nursing his head, he watched blood from a skinned knuckle gather and drip; small scarlet starbursts on the dusty asphalt.

Engine noise and exhaust fumes, agitated voices, robes and incense; Hyacinth rides again. He was whisked into a car and spirited back to the school. There, she dispensed Dettol and recriminations. ''Tis thoroughly reckless you are, didn't I warn you? As well I had the telescope on you all the time. Here, drink this down, now.'

Hot sweet tea, laced with something a good deal harder. He'd lost the capacity for surprise, but she explained anyway. 'Medicinal only, you understand. We keep it for just such emergencies.'

Taped and fortified and reviving fast, Beddoes felt the need for explanations of his own. Not much to say, really.

'Must've tripped,' he lied lamely. 'Clumsy.'

'Is that so? And me thinking that divil waylaid you.'

He met her quizzical stare as squarely as he could. 'No way. He was long gone.'

'Ah well, you'll not suffer in vain. A rare ould fright you gave him. He'll bother us no more.' And in this prediction, she was to be proved entirely correct.

Heading gingerly for the nick, Beddoes contemplated the wreckage of his morning. Mugged by a common peeper, rescued by the Sisters of Mercy, and nothing to show but dishonourable wounds. As near to humiliation as he cared to get, not to be mentioned to the uniforms; or to the Inspector, for that matter. And in future, Evans could find his own way in from the cold.

CHAPTER THREE

STILL BROODING on McKay's treachery, Evans returned to an empty office and an enigmatic scrawl: 'Taking the vows. Expect me when you see me. Roy.' Dull young bugger, what if we got a live one? Chance'd be a fine thing! The bargain basement, this; Evans' emporium for cut-price crime. Nevertheless, when Beddoes eventually showed, his reception was less than cordial.

'Nice of you to drop in, boyo. Glad you could spare the time.'

'Don't *you* start, uncle; not today.'

'Thought you'd be here, see,' Evans explained, coldly polite. 'Left you in charge. Old-fashioned I am, I expect.'

Beddoes moved carefully to his desk.

''Eard a whisper, reckoned it might be big. I was wrong.'

'Duw, there's unusual.'

'No one's perfect, mate. You should know.'

An unfortunate retort, coming hard on Wilson's homily; another snide reminder of the Yardley débâcle. About to lose his temper, Evans took a closer look at his protégé.

Mostly, you'd have to call Roy Beddoes dapper. Lean and sharp-featured, well-groomed and nicely co-ordinated, a bloke the birds went mad for. Not like him to be slovenly: stains on his trousers, an ill-concealed limp, tight arrows of pain around the normally alert brown eyes.

More gently, Evans enquired, 'Rough night, then? You should've said.'

'Not night: mornin'.' Evans waited, eyebrows raised. Finally, Beddoes grunted, 'Told you already – a goose chase.'

'Geese, is it? Tigers, more like. What's this about vows?'

Beddoes began to wag his head; winced, and shrugged instead. 'Bad joke, know what I mean? Forget it.'

Not much fun, being the Manor's permanent dogsbodies. Cooped up like this, it put a bit of a strain on friendship. Evans hated pulling rank; sometimes, though, you didn't have much choice. Heavily, he said, 'I can't let it go; sorry. Dereliction, see, and no reasonable excuse. Come on, Roy,' he urged. 'This is bloody silly.'

The appeal succeeded where sarcasm had failed. Beddoes lowered his guard.

'A peeper,' he admitted reluctantly. 'Down the Convent. Nuns with their knickers in a twist. Saw 'im off, didn't I? Problem was, I 'ad to break into a gallop. Took a fall.'

Only part of the truth, for sure; didn't take a genius to hear the bits missed out. Still, he *did* look ropey; best leave it there.

Trying for a lighter mood, Evans murmured, 'Must've been a pearler. Done over by the All-Blacks, were you?'

'Not me, uncle, rugby's for 'eadbangers. Prefer a touch of skill, I do; the City, fr'instance.'

'Soccer's OK,' Evans conceded judiciously. 'Long as you keep clear of Brussels.' Slipped out, really, he couldn't resist it. It was like that all the time these days; an edge to everything.

For a moment they faced each other, wholly at odds. Then Beddoes turned away, coaxing a flimsy into his typewriter and pecking at the keys. 'No future in this, mate, I got cases to write up. You know – work!' And very soon, the frosty atmosphere and the irritating stutter of inexpert typing drove Evans out, in search of more congenial company.

In vain. At the desk, Warner sat as mournful and dignified as a blue-eyed bloodhound.

'Mornin', Huw. Heard the latest?'

'Going to brighten my day, are you?'

'No chance, cock.' He tapped an official-looking document with a liver-spotted finger. 'Remember that lad you nicked for grievous bodily, coupla months back?'

'Billy Stone? What about him?'

'Just strolled out of court, free as air.'

'Come *on*, Jack! We had him nailed down tight, and a record as long as your arm! How the hell did he swing it?'

Warner sighed, a sound of weary nostalgia. 'Records don't count these days, more's the pity. Told the beak a sob story – hungry kids and his dear old mum's cancer – and one of our witnesses got a bad case of courthouse constipation. Couldn't recall a thing, he said.'

'Darro, Billy put the frighteners on him!'

The desk sergeant shrugged philosophically, waggling his palm to and fro. 'Win some, lose some.'

'Aye,' growled Evans bitterly. 'Next week Billy'll mug some other poor bastard, and we'll be at it all over again!'

He turned, elbowing through a gaggle of startled uniforms without so much as a nod. Back to the basement, boyo; it's tough at the bottom.

'You're quite something, girl, did I ever tell you?'

They'd drawn the curtains as soon as the porter left; mutual urgency had made the outside world irrelevant. Now, his grin a faint Cheshire gleam in the false dusk, Charles sprawled on the rumpled bed and adopted a teasing tone.

Sitting naked at the dressing table, Sara felt languorous and completely feminine. The fine dew of recent lovemaking cooled her skin, and the trappings of luxury bolstered the illusion. Student lodgings, like the world outside, belonged to a different life. Eyeing his vaguely reflected image, she murmured, 'I believe you may have mentioned it, Charles.'

'Call me Charlie: everyone does.'

A subtle dig. She couldn't see herself as good old Charlie's bit on the side. He knew it, and baited her accordingly. 'Don't sulk,' he continued. 'I mean it. Quite a swinger under the educated act. You really turn me on.'

His version of amends, but she had her retaliation ready – a quick, cheesecake full-frontal.

'Thank you, kind sir.'

'Aah, quit it,' he groaned. 'Trading on a man's weakness. Indecent exposure; there's laws, y'know.'

'So call a cop. You're harmless, for the moment. That's a *natural* law.'

'My, the cruelty of youth.' He made his voice cracked and wheezy; he was all of thirty-four. Satisfied with her small victory, she settled to the mirror, brushing tangles from her hair.

After a while, he mumbled, 'Y'know, Sara, I'd do anything for you.'

She answered on impulse, the kind of flip retort much admired in college. 'Why not get a divorce?' For God's sake, she wondered, in sudden panic, what have I done? But he merely said thickly, 'Well, almost anything.'

Vastly relieved, happy to change the subject, she told him, 'Let's eat late. I need a bath, and you can get your second wind. Then we'll dance till dawn.'

'Never heard it called that before . . .' His words faded into deep and regular breathing. It was one of his boasts – work hard, play hard, sleep like a baby.

Reprieved, alone, and pampered by scented water, Sara marvelled at her own rashness. Watch your tongue, my girl, that was a crazy thing to say. In public, Charles was polished and urbane, charming and attentive, an ad man's dream of the rising young tycoon. Behind the façade dwelt another person: someone deeply insecure and unhappy in domestic life, yet ashamed of infidelity; someone who, in business and personal dealings, could be calculating, ruthless and utterly self-centred. Two men, then, neither of whom you would marry, let alone propose to, even in jest. Good job he'd been so dozy – could've been a very uncomfortable moment. The thought depressed her, raised spectres of earlier and far more painful marital disasters . . .

Throughout the entire squalid dispute, her dad had retained a semblance of dignity; the ingrained pragmatism of his native Lancashire. A stocky, taciturn man, he'd risen through apprenticeship and the shopfloor to the status of master crafts-man. He was prudent with money, smoking little and drinking less; every spare penny went on home improvements. Every Sunday she would find him in the gloom of the garden shed, surrounded by tools, up to his elbows in grease, his square, strong face set in a frown of absorbed concentration. He'd met personal crises with the same placid intransigence; she'd never seen him lose either his temper or his self-confidence.

So, one wintry evening in her fresher year, Sara had been amazed to find him at the door of her flat, ill-at-ease and curiously diminished. A suit, baggy at the knees and shiny with age, a white shirt which had seen purer days, and a tie stained by hard use.

"Ow do, lass,' he said, in a forlorn attempt at heartiness. After the ritual kiss, stiff and awkward as ever, he drew back with quite uncharacteristic diffidence. 'Brought someone to show you,' he confessed, grinning in embarrassment and supplication. 'Your new stepmum. Fetch her in, shall I?'

'Of course,' she replied, her heart sinking. Behind her, the flat was cramped and shambolic: pantyhose dangling from the single radiator, unwashed dishes in the sink and books every-where. No time for reparations, he was back already, towing a girl only a few years older than herself.

Ruby - Dad called her his 'little gem' - flaunted skinny legs and an overdose of cheap perfume. Attractive in a bosomy, buck-toothed way, she had an irritating giggle and appalling dress sense. Sara, acutely conscious of the chaos all around, pitched the conversation at a lofty intellectual level; while Ruby, desperately nervous, prattled of Wogan and the weather. They had absolutely nothing in common except the anxious man flicking his puzzled gaze from one to the other like a football fan dumped at Wimbledon by mistake.

Sara unearthed a bottle of cheap sherry which they drank too fast, to cover the awkward silences. Then, to her horror, her father began a plaintive lament about money. Ruby, hanging on his every word, nodded vigorously and exclaimed, 'It's *awful*, reely,' each time he paused.

'That woman'll have me in the workhouse,' he complained; that woman being, of course, Sara's mother. 'When she's 'ad 'er whack, there's scarcely enough to feed a fly.' Emptying his glass once more in a single gulp, he added, 'It's bloody wicked, at my time o' life, watching the pennies. Heartless she is, lass, what with me'n Rube wantin' young 'uns of our own.'

Here, Ruby leaned forward imploringly. 'You won't *mind*, will you?'

'Certainly not,' Sara snapped. 'It's none of my business.'

Another killing hush. Dad looked like a favourite dog who'd just been kicked, and Ruby couldn't control a little gasp of dismay. Suddenly, they were all talking at once, bright, inconsequential and banal; they might have been speaking different languages.

The bottle was empty. Sara could find nothing sensible to say. She felt shame and anger at her father's helplessness, and a kind of pitying contempt for poor, earnest, vacuous little Rube. They must have sensed it; the atmosphere had grown positively frigid. Her father stood up, abruptly and somewhat unsteadily.

'Right, lass, we'd best be getting back'.

'Oh, must you?' Sara said, far too quickly. Briefly, she contemplated an explanation: for the state of the flat, for her own petty snobbishness, for the cruel exposure of their doomed hopes. But pride held her back. You've outgrown him, she told herself silently. There's no need to apologise for what you've become. And besides, he'd never understand.

Ruby managed an effusive thank you and a patently insincere invitation to 'our humble lovenest'. Her father said nothing; just one shifty, defeated, sideways glance. She couldn't wait to get them out.

Leaning on the door, weak with reaction and relief, she heard them giggling their way downstairs. It was a curiously furtive sound: dear God, she thought, in utter disbelief, they're about to fall into bed somewhere! She'd never pictured her father as the ardent male: even now, the leap of imagination was quite beyond her. She didn't know whether to laugh or cry ...

An alien noise intruded, seeping from the bedroom and interrupting her train of thought. And suddenly she *was* laughing helplessly; another black mark against Charles – he snored! At least her mother had been spared that ...

Sara's mother had become, to borrow Charles's phrase, 'something else again'; going home was like entering an emotional desert. A trained teacher from a solidly respectable, church-going family, she'd married young and 'beneath herself'. For her, the divorce was ultimate betrayal, the public acknowledgement of an intensely private defeat. Ever since, she'd withdrawn deeper into apathy and bitterness, neglecting herself to the point of emaciation. Her body, once lithe and slender, was wasted and shrunken, the joints jutting like ridgepoles beneath her drab and shapeless clothing. Her face, always narrow and fine-boned, had slumped into a hatchet-like mask of down-turned lines and unforgiving angles. Only the eyes lived, burning hard and bright with constant, caustic malice.

'If it weren't for me,' she would claim, in precise, well-modulated tones which somehow accentuated the venom, 'he'd be nothing, worthless as the dirt under your feet. Keeping pigeons, swilling beer with "the lads", festering his life away "'oop at mill".' She lampooned his Northern dialect viciously, giving the stock phrase a flavour of vile obscenity. 'Men,' she would continue, her harsh features twisted in disgust, 'they think of just one thing; if you can call *that* thinking! Charm and flattery till they get what they want – even fine promises in the eyes of the Lord.' For this one phrase, her expression would soften – a kind of vengeful piety. In her misfortune, she'd turned to religion, but of the Old Testament variety; her God was nothing if not jealous.

Her purity established, she would launch the diatribe in earnest. 'Then you're only another possession, to be worked and drained and tossed aside like an empty flagon when some passing strumpet takes their fancy.' Here, she would grasp Sara in cool, reptilian hands, fix her with a brooding stare, and urge, 'Don't let them fool you, Sara. Finish your studies, avoid the trap, live your own life. Use them, Sara; how I wish I could start again at your age.' And finally, a tremulous sigh, a note of desolate self-pity. 'When I think what I've been through for you – the drudgery, the humiliation! *You* won't desert me, will you? You're all I have left, Sara; you and the Lord.'

And Sara, moved in spite of herself, would wander fearfully through the gloomy, haunted shell of what had once been home. The kitchen, where they'd toasted muffins and smothered them in peanut butter – she could almost taste the gluey saltness. Now, there was only a dusty, derelict cooker and a whiff of rancid meat. The dining-room, where her mother had once presented a fancy birthday cake to a roomful of wide-eyed little girls; Sara remembered the pleasure and the envy. 'Cor, your mum ain't 'alf clever.' Now, there was just a gloomy room, a motionless, forbidding figure, and the musty, barren smell of a woman grown cold before her time. And here, upstairs in Sara's bedroom, there'd been posters on the wall and furry animals on a flowered bedcover. Her father had sometimes stood here, smiling in quiet pride as she translated smoothly from *Don Quixote* in Spanish.

'Bai goom, lass,' he would cry, laying on the Lancashire, 'tha's a reet genius.' Now only his ghost lingered, pale and ineffectual as the man himself; hankering for money and a child bride.

Always it ended the same way. Her mother, rallying improbably, cackling like a demented witch. 'He has sinned, Sara, against me and against the Lord, and he must pay. I'm going to hurt him, financially and emotionally, just as he hurt me. He won't be happy in my lifetime, he won't have his little trollop and her mewling brats. I'll take my dues; I've earned them.' And she would nod in the chair with her back to the cobwebbed window, retreating into a private world of darkness and righteous retribution; mouthing and muttering, senile at fifty-two. Seeing her this way reminded Sara of that peculiar sketch which alternates as you study it; a pretty girl one minute, a raddled crone the next ...

For years, she'd ignored the signs; hindsight removed the blinkers. The problem, she realised, must have gathered in secret, deep and ugly and painful as a blind boil. It came to a head during her 'O' levels, as she stirred to the rhythms of Romance languages. Gradually, the disharmony had surfaced and she would eavesdrop from her bedroom on the battlefield below.

Seven-thirty. The thud of the front gate, the muffled yapping of next door's moronic poodle. Even from here, she sensed the weariness of her father's tread. His mumbled voice, and her mother's greeting, strident and fretful: 'You're late again, your supper's ruined. Which little *project* were you working on tonight?'

'Hold hard, luv. I'm right done in, and you're not helping.'

'Indeed I'm not! Do you seriously expect me to *condone* your sordid affairs?'

'Hush, woman, the lass is at her studies!'

She'd tried to stay aloof, avoid taking sides, but she was old enough to act both as confidante and judge. Each of them, separately and surreptitiously, had sought her approval and support.

'They're out there somewhere now,' her mother would whisper, taut and intense, 'doing things to each other and laughing about me. That's what really hurts, my girl; they think I'm stupid, as well as plain.'

'But, Mummy, you're not plain!'

'Don't be absurd, Sara.'

'Ah, Sara lass,' he would confide. 'She's driving me away; it's no life for a dog, there's nowt I can do to please her.'

'*Are* you deceiving her, Daddy?'

'Hey, come on lass, not you too!'

Awake in the small hours, she would grasp the rough blanket and fight back the tears. They were driving her into an impossible position from which there was no escape. They wanted her to choose, and she couldn't; because neither would trust her with the whole truth, and because, in her innocence, she loved them both. Worse still, alone and tormented in the unfriendly dark, she began to believe that in some way she couldn't begin to understand, it was all *her* fault.

Until, one evening, as the arguments below grew fiercer, she covered her ears and shut them out. Staring sightless and dry-eyed at a simpering popstar poster, she made her own final decision. From this moment onwards, she cultivated her privacy, kept her mind on her studies, and left them to settle matters as best they could. She cried herself to sleep that night, sobbing for what was lost, and for the loveless years ahead. She hadn't cried much since. The experience had tempered her, made her independent. And yet, as she massaged creamy soap into her skin, she realised she *had* lost something precious; and her mind reached back to recover it ...

At the start, she'd been a typical only child: pretty, pampered and secure. The atmosphere had been gentle and cosy as her parents made the old town house their own. She recalled the struggles with wallpaper and paint; she and her mother falling about at the sight of Dad, a blocky Northern sheikh, boilersuited and beturbaned in a stripy towel, his spectacles bespattered with 'Twilight Blush'. 'Eh, come on, you lot, you're supposed to be t'labour, not laffin' like big soft girls.'

The early days in school, the playground status auction. '*My* dad's the foreman, mends his own car. My mum's got a degree, used to be a teacher like Miss, so there.' Drives in the country, spring on Bluebell Hill, and singing daft songs all the way home. Parental rapture as she played Schubert on the recorder at the end-of-term concert; the way they'd comforted her when a favourite hamster made his successful gaolbreak. Underpinning everything, a sense of oneness: three of them together, winning against the rest.

She was plumbing the depths of memory now, oblivious to the luxurious decor and the cooling bathwater. Drifting, weightless and nostalgic, borne on the images of remembrance, the unmatchable brightness of early childhood. And finally she caught it, the day and the moment, sharp and clear as an Alpine dawn ...

A South Coast holiday, Bexhill probably; they went there every year. The kind of glorious summer day which never seems to end, and happens only when you are very young. Rows of beach huts facing the sea, each door freshly and separately coloured. Warm brown sand underfoot, the sounds of small waves and plaintive gulls, a whiff of salt and the treacly taste of candy-floss. She couldn't've been more than five; an age when each yard of shoreline reveals fresh mystery and fascination. She'd been skipping on ahead, burbling happily to herself.

'What a pretty shell; look, Mummy, a starfish! Does this seaweed pop?' and 'O, how I'd love a donkey ride.'

She turned to make her plea; they were strolling behind, kicking a spray of glittering droplets from the edge of the placid tide. Shielding her eyes against the glare, she saw them through a frame of small, splayed fingers.

He must have said something private, one of those intimate signals all young couples use. They stopped, slightly apart: he, square and well-muscled, she lithe in a polka-dot two-piece considered quite daring at the time. She looked up at him as though nothing and nobody else existed. So many years later, Sara remembered the brief, electric tingle of jealousy which momentarily threatened her own childish joy. They kissed once, tight and tender, and came towards her, their faces aglow. And in Sara's eyes, fleetingly, they were wholly beautiful ...

The bath water had gone cold, and she was very close to tears. She felt lost and melancholy, a stranger in the present. Once, they'd owned it, whatever it was; as a little girl, she'd lived and played in its quiet radiance. Somehow, somewhere along the way, it had faded and died; perhaps she herself had helped to kill it. A kind of love, then; in its absence, only bitterness, solitude, pain and discontent. All that remained resided in her; she who still wept for something which had passed beyond their power to recall.

Get your act together, girl, she warned herself, what's past is over. There's a weekend outside – go and grab it. She hauled herself up and padded through ankle-deep carpet to the separate shower. One thing about Charles – however underhand the rendezvous, the accommodation was invariably five star. Made a girl feel special.

Luxuriating in steamy spray, working the shampoo into her hair, she tried a more rational analysis of her malaise. OK, you feel good but not ecstatic; bed is exciting but the earth doesn't move. Don't knock it, girl, you joined with your eyes wide open and your feet on the ground. Sufficient to the day is the pleasure thereof, so enjoy. Beats hell out of the hop, and the frenzied quest for an acceptable steady. Plenty of time for that, my girl.

Yet she had to sigh for Sara Holroyd, sophisticate and woman of the world. Spawn of a soured trust, budding intellectual, a career for the asking, and a married man to play with. Because, in the end, *that* was the problem: playing at it. Face facts, my girl, you're not so different from poor old Rube – a secret yen for Mr Right, the gilded dreamhouse, and the whole damn domestic catastrophe.

She pulled a rueful grin. Truth strikes at unlikely moments. Groping for the tap, she sensed movement behind her; a hand,

35

firm and knowing, at that delicious spot near the base of her spine.

'Surprise, surprise,' he breathed, nuzzling her ear. 'Nature's revenge. We're dining in tonight, courtesy of room service. Meanwhile, they're playing our tune. Let's dance.'

As she leaned back, melting against his hardness, she thought: Mr Right he isn't – here and now, he'll do rather nicely, thank you.

CHAPTER FOUR

MAYBE HE'D had a decent kip, perhaps it was the prospect of the weekend ahead. At any rate, Beddoes seemed restored: clear-eyed and alert, the limp much diminished, and a natty line in suiting. The tone, rather than the content, of his opening remark declared the truce.

'So 'ow did 'is nibs perform, up in the gods?'

'*The Jungle Book*,' said Evans reminiscently. 'Bloke called Kipling wrote about a python, once. Me mam used to read it. Before your time, of course, reading.'

'Course,' agreed Beddoes cheerfully. 'Used to *make* book down our way. Saw the movie, though.'

'Aye, you would've. About your dab, Disney. I was saying, then – like a python, Wilson. Smooth, pretty and dangerous, weaving a spell. Hypnotised, they were – Kaa's monkeys.'

'There's worse names for that lot,' Beddoes muttered, and Evans shot him an approving smile.

'No doubt. Big on communication and co-operation, our Super is; computers rule, OK? Meanwhile, 'e's up there pushing buttons and setting the world to rights. Not just nicking villains, mind; it's *prevention*, if you please.'

'Give it a year or two, 'e could be right. Doesn't sound so bad to me. Bit of pioneering, touch of glamour in me life: policin' by numbers.'

'Over my dead body!'

'Don't tempt me, uncle. Speaking of temptation, you bin caning the ole iron maiden, lately. 'Ow about a break, night on the town?' He winked knowingly. 'Mate of Gloria's, thirty-ish, on the rebound. Do you a treat, believe me.'

'A kindly idea, boyo, but I'm off women. Look what happened last time.'

'Jesus, that was months ago! You mean you 'aven't ...?' Beddoes leaned forward, very serious.

'Know what they say, do yer, these evolutionists?' His supercilious face, a refined BBC voice: '"Given time, redundant features of the anatomy will atrophy and drop off." Beware, uncle: *this* could 'appen to *you*.'

Evans merely grinned. 'Be all right then, wouldn't I?'

''Ow d'you mean?'

'Like me mam says, sopranos get the best parts.' It was the first good laugh they'd had for weeks.

Richard Wilson's mind arced to the surface, urgent as a breathless diver. Bleary with sleep, his gaze homed guiltily on the bedside alarm, confirming his subconscious fear; Christ, I'm late! He'd actually begun to move, kicking at the duvet, when calmer counsels prevailed. An unusual luxury, an off-duty Saturday: relax and enjoy it.

He rolled on to his side, lapsing into contented drowsiness. A shaft of sunlight edging between the curtains burnished a diagonal on the carpet. He watched idly, held by the play of sparkling dustmotes. Gina's hair was like this ...

He could hear her downstairs, singing softly as she pottered about. It would be a good day for her, too; you had to plan that way, with leisure time so strictly rationed. A trace of her body warmth lingered beneath him. From the pillow, a whiff of her perfume, a tantalising hint of last night's musk. Gina ...

Not for the first time, he marvelled that, given so many eligible suitors, she'd chosen him. Had she wearied of the pinstripe brigade, the Hooray Henries and Sloane Rangers paraded by her parents? Certainly he counted himself worth six of *them*. He had been, after all, the star of post-graduate criminology, the boy most likely; and together they made a handsome couple. Perhaps – treacherous thought – she wanted a middle-class understudy, someone to mould in her private image of masculine ideality. There you go again, Wilson, getting intellectual about matters of the heart. Count your blessings, man!

Mutual attraction had pulled them together across the college dance floor. A happy accident in itself – she'd followed a whim and a former schoolfriend 'to see how the bearded Bohemians carry on'. The spark had smouldered and flamed, despite the social gulf between. Gilded and glamorous, the only child of landed gentry, she seemed fascinated by his intelligence and lofty devotion to justice; whereas he, the third and brightest son of a suburban grocer, had worshipped her from the start. Just as well, he mused pragmatically, that his father had died soon afterwards, leaving the business to his brothers and a modest legacy 'for Richard's further education'. This alone had allowed him to remain within her orbit.

For, whatever her motives, she'd honoured every line of the contract. When, in the early days, he'd flirted with the notion of a university career, she nudged him firmly into the wider world.

'*Really*, Richard! Shut away in an ivory tower, writing little monographs for limited distribution? Is *that* the measure of your ambition?'

During his spell on the beat and in the face of parental disapproval, she'd cut her cloth to the stringent demands of a constable's pay, tiptoeing round him while he burnt midnight oil over police regulations.

'It's no use, dear, not so much as a *glimpse* of my fair white flesh until you've passed the test. Now: standing orders, cases of suspected child abuse. Word perfect, please!' For him, promotion exams had proved almost ridiculously easy; yet she'd greeted each success with genuine delight. Then, grimly determined, she lowered her social sights and mingled freely with the wives of influential officers. It cost her blood, and sometimes he had to bear the brunt.

'The village *fête*, Richard? Surely you can't be serious?' Yet always she'd carried it off, and only the most finely attuned could have noticed the condescension. Behind every successful man, he mused; because, deep down, he still hankered for the calmer realms of academia, where the issues remained abstract and dissent was confined to the printed page. The word dissent raised an image of Evans – the blocky physique, the receding, sandy hair, the pale, implacable eyes – another uneasy relationship. Go away, inspector, it's Saturday.

Now why do you say *another*? he wondered, and grimaced wryly. Because, despite eight years of marriage, some hazardous cross-currents endured. On the subject of children, for instance, Gina was adamant.

'I *refuse*, Richard, I warned you from the start. I won't discuss it: divorce me if you like.' In fact, he held no strong feelings either way, but the sheer vehemence puzzled and disturbed him. Did some hideous disease lurk within her blue-blooded lineage? It wasn't a subject he cared to explore.

She'd always blossomed in company, the darling of any party, the natural focus for every eye. It hadn't been easy, retiring into a limbo of domestic routine leavened only by her parents' generosity. Often, as he embarked on a high-level conference or another tour of night duty, he felt her unspoken resentment like a living force. She'd voiced it only once, after a rare theatre outing and too much wine. As the taxi left in the wee hours, she murmured, 'There goes my link with civilisation; back to solitary.' He'd comforted her as best he could, with words and more intimate remedies; but her silent stoicism troubled him deeply. It was a side of her he didn't know and couldn't begin to understand. Sometimes, in his office, a vision came to haunt him: Gina prowling the empty house and yearning for freedom.

He shifted once more, and the scent of her moved him in an entirely different direction. In this one crucial arena, he entertained no shade of doubt. From the very beginning, her sensuality had delighted him; and continued to do so. She gave herself joyfully and completely, relishing his craving and his need. Recently she had become even more enthusiastic and experimental; at the end of the day and frequently much earlier, all differences dissolved in the sweetness of her hallowed and welcoming cleft . . .

Dear God, Wilson, he thought as the familiar warmth invaded his loins, what's wrong with you? A grown man drowning in erotic fantasy, conjuring poetic porn and a hard-on – and all over a woman you've been married to for years! A lost cause, an intellect governed from the gonads. Should we call her, or will it keep? He sighed and sat up. Down, Rover, we've a needle squash match this morning. And every stew improves for the simmering ...

Harry Mortimer sat at the sports club bar, nursing a shandy and mopping fresh-sprung sweat from his brow. Dressed, he looked dangerously portly and florid; in truth, he was muscular, strong, and surprisingly light on his feet. Highly competitive, too, giving nothing away. To beat him, you had to contest every rally to the bitter end. The weekly squash match was a ding-dong affair, no quarter asked or given, usually decided in the fifth game. Today, he'd been oddly lethargic, surrendering the initiative early and offering only token resistance. Now he was clearly hatching one of his tall stories. Wilson settled back, happy to be entertained.

'Visiting firemen,' Mortimer began. 'Showing 'em the town. Obligations of the trade.' He sighed tragically, to demonstrate how boring it was. 'Some frightful nightspot, right at the death. Enter a dolly, dark, big eyes. One of those crochet jobs, holes and string and nothing underneath to spoil the view. Well made, old boy; bouncy, *nice*.' He made gentle cupping motions with his big hands. 'Points of mutual interest, then. I looked, she stared straight back.' A tone of innocent wonder. 'Took her fancy, it seems. Rates a magnum, at my age, champers all round.' He shook his head wryly, mocking his own naïveté. 'Firemen already *suited*, d'you see. So, smooch round the floor, more bubbly. Hollow legs, she had, sloshing it down like scrumpy. Cometh the witching hour, hotfoot for my little hovel. Old boy, she was *panting*! Ever driven a Bentley with a dolly bent on Kamasutra? Tricky, that. Not boring you, am I?'

Wilson grinned. 'Not a chance.'

Mortimer drained his glass and ordered another round, riding serenely over Wilson's protests. 'Nonsense, old boy. Corrupting the constabulary, my pleasure. Where was I? Ah yes. Back at the hacienda, thirsty dolly. Discovered cognac, shed all inhibition and most of her clothes. Very fetching.'

From across the room, someone called his name. He produced a generous wave, a genteel bellow of greeting. 'Wotcha, Nige! In the pink, I trust?' Then, distracted, he hunched over his glass with the air of a man beset by life's misfortunes. 'Bloody fiasco,' he announced glumly. 'Legless. Flop and giggle, dead to the world. Rag dolly. Sad Uncle Harry tucked her in, pushed out a few zeds.' He glanced up, righteously indignant. 'Four in the morning, Taittinger's revenge. Sat herself up and puked all over the Aubusson. Don't cackle, old boy, it's the gospel truth.'

Odd thing about Harry, Wilson reflected, as the guffaws subsided. You only heard the disasters; never the ones that *didn't* get away.

'Serves you right, man. Shouldn't keep valuables in the fornicatorium.'

Harry contrived a suitably huffy frown. 'A fella has standards, Richard. I'm very attached to the place. So, come the dawn, black coffee and detergent, everlasting apologies. No contest today, then; put it down to Cupid. Fear not, Mortimer rides again. Next week, I'll have you.'

'Promises, promises. Besides, we're expecting you tonight.'

Mortimer nodded solemnly, the whimsy fading. 'Roger. Bridge with demon wives, your place. Remind me of the route notes.' More diagrams, this time with Harry's gold pencil on headed club stationery. 'Got it, old boy. Eight for eight-thirty, best bib and tucker. We'll be there.' He drained his glass, collected his bag, and strode off. Moments later, Wilson saw the big car purr past the window.

It was, he acknowledged, picking his way homewards through the lunchtime snarl-up, a pretty unlikely friendship. Gina had introduced them, soon after the engagement. She and Harry had been childhood neighbours – apparently they'd baited nannies and ridden gymkhanas together somewhere in pseudo-rural Sussex.

'Richard, you simply *must* meet Harry,' she'd insisted. 'He's going to be the *youngest* millionaire, aren't you, darling?'

'Next week, old thing,' he'd said, easy and assured; and offered a rock-like paw.

Wilson detested him on sight. Everything about him proclaimed his origins – Winchester, Caius, and the Greys, it transpired – from the top of his rakish bowler to the turn-ups of his Blades broadloom. His every pronouncement echoed

42

High-Tory orthodoxy, delivered in the clipped military manner of the long-discredited Raj. A mindless bundle of aristocratic reflexes held together by an old school tie and cushioned by thoroughly unmerited wealth.

The contrast could scarcely be greater. Wilson was lower middle-class and proud of it, the product of an early comprehensive and a new university, pledged by instinct and education to the elimination of hereditary privilege. To him, Mortimer represented a living anathema; the ruddy, complacent face of the ancestral enemy. Thus, while his status and social graces might be secretly envied, his politics and lifestyle must be undermined at every turn.

Gradually, drawing on snippets of Gina's conversation, police and media sources, and first-hand experience, Wilson discovered the full extent of his own misjudgement. Far from a fortune, Mortimer had inherited a derelict country estate and a family printing firm teetering on the brink of liquidation. Inside five years, through shrewd management, ruthless pruning, and technical innovation, he had stopped the rot. Marriage to Clare turned the financial tide; sheer hard work brought it to a flood.

Beneath the witless, hail-fellow pose, Harry concealed an astute brain and an inherent commitment to justice. From time to time, he'd furnished valuable insight into the City's more dubious dealings; once, his informed analysis had helped to expose and dismantle a complex insurance swindle. By degrees he had become a regular squash partner, an amusing confidant and a firm friend. Because, though many might deride his outdated values, you had to respect his devotion to them. A mutual acquaintance had put it rather neatly: 'If ever I had to walk on the wild side, I can think of worse people than Harry to watch my back.' Quite simply, Harry was a man you could trust; and trust was something policemen usually reserved for one another.

All of which made him perfect company for Gina, on those rare occasions when he could be persuaded to bring his wife. He was also reputed to play a mean hand of bridge ...

An intimate dinner party. Candlelight playing on good

crystal, polished wood, and what even Harry acknowledged as 'very decent silverware'. An easy flow of conversation, a good deal of genuine laughter. Beyond the soft focal glow, the shadowed room provided an ideal backdrop; rich leather upholstery, an embossed Chinese carpet, russet velvet curtains drawn against the autumn night. In this setting, the Mortimers could be treated as equals; on such occasions, Wilson had to concede, generous in-laws conferred distinct advantages.

Gina had spent all day on cheerful preparations: cooking, cleaning, getting things *just so*. Now, sporting The Diamonds above a backless little black dress, she was in her element, playing hostess to people she knew and liked. She did it beautifully, too. The food might be a little rich for Wilson's palette – deep-fried Camembert, Hungarian goulash, Gâteau St-Honoré – but the Mortimers made complimentary noises, and she basked in their approval. However briefly, she was back where she belonged, the centre of attraction; her obvious delight captivated them all.

The leisurely meal was completed, the debris consigned to the dishwasher. At the card table, Clare Mortimer took control. An angular, plain woman, she escaped caricature of the squire's lady by virtue of a warm contralto voice and a robust sense of self-mockery.

'We will *not* cut for partners,' she declared firmly. 'It could lead to unhappy families. Harry and I fight' – a frown of comic distaste – 'and he *invariably* wins. Harry and Gina can't be paired. Doubtless, they worked out some frantically clever signals in their misspent youth, playing snap for matches.' Despite large, horsey teeth, her smile was almost girlish. 'A battle of the sexes, then. *So* much more interesting, don't you think?' Not a hint of innuendo; mindful of Gina's revelation, Wilson considered this a brave, if risky, proposal.

'Agreed, my dears? Splendid. Do the honours, Harry.'

At first the cards brooked no favourites; part scores and sacrifices, fiercely contested, were the order of the day. Harry, sipping wine and deploring the abuse of the Welfare State, nevertheless played cannily. The women remained cautious, learning each other's game. Eventually, they took the rubber, then another in two lay-down hands. 'Buck up, partner,'

Mortimer urged. 'Never hear the end of this.' Under pressure, his concentration hardened. He won the next game with an outrageous double finesse, having overbid in no-trumps.

'Fortune favours the bold,' he said, quite unabashed, and proceeded to make six clubs.

Here, Gina called time-out. 'Toasties and coffee,' she explained, 'and high-level strategic discussions at the sink. Come along, Clare.'

Mortimer rose, stretched, and ambled across to toast his rump at the fireplace. His knowing eye traversed the room; what he saw clearly impressed him.

'Lucky fella, Richard. All this, and the lovely lady too. Touch of the upward mobility, I hear. How's policin', then? Got 'em jumping through hoops?'

Wilson shrugged.

'So-so. Very conservative, the Police Force; not necessarily a small c, either. Hidebound, some of the senior men. Natural immunity to change and the march of time.'

'Hm. Got something special in mind?'

He seemed to be listening, head cocked, to the suppressed giggles issuing from the kitchen. It was another of his unlikely accomplishments: the ability to absorb information from several sources at once.

'Nothing dramatic,' Wilson admitted. 'Setting up basic data networks, making use of the media. Old hat to you, I suppose.'

'We're computerised, naturally. Have to be, the cost of labour. Useful tools, but limited.'

'Really? In what way?'

'Computer's a fast idiot. Does what you tell it, no more, no less. Can't *think* for you, old boy. Be a frosty Friday, that would.'

Wilson was disposed to argue, but the women were back, bearing caviare and other goodies; the talk broadened out to include them. Clare Mortimer, squatting straddle-legged and unladylike on a straight-backed chair, set out to amuse: farmyard stories. She began with the joys of muck-spreading – 'Such a rewarding pastime, my dears' – and graduated, at Gina's mischievous prompting, to artificial insemination. 'Poor old Ferdy the bull. Supporting two tons on those dumpy little hind legs, bellowing and wheezing like Harry's Land-rover. And all for a cardboard cut-out of bovine paradise and a warm rubber glove! So undignified really. Still, it works. The results are *much* more satisfactory.'

'Prefer the traditional method, myself,' Mortimer muttered darkly, and preened in their hilarious applause.

'Enough of this fraternising,' Clare said. 'Time for round two. Back to your corners, please.'

'Half a mo',' Harry protested. 'Gotta powder my nose.' He strode purposefully to the door.

'Down the corridor, second left.' Gina instructed him; and he called, 'I *know* where it is, old thing.'

Wilson, shuffling cards, became aware of a sudden tension between the women. Gina had gone very pale; Clare was regarding her with a strange, almost pitying expression. As he watched, Clare sensed his interest and began to chatter brightly. 'A super meal, Gina. I simply *must* have the recipe. Harry will badger me for weeks.'

Gina seemed to wake, raising a shaky smile and picking up the cue. Good rump steak, she said, and some rather special herbs; sherry and sour cream were *vital*. Presently, to her obvious relief, Harry reappeared, raring to start. 'Right then; lambs to the slaughter!' And the moment faded in the glow of renewed hostilities ...

Much later, in bed, Wilson acted out his earlier fantasy. Pliant and jointless with wine and contentment, Gina excelled herself – gentle, moist and velvety. In the blinding heat of his climax, he sensed her rhythmic clenching and heard her lost little cry; afterwards, he caressed her into instant sleep.

Whereas he lay tense and wakeful. Something had happened at the card table, something which stirred his policeman's instincts. It had to do with Gina and Clare, perhaps with Harry, too. A small mystery, probably; something from their common past in which he couldn't share. Yet, in a curious and disturbing way, it had already touched him. Therefore, after his own fashion and with due caution, he would investigate.

Because tonight, for the first time and without the slightest cause, he suspected that Gina had faked it.

CHAPTER FIVE

SHE MADE her entrance quite early one morning, trailing an aura of musky perfume. It was raining outside, and she took her coat off before she sat down. She did it slowly and gracefully, the calculated provocation of the artiste she had once been. Beddoes stopped typing and watched avidly; Evans merely watched.

She swivelled sideways on the chair, offering long, elegant legs for their inspection. Handsome woman, mind, firm-bodied and high-breasted; good bones. Still capable of turning heads in the High Street, even though she'd never see forty again. Beneath the demure, well-to-do façade, she carried an unmistakable air of sexual promise. Beddoes had sensed it already; she returned his frank appraisal with cool amusement. Evans, who knew better, felt a different kind of arousal, the awakening of a purely professional interest. *Something's brewing*.

'Word in your ear, inspector,' she said, low and throaty, and only a trace of Cockney.

These days, she called herself Lily Mendoza, and ran a 'retreat for the amusement of gentlemen'. Once, when they were both much younger, Evans had done her a kindness: copper's blind eye to a kid from the Sticks with showbiz ambitions turning the odd trick to keep body and soul together between infrequent auditions. She never forgot. Then, and later, he'd politely declined the obvious reward; instead, she repaid him in the most valued coin of his trade – information.

'An honour and a pleasure, Lil. Make yourself at home, girl.'

She raised her head, an imperious glance at Beddoes, who was now watching them speculatively.

'A *private* word, know what I mean?'

Beddoes climbed to his feet, grinning. 'Beg pardon, duchess. Three's a crowd, right?' He had a passing leer for Evans, too. 'Go steady, uncle. Out of practice, remember?'

'Bugger off, Roy.'

'I'm going, already.'

As the door closed, she cast a distasteful eye over the cramped office. 'Gives me the creeps, this does. Never thought I'd come here of my own accord.' He nodded, conscious of fading cream paintwork, tired furniture and archaic radiators.

'Hardly the Ritz, is it? You get used to it, I suppose. What's on your mind, then?'

She rummaged in her handbag and tossed a handful of flimsy lace on to the desk. The perfume was suddenly stronger; heady. 'Take a butcher's at that lot.'

Evans wagged his head sadly. 'Ah come on, Lily; pawing your lingerie at my age?'

'Look at them, for Chrissake!'

She shook them out angrily, two small black scraps in each hand. Panties neatly severed from crotch to waistband, the separated cups of a bra. Evans sighed for the destruction.

'Awful, really, fancy gear like that. Been at your clothesline, have they? Some'd call it vandalism, I grant you; hardly inspector fodder though.'

He'd misread her mood. To his astonishment, she was blinking back real tears.

'Never mind the funnies, it's hard enough already. Just listen, can't you?'

He nodded contritely. 'Sorry, girl. Go on, you.'

She sniffed and sat straighter, under control again. 'It was nice last night,' she began, calmly enough. 'Mild and gentle, bit of a moon. Fancied a stroll in the park, taking the air, OK?' He let his scepticism show, and she snapped, 'Oh, all right, I was touting! Still do that once in a while, keeping my eye in. I'm over twenty-one.'

'Aren't we all,' Evans murmured, and won a tight smile.

'You're so bloody gallant, mate.'

'Listening, aren't I?'

'Ta very much. So I was cruising, doing the circuit. Out on my ownsome, not a mug in sight. What the hell, I thought, a write-off, the early night'll do me good. Beauty sleep,' she explained, with a flashing grin which belied her need for anything of the sort.

Evans was concentrating, his instincts fully alert. She looked older, somehow. Tiny crow's-feet under the make-up, the tendons in her neck starting to show. Worn well, mind; but worn, just the same. Her voice fell, her eyes turned glassy and opaque.

'There's a shrubbery, near the playground. Laurel, I think. Those big broad leaves. Lot of rustling, right?' He nodded and she swallowed noisily. 'He was just *there*, suddenly. Only an outline, the streetlights behind him. Gave me a bit of a turn, see. Still, plenty of punters like the shadows, it's part of the game. "Hullo, there," says I. "Lonely, are we?" "Strip," he grunts, just like that. You have to laugh, don't you. "My, you *are* impetuous," I says. "Come on home, luv, it's a bit parky for outdoor sports ..."' The words tailed off. She sat bolt upright, clawing sightlessly at the material in her hands.

'Go on Lil,' he urged, very soft, and she shuddered at the sound.

'Moved round a step, didn't he,' she whispered, 'into the light. No face, was there. Eyeballs and teeth was all I could see. It was – ' She stopped, taut and trembling, lost for words.

Slow and easy, he reached across and took her hands. 'No hurry, mind; take your time.'

She mustered a mirthless grin. 'Met 'em all, in my day: nippers, strippers and whippers. Not a lot of complaints, either. So jolly him along, I thought. 'Til he showed me the steel.' Her fingers closed convulsively, long scarlet nails biting into his palm. 'Held it straight and level, gave me a good look. Reddish, it was, in that light. Like blood.' A small tremor seized her. 'I *hate* knives.'

'Need a few stitches myself, girl, if you carry on.'

She released him, staring down distractedly at the small pink half-moons printed on his flesh.

'Yeah, sorry. Lost my nerve, don't mind telling you, started looking for a nice handy uniform. Fat chance; never around when you need 'em. "OK," I says. "You sweet-talked me. For you, I'll make an exception." Couldn't see the joke. "Strip," he says, and gives the blade an ugly little twist. So I stripped.' In spite of the tough talk, she was slipping away again, lost in the horror.

'I was *freezing!*' she breathed. 'Stood in my undies, clothes neatly piled, about to make the headlines after all. Eyes closed, shivering like a leaf, just waiting for the knife. Where'll he put it? I wondered.' She lifted her head, fighting her way back. 'Don't often have *that* problem! I felt two little tugs, the smallest of pricks – pardon the language. Know what the bastard did then?' For the first time, she was truly angry, a kind of incredulous outrage. 'He *groped* me! Could have had anything, the ride of his life, and all he took was a measly *feel!*' She was crying in earnest now, squeezing words between great rasping sobs. 'The filthy great animal made me *wet* myself, Huw. Can you imagine, me, *unclean?* Oh my God.'

He waited while she pulled herself together; a visible struggle for control, a deep breath, a glimpse of creamy cleavage at the V of her jacket. Quite a lady, our Lil, even in distress. She hadn't finished yet, either; he could actually *see* her sifting the facts from the terror.

'Big cold hands, Huw, like slimy codfish. Dark clothes, dark hair, I think, but it could've been the mask. I kept remembering that looney in Yorkshire. Christ, Lil, I thought, you chose the wrong profession.' And finally, the heart of it, the words she'd come to say; spoken with utter conviction, from the very depths of her being: 'Listen – *you've got to get him.*'

Evans nodded briskly, very pleased. Nice to have a hunch pay off, once in a while. 'Right you are, girl. Walk it through once more, shall we, get it down in black and white?'

She was already on her feet, shovelling stuff into her bag. 'Do us a favour! A statement, me?'

'Sit down, Lil!'

She stopped short, stunned by the sheer violence. 'Hey, don't you talk to me like that!'

'All right,' he agreed, much quieter, 'only sit down, then.

You've had your say; it's my turn.' And after a moment, she complied, doubtful and apprehensive.

Evans leaned back in his chair and adopted a reflective tone. 'Come in their droves they do, the Queens of the May. Every year, up from the villages and valleys, up to the Smoke for a sniff of Real Life and a crack at the big time. Remember the feeling, Lil? Striking a chord, am I? Is that what you want, then, a trail of sweet young bodies carved and defiled, and all because an old pro's got stage fright? Get him, you say. How shall I do that, I wonder, and nothing on paper?' He gave it a second to register, then came down hard and heavy. 'Be your age, girl!'

And suddenly she was grinning, hardboiled as ever. 'Bloody coppers, I should've known better. Give 'em a wink and they'll have your soul. Oh, what the hell!'

Her statement took an hour to type, by which time she'd grown quite perky – the retroactive bravado of unlikely escape. Even offered him a quickie on the house.

'Run along Lil, or I'll have you for corrupting a minor.'

For quite some time afterwards Evans sat nursing the typescript. A break at last, a real case, something to get your mind around. But these days, he wasn't his own man; holism and Wilson must be obeyed. On probation, too. Not the best time for personal initiatives. Only one thing for it: an unscheduled sortie upstairs ...

It's unnatural, really, Evans mused, in genuine concern. From here, you could easily believe machine controlled man. He'd entered the big office uninvited and apparently unobserved. Wilson sat hunched over the desk. Around him, consoles glowed, printers muttered, and paper spewed forth in irregular spurts. The sorcerer's apprentice; what happens when the music speeds up?

Presently, the superintendent moved, flicking switches and pressing buttons; the mechanical noises dwindled into silence. Without looking up, Wilson said, 'You wanted to see me, inspector?'

Evans came forward and laid the statement before him. 'I think you should read it, sir. Urgent, mind; it won't wait.'

'I'm busy, man; surely you can see.'

Evans shoved his hands in his pockets and stood his ground. Wilson gave him a cold glance and an exasperated sigh.

'I gather dumb insolence is the tactic of the week. Oh, very well. You'd better sit down.'

'I'll browse, sir, if it's all the same to you.'

'Suit yourself.'

Conscious of the rustle of paper at his back, Evans prowled the newly installed bookshelves. Before, this had been uncluttered space, emulsioned wall and peaceful watercolours. Smythe had attached small value to the printed word, putting his trust in practice and experience. Whereas Wilson ... He sidled along, noting titles at random: *An Interpretive Approach to Adolescent Criminality, Holism – the Preventative Paradigm, Paranoid Schizophrenia: A Diagnostic Analysis*. Duw, duw, there's pompous; why not call it *Spot the Nutter*?

Speaking of which ... He found himself by the window, peering through layers of drizzle and murk at the city below. According to Lil, there'd be a nutter loose right now. Going about his business, no doubt, mending cars or flogging insurance, indistinguishable from the common mass of humanity enduring another foul day. Unknown and unknowable until the private lightning struck, and he took to the sodden streets with his camouflage and his evil little urges. Evans' mind dawdled reluctantly back to the Yardley girl, last year. Same thing, really, except they'd got lucky. He smiled bitterly to himself. If you could call *that* lucky.

Behind him, all sound ceased. He turned to meet Wilson's quizzical stare.

'Enjoying the view, inspector? Or just trying the office for size? Never mind; I'm ready now, if it's not too much trouble.'

He strode to the desk and took the offered chair. Wilson, indicating the statement, demanded, 'What would you have done with this, before I came?'

'Stuck it on a file,' said Evans promptly. 'I'd've asked around, paged the snouts, done some legwork. Making a case, see.'

'Indeed I do. Superintendents should be kept in the dark, left to push paper and hoodwink the press.'

'You said that, mind, not me. It's only a sniff, at present. Not worth your time. You being so busy.'

Wilson frowned, but chose to ignore the challenge. 'Wrong, inspector. Need to know, remember – *my* need. Anyway, you did the right thing and I appreciate it. We'll take the necessary action at once.'

A royal we, thought Evans, if ever I heard one. Aloud he asked cautiously, 'What action?' You're not going to like it, bach, you can tell by his smirk.

Wilson folded his arms, a posture of relaxed self-confidence. 'I'd say this was ideal *Crimewatch* material. Your Miss Mendoza makes the position admirably clear. A rapist at large, armed and dangerous. We're overburdened and understaffed; very well, let's mobilise the populace. He might have been spotted already; millions of *Crimewatch* addicts out there' – he waved at the rain-blurred glass – 'and the sooner we get them working for us, the better.'

Evans had listened to this with a growing unease he couldn't wholly conceal.

'Something bothering you, inspector?'

'Looking at the weather, I was.'

'You don't approve?'

'I've seen worse. Rains a lot, in the Valleys.'

Patiently, as to a wilful child, Wilson explained, 'I want your professional opinion, not your meteorological heritage.'

'Do you, sir? Had one up-and-downer already, 'aven't we.' He was allowing more of the Welsh into his voice, a trick he'd used on Smythe. Didn't sound quite so impudent, somehow; and it seemed to be working. Wilson grew more conciliatory by the minute. 'Sycophants have their uses, Evans, but a healthy herd needs at least one maverick. What's so funny?'

'Novel idea, sir, never saw myself like that.'

'Then you'd better start. I want you to play devil's advocate; I'll make it an order, if I must.'

Evans hid another smile, thinking about taking a maverick to water . . . Then, picking words carefully, gaining impetus as he went, he began his tilt at the windmill: 'First, he's not a rapist, only a groper, far as we know.'

'Hair-splitting,' said Wilson at once. 'We'll stress the "armed and dangerous".'

An ethical issue here, mind; let it go, for now.

'Sure, there's millions of watchers, all dying to play Sherlock. But they're *amateurs*, see; find me five witnesses, I'll show you six conflicting stories. He'll be spotted from Perth to Pevensey, the phones'll never stop. Have to check everything, mind, that's the catch with amateurs: every so often, one of 'em strikes oil. Give it a month, you'll 'ave more grey hairs, a stack of paper to burn, and the Manor gone to pot while your back's turned.'

'Nonsense,' declared the superintendent flatly. 'You're years behind the times.' He aimed a pointed stare at the computer. 'One decent programme, a couple of competent ears on the switchboard, you can sort the wheat from the chaff in no time. Remember the London rapists, inspector? Never underestimate artificial intelligence.'

It wasn't the artificial kind that bothered him; but Evans didn't say so. 'Look, you go on the box, make a little drama, enlist the aid of the masses. Lovely. But you're telling Chummy, too, showing him what you know. If he's not dead simple, he'll change his patch and his MO, and you're back to square one.'

Wilson stroked his moustache absently, not in the least put out. 'Swings and roundabouts, certainly. In my view, we gain more than we lose.'

'Only if you nick 'im.' And, as Wilson blinked and hesitated, Evans pressed the attack. 'Either way, he's under pressure, alerted. Goes to ground, probably; bottles it up till it explodes. Accept that, will you, blood in the gutters? There'll *be* a next time, sir, if he's a nutter: carnage. Only a matter of where and when.'

But Wilson was recovering, yielding no more ground. 'Desperate men are careless, inspector, which gives us the advantage. Besides, he's out of action, off the streets: prevention, right?'

Evans shook his head in frustration. 'Chummy's on the run, you've got a mugshot: fine, show the viewers. A dormant case, you're stuck for leads: great, go public. Educate the population, man the *Crimewatch* lines, put a bit of gloss on enforcement. But it's got to be an alternative, a last resort. Darro, mun, it's *entertainment* we're talking about; you can't give 'em first bite!'

Wilson nodded, aloof and superior. 'As I suspected: reactionary prejudice masquerading as reason. I'm disappointed, Evans. That's not an argument, it's an apologia for a bygone age!'

He was right, of course, and no wonder. When it came to the media and matters of information technology, *he* was the expert: his choice of weapons, his victory. Cool head, boyo, try another tack.

Evans had done some homework, a quiet check on Wilson's pedigree. Apparently, he'd made his name in supertax territory, spying on the City's nabobs. Listening jobs, mostly – picking the false notes of high finance, sorting one-note fiddlers from your actual Strads. Good at it, fair play, some spectacular coups. Bloodless, though, and a long way from the streets at night. Question was, could he fight dirty?

'Not quite done, mind,' Evans warned him. 'Saving the best for last, I was.'

'Do your worst,' Wilson invited; he sounded almost bored.

'Aye, well it could be eyewash, see; thieves fall out.'

The superintendent stiffened, delivering the caution. 'You'd better explain that.'

Evans chose a nostalgic tone, the voice of experience. 'It's a dodgy life, on the game. No telling who you'll meet, in the small hours.' He flicked a casual hand at the statement. 'It's all there, isn't it? Girl like Lil needs protection; a minder, then. Pays well, but it's low status. Apprentice hardmen, short term only.'

Wilson's fingers drummed an irritated tattoo, echoing the patter of sudden rain on the glass outside. 'Get on with it, man!' But Evans wasn't to be rushed. 'Suppose, just suppose, Lil's minder got uppity, gave her a hard time, and she's looking to stitch him up. It happens; hell hath no fury ...'

'So what? What's it to us?'

'Oh, not a lot. Time we can't afford, a slice of the taxpayers' cash; nothing tangible, really. Not for the moment, anyhow.'

'But?' Looking a bit hunted, Wilson, a stranger in badlands. Been brought up too decent, poor dab.

Enjoying himself now, Evans developed the theme. 'Lil's prepared the ground, see; biding her time. Minder gets ambitious, breaks in on the heavies, makes a few steps up the ladder. One day he hits the jackpot, a big bank job. Week later, the phone rings; Lil, passing the time of day. "By the way inspector, this business on the telly last night, when the guard got stabbed? Have a word with young so-and-so, lives down the docks. It was him that threatened me, you took the details, remember? Can't stand violence, myself; have to walk the streets at night."'

'Pure conjecture, Evans, a figment of your imagination.' But it was a token thrust, lacking both passion and conviction. He hadn't caught the drift, he was striking out at random. No alleycraft, then, a weakness to be exploited now and in the future.

'It wouldn't be *public*, of course,' Evans murmured, salting the wound. 'Only gossip in pubs and massage parlours. "See that *Crimewatch*, did you, local Jack the Rapist? Well, it's all cobblers. Ole Lil got shirty with what's 'is name, the 'eavy they done for the bank job. Filth got their lines crossed, spent a bleedin' fortune on *Coppertunity Knocks*." Actually call it that, see. Sorry, sir.' He paused, letting it soak in; then added softly, 'Could get someone a bad name, gossip.' Foul blow, really, aimed at the Super's most vulnerable spot – The Image. You could see him writhe as the full implication went home.

'Let me understand you, inspector,' he began, eyeing the typed pages warily. 'You're saying she committed perjury?'

'Not at all, sir. Shattered, she was, and very convincing.' And, meeting Wilson's truculent glower squarely, he lowered the boom. 'Thing is, it's just her word. Hasn't been checked, there wasn't time. Trotted up here, I did; following orders, see.'

Wilson was on his feet, striding furiously to the window; the traditional launch pad for heavy artillery. Hard to blame him, really. If I was you, boyo, I'd be *bloody* mad! But in the end, you had to make a stand or you couldn't do the job.

The superintendent watched the weather for what seemed a

very long time. Once he half turned, and thought better of it; once he laughed, sharp and bitter. Eventually he came back, his gait steady, his face clear and composed. Seated once more at the desk, he toyed with the statement, lining the edges of the paper into a tidy pile. To Evans's amazement, he even found a wry smile. 'You've made your point, inspector. Too early to rush into print; or on to the airwaves, for that matter. We'll keep the option open, of course.'

Evans let his breath out, very relieved indeed. The Super had been fair, you had to give him that : open to reason. 'I'd really appreciate the extra time, sir. With your permission.'

No harm in a little diplomatic grovel, even if he had caved in. 'Granted.'

Wilson was crisp and good-humoured; and determined to have the last word. As Evans made for the door, he warned, 'Do it right, inspector. He may be only a groper, but I want him off the streets.'

'Amen,' said Evans, and got out fast before he changed his mind.

CHAPTER SIX

Taffy was a thief, thought Wilson grimly, as Evans bore his stolen victory away. How do you refute a man who sits, craggy and unyielding as Welsh rock, deflecting each thrust with barely concealed contempt and enjoying your discomfort? You don't, not by debate, anyway; not while he chose to cite working knowledge you didn't share and couldn't challenge. Exploiting this weakness, Evans had vetoed the *Crimewatch* option without the slightest compunction, thereby stealing both initiative and responsibility. Impressive loot; small wonder he looked so smug. Here endeth the first lesson: in future, don't ask him, tell him. Get a grip, or he'll end up running the whole damn show.

Meanwhile, there was a deadline to meet. He'd promised the commissioner a programme, something to streamline the matching of psychiatric profiles and *modus operandi.* Contemplating the silent consoles and a strew of raw print-out, he realised that Evans had wrecked his evening, too. He was due for squash with Harry in two hours. Debugging would take much longer; he'd have to call and cancel. And tell Gina he'd be late. She'd *love* that. He sighed and picked up the phone. Demands of duty; might as well kill two birds ...

She answered at the second ring, blithe and breathless as ever. 'Richard, how *nice!* I was just thinking of you, and planning a *delicious* dinner!'

He swallowed hard, biting the bullet. He explained as gently as he could, her cries of disappointment cutting to the quick. *Blast* you, Evans!

'Listen,' he pleaded, 'do me a favour, please?'

'I can't think of any reason why I should!' A pause, a familiar note of resignation. 'Of *course* I will, silly!'

He told her about Harry, asked her to break the news. 'It might come a little easier from you, my love.'

There was a long, curiously tense silence. At last she said, 'Do you really think that's wise?'

'Tell him something's come up, and I can't get to the phone.'

'Richard, that's dishonest! It's your arrangement; do your own dirty work.'

'Not dishonest, just diplomatic. Come on, darling. You're so much better at this kind of thing.'

Again, the hesitation: and an unexpected question. 'How late will you be?'

Briefly, he considered fudging it, but the least he owed her was the truth. 'It's expected tomorrow, I daren't let him down. Half-ten at the earliest; could be as late as midnight.' Finally, with a reluctance he could almost taste, she gave her consent.

'Bless you, Gina. I'll make it up to you later.'

'Don't be too sure of *that*!'

But he *was* sure, and the prospect sent him to work with renewed vigour. As the day faded and the sky outside grew dim, he lost himself in the intricacies of probability. It was an intellectual exercise, pure and demanding; the kind he liked best. Because the computer acknowledged no shades of opinion, no clash of personalities, and logic remained the sole impartial arbiter of achievement.

'How about you, princess? One for the road?'

Rodney the rugger hero speaking, a trifle glazed and very imposing: more a demand than an invitation. Why not? Sara sighed inwardly, acknowledging the risk. Already he'd assumed a certain licence, looming over her with an insinuating grin and a subtle air of ownership. In this mood, he would take consent for the wider acquiescence he so clearly expected; and which she did not propose to grant. The evening would end in a niggly rearguard action; men like Rodney, once aroused, were never easy to divert. Reluctantly, she covered her glass.

'Not for me, thanks.'

'Aw, come on!'

She shook her head, sorrowful but firm. 'No, really.' Scowling ferociously, he turned and made for the bar. Half-cut, he nevertheless moved with the graceful economy of the gifted sportsman, casually balancing a tray of empties on one enormous hand. His departure provided breathing space. Briefly, she sat alone in the crowd.

The Black Lion typified a certain style – mock Olde Englishe. Rambling, low-ceilinged rooms, heavy timbers and stone facings, an artificial log-fire glowing in the massive hearth. Hunting prints on the walls, horse-brasses everywhere, and the furniture determinedly rustic: a place to visit for leisurely drinks and intimate conversation. Amazingly, half an hour before stoptap on a Monday night, the lounge was going full blast; an atmosphere thick with noise, tobacco smoke, and too many bodies. Student bodies.

Smiling at her own private joke, she eavesdropped on snatches of conversations heard above the babel.

'. . . yes, but Molière is *so* much funnier in the original . . .', '. . . chip into the box, win second phase, roll the maul to suck in the flankers . . .', '. . . but, darling, didn't you know? He's *completely* gay, poor thing . . .', '. . . big ends, old son, by the sound of it. When did you last have her serviced? . . .' And all the time, she was pleasantly conscious of stagestruck Fran's furious glare from the other end of the table. Too bad; it was *her* idea in the first place.

Whereas Sara had never intended to be here. The prospect of a 'hen party for the language lasses' – Fran's words – offered little appeal; merely a different setting for the same semi-incestuous bitchiness. But, early in the evening, study palled, the French unseen turned stubborn, and she began to regret her self-imposed isolation. The pub was a five-minute bus ride away; she grabbed a coat and came in search of familiar company.

Even then, she'd almost changed her mind. At first she thought she had the venue wrong; hardly a hen party! A pretty fresher, pink with plonk and excitement, gave her the low-down. 'Someone spilled the beans! The rugger crowd took us by storm – no casualties and *very* token resistance!' Sara nodded, reading the signs and planning a rapid withdrawal. Any minute now they'd be singing. But she'd been spotted, surrounded, and awarded a brimming glass; might as well relax and enjoy it. Oddly enough, she *had* enjoyed it – the more so when, as she shrugged out of her coat and pushed her hair into place, Rodney had forsaken Fran and ambled straight to her side.

He was on his way back, half-a-head taller than anyone else, his battered features tight in concentration as he steered the laden tray through the mêlée. He made it with only moderate spillage, using his elbows to good effect and apologising to no one. 'Barging in the line-out,' said an admiring female voice. Welsh, by the accent, which explained the knowledgeable tone.

Settling himself beside her, Rodney downed a mammoth swallow of beer and pursued his clumsy advance. 'What are you doing later?'

'Going home to bed.' She meant it as flat rejection. Recognising, too late, the alternative interpretation, she hastened to make herself clear: '*Alone*, Rodney.'

'Live for the moment, princess. We're only young once.'

'Exactly. I'm working hard. I need plenty of sleep.'

He wagged a large finger under her nose. 'I won't believe it: she walks in beauty, like the night.' And, seeing her astonishment, pitching his voice for her only, he intoned:

> 'Good-night? ah! no; the hour is ill
> Which severs those it should unite;
> Let us remain together still,
> Then it will be *good* night.

There. Beneath this rough exterior beats the sensitive heart of a poet.'

Impressed and careful to hide it, she wondered sarcastically, 'How many innocents have swallowed *that* line? What else can you quote, excluding Eskimo Nell, of course?'

'Hurtful words, my lovely. Percy Bysshe Shelley, a great man. Alas, I knew him well.' Grinning owlishly he confessed, 'Had to cram him for "A" level.'

'Then you're a great fraud!'

'And you are a *belle dame sans merci*, who spurns my tender approaches.'

'About as tender as the average rhinoceros.'

The level of noise was steadily rising. Their faces, she realised, were very close together. She was aware of his healthy male odour, the extraordinary length of his eyelashes; and the unwavering force of Fran's hostility. Serves you right, shouldn't have pinched him from Jenny. You can have him back when I've finished.

Which wouldn't be long, she thought wryly, as someone nearby launched the inevitable song. 'Four-and-twenty virgins came down from Inverness ...' Rodney winced and gazed heavenwards; the publican, evidently a man who rated prudence above profits, called time seven minutes early. Denied further excess and sensing a sordid finale, the crowd broke up. Fran commandeered the most presentable rugby type and made a flamboyant exit; though whether for Rodney's benefit or her own, Sara neither knew nor cared. Quite soon, they were alone at the table, enduring the obscene and tuneless serenade.

'Knock it off, you chaps,' Rodney bawled, making a passable show of righteous indignation. 'Can't you tell a lady when you see one?'

Raspberries and catcalls, and a beer-flushed youth who rashly enquired, 'No, can *you*?'

A sudden, bated hush. Rodney came smoothly to his feet, very large and very angry: awesome. Icily, he advised, 'Grow up, drink up, and go home, Bobby, while you can still walk.' Beer, apparently, made Bobby suicidal; he was actually prepared to contest the issue. But team solidarity prevailed, and he was hustled smartly out of the firing line. Rodney's big fists opened. He turned to her, a posture of genuine humility.

'Sorry, princess, honest. He's only a kid with a skinful.'

An improbable and affecting gentleness, and she gave him her best smile. 'Of course. I understand.'

Sensing concessions, he suggested hopefully, 'Change your mind? About later, I mean?'

'Certainly not!'

'Well at least let me see you home.'

Again she was tempted, again she resisted. It was by no means too late for one thing to lead to another.

'Don't bother, I'll catch a bus.'

He glanced at his watch. 'Not now, you won't.'

'It's a very short walk. I'll be fine.'

He frowned threateningly. 'I'll follow you, anyway, so I know where you live.'

Time to call a halt, once and for all. 'Back off, Rodney, or I swear I'll never speak to you again!'

He shook his head, his ugly-handsome features creased in comic woe. 'I *do* like a girl with spirit. Let me help you with your coat.'

He made a production of it, ending with a flourish and a protective arm draped around her shoulders.

'I'll say this for you, Rodney – you're very determined.'

'Only when there's something I really want.'

She freed herself briskly. 'You mean some*body*, don't you?'

He let that pass, preferring to pick up a much earlier remark. 'You promised a raincheck. I won't forget.'

From the corner of her eye, she could see the publican fidgeting. Anxious to lock up, of course, but wary of Rodney's displeasure. Prudent. She was impatient herself now; anything to get away. 'Well – we'll see.' And finally, he let her go.

It was quiet outside, and she was grateful. If nothing else, Rodney's persistence had spared her the leers and whistles of after-hour stragglers; apart from a distant and solitary policeman, she had the High Street to herself. Briefly, she paused to covet fashions in a boutique window, pursing her lips at the price tags. Outside the bank, she confronted her own reflection, slender and white-coated, the blond hair drifting behind. Run along home, pretty lady, before yon fuzz gets the wrong idea and does you for loitering. A night wind sprang from nowhere, as though to stress the point.

She crossed the road and turned the corner. Shivering, wishing she'd dressed for the weather, she raised her collar and hugged the trenchcoat tight against her cotton T-shirt. Gesture and clothing, she realised, had prompted Rodney's abrupt and mysterious change of partners. Sara had been adjusting her hair, both hands behind her head, the thin material stretched across her breasts. A simple, reflexive action, devoid of artifice or intent, yet it drew him like a beetle to the flame. And suddenly, she understood, moment and motive. He'd come hotfoot and panting because she *wasn't wearing a bra!* A dino, not a rhino, our Rodders, couldn't tell a libber from a libertine; no wonder he'd been so aggressive.

She paced the avenue's sweeping bend, the main road a receding orange glow. Rocked by the fitful breeze, individual street lights cast shifting pools of paler light. Between them, stark and black, the urban trees stood almost leafless. Sara's breath made feathery plumes; already, a thin rime of frost gleamed from rooftops and the windows of parked cars. But activity warmed her, and she'd always liked walking at night. Peace, solitude, and the comforting rhythmic echo of her own footfalls.

The way ahead lay windswept and deserted. Here, the street broadened, detached mansions set well back and screened by dense hedges. Why, then, an echo? Someone else walking, of course. It wasn't *that* late. The final constitutional for a house-bound alsatian, a wayward husband getting his excuses down pat. Her private smile broadened. Perhaps, after all, PC Plod dogged her steps, his notebook poised to log each illicit contact. Sorry, little man, the Harlot of Jerusalem is taking an evening off. She suppressed a giggle, lengthened her stride, and let her mind roam free.

Only tonight, it didn't: events at the Black Lion continued to absorb her. Over the past year, she'd grown accustomed to Charles' public manner – smooth, mature and laid-back, lacking any hint of possession. For all his gaucheness, Rodney's lusty attentions held a certain refreshing candour. Behind the macho façade, she'd glimpsed a more complex being – the innate gentleness of the very large, a genuine regard for the power of language. Kindred spirits? Mutual attraction, anyway, and stronger than anything she'd felt before. Forget it, girl, no time for complications; degree exams are only months away.

Work again, she couldn't escape. She was stuck on a passage

from Saint-Exupéry, the Milky Way above North Africa. In French, it read with a delicate grandeur which, hard though she tried, she simply couldn't reproduce. Her translation limped along, a procession of lifeless clichés. She dawdled, stargazing through an iced trellis of TV antennae, struggling to capture the images. Diamonds on blue velvet, wisps of pearly opalescence. Good grief, it sounds like Hatton Garden. You're getting worse, not better!

And the echo had drawn nearer.

There was a slurred, secretive quality to it now, a suggestion of menace which stirred darker reaches of imagination. Alien eyes at her back, an unseen presence, calculating and watchful. The lamps seemed dimmer and further apart, the blackness in between deeper and more sinister. She was isolated and uneasy, and still a long way from home. Unconsciously, she began to hurry, her heels ringing staccato, the coat flapping against her knees.

Don't be absurd, she reproached herself, slowing and steadying, you are *not* alone. On either side of this chilly corridor, people are eating, watching TV, making love. You have only to call and they'll come. Thus reassured, proud of her own good sense, she could face whatever or whoever lurked behind. She took a deep breath, checked, and glanced back.

As far as she could see on either side, the empty pavements mocked her, prompting a state of real alarm. *He didn't want to be seen!* Then, at the very edge of vision, stealthy movement, a shadow crabbing from one ghostly tree to the next. Her pulse lurched and fear caressed the nape of her neck. She had actually started for the nearest front gate when recognition and realisation flooded in, reducing her to furious relief. Though foreshortened by distance and weak light, the bulky silhouette was unmistakable – Rodney! A moment to recover composure and she spoke; loud enough to carry, low enough not to wake the neighbours.

'Rodney, you ass, I nearly had a heart attack! For heaven's sake, go home!'

No response, no sheepish laugh. She ought to go back and give him a piece of her mind. But the wind had turned vicious, she was embarrassed at her own groundless panic, he simply wasn't worth the trouble. She tossed her head defiantly, whirled, and struck out once more. Twenty yards, thirty, fifty, her footsteps falling crisp and clear; and no echo. Should jolly well think not!

She branched off the avenue, passing along meaner, narrower pathways. Students couldn't aspire to a chic address : I wonder which squalid little hovel Rodney and his cronies occupy? Must be nearby, he was obviously coming here anyway. Her enjoyment was dead, smothered by fatigue and lingering anxiety. She couldn't quiet the secret dread he'd raised – and she *hated* practical jokes. What a fool he'd been, how callous, how immature, how *young*! Charles would never ruin an evening like this; *his* surprises came gift-wrapped and labelled 'Harrods'.

On the other hand, neither would Charles rise like a wrathful warlord to avenge her slighted honour. Charm his way out, Charles would, and devil take the hindmost. She rounded the last corner, the flats loomed up ahead. The nearness of home lifted her spirits and inclined her to charity. Perhaps, after all, she should feel flattered by Rodney's protectiveness. Maybe, in his quaint, outdated way, he was only being gallant, making sure she came safely to harbour.

So, when the echo started again, fast and urgent and not far away, she merely waited, folding her arms and tapping her foot. Should she offer coffee or slap his face? She glanced over her shoulder into the icy wind which flayed her skin and stung her eyes. And at last, as vision cleared on the empty, silent street, true fear was upon her; the price of her own foolhardiness. It wasn't Rodney, it never had been! Only a few more steps, dear God let me make it! She ran blindly forwards, blundering straight into him – faceless horror and a glittering blade.

A feral smell, eyes that blazed in cruel malice. He bared his teeth, aiming the knife directly at her heart.

'Quiet, whore! One sound and I cut.' Crippled by cold and shock, her brain cast about for anything she'd ever heard or read. Keep him talking, don't give in.

'I – I have money,' she whispered. 'Please take it and go.'

A pitiless chuckle, striking sick terror to the very depths of her soul. Already, his free hand was wrenching at her skirt.

'Don't! I'll do it.' Fumbling her coat buttons open, she knew she was lost, knew with utter certainty what must now follow. He bore her downwards, hard and heavy and uncaring, and she was screaming silently; Rodney, where are you? Please, please help me! With rank breath in her face, a knife at her throat, and the roadside gravel raking her naked flesh, she must simply submit and endure. But somewhere beyond her quivering, brutalised body, aloof from pain and his foul animal rutting, a tiny part of her mind stayed cool and remote. In this moment and the next, and the one after that, there is only one thing to do. Survive.

Richard Wilson sidled through his own darkened hallway, shrugging off his coat as he went. It was after midnight; often, when gently coaxed from sleep, Gina could be quite magnificent. It would be better that way – passion before recrimination. The programme nestled safe inside his briefcase – fool-proof, he believed, though only working trials would tell.

He had risen from his labours mentally exhausted, famished, triumphant, and totally disoriented. Blackness outside and an unbelieving glance at his watch told him the worst. A wild-eyed dash through the station, his heels ringing in the quiet corridors, a breakneck drive across town. Privileges of rank, he'd thought, gambling on amber, God help the uniform who stops me tonight.

He started up the stairs, carefully skirting the one that creaked; to no avail. Gina's voice came high and shaky. 'Is that you, Richard?' Idiot! On top of everything else, you've frightened her. Aloud, he called, 'I thought you'd be asleep. Can I bring you something? Coffee? A drink?'

'Please yourself.' He was prepared for anger; at times like this she could be very scathing. Instead, she sounded distant, almost apathetic.

He entered the bedroom cautiously, wearing a supplicant's grin. 'If I had a hat, I'd toss it in first. What can I say? *Mea maxima culpa.*'

She sat severely on the edge of the bed, her hands folded in her lap. Her skin was creamy, recently bathed and perfumed, revealed and offset by the lacy apricot nightgown; she looked and smelled ravishing. But her eyes held nothing for him, neither welcome nor reproach. She seemed absorbed in some deep and private pain. 'You should have come home, Richard.'

A blend of loneliness and fear, he decided. You couldn't blame her: the screen was full of housebreaking and rape. Remorse overwhelmed him; he hated to hurt her.

'I'm sorry, I've been thoughtless. I'll see to it first thing in the morning – an extra patrol whenever I'm away at night.'

She stirred, a hollow laugh, a pitying stare. 'I've *got* a policeman. The trouble is, he's never here when I want him.'

'We'll soon change all that,' he promised, throwing off his clothes; but when he returned from the bathroom, the lamp was out, and Gina was feigning sleep.

She lay beside him, cold and unresponsive, refusing to be roused. 'Leave me alone, please,' she mumbled. 'I'll feel better in the morning.'

'You feel marvellous right now.'

'Richard!'

And as he rolled away in sorrow and frustration, he was already apportioning the blame. Thank you and good-night, Inspector Evans.

CHAPTER SEVEN

AN INSISTENT clamour chivvied Evans awake. The covers had slipped, his shoulders were icy. Quiet as the grave outside, you could almost smell the frost. The digital clock glowed palely: 01.26. Phone calls at night, a copper's delight; it's getting too much for you bach. Creaky and shivering, he stretched for the receiver. Warner's voice, ponderous but urgent: 'Sorry to disturb you, sir. Young lady claiming rape. Get over quick and you can log it, know what I mean?'

Gathering his wits, noting the light stress on the word *you*, Evans nodded in the dark. Looked out for his mates, Warner did.

'Aye, good thinking. Sent for the police surgeon, have you?'

A defensive note, Warner playing it cagey. 'She's acting very odd, sir. Too chirpy by 'alf, if you ask me. Car's coming: best see for yourself.'

Not so good; just one more false alarm. Resignedly, Evans grunted, 'Better page the understudy.'

'Already did, mate.' He chuckled slyly. 'Some bird answered. Said a naughty word, didn't she? Sar'nt Beddoes was not amused.'

This thought, and a healthy dollop of Johnny Walker, sustained Evans while he dressed. Only sleep, *he* was missing.

The police driver was little more than a boy and much too eager, taking the first roundabout on two wheels. Evans snarled, curt and obscene; thereafter, progress was sedate. Slumped against the shiny upholstery, watching the deserted streets through gritty eyes, Evans felt about ninety years old.

Beddoes hovered at the nick, morose and monosyllabic.

'Cheer up, boyo,' Evans advised. 'Nice night for it.'

'It *was*.' Evans sighed in false commiseration. 'Interrupted, were we? Ripped untimely from the womb, or thereabouts?'

Beddoes gave him a blank stare. 'Dunno what you're on about.'

'Course not. Shakespeare, see.'

'Oh yeah? Geezer 'oo makes fishin' rods?'

'Duw, there's culture for you. *Fishin' rods!*'

From his post at the desk, Warner brought them to order, stolid as suet. 'Name of Sara Holroyd, student. Raped, she says, goin' home from a pub. Soon as 'e'd done, she 'ops up, dusts 'erself off and swans in 'ere bright as you please.' He shook his head. ''Ard to believe, innit? She's down the rest room, 'avin' a cuppa with a WPC.'

'You just broke the law, mind,' Evans informed him.

Warner blinked, uncomprehending. ''Oo, me?'

'They're plain PCs now; *very* plain, some of 'em. Double-yous not allowed. Sexist, see: discrimination.'

'All the same to me, mate.'

'You're joking!' said Beddoes, incredulous. 'If you can't tell 'em apart, you're older'n I thought!'

'*Vive la difference*,' muttered Warner, surprising them. 'Go to it, *mes braves*.' They left him still rocking with suppressed mirth.

They trudged the dim corridor, sobering by the moment.

'Preliminary enquiries, boyo,' Evans warned. 'Take it nice and steady.'

Beddoes snorted scornfully. 'You 'eard the man: a fairy story. Some little tart making trouble.'

'Even so.'

''S'all right for you, uncle. I got unfinished business.'

'And *vive le sport*,' said Evans, receiving a surly glower for his pains.

A windowless cubicle at the heart of the building, the rest room boasted a Red Cross wall cabinet, a grey-blanketed divan, and a pervading whiff of disinfectant; the four of them filled it to capacity. The choreography of interrogation took

Evans, unobtrusive, to a corner, and left Beddoes facing the girl across the formica-topped table. Catching Evans' eye as she perched on the divan, the WPC slipped him an almost imperceptible nod. One believer, then, Warner notwithstanding. While Beddoes began the litany, restrained but terse, Evans took stock of the plaintiff.

Attractive piece, if you liked 'em slim and vulnerable; and she did seem remarkably self-possessed. Her answers came readily, a husky alto and just a suspicion of the North. Sitting upright, meeting Beddoes' stare head-on, she might have been reporting a lost dog.

She described an impromptu party at the Black Lion, and the need to discourage a persistent admirer.

'Name?' demanded Beddoes at once.

'Oh, it wasn't *him*! Just a rugger type taking too much for granted.' She made it sound commonplace, as though she faced such irritations daily. Her responses were *too* ready; unguarded.

'We'll find out,' Beddoes warned. 'Might be better coming from you.'

'Rodney,' she said, casual and indifferent. 'I don't know his surname.'

Beddoes let that hang, then wrote in his notebook, very deliberate. The heavy silence prompted her first nervous gesture, an unsteady hand touching her forehead.

As she told of the walk home and her 'silly fear of being followed', Evans focused on appearances. Her long blond hair lay dull and tangled; the single light bulb struck no answering gleam. Odd, that. You'd expect her to keep it nice. Despite the heat in the room, her coat was buttoned to the neck and held protectively to her body; wonder what she's nursing underneath? As he watched, her green eyes welled with unshed tears. *Something* had rattled her, no question.

'It happened so fast,' she was saying, jerky and compulsive, 'it was so unexpected. I was *home*, you see, only yards from the flat.' He'd sprung out of nowhere, she said, and forced her to undress. 'He didn't hurt me much, it was over almost at once. I was lucky.' Funny thing to say, having just been raped, but she seemed unaware of the paradox. She'd waited a while, to be sure he'd really gone, then come directly to the nick. On foot. 'Most of all, of course, I wanted a bath,' she continued, with a forced brightness painful to behold, 'but I've read about these things – the medical side, I mean – so I came straight here.' And, waking at last to Beddoes's patent disbelief, she threw him a rash challenge.

'Well, isn't that what one's *supposed* to do, in these circumstances?'

A doomed echo of her earlier worldliness, and Beddoes brushed it aside. 'You walked? After all that, alone in the dark, you walked the best part of a mile?'

The WPC, a placid, matronly type hand-picked for this work, had been regarding Beddoes with growing distaste. The divan creaked as she leaned forward and suggested gently, 'Tell him, luv. Tell him what you told me: why you weren't afraid.'

The girl swallowed, suddenly very pale. Her glance slid desperately around the cramped room, her hands opened in appeal. 'Don't you see? There was nothing left to fear!' A ring of truth there, thought Evans, or she's a great little actress.

She shifted uncomfortably on the chair, and the coat divided over her knees. Bare legs, in this weather? Worth noting, anyhow. In Evans's experience, tights seldom survived a sexual assault.

Beddoes pressed on, cold and remorseless. What did she mean, *forced*? She raised her left hand and laid a shaky red fingernail against her neck. An awful lethargy settled over Evans's brain; he knew what was coming.

'He had a knife. He held it at my throat: here.'

Beddoes, unwitting, merely nodded in satisfaction. 'Won't have any bother picking him out, then.' And, as she waited, uncomprehending, he rammed the point home. 'Face to face, like. Know him again, won't you?' It hadn't occurred to her, identification, you could see the horror it provoked. 'A mask,' she murmured, her eyes wide with agonised remembrance. 'It was ... very grotesque.'

Good word, grotesque, Evans thought distractedly, not one Lily would use; but the tone, and the depth of revulsion conveyed, was identical. As, no doubt, was the creature who

72

inspired it. Own up, bach, you've been ducking it since Warner first said 'rape'. Daft, really, hoping against hope. He leaned back and closed his eyes, past caring. The exchanges continued, half-heard, irrelevant.

'Ah, a mask,' Beddoes grunted, tart and sceptical. 'Big guy, was he?'

'Yes. Not tall, but very broad.'

Aye, Lil said the same. Call it a day, then; summon the surgeon, record the statement, ferry the girl home. Start the machinery, oil the wheels – and get the excuses ready for Wilson. Darro, what a shambles! He was collecting himself, forcing his eyelids apart, when she whispered, 'Oh! I've just remembered. He was wearing a tracksuit, a dark colour.' Her voice rose, the raw edge of hysteria. 'He had trouble with one of the zips!'

Evans saw Beddoes recoil, his features pinched, his nostrils flaring as if she'd delivered a mortal insult. He looked raw and badly ruffled – a bit like that morning, after his convent caper. From this moment, the interview developed a strange distortion of scale and logic. Beddoes assumed the spotlight, imposing his will, hounding her towards an obscure purpose of his own. No mercy, mind; every question barbed and hurtful. 'Forced, you said. How come your coat's all lily white? Show me the bruises!'

'I told you, he made me undress.'

'Oh yeah? Folded it up, did you, neat and tidy? Good of 'im to spare the time. Where's your tights?'

'I – wasn't wearing tights.'

'What else, I ask myself? Stand up! Take your coat off!'

The WPC half rose: 'Here, wait a minute, what d'you –?' and Beddoes rounded on her, furious. 'You're a spectator, not a bleedin' umpire. Sit down and shut up!'

Discipline held, just. The WPC obeyed. In a low, choked voice she muttered, 'Please do as he asks, Miss Holroyd.'

The girl was trembling, either from fear or anger. Bit of both, probably. She removed the coat in a series of violent, slashing movements and faced Beddoes defiantly. For Evans, wounded as she was, she brought a touch of nobility to the dingy little cell; but Beddoes merely smiled, icy-cruel.

73

'No tights, no bra? 'Oo's the lucky man, sweetheart, 'oo were you off to, 'alf-naked?'

'For God's sake, I'd been studying! I only went out for one drink!'

'And stayed till after stoptap.' Beddoes came slowly to his feet, looming over her, his eyes bright with triumph. 'You've bin lying, Sara, you shouldn't 'ave mentioned the bath. There *is* something worse, and we all know what. First thing *any* woman'll do is clean up – unless she's sure it can't take.'

As they stood, their faces harshly lit and inches apart, their mutual contempt plain to see, Evans caught her fleeting change of expression. Dismay, perhaps, or maybe self-disgust? Something she couldn't handle, anyway. Somehow, finally, Beddoes had stolen her innocence; and with it, both courage and composure. All at once, she was just another victim, bone-weary, out of her depth, and sick in spirit. She sank back to her seat, her head bowed, her shoulders quivering.

Beddoes prowled, pacing the confined floor like a caged predator. The sweat surged from his brow, furrowed in fierce concentration. The WPC watched him with loathing; the girl simply ignored him. Suddenly he checked and whirled around, incandescent with discovery. He was like some vengeful prophet, one arm extended in accusation, a voice of absolute conviction.

'You were out lookin' for a mug to set up! Got a bun in the oven already, 'aven't you? All right – *'oo's is it?'*

The WPC could contain herself no longer, coming like an Amazon to the fray. 'You bastard, leave her alone! Can't you see ...' Briefly, the room was a cockpit, brimful of heat and noise and emotion. Evans leaned forwards and crashed the flat of his hand against the table. 'That'll do!'

In the frozen, shamed silence, he set about restoring sanity. 'Thank you, Sar'nt Beddoes. Wait outside, please.' As Beddoes stormed off, he told the WPC, 'He's right, you're only an observer. We'll talk later.' She flounced back to the divan, and Evans was left confronting the girl.

She sat slack and drained, her green eyes empty, her small face ashen. With a massive effort, he pulled himself together. Come on, bach, there's work to do after all. Patiently, doggedly, he drew her story out; parental feuding, academic ambition, and a man named Charles. Here, she rallied momentarily, making her one confession. 'In a way, your precious sergeant was right. I'm on the Pill, you see. For Charles.' Her reserves failed: she sank towards total collapse. As the sobs broke and her body began to heave, he noted the address of her lover. Then, breathless and desolate, she cried, 'Why are you treating me like a criminal?'

Routine, he could have said, because things often aren't as they seem. Too complex for here and now; besides, it was comfort she wanted, not explanations. He made soothing noises, consigned her to the WPC, and went in search of Beddoes.

He was loitering in the corridor, still seething.

'You want to ease off, boyo,' Evans advised him. 'Over the top, you were, at the end.'

Beddoes fell into step, his lip curling in disdain. 'Oughta get an Oscar, that kid. An act, uncle, believe me.'

'You'd decided in advance, see,' Evans went on evenly. 'Dangerous, that, I told you before.'

'Give over, you know the figures! 'Appens mostly in the mind, rape does.'

'Could've saved you the bother. Still, you weren't to know.'

Beddoes had slowed, watching him narrowly. 'Know what?'

'Remember Lil? Handsome lady you were oglin' a few days back?'

'Your fancy piece? Course I do.'

'Nasty experience, she had; got groped in the park.'

'Nasty? At 'er age, she oughta be grateful!'

Evans played along, nudging him back to normality. 'Many a good tune on an old fiddle, mind. Thing is, she gave a description. Masked, chunky, and handy with a knife.'

Beddoes halted in his tracks, his youthful face made gaunt by doubt and shadows. 'You *knew*? And you let me work 'er over?'

'Give us credit, mun; couldn't've stopped you with a Panzer!'

Beddoes nodded grimly. 'You're right there. Jesus!'

Walking again, Evans explained about Wilson. 'Not feeling too clever myself, if it's any consolation. Listen, you did what you had to, dredged up the truth. She's not pregnant, by the way: on the Pill.'

Beddoes revived immediately, loth to relinquish the scent. 'Got a name?'

'Oh sure.'

'Pay our respects, shall we, while I'm in the mood?'

'That's what I mean, see: ease off. It's four in the morning and nothing to go on. He'll need checking, no doubt; but not now.'

They approached the broader, brighter area round the desk. Warner sat in regal isolation, bolt upright – and fast asleep.

'A man after my own heart,' murmured Evans admiringly. 'Takes years of practice, that does.'

'Balls,' said Beddoes, rude and loud. ''Orses do it from birth.' He still looked edgy, at odds with himself and the world; and Evans lost patience. 'If you're so bloody keen, get yourself out with the incident squad. Have a good rummage, burn off some of the vinegar.'

'Reckon I will, uncle; 'ow about you?' He jerked a thumb at the somnolent Warner. 'Go thou and do likewise, eh?'

Evans sighed tiredly. 'Whatever *you* think, boyo, the complaint stands: I'm calling the quack. And, Roy? You'd best avoid that girl.'

Halfway to the door, Beddoes paused. 'Like the plague, uncle,' he said feelingly. 'Like the bleedin' plague.'

The police surgeon was a tall man, the kind the media call 'distinguished-looking'. Respected for the precision of his work and feared for the vitriol of his tongue, he was also rated a formidable tippler. Twenty minutes later, immaculate despite the ungodly hour, he strode past Evans without so much as a glance. A faint boozy miasma lingered in his wake; mine, too, I expect, thought Evans, mindful of the Johnny Walker.

Waiting, Evans fell to a state midway between sleep and wakefulness. His mind, beset by fatigue and reeling from the events of the past two hours, grappled with alternatives and shied away from any sort of judgement.

The essence of Sara Holroyd continued to elude him. Unnaturally controlled one minute, utterly distraught the next, her visible emotions had covered an impressive range. Acting, Beddoes called it. Well, maybe. Certainly, there were at least two different men in her life. Not your actual vestal virgin, either. Yet there was a certain quality about her, an air of innocence defiled and grieving. If you believed her – the WPC surely did – every reaction could be readily understood. Give it a rest, bach. Time and routine will tell.

A can of worms, mind, rape; Beddoes had at least that much right. If you weren't damn careful, a case like this could get thoroughly messy. Private vendetta spilling into the public domain, daylight forced into the dark and grubby corners of personal lives. Apologies all round and everyone back to their own beds; very tasty. Even so, this ever-present copper's nightmare couldn't fully justify Beddoes' behaviour. It had started, he reckoned, as the girl described her attacker; yet Beddoes knew nothing of Lily Mendoza's testimony, nor of the subsequent clash with Wilson. So, what the hell was eating the daft young sod? It made no kind of sense.

A hand on his shoulder; Warner waking him for the second time tonight. 'Surgeon's leaving, sir. Better hustle, if you want a word.'

Evans lumbered groggily to his feet. The doctor stood nearby, wrestling into a camelhair topcoat.

'All done, sir?'

'Yes.' Brusque and dismissive, and a distinctly icy glare.

'Something to go on?'

'You'll have my report as soon as is humanly possible.'

Offensive, really, but Evans couldn't afford the luxury of temperament. 'Don't like to press, sir, only – we have to take a decision.'

'I'm aware, actually. It's hardly my first experience.'

Evans swallowed. Older you get, the harder it is to grovel; but still. 'I'd appreciate a hint, sir.'

The surgeon buttoned his coat and adjusted his silk muffler, just so. A sniff, a supercilious glance for the plebeian surroundings. 'Very well, if you insist. Unquestionably, intercourse took place. Doubtless, forensics will inform you on timing in due course. Penetration was brief and transient; there are few indications of undue force. In my view, therefore, the physical evidence is inconclusive.'

Evans sighed, knuckling his inflamed eyes. 'Aye, well, thanks anyway.'

The doctor bristled, drawing himself to his full height. 'You asked my opinion, inspector. Do me the courtesy of receiving it uninterrupted!'

Do as the man says, boyo, what else is there?

'The young lady's *mental* state, however, is entirely conversant with extreme trauma. I am not a psychiatrist, but from what I have just seen and heard, I suspect that the trauma was induced at least partially by events *subsequent* to intercourse. Do I make myself clear?'

Dangerous ground, this. Cautiously, Evans muttered, 'Routine enquiries, sir, properly witnessed and supervised.'

The doctor was breathing heavily, his contempt open and awesome. 'Indeed! There are times, inspector, when I despise my job. Tonight is one of them. I hope, in the name of whatever little humanity you may possess, that you feel the same. Good-night to you, sir!'

He swept out, slamming the door. Warner, dozing again, woke with a start, and a gormless geriatric grin. 'Evenin', inspector, what're you doin 'ere?'

'Leaving,' said Evans.

CHAPTER EIGHT

EVANS STAYED, doing the necessary; duty, you couldn't shirk it. Irregular comings and goings, paperwork, and crushing weariness. Almost imperceptibly, night became morning – uniform greyness, a persistent drizzle, and the city oozing out of slumber. At some point, Warner brought the statement; then the WPC emerged. The girl, blank and teetering under her motherly wing, was gentled away to the scene of the attack. An hour later, Beddoes returned, bloodshot and unrepentant.

'Building site near 'er flat,' he reported. 'Forensic's goin' frantic, fillin' testtubes before the brickies trample it to pulp. Waste o' time, they'll find sweet FA. She's connin' you, uncle.'

'Cooled off, have you?' Evans asked him hopefully. He sounded less certain, somehow; defensive.

'Course I 'ave.'

'Right. Let's make eyes at the sugar daddy.'

Heedless of the weather, Beddoes drove with inspired aggression. Rush hour, mind, and hard on the nerves. Once, red lights blazed just ahead, a delivery van making an abrupt halt. Beddoes swung out and squeezed past a looming, on-coming bus. 'For Christ's sake!' Evans muttered over the blare of protesting hooters, and Beddoes gave him a four-lettered reply. So much for cooling off.

The factory office was a low modern box made of glass and pastel colours. A quiet location, landscaped surrounds, and the legend 'Thompson Technics' in large letters. They parked and trudged through the frigid murk, hunched and morose. A red Porsche lurked like a waiting bullet in the managing director's bay.

'Last of the big spenders,' said Evans, but Beddoes wasn't to be drawn.

Inside, behind a veneered partition, the pert receptionist offered a tight sweater and a professional smile. 'Can I help you, gentlemen?'

'A word with Mr Charles Thompson, please,' suggested Evans.

'Do you have an appointment, sir?'

Beddoes stepped forward, warrant card at the ready. 'Police business. Urgent.'

The smile faded fast. 'I'll show you through.'

She led them among spacious, well-lit passages, undulating prettily on spiky heels. A natural for the Beddoes chat-up, but today he followed in stony silence.

The private secretary, a fifty-year-old dragon with iron-grey hair and spinsterly eyes, offered a show of resistance. 'It may not be convenient. Mr Charles is a very busy man.'

'So am I, lady,' Beddoes retorted. 'Tell him, will you?'

Bridling at his tone, she swept into the inner sanctum, reappearing seconds later, much subdued. 'He'll see you now. This way.'

He was waiting, a poised, slim individual; mid-thirties, regulation business suit, sleek hair and a sharp grey gaze. There was an air of contained energy about him – edgy, but not apprehensive, a go-getter. The office was palatial, an egomaniac's desk, luxury wall-to-wall.

'Make yourselves comfortable, gentlemen. Coffee, or something warmer?'

Evans fancied either or both, but Beddoes had no time for amenities. 'Sara Holroyd. Know 'er at all?'

'Never heard of her,' said Thompson immediately; then he flicked a switch and spoke to the intercom.

'Miss Beecham? No visitors, no calls. I'm in conference, got it?'

Flat and decisive, and no concessions to courtesy; a touch of steel under the velvet, then. He settled himself, taking his time, exuding expensive cologne in small wafts. 'What's she been saying? Has she been making trouble for me?'

'Nothing to fret about,' Evans interposed smoothly. 'Just a few questions, see.'

'Yeah,' added Beddoes, 'like, where were you last night?' He could handle this one, you could see his confidence rise. 'Home, watching England on the box. Rubbish, as usual. Now, if I was picking them, I'd have –'

'On your tod, were you?' demanded Beddoes, cutting straight across him.

He took it in stride, not a flicker. 'With the wife, actually. Her brother used to play for City reserves.' He smiled, warm and confiding. 'Should've heard her, when he gave that penalty: my word, the language!'

'Good decision, I thought,' Beddoes said, apparently climbing down. Then, as Thompson nodded eagerly, he sowed the first seed of disquiet. 'Saw it meself – on TV-am.'

'You'd be having a video, Mr Thompson,' Evans added softly. 'A man of your status, I mean.'

Thompson paled, catching the drift. 'Yes, but ...'

'Makes no odds,' Beddoes declared. ''Ow about the girl, then?'

Thompson, selecting a silver biro from the array on the desk, was doodling on the blotter; great shapeless scrawls which seemed to demand immense concentration. Eventually, he looked up, the light of male conspiracy in his eyes.

'Marry in haste, they say, repent at leisure. That's me, I'm afraid, gentlemen, I have to admit it. Came up off the streets, I did, and got hitched to a sexy little typist while I was still selling paperclips. Since the kids, Joan's filled out, lost a bit of oomph. She can't keep up with all this.' He waved a negligent hand at the splendour around them and added, 'The wife, I mean,' in case they'd missed the point. 'No, I have the odd flutter on the side, to keep the juices flowing.' He edged forwards, making his appeal directly to Evans. 'You're a man of the world, inspector; you understand.'

''E's Welsh,' explained Beddoes crisply. 'Narrow-minded, see. If you was to ask me, it might be different. 'Ow long 'ave you known 'er?'

'The biblical sense, he's asking, mind,' Evans cautioned, pleased to have the teamwork going so smoothly.

Thompson's glance flitted between them like a trapped bird; the doodling began again. 'A year; eighteen months, perhaps. Look, it's not *serious*. She's no threat to Joan, I wouldn't allow it. She's a student, she likes a good night out. Mutual benefits, if you get my meaning.'

'Oh sure,' murmured Evans amicably, 'and tax-deductible, too.'

'Give a man a break, inspector! Let the Revenue do their own dirty work.'

During this exchange, Beddoes tipped him the wink, wanting to go solo. 'You're right there, sir. Swamped, we'd be, in extra-curricular activities.'

In the brief hiatus of nervous laughter, he gave the nod and settled back to watch. Sound technician, Beddoes. He got up and prowled the office, pausing with his back to Thompson, studying a regional sales graph on the wall. Over his shoulder, very casual, he enquired, 'Part of an 'arem, is she, girls in every port?'

Watching him, Thompson said cautiously, 'I travel a bit, I'm your normal red-blooded type.'

'You want to ditch the Manchester rep,' Beddoes told him. ''E's rippin' you off, mate.' And before Thompson could react, he continued, 'So 'Olroyd's just another name in the little black book, eh, good for a quick tumble on a slack weekend?'

'I suppose you might say that.'

'Yeah, I might, if she 'adn't been assaulted last night.'

Thompson recoiled, genuinely shocked. 'Assaulted? Good God, inspector, you're not suggesting . . .? Look, the amount I pay for the privilege, there's no way I'd need to knock her about!' His hand shot out and hovered over the telephone, revealing an inch of snowy silk and a monogrammed cufflink. 'Think I'll bell my lawyer.'

'You do that, sir,' said Evans comfortably, 'and we'll nip off and check things out. Home with the missus, you said, right?'

Thompson hesitated, thinking it through. His hand fell limply to the blotter.

'That's right,' he murmured; and to no one in particular, 'What have I got to fear?' Then, more strongly, 'So what's going on, inspector?'

'Call it a character reference,' suggested Beddoes, motionless. Nice one, Roy. Didn't say *whose* character, see. 'She's a slag, you're saying, sleeps around, can't get enough. Could be anyone, you reckon, maybe she made it up.'

Thompson was still staring at Beddoes' impassive back. Evans saw him measure the openings and recognise the escape being offered.

'*Yes*,' he said finally, with an unpleasant note of relish, 'she was great in bed – very practised. You've got her number, sergeant.'

'Won't be putting a word in for her, then, down the courthouse. Can't expect it, can she?' Evans asked.

'Certainly not! I'm a married man, inspector. I've got a business to run.'

At last, Beddoes turned, pale and expressionless; but you could sense the anger burning somewhere deep inside. Evans had seen him like this once before. A year or so back, it was, just before he won the divisional judo championship. Coming to the desk, he said quietly, "'Ow old are you, Charlie-boy? Thirty-five? Nice set-up, this, see you comfy in your middle age. Seen the quack lately?'

Thompson faced him, bewildered. 'What for? I'm as fit as a fiddle!'

'Can't be too careful these days, a lot of AC–DC folk about. Goes both ways, know what I mean?'

Thompson wagged his head, sullen and nervy with it. 'I haven't the faintest idea.'

'AIDS, mate, that's what,' snarled Beddoes. 'You get it sleepin' with slags! Now tell us the truth, you bastard!'

Thompson blanched, drawing back sharply. 'He can't speak to me like that! Tell him, inspector.'

'Mmm? Sorry sir, did I miss something?' Evans murmured blithely. 'Wool-gathering I was, wondering what we'd say to Joan.'

And, as Thompson digested the new threat, Beddoes delivered a second broadside. 'You 'andpicked that girl,' he insisted. 'No way you're going to trail scrubbers through the fancy 'otels; bad for the image, innit?'

Thompson held up his hands, fending them off.

'OK, OK, she's a decent enough kid! I've never hurt her. What the hell do you want from me?'

'Taught her about deception, did you?' Evans wanted to know; and Beddoes followed up promptly. 'Keepin' it dark, 'e means, connin' the trouble and strife: doin' things on the sly.'

Thompson was doodling once more, refusing to meet their eyes. 'She never liked that part of it.'

Evans stood up briskly. 'There we are then, sergeant, a nice, clean kid who doesn't like lying.' And to Thompson, reproachfully, 'Could've saved a lot of bother, sir, if you'd said so straight off.'

Thompson rose, shaky with relief. 'Caught me on the hop, inspector. Look, there's no need to trouble Joan about this, surely?'

Beddoes checked in midstride, his fury cold and naked. 'You're a real toff, Thompson, a warm an' carin' 'uman being. You've never asked, not once – 'ow is she then? Could be dead for all you care. AIDS? Couldn't 'appen to a nicer guy!'

'Changed your tune, 'aven't you?' Evans enquired, as they drove back. 'Roasting her one minute, wearing her colours the next?'

Beddoes pursed his lips. 'Been thinkin', uncle. *If* she's sellin' a true bill, she'll be wanting a bit of succour. Won't get it from Bonny Prince Charlie, neither.' He was holding the wheel at ten to two, concentrating hard, taking it much steadier. There was an air of maturity about him which Evans had never seen before.

''E'll 'ave given 'er the treatment,' he explained. 'Soft lights, music, wine, the lot. Made 'er think he cared, see. OK, so it's part of the game, I'm not talkin' about the forever bit. Then 'e drops 'er like a hot brick. Charming.' He came to a gentle halt, beckoning a couple of kids across a zebra. 'Tell you what, anyone 'ad a go at *my* bird, I'd be out there 'untin'.'

'Watch it, boyo,' Evans warned him. 'You're going soft.'

'Not me, mate, ask anyone: ask the 'Olroyd girl.'

A definite note of regret there, which made it unanimous – a case to answer. And *that* meant more aggro from Wilson.

* * *

Mid-afternoon, and for once the big office blazed with light. Evans had honoured the Inspector's Code – bad news must be delivered in person. Four double-spaced pages, the bones of the case laid bare for easy post-mortem. He sat to attention, steeled for the onslaught, while Wilson read like the academic he was : hunched and absorbed, a pen poised to strike at any inconsistency.

The Super, Evans noted, had made an addition to the decor; a studio portrait of his wife, smack in the middle of the desk. One of those misty stargazing jobs, all highlights and pallor. Did her no justice, really. Didn't catch her vivacity and purpose, or the snooty touch she'd shown at the dinner. Good-looking woman, though, fair play.

Wilson finished reading and shoved the papers aside brusquely. His first question took Evans by surprise. 'How did you get involved in this?'

'Beddoes was on call,' Evans replied, stretching the point and mindful of Warner's complicity.

'Mm. Pity. You're out of practice, having been under-employed recently.'

Sensing deliberate provocation, Evans held still. You got something to say, boyo, you go ahead and say it. But Wilson, leaning back and stroking his moustache absently, seemed to be seeking inspiration from somewhere above. As the silence lengthened, Evans's attention wandered back to the picture.

What was it Beddoes had said, that night? 'Lotta woman there, uncle, I know the type. Hard on the outside, gooey in the middle. Melts in the mouth *and* the 'ands!' Maybe, bach, but not for the likes of you and me.

'The evidence at this stage,' Wilson quoted, breaking the deadlock, 'remains inconclusive. Nevertheless, the complaint seems genuine, and further investigations should be pursued with maximum priority.' He hadn't moved, he was still staring at the ceiling. Impressive memory, then; he had it verbatim.

'Something wrong, sir, is there?'

Wilson heaved himself upright and laid both hands on the desk, ignoring this mild enquiry. 'Stocky build, dark clothing, a mask and a knife. A familiar ring, wouldn't you say?'

'Lily Mendoza; sure.'

'At that stage,' Wilson went on, with growing force, 'I was told a cock-and-bull tale about feuds in red-light country and threats to our credibility. A serious misjudgement, Evans.'

Evans wagged his head. 'Only making the point, I was; a little parable. You get cuddly with the media, you give away secrets. It's not cock-and-bull, mind; just the facts of life.'

'Ah, I see. The streets teem with budding rapists, all auditioning for *Crimewatch*. Very persuasive.' His eyes narrowed, a finger came up in warning. 'Spare me the *parables*, inspector, until their source is a little less fallible!'

He came smoothly to his feet and began a circuit of the office. Not to the window, this time, no point really. With murk outside and the big fluorescents going, there was only a blank hole in the wall.

'I predicted this,' Wilson said, walking, and Evans had to swivel the chair to keep track. 'And you talked me out of it. Not an auspicious start: my first serious case.'

Very touchy on appearances, the new Super. Time to lighten the mood. Evans laid a finger against the side of his nose. 'I won't tell, mind, if you don't.' Another mistake, and a big one.

Wilson turned on him, livid with anger. 'Good God, man, I don't give a fig for reputations! The Holroyd girl's been raped, and we should've prevented it!'

Evans sighed inwardly. A new breed of copper, Wilson. Didn't even understand what passed for humour. Arguments with him were like crossing a minefield at night. There'd been rows aplenty with Smythe, but at base they'd understood one another. Same experiences, same attitudes, fight like buggery in the office and a pint of peace after. Wouldn't catch Wilson *boozing*; probably drank sherry in the snug. Gracelessly, Evans growled, 'My responsibility, sir. I'll carry the can.' And that wasn't right, either.

'You'll do no such thing!'

Wilson strode to the desk and sat down. Tapping himself on the chest he said, 'It was *my* decision; against my better judgement, admittedly, and it won't happen again. I'll be taking the case to the Commissioner, requesting immediate negotiations with the BBC.'

'Oh aye? Going public after all, then; paging the old lags?'

Evans still didn't fancy it, there was still a deep reservation he couldn't quite explain. Didn't get the chance, anyway. Wilson shoved a flat palm forward. 'Your objections are redundant, the doubts are resolved. We have a definite rape now, the sort of thing *Crimewatch* does best. Drama, sex and violence to capture attention, the actual scene revisited, and an actor to match the description and stir memories. You'll see – the leads will come pouring in before the programme's over.'

'Aye, right. Leave the file, shall I? You'll be wanting someone else on it, I expect.'

At this, Wilson looked truly shocked. 'Don't be absurd, man! Judgement's the issue here, not competence. Just get on with your job, and don't presume on mine.' A note of dismissal, if ever he heard one. Evans gathered the typescript and let himself out.

As he closed the door, he caught a glimpse of Wilson, sitting very straight, gazing at the portrait. Aye, it's all right for some, boyo. At least you've got *that* to go home to.

For Sara Holroyd, the long night finally ended with a massive sedative and the familiar comfort of her own bed. At the building site – transformed by tapes and flashing blue lights – the nature of the questioning softened. The evil sergeant kept his distance, and the others treated her kindly. At last they seemed to believe her, and she clung to this thought as the drug sucked her down.

There followed a two-day period of permanent twilight. Her physical hurts were healing; her mind had yet to emerge from numbed paralysis. The WPC, motherly and ever present, urged her to go back to college. 'Something to occupy your mind, luv, that'd be best. Keep yourself busy, try not to think about it.'

Mostly, she took refuge in the oblivion offered by the bright and blessed two-tone capsules.

Then the WPC left her alone, and time dragged. Following doctor's orders, she set the pillbox aside. Sleep, so lately her faithful ally, became the enemy to keep at bay. The nightmare was always the same.

She stood in a green and sunlit land, facing a plain wooden

door. There was birdsong and brightness, and the scent of summer flowers. Then, gradually, from far off, a rustle in the woods at her back. The air cooled and darkened, the hunting sound grew closer, and the door began to creak slowly ajar. She stood, rigid and trembling, with an unknown horror behind her and something she dare not confront ahead. At the last instant, as hot animal breath seared her neck, she leaped forwards and wrenched the door open. There, facing her, upright, open-eyed and smiling serenely, stood Sara Holroyd – encased in a block of ice. She screamed ...

And lay sweating in the alien dark, vainly seeking sense and meaning. Then the waking images came to haunt her. The dreadful sergeant, fierce in his holy wrath; her mother, gaunt and bitter – 'He has sinned, Sara'. It had to be that, she thought desperately, she was being punished for *something*, else why should she suffer such torment? Finally, as faint late dawn touched the sky, she acknowledged the worst nightmare of all; she was *not* dreaming.

Time passed, the day crept in, and the rigour left her. She needed someone to tell, someone who would listen and understand and love her anyway. Who? Dad and Ruby had troubles of their own. Her mother? Even in this extreme, she managed the hopeless shadow of a smile at the absurdity. Charles, of course, would write her off as a bad risk. She got up and prowled the empty, echoing room. She was searching for something; she'd know what it was when she found it.

Following some deep-rooted instinct, she ransacked a drawer for her sewing basket. Among tumbled and rainbowed cottons, the scissors lay; slim, long-bladed, dully gleaming. She carried them ceremoniously to the dressing table. There, she fitted the handles firmly to the fingers of her right hand, and laid the cold sharp points against her neck; probing, seeking. Until, at last, reflected in the mirror, she saw the metal rise and fall to the pulse of the great slow artery. She raised her arm, tilting her wrist and cocking her elbow so that the blades came horizontal, poised and perfect. Amazing, she thought fleetingly, my hand is as steady as a rock. A last breath, and she summoned the single, convulsive thrust which would end the horror and loose a scarlet tide above the virgin white of her nightdress ...

CHAPTER NINE

GLORIA, BEDDOES' erstwhile bedmate, had drawn the line at midnight desertion.

'You *pig*, Roy!' she hissed down the phone. 'I bin stood up by experts, but never in a water bed!'

'Call o' duty,' muttered Beddoes, his mind on other things.

'Oh *sure*! Keep it warm for me, 'e says, be back in a jiff. And what 'appens? A big fat zero. You were at the nick: why not bell me?'

'Leave it out, lovely. Official business only, right?'

'What're we doin' now, then, solvin' the inner city crime-wave?'

'*You* called *me*, lady.'

'Yeah, well, I won't be makin' *that* mistake again!'

Thus condemned to an excess of his own company, Beddoes lapsed into uncharacteristic introspection. Taking time off in lieu, drawn to dockland by forces he could neither understand nor resist, he found himself on a rotting wharf where a sullen eddy coiled. He knew it as a place of lingering evil; here, a year ago, a mutilated youthful corpse had surfaced. This afternoon, beneath a late autumnal sun, the water gleamed bronze and benign. No mysteries now; just the river, rolling on.

Later, he patrolled the seedy street where they'd snared the culprit. The derelict row had gone. In its stead, a new development rose: little boxes turreted in scaffolding, men in parkas wielding trowels, and a ghettoblaster blowing Force Nine. A scene of utter normality, the past not only buried but transformed. So, what are you lookin' for, my son, a bleedin' monument?

As he loitered, hands in pockets, collar raised against the

encroaching chill, school let out; a gang of kids came bawling and brawling by. At its hub, inevitably, the smallest, and he was taking stick.

'Garn, Willsy, you're an effin' sneak!'

'Teacher's pet, poxy ghet!'

'Willock the pillock, tell-tale tit!'

The subject of their jibes was neatly dressed, pale and taut and very close to tears. The leader, a fifteen-year-old with razor stubble and vicious eyes, grabbed the dangling school tie and hauled it tight.

'Nar then, Willsy, let's see 'ow brave you are away from sir.'

Willsy was hoisted on tip-toe and slammed against a wall.

'Lay off, Stubbs,' he gasped. I didn't do nothin'.'

Beddoes stepped forwards purposefully. 'All right, you lot, pack it in.'

Stubbs turned slowly, insolent and menacing. ''Oo the 'ell are you, mister? Mind yer own business.'

What *he* needed, Beddoes reckoned, was a good thick ear, punishment to fit the crime. A sanction restricted largely to parents these days, more's the pity. Heavily, he said, 'The law, that's 'oo. Move along, before I get official.'

They drifted away, wary but not in the least cowed.

'I'll 'ave you, Willsy,' Stubbs boasted. 'Soon as the filth butts out.' And he was off, with a smirk, a derisive 'V' sign for Beddoes, and cocky swagger. The gang followed, frisky and raucous.

Beddoes dusted the victim down.

'Ta, mister, but I ent scared of Stubbsy on 'is own. Take care of meself, see.'

He scooted round the corner, the school bag bobbing against his narrow back. There were shades of Beddoes' own past here, and they led him, reluctant, down Memory Lane ...

Alf and Dora Beddoes were middle-aged when Roy was born. One of his earliest recollections was his mum's fury during a Christmas party. An uncle, drunk and indiscreet, suggested, ''Is initials oughta be PS – the little afterthought.'

''Ow *dare* you!' Dora snapped. 'Four smashing girls we got, and always wanted a boy. Answer to our prayers, 'e is, archer darlin'?'

They treated him that way, his sisters did, too. Spoilt rotten, actually.

A stevedore, Alf Beddoes took justifiable pride in physical strength. 'See them muscles?' he would bellow, flexing a brawny bicep for Roy's pop-eyed admiration. 'Grown on God's honest toil, they were. Sixteen-hour shifts, boy, and none of your bleedin' lead-swingin'. Work? Kids today don't know the meanin'!' The mid-sixties, and overtime yours for the asking. Alf laboured, and Dora kept the little house shipshape despite teenaged daughters and a hopelessly untidy son. Happy times, growing in the warmth of sisterly approval, wits sharpened on constant banter and seeing him right in school.

But years and the effort were catching up with Alf. Success at Eleven-plus and subsequent entry to the Grammar were marred by an insidious echo; the echo of a raking cough which seized Alf, night and morning, and shook him as a ferret shakes a rat. Weakened and failing, the old man nevertheless maintained his grip on standards and family. One Saturday, when Dora and the girls were shopping, he summoned Roy to the bedroom.

'Bin 'earing rumours, boy. Goin' bent, arncher, like the rest of the oiks round 'ere. Thievin'!'

'Leave off, Dad! Scrumpin' ole Barnsey's apples, a coupla cheap biros from Woolies? S'only a game – for fun, see.'

Alf sighed, grim and reflective. 'Near forty year, I bin a docker,' he confided. 'What we don't 'andle ain't worth worryin' about. Provisions, furs, electrics, the lot. Crates is fragile, see, accidents 'appen. There's men I could name got fat that way; but not me or mine. Everythin' in this 'ouse I earned, fair and square. Gettin' the drift, are yer?'

Roy, shamed and miserable, nodded eagerly. 'Sorry, Dad.'

'Oughta belt yer,' Alf rumbled, holding up a calloused hand. 'Don't smirk! Ain't the man I used to be, but you still wouldn't sit fer a week.' His tone softened. 'Come 'ere, boy. 'Ave a butcher's in the mirror.'

Out of his depth, Roy obeyed.

'Yer different, can't you see? Honest face – came from yer ma, no doubt. Yer at the Grammar, a cut above the local rubbish, you got a chance to get outa this. And you're gonna chuck it all away for *fun*? Do me a favour, son; think about it.'

Thereafter, Roy avoided the gangs, coming home early, hammering the studies, keeping his nose clean. It wasn't easy; a despised Grammar boy, small for his age, he'd been a natural target for the Stubbsys of his day. Dodging them had called for speed, cunning and considerable street craft; he'd always have a soft spot for kids like Wills ...

He'd turned his back on dockland, the old stamping ground. He walked mechanically, only vaguely conscious of the cold; because his mind stayed behind, as yet unable to escape nostalgia ...

Alf's cough worsened. Soon he was carted, protesting, to the infirmary. The weekly visits were agony for them both. Roy was too young to dissemble, unable to hide the dismay he felt in the presence of this querulous stranger; and Alf hated anyone to witness his weakness. But always, as the bell shrilled and the exodus began, he asked the same urgent question, 'Still goin' straight, boy?'

'Course I am!'

He died in May. Six months later, Dora followed, for no apparent reason; simply turned her face to the wall. She'd been, it transpired, as prudent as Alf was honest. She left her daughters the house – no strings, no mortgage – and the care of her thirteen-year-old son. Else, the eldest, pretty, level-headed and twenty-two, took on motherly duties; the others pooled their wages and paid Roy's way.

Maturing in a household of young women, Roy grew accustomed to the female form in all its stages of development and undress. An era of liberation; talk was frank and free.

'That bloody Arnold,' moaned Liz, the plump one, 'like an octopus wiv Brylcreem!'

'Watcha mean, Liz?'

'Feelin' me up, stupid!'

'Feelin' *what*?'

'Gordon Bennet, 'ark at 'im! Me boobs, o'course!'

So Else had instructed him on birds and bees. She did it simply and unselfconsciously, stripping to the buff and providing a guided tour of the human anatomy.

Watching, hypnotised, Roy gulped. 'The boys in school call it fuckin'.'

'Smutty little sods,' said Else, scornfully. 'Grown-ups make love, and they don't broadcast it, neither. Just you remember!'

Gawping at her naked roundness, his throat tight and gritty, he mumbled, 'They say it turns you on.'

'Not with yer sister, silly.' Then she explained the mechanics of the affair, crisp and matter-of-fact.

'Crikey,' he breathed, stunned. 'If it's that much trouble, don't reckon I'll bother.' And wondered what she found so bleedin' funny.

Of course, there'd been other girls in the house – his sisters' mates – most of whom ignored him. And one in particular who didn't. Looking back, after all these years, he still found a special grin for Rosie ...

It was like Pearl Harbor now; a real, nasty nip in the air. He wasn't dressed for it, hadn't intended to be out this late; oughta take a bus, really. But somehow, he didn't fancy it, he still wasn't ready to come in from the past. Walk quicker, my son, get the old blood circulating ...

Rose was plain as sago, flat as an ironing board, and a cripple: one withered leg and a built-up boot. At eighteen, she owned little more than a generous nature and a hankering to share the experiences of her better-favoured friends. In the young Roy Beddoes, she discovered an undiscerning and enthusiastic pupil.

She took him, quite literally, in hand. Then, awed by the effect, she went a good deal further. 'Put yer fingers 'ere, Roy. Gently does it – a little 'igher – aaaah, Roy! Talk to me, darlin', tell me 'ow nice I am.'

Indeed, flushed and soft-eyed and spread for him on Else's bed, she *was* nice.

'*Now*, Roy, come on in! Oh, you're so big, you're so good ...'

Blessed by natural aptitude and beginner's luck, she carried him on the short, explosive journey out of childhood. Afterwards, she held him with a fierce tenderness he'd never known before; or since.

Taught him the lot, Rosie did. How to chat up a girl, make

her feel special; when to be patient, respecting a mood, and when to take charge; and much more besides.

'You wanna forget that Sunday School guff, Roy; girls like it, too. Well, it's the way we're made, innit? Nothin' to be ashamed of.'

Best of all, she showed him how to end things, keeping the pain small, leaving pride intact.

'Gotta regular fella of me own, Roy. Walkin' out, know what I mean?'

A loving smile, a grateful hand on his shoulder. 'You bin terrific, Roy, but you're growing up, see. Deserve better, you do, you've got the gift.'

She took his face in both her hands and kissed him once, sweet and chaste. 'Promise me one thing, Roy. Never force it, right? Be gentle, that's all you 'ave to do.' The best ever, Rosie.

Before long, the girls were treating him as an equal, confiding their closest secrets and seeking his advice. Between them, they rounded his education; ever after, he'd be at ease in feminine company ...

Nearly home, passing the alley where the local uniform had his surreptitious mid-duty fag. The cold was bitter, the pavements deserted; a night to be glad you'd never walk a beat again. He had to smile, remembering how keen he'd been to join ...

Beatlemania, and a Mersey sound which rocked the world; but Beddoes' blood had stirred to an older scouseland anthem. Fifes and drums, one Johnny Todd who crossed an ocean. *Z Cars*, the original warts'n'all portrait of police work. Gutsy and grainy, real people who talked normal and did a real job. At the centre of it, Inspector Barlow; larger than life, hard as nails, bullish and irascible, a man who took chances and usually got a result. It wasn't a time or a neighbourhood in which to idolise the Old Bill; but Barlow personified every virtue the late Alf Beddoes had held so dear.

Roy kept his adolescent dream to himself, being too young and too small to join the Force. He couldn't go on sponging off the girls, either, though his 'O'-level passes qualified him for the sixth form. For three years, he drifted – clerking for an insurance firm, tending the bar at the Rose and Crown, playing the dogs at the nearby stadium. Back on home ground, mainly an innocent bystander, he learned the local capers and the lie of the streets at night. He had threads on his back, readies in his pocket, hope in his heart – and no responsibilities. Twice a week, in deathly secret, he trekked across town to a seedy boxing hall and worked on the weights. He was growing taller, filling out, and laying the foundations for his futute.

Else married a plumber and flew the coop; Liz was already engaged. Roy himself did nicely, ta, seldom short of a tasty partner for the long winter nights. Casual, mind you. There'd never been another Rosie. He was getting restless, too, scenting a watershed; time to make something of himself. He was going on twenty, five nine and a bit in his socks, and dying to be a copper. It must've shown in the interviews; he got in at the first attempt.

And took to it as to the Manor born. On the beat, a keen eye and a feel for the neighbourhood stood him in good stead. Contacts established in the years of waiting and watching gave him an inside track; he achieved an outstanding record of pinches. His wiry slightness proved a bonus rather than a handicap. Coupled with an instinctive grasp of balance and leverage, it enabled him to confound much bigger men, trading on over-confidence and using their greater power to his own advantage. Even the judo instructor found him a handful, and the news travelled fast; hard cases in and out of the Force gave him respect and a wide berth.

His probation over, he found his own pad and studied for promotion. Exams came easy to one of his relatively academic background and native intelligence; the CID snapped him up and sent him for marksman's training. Once more, he proved an adept, relishing the precision, the discipline and the pungent whiff of cordite, using the weapon as a natural extension of himself.

When, eventually, he made sergeant and was assigned to Evans, this ability provoked their only serious difference. 'Your funeral, mind,' Evans had told him, very heavy indeed. 'Trot off to your targets, have your little war games, but don't you ever bring one of those things on a job with me.'

'What's up, uncle? Don't tell me you're windy?'

'Windy, is it? Shooters scare me witless, boyo; me'n' anyone else with a grain of common. Join the army, you should.' And that was that.

Nevertheless, at Evans' direction and with Smythe's growing approval, his star had moved onwards and upwards.

He emerged from his daydream on the doorstep of his own bachelor pad, older, colder, and not a whit wiser. Give it a rest, my son. Time for grub and something to warm the cockles.

But later, pleasantly bloated with ale and take-away vindaloo, dozing to John Denver on the stereo, he still felt liverish. The past, ancient and modern, continued to taunt him.

'*Still goin' straight, boy?*' Alf's ghost demanded; and of course, he wasn't. For starters, he should've come clean about the peeper. An early warning there, for sure; at the cost of humble pie, he might've saved a pile of trouble. Instead, he'd gone all prickly and macho. A sin of omission, and consequences more serious than anyone could predict. Sorry, Dad.

Evans had a point, too. '*Made up your mind in advance, you had.*' And rejected the truth, even when she told it. The description had triggered alarm bells and he'd ignored them, sweeping his own error even further under the carpet, casting *her* as the liar and treating her like dirt. Barlow'd be proud of you, my son.

Rosie, likewise. '*Never force it, right?*' But he had, worse than bullyboy Stubbs and his pimply oppos. An act of gross indecency on the girl's psyche, if not her person; and all because her description of the rapist fitted the convent peeper. You got a nerve, Roy Beddoes, going for Thompson so savage: the pot and the kettle.

He squirmed in his chair, disgusted with himself. Spoilt rotten, see, starved of responsibility. First sign of a cock-up, you lash out at random, everyone's fault but your own. First taste of failure, you sick it up in the nearest female lap. Charming.

Denver was warbling: 'Rhymes and reasons', very apt. Because finally, he began to understand the dockland odyssey. Unable to stomach failure, he'd fled to a scene of past success.

Like a senile, discredited general, he'd retired to fields of forgotten glory; the places where, long ago, arithmetic, routine, logic and luck had fused triumphantly, and Chummy had blundered into a perfect ambush. The high-spot of his own career to date. No wonder he'd found so little satisfaction. 'You're only as good as your last game,' Evans said; and he was right, as usual.

He poured another beer, watching the bubbles trickle upwards. Put it down to experience, my son. There's no need for sackcloth and ashes. Even Evans admitted as much '*You did what you had to, see.*' But, somehow, it wouldn't wash. Beddoes, CID, might stand acquitted; but Roy, brother to Else and Rosie's novice lover, was guilty as hell. For his own sake as much as Sara Holroyd's, he had to clear the slate; he had to be able to face himself, shaving. In the end, from beyond the grave, old Alf had the last word – something he'd once confided after a rare barney with Dora – 'It takes a big man to say sorry.'

Richard Wilson's day began badly and grew steadily worse. He arrived to find the programme on his desk, a curt note appended: 'Unsuitable in this form. Please amend and resubmit soonest.' Compliments of the Assistant Commissioner. Very illuminating; unsuitable *how*? The AC's line was engaged and, in any case, Wilson was due at the *Crimewatch* conference at nine-thirty.

There, under pressure from rival chieftains, the Commissioner's sponsorship for the Holroyd presentation wavered; one of the media men questioned its 'ratings value'.

'The proles are growing blasé,' he declared flatly. 'Why watch mock-ups when you can see it for real on video? Seriously, gentlemen, they're bored by menace; they want blood.'

In the end, victory cost Wilson a morning of delicate wrangling, a couple of dents in his reputation, and most of his peace of mind. Someone accused him of hogging the spotlight, a charge the Commissioner neglected to contest. Several of the doubters sounded very much like Evans; though he silenced them reasonably enough, they caused him some private misgivings. It was the price you paid for academic advancement – an ingrained receptiveness to contrary opinion.

Lunchtime passed unremarked, the AC remained unobtainable. An obliging secretary rustled up a cardboard sandwich and a mug of caffeinated dishwater while he fretted over a programme he couldn't correct because he didn't know what was wrong with it. Finally, turning in desperation to the day's unopened mail, he encountered a blueprint for domestic strife. Gina had clearly run amok with the plastic money; the credit card account was horrendous.

At home, he parried her welcome bluntly, demolished dinner like a famished navvy, and slumped in the lounge nursing the monetary timebomb and a large brandy. When Gina emerged from the kitchen, very fetching in a frilly apron and a pink leisure suit, he launched the offensive. 'The Barclaycard bill came this morning.'

She paused in mid-stride, one hand coming to her mouth in a gesture of mild remorse. 'Oh! I meant to tell you about that. Winter sales, an absolute bargain – *super* curtains for the guest room.'

'We're hardly overrun by guests, dear.'

Her eyes narrowed. He never called her dear when he meant darling.

'Maybe now we will be.'

He set the brandy down, opened the briefcase, removed the bill and spread it on his knee. She watched coolly, head cocked, one fluffy mule tapping impatiently.

'Curtains,' he grunted, running his fingers down the long list. 'That would be House of Fraser, I presume. What's this payment to the off-licence: fifty-three pounds?'

She raised one hand and counted on her fingers. 'Clare and Harry had the last of the white; vintage port was on special offer, and I bought some liqueurs.'

'Good God, who are you inviting, the London Philharmonic?'

'Don't be so *silly*, Richard!' She plumped herself on to the chesterfield and faced him defiantly. 'Do you propose to *grill* me over every little bill? For goodness sake, you're a superintendent, you *deserve* a few luxuries.'

Perhaps there was a note of appeal; if so, he chose to ignore it.

'Only those I can afford.' He laid subtle stress on the 'I'; it had always been a sore point.

She sighed, spreading her hands, offering the olive branch. 'I *hate* arguing about money. Surely *I'm* allowed to pamper you?'

She was wholly sincere, and normally he would've surrendered gladly. Tonight, an ugly mood possessed him, and he quoted one of Harry's favourite maxims, tapping the paper on his knee. 'The surest way to become poor is to spend like the rich.'

Perhaps it was the tone, maybe she recognised the source. At any rate, she came stiffly to her feet, pallid with fury. 'Very well, Richard. If you're such a financial wizard, *you* can run the house. Shopping, cooking, furniture, the entire domestic budget. I will *not* be interrogated, I will *not* be treated like an accountant, I will *not* be told how and when to spend *my* money.'

As he folded the bill away, she swept to the bottom of the stairs, paused, and delivered the second barrel. 'Starting next month, we'd better have separate accounts.'

Her heels clattered upwards, the bedroom door opened. Her voice floated down, cold and disembodied.

'Starting *tonight*, the guest room *will* be occupied. By you!'

The door crashed shut, the key rattled in the lock. Congratulations, Wilson, on another unenviable first.

He got up and poured himself another brandy; it gave him no pleasure at all. The row, their worst to date, had been cruelly provoked and pursued; Gina had been almost entirely blameless. True, it had been an evil day, maybe he needed to take it out on someone, perhaps every marriage generated squalls like this.

But he had no real financial worries, and no *reason* to make her miserable. She remained, as she'd always been, the focus of his life; he was allowing vague suspicions to blur her lovely outline.

Nevertheless, the situation was getting badly out of hand. He'd have to do something positive about it very soon …

Chapter Ten

Penance, Beddoes found, was like a pretty virgin; much desired but hard to get done. For days he deferred it, taking the official line, gathering corroboration, searching for Sara in the people she had known.

It was a halting, irksome journey through wholly unfamiliar territory; the concrete groves of the New Academia. Few students troubled to hide their opinions of the police in general and him in particular. He read it plain in superior smiles and disdainful eyes – Fuzz, Brown Shirt, mindless apparatchik. Yet, beneath the posturing, he sensed their greedy fascination. They swarmed to him like flies, drawn by the whiff of the underworld, a darker side of life they'd never know. Brains at the bullfight, then, panting for vicarious horror and blood on the sand. They were like those masks you get on theatre programmes: two faces, and both of them ugly. Sod you, he thought, and dismissed them with the contempt they deserved.

Nevertheless, they painted a portrait which tallied well enough. Sara was reserved, self-contained and studious; they could imagine no one less likely to fall foul of a rapist. They were genuinely appalled, too; big Rodney, the rugger captain, made the point pungently. Looming like a large unhappy puppy in an empty lecture hall, he said, 'I'd just met her, we were getting on famously. Then some *animal* –' He broke off, smashing a huge fist into the palm of his hand. 'I hope you catch him, sergeant. Men like that should be bloody well gelded!'

Beddoes smiled grimly to himself. Even the liberal young, it seemed, could turn Fascist when Chummy struck too close to home. They'd all become adult, probably, once they were free of this over-age kindergarten.

The lone false note came from a dark girl with bedroom eyes; one Fran, aspiring actress. Lounging at a coffee bar, offering too much thigh and a seductive pout which could've led to something big, she confided, 'Sara Holroyd fooled a lot of people; she didn't fool *me*.'

''Ow d'you mean?'

She blew smoke haughtily. Seen Dietrich do it on Channel Four, no doubt, and fancied the aloof, mysterious touch. 'Still waters, sergeant.' She swayed forwards, close and confiding. 'It's the quiet ones you have to watch. I'll bet she had a whole secret life going.'

'I see. Female intuition.'

She shrugged, hauling her shoulders back, revealing the thrust of pert young breasts. 'Just a feeling I have. I'm very sensitive to atmosphere, you see.'

Lowering her voice and her cigarette, glancing around like a modern Mata Hari, she breathed, 'She was seeing some *man*, I'm sure of it.'

Sure, thought Beddoes meanly, and pinching *your* limelight. Closing his notebook firmly, he told her, 'Yeah, thanks a million. The casting couch is vacant, but you didn't get the part.'

She sneered and exited left, wagging her rump indignantly. Had the last word, though. Over her shoulder, smiling sweetly, she hissed, 'Arrogant pig!'

Women.

But he couldn't escape them. Sara's tutor was next: Dr Mary Timms, it said on the door. Plain, squat and bespectacled, sporting a vast pullover and tattered jeans, she admitted him grudgingly to a room the size of a wardrobe.

'Shove those things on the floor,' she ordered, indicating a book-strewn chair. 'Make yourself at home.'

He grinned, taking it for sarcasm, but her expression remained completely devoid of warmth or humour.

Hauling back a baggy sleeve and glaring pointedly at a man's Rolex, she announced, 'I have a lecture at three; I can spare you twenty minutes.'

101

Settling, he risked a glance through the tiny window. Redbrick and starlings, punk scalplocks and double-glazing. Hardly your actual dreaming spires. He brought himself to business, stating his request concisely.

'Sara Holroyd?' she echoed icily. 'I'd've thought you'd done sufficient damage in that quarter.'

It figured. The walls screamed with slogans. 'Oppose the Cuts', 'Vegetarians Rule', 'Coal Not Dole', 'Viva Greenpeace'. Nothing about supporting your local sheriff.

'Routine enquiries, ma'am,' he reassured her. 'Just for the record, OK?'

'*Doctor.*'

'Huh?'

'Universities remain bastions of chauvinism, sergeant, despite the contrary rhetoric.' She nodded in emphasis, her glasses glinting coolly. 'I earned a title; I expect people to use it.'

Yeah, I bet. 'Specially men. 'Good for you. Doctor, then.'

'I'm sorry you find it amusing, sergeant. It's a very serious problem.'

Beddoes sighed and spread his hands. 'Look, they said you knew 'er best, but there's no obligation and no warrant. Want me to push off or what?'

Momentarily, her plump body stiffened and her mouth set thin and sulky. Then, for some reason, her mood changed. She wrung her hands, letting distress hang out. No one else to tell, perhaps.

'She has this ... *instinct* ... for linguistics. Good written style, a penetrating mind. Conscientious, too; she wasn't work-shy, like so many these days.' She paused, studying him for signs of mockery. Finding none, she continued, 'Basically, Sara's such a *nice* child.' Real concern there, no one could mistake it. Beddoes murmured something sympathetic and she seized on it gladly. 'She came back, you know. Actually attended a few seminars. Very courageous, even if it did prove premature.'

She sat straighter, letting the contempt show.

'Undergrads are so *crass*! Treading on eggs, minding their Ps and Qs, treating her like some kind of ... *leper*! I'm sorry, I shouldn't't've said that.'

'I dunno. Find 'em 'ard-going myself.'

She shot him a doubtful glance, but was too well launched to take issue. 'The last time she came here she looked dreadful. I went straight to the Prof and demanded a moratorium.' An apologetic note, treating him like the thick copper he wasn't. 'Time off for recovery, I mean. A battle, of course; he's a thoroughly callous man.' Like *all* men, she clearly implied. Her attitude altered subtly; she was desolate now, and fearful with it. 'She's been absent more than a fortnight. I'm sure she's dropped out,' she cried.

She had taken off her glasses. Her prominent blue eyes looked naked and vulnerable; she might have been any mother mourning a lost child. Then she spoke, broken and unguarded – and destroyed the illusion – 'Such a waste of effort and talent. She was bound to get first-class honours. It would've been a first for *me*, too.'

So much for the maternal instinct, Beddoes reflected grimly; Doctor Timms grieves only for herself. A harsh judgement, maybe; but he'd *had* academics, right up to here.

She must've sensed it; she rounded on him once more. '*You* destroyed her – you and that frightful creature of the night; and still you're not satisfied! Why don't you leave her alone?'

I'm bleedin' tempted, believe me, he thought; aloud, he thanked her curtly and legged it for the real world.

Back home that evening, he thought of calling Gloria; burying the hatchet and other tokens of friendship. Somehow, he couldn't quite bring himself. For the first time in his life, he felt alienated from the entire female sex. No – just alienated. Something to do with being a copper; *that* had never bothered him before, either.

It wasn't merely the social ostracism. Nobody, peasant or professor, could be entirely easy with enforcers; it was something you learned to expect. The intelligentsia didn't *have* to patronise you, though, did they? He grinned suddenly. Well, maybe they did; maybe it was an essential part of college life, like losing your virginity and ripping off the DHSS. Perhaps old Evans had a point about the new Super, after all.

He got up and poured himself a beer. Admit it, my son, you've been hunting someone to guide her through the shadowed vale of rape; someone *else*. And found no one. Was there ever a bird more truly alone? Forsaken by warring parents, ditched by a callous lover, already cast out by priggish classmates, and counted lost by a thwarted tutor. Big Rodders might be co-opted; his clumsy passion would be as welcome as a fart in a phone booth.

Which left Roy Beddoes, the prisoner's friend. Speaking of welcomes – Jesus, mate, you gotta few housemarks to make up! He emptied the glass in two long swallows, a trifling reward for a dodgy day. No point in ducking it; he owed her, simple as that. And tomorrow he would take time off and pay the deposit.

Carnations would be best, he decided. According to a former flame, you only gave roses when you were looking to stay for breakfast. He bought them in town, a dozen white ones to signify surrender and honourable intentions.

At first sight, the locality had seemed a bit upmarket. How could she swing it, a single bird on a grant? Languages, he remembered; moonlighting, perhaps, translating dirty books from the foreign for some greasy Soho porn merchant. Leave it out, sunshine, you're off-duty; an ordinary punter come to mend fences.

A survey of the venue reassured him. Pre-war mansions, these, and somewhat worse for wear. Once they'd been pads for the upwardly mobile: doctors, solicitors and your rising media celebs. Then fashions changed and the rent sharks moved in, carving 'em into umpteen dinky flatlets. Bedsits, they called them. Unless he missed his guess, the accommodation would be a hair's breadth above ghetto level. Another theory bites the dust. Whatever he tried, she came out Simon-pure.

She lived on the second floor. He trod the dim and rancid stairway, flowers upfront to disarm the curious. He needn't have bothered. Half-two in the afternoon, dead as a tomb and about as comfy.

He had to knock twice and wait a long time. Eventually, the door eased ajar and a ghostly figure appeared; an incurious stare, a voice without life or colour. 'Yes, what do you want?'

He was actually going to ask for Miss Holroyd when recognition dawned; and was instantly reflected from her sunken and shadowed eyes.

'You!'

A sharp and violent accusation, but he was already herding her back from the entrance.

'Not interruptin', I 'ope,' he began, giving his natural Cockney free rein. 'Came to read the meter, see, brighten up your day.'

She retreated further and he followed quickly: phase one complete, a beachhead temporarily secured. As she hesitated, he took a swift mental inventory. A minute kitchen, a living area with the bare essentials: table and chairs, a divan, and several overloaded bookshelves. The privy would be down the landing, he guessed, first come first served and baths is extra, luv. Very salubrious.

'Hey,' he asked jauntily. 'What's a nice girl like you doing in a place like this?'

She turned slowly, gaunt and ravaged, her hands rising in a gesture of total rejection. 'How dare you come here? How *dare* you?'

'Took a bit of nerve,' he admitted cheerfully. ''Ere. Small token of my esteem.'

She shrank from the bouquet as though it were tainted. She looked *terrible*, stooped and swamped in a shapeless shift, and just a blink away from collapse. Her long blond hair had been roughly cropped to a tufted stubble: not your actual styling, more an act of war.

'Go on, Sara,' he coaxed her. 'Shove 'em in some water. Thirsty, aren't they, like me.'

She cracked then, clean over the top, spitting hate and outrage. 'You *bastard*, get out!'

The first blow, a long, open-handed lunge, caught him flush on the mouth. Its force brought her close where she sobbed and flailed and battered his ribs with sharp little fists. He took it, firm but unresisting, staring sadly at the scatter of fallen flowers on the highly polished floor. The whole place was spotless, he realised, witness to the need for mindless action in times of intolerable stress.

The attack faltered. She sagged against him, blind and spent, keening helplessly, her body wracked and convulsive. Cautiously, he ran his hand across her back, over the spinal ridge and the jut of her shoulder blades. 'There, there,' he muttered foolishly, his voice thick with shame and pity. 'There, there.'

She held him fiercely, weightless and fragile and sexless as a terrified child. Something inside him stirred and shifted; for no reason at all, he was reminded of Rosie.

Gradually the spasms eased and she pushed herself away. Her face, pale and uptilted, had been washed of all emotion. She stooped gracefully, gathering carnations with a kind of absent tenderness. Still wordless, she selected a vase and filled it, dropping the entire bunch in casually, heedless of effect. At last, her voice low and controlled, she said, 'Thank you, it was a kind thought. Please go now.'

''Old on,' he protested. ''Ow about a cuppa for me pains? I'm parched, honest.'

She seemed beset by conflicting demands; privacy versus manners. 'I owe you *nothing*, sergeant. But if it will help be rid of you ...' and she was gone, gliding silently into the kitchen.

Outside, behind the single window, the light had started to fade. Traffic rumbled somewhere near by, and a neighbouring watchdog challenged the advancing night. Sounds of normality, returning. From the kitchen, a steamy whiff of fresh brew and the rattle of spoon on china. In another time and place, it might've seemed quite homely. Strictly business, my son, and you haven't done it yet.

She poured his tea and he downed it gratefully. Then, sitting upright, keeping the dialect under wraps and looking her full in the eye, he made his prepared speech. 'I'm paid to ask questions. Believe it or not, I'm good – mostly. But there's a hard way, and I used it on you; read you all wrong, see. Unforgiveable, no argument, no good pretending otherwise.' He nodded at the vase on the table. 'Anyhow, I came to say ... sorry.'

She was sitting sideways, profiled against the darkening window. Failing light picked out the angle of her jaw, the line of her neck, and a hint of litheness beneath the spinsterish shroud. Jealous Fran's words came back – *'It's the quiet ones you have to watch.'* If this quiet one gave herself a chance, she'd be well worth watching.

Calmly, speaking to a space somewhere in front of her, she said, 'And now you've got it off your chest.'

He nodded, taken aback, too surprised to dissemble. 'You could say that. Yes.'

She swivelled to face him gravely. 'Very well. You're right about forgiveness; but I accept the apology and the unnecessary gift. For me, the matter is closed.'

Time to go, then. She could scarcely make it plainer. You've done right by old Alf and other childhood heroes, why outstay your welcome? And yet he lingered, held by forces he couldn't begin to understand. An unfamiliar species, a high-flier with one wing down; not his usual mark at all. Astonished, he heard himself saying, 'I know a few things about you, lovely; been askin' around. On your tod, aren't you? Ashamed to go to college and afraid of going home. Bet you 'aven't seen too much of lover-boy, either.'

'That's none of your business!' The tightness was eking back, you could see her coiling in on herself.

Gently, persuasively, he explained, 'I've got the time, I've got the inclination; I can't see 'em queuing for the job. I'm *here*, Sara: I'll listen.'

Again the sharp involuntary recoil. '*You*, sergeant? We seem to be back where we started.'

'Yeah,' he agreed. 'Remember what 'appened next?'

Clearly she did, and the knowledge pained her.

He moved on briskly. 'Let's play confessions; me first.'

It was hard to make her out, the day had nearly gone. Her voice came low and toneless, thoroughly disinterested. 'You're the policeman; I can't stop you.' Still in there, then, still punching.

His own stubborn pride might well have brought her to this; hardly the time to tell her so. Instead, he improvised, trying for a suitably discursive style. 'There'd been a bit of a nonsense. Personal and professional problems, as they say on Beeb Two.' If she found this amusing, she hid it well. Press on, my son. 'Livin' on me nerves, then. It wasn't a *likely* tale, the one you told, in the light of experience, I mean.'

'*Your* experience,' she murmured, and he smiled wryly. Love-fifteen.

'OK, put yourself in my shoes. This bird comes in, not too banged up and dead chirpy. Thought you were on a high, know what I mean? Drugs.' A curious sound in the gloom: contempt? Disgust? He wished he could see her face. 'Thought I knew the answer, see, before I asked the questions.'

'Lawyers,' she murmured. 'That's how lawyers do it.'

'Yeah, well, it doesn't work for coppers. You put me straight, I lost me rag, and Bob's yer uncle. Unforgiveable, like I said. So here endeth the first confession. Shall we 'ave a bit of light on the subject?'

'No!' Very emphatic, she was, and just a hint of alarm.

'OK, OK, sorry I spoke. It's your go, anyhow.'

He hunched forward in the dimness, sensing the conflict within her. On the one hand, an urgent desire to be rid of him; on the other, the need to talk it out with someone – *anyone*. Passing headlights held her briefly and moved on. She was sitting very straight, and he thought her cheeks were wet. Nice try, he thought, but she's going to chuck you out anyway.

Night returned, and with it the sudden and delicious waft of carnations. Remember it well, my son; a crippled girl and the smell of cut flowers. Then, amazingly, she *did* speak.

'You have to understand,' she said; pleaded, actually. 'I'd *survived*! Despite what that ... *creature* ... did, I was still alive, I wasn't even badly hurt ... physically, at least. It kept me going all the way to the police station. You were right, in a way – on a high.' And he did understand; about not wanting the lights on, anyway. What she said made more than sense; it had the ring of absolute truth. Eerily, unseen and apparently reading his mind, she went on, 'Truth, sergeant, is what *you* offered. There was more of it later, at college. Friends staring, people watching, classmates avoiding me.'

Another long, charged silence, broken only by the muffled wail of pop song from one of the flats upstairs.

She spoke again; a quiet, relentless monotone. '*You* showed me, sergeant, long before any of the others. Showed me I could never be the same again. To other people I would always be a victim, a number in a table, an object of pity and revulsion.' She chose her words carefully, giving each one equal emphasis, sparing herself nothing. 'A broken, degraded, shop-soiled little tramp!'

He was already moving, leaping for the light switch, knowing he would be too late. The brightness hurt his eyes; he had to squint to make her out. She was lying across the table, her eyes closed, the tears squeezing under long lashes and coursing down. Her head rested on the crook of her left forearm; her right arm lay limp and fully stretched towards him, the fingers curling lightly round a single white carnation. He took it gently from her and put it with the rest.

'Pity to spoil it,' he said. Then, more strongly, 'You're talkin' rubbish, lovely!'

She hauled herself upright, weary and distraught. 'Am I, sergeant? Look at me, please!' She had lifted her hand to the ruins of her hair. 'When the drugs wore off and your nice police lady went away, I kept having this dream.' The faintest of shrugs, the bitter ghost of a smile. 'The shape of things to come. I found a pair of scissors and sat in front of the mirror. I was going to finish the job, you see; an end to Sara Holroyd.'

'Jesus!' he breathed, and she gestured impatiently.

'You needn't worry. I didn't have the courage; I couldn't bear the mess. Anyway, it wasn't necessary; he'd done it already. The girl in the mirror was a stranger so I cut off her hair.'

'Do us a favour,' he pleaded, still trying. 'Let it grow.'

But intimacy was fading, unable to withstand the light. She looked worse than ever; empty. Coldly, she said, 'You're sorry and I'm grateful. We've played your game and purged your guilt. What more do you want?'

'The real Sara Holroyd.'

Momentarily, he thought there might be a flicker of hope somewhere deep in her haunted green eyes; if so, it died at birth.

'I'm tired,' she said. 'I can't take any more tonight. Go away, please. Leave me alone.'

* * *

He clung to this statement, driving home. It was all she had given him, apart from a fat lip. Carries a fair old dig, he thought, probing the soreness with his tongue. You'll have to keep your guard up. No more tonight, she'd said. Well, that left tomorrow; and the day after; and the day after that ...

CHAPTER ELEVEN

THE PERFECT October morning; an early sun to burn off the mist, a cloudless sky, the chill already in retreat. So it was nice to loiter in the car park trading rugby gossip with a uniformed fellow Celt-in-exile; to shove the brain into neutral and soak up the warmth; to remember, fleetingly, that there was life beyond the nick, and issues other than real and imaginary sexual assault. But not for long, of course.

Inside, spotlit by a yellow beam through the dusty window, Warner was briefing the dayshift beatmen. Carving up the Manor, he awarded a tidy piece of street work to each individual.

'Knock on every door,' he insisted. 'If they didn't see the programme, give 'em the description and tell 'em to report any gen to the office. If they're *Crimewatch* fans, ask your questions and record *all* the answers.'

Shuffles and sighs, and the inevitable would-be-humourist trying for a cheap laugh. 'What if 'e was boffin' the wife, sarge?' Before Warner could squash it, insurrection spread. From somewhere among the clustered blue ranks, a second voice: 'What if 'e was boffin' *someone else's* wife?'

Lurking in the shadows, Evans was tempted to intervene; but Warner needed no assistance. He drew himself up, mature and weathered and immaculate, mustering the full authority of rank and a lifetime's service.

'See *those*?' he demanded, tapping the gleam of stripes at his shoulder. 'You earn 'em by persistence and devotion to duty – not by taking the piss out of your betters! The Force and the Beeb spent a fortune getting that reconstruction right. If just one person caught a glimpse of him, *you* could point us in Chummy's direction. Now get out there and do the job!'

The men obeyed, shamefaced; but you could sense the air of renewed purpose.

Fair enough, thought Evans, treading the unseasonably bright corridors. But you couldn't really blame the lads. Routine, see, and about as exciting as flat beer. He'd checked on a few 'sightings' himself – like yesterday, for instance.

Mrs Wilkins lived opposite the Holroyd girl's flat. Seventy-five in the shade, she was, wearing thick bi-focals, a hearing aid, a threadbare mauve housecoat; and a fag in her mouth which squirted smoke into pale and milky eyes. Squinting near-sightedly, she led him through an aura of boiled cabbage and none-too-clean old lady to a window overlooking the scene of the attack.

'A big, shiny motor,' she was saying breathlessly, 'like the film stars use. Blood red, it was, real creepy.'

Questioned much earlier, she had reported nothing untoward. Since then, it seemed, *Crimewatch* had sparked her memory – or her imagination.

'Sure, are you?' asked Evans, noting the distant, solitary street lamp. 'Couldn't have been much light out there.'

'I'm deaf, dearie, not blind! She was tripping past in her white coat and her pretty blond hair. All of a sudden, out he pops, waving a dirty great meat-cleaver. Gave me a right old turn!'

'What time was this, Mrs Wilkins?'

'Ten past ten,' she said at once; and probably at random. 'He ripped her clothes, chucked her on the back seat, and had his evil way. Heard the screams, didn't I, and came running over here.'

Evans sighed, putting his notebook away. Sara had still been in the Black Lion then. 'Miss Holroyd tells it different, mind.'

'*Who?* Oh, I never knew her name.' Stubbing the cigarette, she gave him a cunning, senile grin. 'Bound to, isn't she, what with the shock. One of them mental black-outs, see.' She leaned forward, breathing nicotine into his face. 'He done it in the car! Didn't show *that* on the programme, did they?'

112

'How come you didn't call, being so upset? Why didn't you tell the sergeant when *he* came?'

Her ready answers dried. She shook her thin grey locks in confusion.

'Hanky-panky,' she mumbled, finally. 'Thought they were larking about – till I saw *Crimewatch*. Here, when you catch him, will they put *me* on the telly?'

'Come on, lovely,' he coaxed her gently. 'It's just a story, right?'

'Shall I make tea, then?' She smiled up at him, relieved and hopeful as a kid caught fibbing. 'Don't get much company, these days, and I *do* love a nice chat.'

He granted her this small comfort, even though he had other calls to make; which, if less poignant, proved equally unproductive. Negative evidence, Wilson would say; the Crimebotch Gavotte, more likely.

The basement gloom did nothing to lift his depression. Beddoes was missing again, very late if not actually deceased. Overworking, he was, but only on the *personal* angle – ducking the footslog and spending too much time with the girl. The Holroyd casefile was inches thick and growing, most of it down to Roy. An unhealthy business, obsession, 'specially with a woman on the scene: time for a quiet word of warning.

At which point, Beddoes himself sidled in, looking pensive and subdued.

'Taking the air, were you?' Evans enquired. 'Nice day for it.'

'Cracker,' Beddoes agreed, without much enthusiasm. 'Been upstairs, actually. Confab with 'is nibs.'

'This week's campaign, I expect,' said Evans comfortably. 'Rubbing shoulders with the drones.'

'Not exactly, sir. Sorry.'

Evans looked up sharply, scenting a put-on. Beddoes rarely gave him the courtesy, and *never* apologised.

'Should've cleared it with you first, uncle; thing was, you weren't *'ere.'*

Evans wagged his head, thoroughly bemused. 'Cleared what?'

''Ad a funny on the blower,' Beddoes explained. 'Wouldn't use the 'ot line, insisted on me, personal. Rabbitin' on about the rapist; Irish, too, know what I mean?'

'Oh sure,' grunted Evans. 'Down to the leprechauns, is it?' But Beddoes wasn't smiling.

'That's what *I* thought; 'til 'e said 'e'd 'eard this bloke braggin' in some posh club. Talking about Sara, mind you; called 'er the bra-less bar fly.'

Evans whistled softly. 'Duw, duw. Never made it public, did we?'

Beddoes nodded, settling at last into his chair. 'Odd, like I said. 'Ung up, of course, before I could start a trace. OK, I thought. Take it to our leader.'

'You did right,' Evans assured him. 'Got a name, have we?'

Suddenly, Beddoes seemed wholly engrossed in paperwork. 'Better ask Wilson,' he muttered. 'Wants a word. Like, now.' Seeing Evans' angry frown, he added, 'Orders. Sorry, already.' And starting potching with that bloody file again.

'Aye, well, thanks,' said Evans drily. 'Thanks very much!'

A slant of sunlight from the picture window caught Wilson behind his desk, suave as ever in pale grey suiting, yet solicitous. Lovely day and would Evans like tea or coffee? This established, he asked, 'Beddoes gave you the gist?'

'Anonymous call, he said; suggestive but not conclusive.'

This, Wilson insisted, was precisely the point. The subject – he carefully avoided the word *suspect* – had previously assisted with fraud investigations, and was much too influential to be harassed on such slender evidence.

'Aye,' murmured Evans. 'They said the same about Nixon, once.'

The Super flushed angrily. 'I hope you're not implying complicity, inspector!'

Hospitality to the rescue. There was a brief knock, and a secretary distributed refreshments. When she'd gone, Evans enquired cautiously, 'What would *you* call it, sir?'

'A special assignment.' Stirring coffee and allowing himself a tight smile, Wilson added, 'Under cover, perhaps: a cover-

114

up, most certainly not. No doubt he'll be able to account for his movements on the night in question.'

'Testing his alibi, are we?'

Wilson frowned, looking hunted and shifty. 'It's rather more delicate than that. We play squash regularly. I've entertained him in my house. A *personal* dilemma, then: on the one hand, a valued friendship, on the other a case I daren't relinquish. Which is where you come in.'

'Why me? Hardly the blue-eyed boy, am I?'

'Exactly. Our differences are well known; with *you* on the case, I can hardly be accused of favouritism.'

Evans leaned back, weighing the implications. A bit of a shaker, mind, the Super rubbing shoulders with a possible rapist. No wonder he's been edgy. On second thoughts, not edgy enough; almost as if he *knew* it was all eyewash. Somewhere far below, an ambulance raced by; the two-tone bray of a distant, demented donkey adding to the already somewhat crazy atmosphere.

'Think of it this way, inspector – a chance for you to retrieve lost ground.'

Crazy like a fox, Wilson; a solution which had something for everyone.

'Get it clear, shall we?' Evans suggested. 'My case, no interference and no mentions in despatches?'

'Correct. Are we agreed?'

'I'll need a proper briefing, sir – just the normal background stuff.'

The Super didn't fancy that, either, you could tell by the way he fingered the moustache. Well, no one cares to rat on a mate. Grudgingly, like a miser forced to dispense largesse, he released a few more crumbs of information.

The mate in question was one Harry Mortimer, landowner and City whizzkid, who kept a farm-bound wife and a town flat for the away fixtures.

'A womaniser, then,' said Evans, stating the obvious; and adding to Wilson's embarrassment.

'I know all too little of his private affairs.'

An odd note, this, a mixture of envy and anger; but before Evans could press the point, Wilson staged one of his unpredictable rallies. Very much the superintendent again, he gave the orders crisply. 'You're to go there as soon as possible, unofficially and out of working hours. Ask, discreetly, where he was that night, and take *no* other steps whatever without my consent. If, as I expect, Harry is cleared, the investigation remains strictly confidential between us. At present, no one else knows.'

'Except Beddoes.'

'Have no fears on that score; the sergeant's sworn to secrecy.'

'Aye,' said Evans. 'I noticed.'

He mulled it over, making his way downstairs. A dodgy business, mind, he'd never cared for clandestine stuff. Nor anonymous tipsters, for that matter. No credibility, see. Still, it was something to sink your teeth into; need your wits about you, dealing with the likes of Mortimer, and it beat the hell out of chasing unlikely sightings.

Beddoes was waiting, curious and eager. 'Took your time, uncle; what's the story?'

Evans smiled coldly. 'Drew the short straw, I did. Mission improbable.'

'So when do we start?'

'You want to listen. *I*, not we.'

'Oh yeah, and what'm I supposed to do, fester?'

Evans took his coat from the peg behind the door. 'More research for "This is Your Life, Sara Holroyd"; shooter practice; an hour a day on the files. You're a resourceful lad, Roy, you'll manage.'

'Do us a favour, uncle. We're a team, remember?'

'Sorry, boyo,' said Evans nastily, savouring the moment. 'Orders, see.'

Bleedin' typical, mused Beddoes acidly, holding the fort and twiddling his thumbs once more. The first sniff of a lead and the Brass close ranks. First Wilson, bland and slippery as jellied eel, and now Evans doing a Garbo, wanting to be alone. Going bush, Evans was, opting out of the twentieth century. Carrying on about *Crimewatch* and computers like they were the Black Death, or something. Getting senile, poor old sod.

Must be the strain of inactivity. Slagging off Wilson one minute, holding hands the next. Dead peculiar, that.

Worse yet, Evans had lost his sense of fun. Not much friendly backchat these days, more your verbal fisticuffs. Evil crack, the one about the girl, well below the belt. The thought took his mind beyond the peeling paint and asthmatic radiators, all the way to Sara's flat: two days ago, moved by pity, rebellion, and a more private inclination he didn't care to examine too closely, he'd made a second visit . . .

She had answered his knock promptly and admitted him without demur. The carnations still held pride of place, but her greeting offered little encouragement. 'Oh. It's you again.'

'Right. Unfinished business, remember?'

'Yours or mine?'

He ignored that, moving straight to the table. After a moment, she followed, listless and dowdy beneath another sacklike dress. Her compulsive industry had paid off. Sunlight broadened the room, lingering on polished wood and striking sparks from the shiny glassware.

'Got the place lookin' good,' he commented, but she had no time for pleasantries, watching him steadily beneath the awful crewcut.

'Just ask your questions, please.'

'No questions, more of an explanation, like.' Along the landing, a lavatory cistern erupted violently, startling him; she paid it not the slightest heed.

'We're public servants, the police,' he began, conscious of the pomp, 'funded from the taxpayer's pocket.' Seeing her expression, he added quickly, 'Yeah, well, you'd know that, wouldn't you? Thing is, the brass get twitchy over waste: duplication, wrongful arrest, botched prosecutions. There's standing orders, see. A case gets on paper, it's 'ard to stop. Costly, too.' It wasn't going as planned; consolation, she needed, not bleedin' excuses. Doggedly, conscious of her evident disinterest, he tried again. 'I'm sayin' you can't take things for granted. Bedlam, some nights, believe me. Acid freaks, dream-pedlars, and some just plain lonely, fancyin' the attention. 'Ave to be tested, see, before the machine starts rollin'. Nothin' personal, just doin' the job.'

117

'I noticed.' Sitting severely, she looked pale but composed.

Reassured by the mildness, he continued, 'Eight out of ten rape complaints never go on the books. They're eyewash, see, three other blokes. That's what we're up against; it's why you 'ad a rough ride.'

Finally, she woke, the welling of a deep, long-suppressed fury. She rose abruptly, pacing the meagre space, the dress wafting around her. Colour flooded to her cheeks; in the sun, her eyes burned cat-like and tawny. 'How many girls have you bedded, sergeant? Don't bother to count! Do you bully *them* into submission?'

''Ere, go steady!'

'Of course not! That's reserved for *victims*, isn't it? The unfortunates who must be probed and humiliated in the name of the taxpayer's mite!' Two sharp paces and she whirled again, her head high, a finger aimed in accusation. Her silhouette sprang from the backlight, slender and vibrant and unmistakably feminine; despising Charles Thompson, you had to admire his taste.

'Nothing *personal*!' she cried contemptuously. 'How blind can you be? Is *anything* more personal than rape? You come here with your feeble explanations and your bleating conscience and you know *nothing*!' Even as he reeled under the ferocity, a part of him welcomed it. This was how she'd once been; quite something. As if rejecting the very thought, she made a sweeping, slashing gesture taking in the whole room.

'Looks good, you say. And so it should; it's all I can do! Why should physical assault damage the mind, sergeant? How, stupid of me; policemen only *ask* questions!' Already the anger was fading. She sank wearily on to the chair, her eyes vague and fearful. 'I don't know who I am any more,' she confessed. 'Only what I'll never be again.'

Cautiously, he reached over and took her hand. The brief contact filled him with compassion, and a curious kind of contentment.

'I didn't know you before,' he reminded her. 'I volunteered, remember?'

Gazing in wonder at the intertwined fingers, her voice small and far away, she murmured, 'How could I ever trust you . . .?'

Not a lot to be done about *that* question; time will tell, my son. Meanwhile, the guilt simply refused to go away, and her earlier taunt – *'You know nothing!'* – struck uncomfortably close to home. Confined to the nick he might be, but not to solitary. By this time thoroughly inured to apologising, he went in search of the WPC who'd witnessed the fateful interrogation. Her name was Mary Parrot. Inevitably, she was known throughout the nick as Pol.

Equally inevitably, when eventually he cornered her in the canteen, she gave him short shrift. 'You've got a bloody cheek, Roy Beddoes,' she snapped, her eyes flashing; nice eyes, he noticed, sort of velvety brown. 'After what you put her through!'

She made to get up and he forestalled her, taking her arm and pleading, 'Line of duty, Pol, someone's gotta do it. I'm sorry, honest.'

'Don't tell me, tell *her*!'

'Yeah, well, I'm trying, know what I mean?'

As she hesitated, he made his pitch, coming down heavily on his own bad conscience and exerting a maximum of charm. Not the most romantic of settings, mind you, boiled beef on the menu and the extractors on the blink; but it was emptying fast, and at least he had her to himself.

'I need your help, Pol, I dunno where to start.' A warm-hearted girl, WPC Parrot, under the matronly and somewhat forbidding surface. Not averse to a touch of aid and comfort herself, either, judging by the occasional sideways glance she sent his way. He moved closer, pressing his luck.

'Tell you what,' he suggested warmly. 'Quiet evening, just the two of us. I could pick your brains, like, make use of all that expertise.'

'It'll cost you a decent nosh,' she warned. 'Partial to Chinese, me.' A nice, conspiring grin. 'I eat well, I'm a big girl.'

He let his eye wander over her well-filled tunic. 'So I see. You're on.'

Bit of a dark horse, Pol. She arrived bang on time in a high-necked blouse which underplayed her formidable bust and a skirt which revealed slim and lovely legs. Oriental lanterns made magic in her eyes and did wonders for her cheekbones. She was a knockout, and over the special for two he told her so.

'Do leave off, sarge, you can't mix business with pleasure.'

"Oo can't?"

Later, back at his pad, he proved the point, to her noisy and athletic rapture. Pink and breathless, she crooned, '*Nice* to 'ave a man who knows the score! It's the knockers, see, turns 'em on too quick. Wham, bam, an' I'm still warmin' up.' Then, brisk and businesslike, she wriggled into his shirt and declared, 'You've done your bit, an' I'll do mine.' And delivered a full and frank brief for the sympathetic handling of rape victims.

Beddoes reckoned he'd remember it a good long time; learning by doing, you might say. 'Don't take *my* word,' she cautioned, at the end. 'Enthusiastic amateur, me.'

Which led, naturally enough, to a second bout of sympathetic handling.

'I know a good shrink,' she murmured, afterwards. 'I'll give you 'is name and address.'

'Intensive care'd be better,' gasped Beddoes. 'Tell us in the morning, there's a good girl.'

When he woke, she'd already gone; the details were printed in lipstick on the bathroom mirror. Good value, our Pol.

Which couldn't be said for her psychiatric mocker. Had to be an imposter, for a start. No beard, no facial tics, and no mid-European accent; didn't even look old enough to smoke. Second, he insisted on a meeting in the lounge of a very posh hotel, and drank doubles like there was no tomorrow. Not the greatest of communicators, either; so laid back that at times you had a job to know whether he was even conscious. Mostly, he acted like a Savile Row tailor's dummy with hollow legs, listening with his eyes closed, bending his elbow at regular intervals, and nodding about once every twenty minutes.

Towards the end, though, he did let slip a couple of hints for DIY analysts. Maybe booze made him talkative.

'My dear chap,' he drawled, 'don't confuse us with *doctors*, dear me no. It is not our function to heal the sick. Rather, we assist individuals to identify and discuss their own problems.'

'Talk it all out, you mean?' Beddoes suggested, wincing as another large malt went the way of all spirit.

'Doubtless the uninformed would put it that way. The idea, you see, is for the patient to cure *himself*.' He glanced at his watch. 'Time's up, old man, I'm afraid. Mustn't give away any more trade secrets.'

Somehow, Beddoes figured you'd need to know a bit more than that to rate a Harley Street practice and holidays in Bermuda ...

All the same, he'd done his best, and picked up some useful knowledge along the way. He reckoned there could well be further exchanges with PC Parrot; some might even involve information. Meantime, Sara Holroyd continued to occupy a good deal of his waking and working hours; next time they met, he would be able to offer more than just a sympathetic presence and a shoulder to cry on.

CHAPTER TWELVE

THE PROBLEM with fashionable addresses, Evans thought testily, drumming his fingers on the wheel, is finding somewhere to park. Six in the evening and you couldn't see the kerb for Mercs and BMWs; only proles and coppers buy British. Eventually, he abandoned the unmarked Ford on a double yellow, shoved his card under a wiper, and hiked two blocks back to Mortimer's place. Fraud Squad country, this; leaded windows and ornate Edwardian lampposts. Hardly your normal setting for Hunt the Hitman.

Hardly your normal approach, either, pussyfooting around a mogul and no paperwork. Still, Wilson wanted it this way, and he was calling the shots. Accordingly, Evans had opted to beard the suspect – sorry, *subject* – in his own lair. Mortimer would believe his home was his castle; probably owned one, somewhere. Preserve the illusion, then; he might be more amenable that way. He'd sounded OK on the phone, no more patronising than you'd expect. 'The men in blue, old boy? Happy to oblige.' And had given directions with soldierly precision.

He was waiting, though; answered at the first ring. During the hiatus for handshakes and coat hanging, Evans measured his man. Blocky, and taller than you'd think: their eyes locked at pretty much of a level. Florid complexion, a head of dark wavy hair, an air of complete self-confidence. Well set-up, physically and financially in the pink; his chukka boots alone would rupture a copper's monthly pittance.

'Sun's past the yardarm,' he announced, leading the way in. 'What's your poison?'

Evans hesitated only briefly. Clandestine, he was, almost a social call. 'Very civil, sir. Scotch then, a small one.'

Mortimer padded to the well-stocked bar. An unlikely rapist, but you couldn't write him off, whatever Wilson might say. A squash player who moved well, and hands like shovels. A vague description, mind, but it fitted like a glove; wonder where he keeps the tracksuit?

The drinks came in crystal tumblers, smooth and heavy to hold.

'Mud,' said Mortimer sipping formally; then, 'Money problem, I assume?'

'A bit of background, more like. All the best, sir.'

'Fire away,' Mortimer invited, not a care in the world, and planted himself four-square in the massive club chair. The masculine corner, this; state-of-the-art stereo on one side, the bar on the other, and team photos lining the walls. Hockey, with Mortimer in the middle, padded but unmistakable. Loonies, mind, the goalies, men who thrive on hazard.

Evans began cautiously. 'Your name was mentioned, see, in connection with a certain investigation.'

'Hm. Witness for the prosecution, eh?' He sounded quite pleased.

'Not exactly. A question of times and places.'

Mortimer frowned, mystified. 'Not with you; sorry.'

'An incident up west, about a month ago; near the Black Lion. Know it at all, do you?'

'Know *of* it; never use the place.'

Evans cropped his drink, taking his time: an official pace. 'Twentieth of September, midnight or thereabouts. Recall what you were doing, then? Offhand, I mean?'

Mortimer tested the subtly inquisitional note, his eyes narrowing, the joviality slipping. 'What *is* this, inspector; third degree?'

Evans shrugged, very casual. 'An account of your movements. Only asking, mind.'

'You *asked* for help,' said Mortimer coldly. 'You're drinking my whisky. Damn bad form, old man!'

'Assisting with enquiries was the phrase, sir. Very careful about that, I was.'

Mortimer came to his feet, a formidable physical presence. 'False pretences, *I'd* say.' An expression of utter disdain, the officer's response to a loutish squaddy. Then, astonishingly, he snapped, 'I'll make a call, d'you mind?'

Darro, thought Evans, he's paging the mouthpiece already; must have *something* to hide. Aloud, mildly, he advised, 'No need for solicitors, yet. We're off the record, see; no witnesses.'

Mortimer's downward glare was withering. 'Chum of mine, actually; police superintendent.'

Naked condescension, mind, enough to lift anyone's hackles. Evans nodded, worldly and cynical. 'That'd be Wilson, no doubt. The old pals act, then.'

Mortimer caught the implication at once, halting incredulously in his tracks.

'He's *aware* of this ... tomfoolery?'

'Tomfoolery, is it?' Evans echoed, priming his retaliation. 'Funny way to talk – about rape.' And sat back to savour the effect.

Mortimer's broad face went completely blank; his jaw actually sagged. 'Rape? D'you say *rape*?'

For a moment he stood stunned and motionless, the high colour having bled away. Then his eyes flickered and he dredged up a sickly grin. 'A joke, of course; Richard put you up to it.'

Evans took out his wallet. Slowly and deliberately, he produced the warrant card and laid it on his knee. Mortimer watched, mesmerised.

'No joke, sir. Call the lawyer now, shall we?'

The room was very quiet, you'd never know there was a main road outside. Double glazing, Evans mused distractedly, and those thick brocade curtains. On second thoughts, much of the decor had been chosen with women in mind; the generous sofa, the fireside sheepskin, a couple of romantic, impressionistic prints. *The man's a seducer*, he remembered. What would he want with masks and dark alleys?

And indeed, Mortimer had rallied, fixing refills without so much as a by-your-leave. Clearly, action soothed him; Evans' last crucial question might never have been asked. From the bar, tense but unyielding, he demanded, 'We'll get it straight, d'you mind? Richard's accusing me of rape?'

'I never said that, sir,' replied Evans at once. 'Assisting with enquiries, remember?'

'Hmph!' Mortimer offered the fresh drink brusquely; duty not hospitality. There was a hint of animal power about him, the truculent stance of the baited bull. 'So who's the victim, eh? Assuming I'm allowed to know?' Lurking beneath the hectoring tone, Evans sensed real apprehension. For some reason, the answer mattered very much.

'Girl called Sara Holroyd. She's a student.'

It was very odd. The name meant nothing to him, anyone could see; yet suddenly he had the air of a man vindicated. His composure returned, and with it, command. 'Twentieth of September, you said,' he murmured, lowering himself into his chair. 'Around midnight.'

'Right.'

Mortimer swigged his gin, setting the glass down carefully. 'Very well. I was here, all night.'

Flat and anticlimactic, after all the foreplay; and too definite altogether.

'A while ago, mind, sir, memory can be tricky. Sure, are you?'

'Positive.' He threw it down like a challenge, take it or leave it, almost as if he didn't *expect* to be believed.

'Just wondering, I was, see,' Evans murmured. 'A date and time, off the cuff, like that.' He allowed a short, insinuating pause and added curtly, 'Alone, were you?'

Suddenly, there was complicity in the air, and Wilson's veiled warning made some sense.

'Not for a moment,' said Mortimer; and meeting Evans' stare head-on, he continued, 'I won't identify her; not now, not ever. A matter of honour, d'you see.'

'Very discreet, I am,' Evans declared. 'One word from the lady'd do it.'

Mortimer leaned back and took a long, untroubled swallow. 'Inspector, wild horses couldn't persuade me.'

'Pity,' said Evans, meaning it. 'What am I supposed to think, and no corroboration?'

Mortimer grinned savagely. 'Old boy, you can think what you damn well please!'

You had to admire him, really, whatever he'd done. The Sidney Carlton touch: 'Tis a far, far better thing ...

'A serious charge, mind,' Evans murmured. 'Being a bit noble, are you?'

And that didn't bother him, either. 'See nothing wrong with nobility, Evans. Rather the opposite, actually.'

A moment of truce, a fleeting atmosphere of mutual respect. Mortimer broke it with an incongruous question. 'Richard's top dog, I take it? Man you report to?'

'Oh sure,' admitted Evans. 'Me and a few others.'

Mortimer nodded grimly. 'Tell him from me, will you? Rape indeed! Balderdash, old boy. I know it, he knows it. Wild horses, then; don't forget.' Very insistent, he was, and much of the arrogance back in his bearing.

Rising to leave, Evans delivered a caution of his own. 'Give us a name, I would; or see a good mouthpiece.'

Mortimer saw him out, saving his best for last.

'You want a rapist, inspector, you'd best look elsewhere. Before it's too late.'

Food for thought, mind, and Evans chewed it over, driving home. The mews had cleared miraculously, the toffs all headed up west to spend like drunken sailors. Mortimer was a toff, no question; did it make him incapable of rape? Walk softly, bach, don't confuse honour with innocence.

Oncoming lights blinded him: dip, you mad bastard! The little gold afterblobs cleared slowly, and the road opened ahead. A lull in the traffic, a chance to engage the automatic pilot and give the forebrain a chance.

Never mind impressions, consider the facts. According to your friendly but nameless snout, Mortimer was privy to information known only to the rapist, the victim, and the cops. He looked the part, was physically capable of playing it, and his alibi stunk. Throughout the curious, shifting interview, the first impression held: he was hiding something. And leading the field, no question, not a challenger in sight.

A taxi overtook him, travelling much too fast. Don't push your luck, boyo, Traffic'll have you. He tootled on steadily, still immersed in the Mortimer enigma. Philanderer he might be, and shifty with it; but hard as he tried, Evans simply couldn't see him taking a woman by force. Neither could Wilson, obviously, which explained *his* painful embarrassment.

Back home, he parked and locked the car. Freezing again, the stars bright and close. Looking up, shivering slightly, Evans thought, build up a profile. Check his past, talk to his contacts, unearth the distaff side. Routine, then; he'd put it to Wilson in the morning ...

'Absolutely not!' hissed the Superintendent, cornered in a quiet corridor. 'I won't have you sniffing about publicly, raising groundless suspicions, creating a scandal!' He had a point, no doubt. If Mortimer *was* clean, someone'd be eating an awful lot of humble pie.

'If you say so, sir,' said Evans, glancing furtively around, feeling like a heavy in a bad spy movie. 'What d'*you* suggest?'

Wilson paused as two WPCs passed by, then whispered, 'We wait. An additional uniformed presence around his flat, make them very visible.'

Evans whistled softly, much impressed. 'I like it, sir. If he's our man, it'll keep him off the streets; no more attacks, negative evidence. If he's not, the pressure'll loosen his tongue, p'raps.'

'The two-way squeeze, inspector.' A rather twisted smile, a curiously wistful note; he still didn't fancy it, obviously.

'Hard, is it?' asked Evans sympathetically, 'putting a collar on a mate?'

The Superintendent drew himself up, affronted. 'That's *my* problem.'

Excluded from the investigation, left once more to his own devices, Beddoes gravitated to Sara's flat; time to test the Parrot theory. Today, there were hopeful signs: a certain eagerness to her step, the suggestion of a welcome somewhere deep in her eyes, a little less of the obsessional tidiness, and a book open on the table. He nodded towards it, approvingly.

'On the come-back trail, are we?'

She shrugged, indifferent and lethargic. 'I've tried; it's

pointless. The Romantics are so artificial; I simply can't take Hugo.' She gave him a tortured, sarcastic glance. 'No doubt you can solve that problem, too.'

Outside, it was cold and gloomy, a chill wind and a leaden sky. The room seemed mean and isolated, and her mood was changing to match. Somehow, he'd have to jolt her out of it.

'As it 'appens,' he began breezily, 'I've bin doin' a bit of 'omework. Take a pew; Doctor Beddoes will reveal all.'

'My,' she murmured sceptically, 'home-grown psychology.' But she obeyed readily enough, an encouragement in itself.

'First off,' he said, 'there's special clinics for people like you.'

Bull's-eye. She awoke immediately, bitter and scathing. 'More *victims*, you mean, wallowing in communal self-pity! No thank you, sergeant, I have sufficient troubles of my own.'

He moved on quickly, stating the gospel according to Pol. 'Listen, lovely, you were in the wrong place at the wrong time. It's like a traffic accident, nothing to be ashamed of. Understand that, and you're 'alfway 'ome.'

She was sitting rigid, gazing at the wilted carnations. 'Understand?' she repeated blankly. *'Understand?'*

He hunched forwards, warming to the task, counting the arguments on his fingers. 'Rape's about dominance,' he told her blithely, with all the authority of recently acquired knowledge. 'The revenge of an inadequate man against the entire female gender. It's not a sex act, there's nothing personal. It's plain aggression, see, and any woman'll do.' Seeing her expression of patent scorn, he added, 'Outcome of research, mind you, all the boffins agree.' Somehow it had sounded better coming from Pol.

'The boffins in question being men, no doubt,' said Sara.

He made to protest, and she stood up decisively. 'Just wait. I'll make tea.'

As she busied herself in the kitchen and the illusion of domesticity returned, he noticed the title of her book – *Les Misérables*. Very apt. Presently, she came back, carrying a loaded tray. Her movements were controlled and oddly ceremonious; he sensed the approach of a watershed.

'You're a man,' she said evenly. 'You can't begin to understand, so I'll tell you. Then perhaps you'll leave me in peace.'

'I doubt it,' he breathed, but she ignored him, pouring tea. Her eyes were glazed and remote, seemingly focused on something deep and inward.

'I was quite calm when he finished – rational. Walking to the police station, I tried to get it clear in my mind; the timing, the location, what he'd said and done. I never imagined anyone would doubt me.' He stirred, starting yet another apology. 'It doesn't matter,' she said, and the finality reduced him to silence.

She sat down, propping her elbows on the table, resting her small chin in her hands. Her steady gaze demanded his total attention, and he gave it willingly.

'It didn't last long,' she admitted. 'Rationality, I mean. He was still with me, you see. The stench lingered, a rancid, animal vileness. His wetness was on me and inside me, burning with every step. I felt *corrupt*, sergeant; do you understand that?' Again she dismissed his appalled exclamation. 'Of course you don't!' Somehow, she managed the travesty of a smile. 'If it's any consolation, you were right about one thing. I spent hours in the bath, trying to be rid of him. Sometimes, even now, the smell and the corruption come back.'

She paused, erect and dry-eyed. A wisp of steam rose from her untouched cup and she watched it tightly, as though it harboured all her ghosts.

'It could be anyone, you say; but it was *me*! Imagine it was a traffic accident, you say.' Her eyes narrowed and she leaned in towards him. 'Tell me, do people avoid accident victims? Do they shrink away and stare sideways with eyes that say – *tainted*? Aggression, you say, and dominance, it has nothing to do with sex.' She shook her head at the sheer absurdity. 'I was violated, sergeant, coldly and deliberately, in a freezing alley with a knife at my throat. Something I valued, something I had given freely and with joy, was ripped away. Nothing and no one can ever give it back.'

Her eyes held him mercilessly; she wasn't finished yet.

'Another thing the "boffins" always say.' She gave the word the full weight of her contempt. '"Don't struggle, don't antagonise, try to keep him talking." They're wrong about that, too.' At last the tears began; she could deny them no longer. 'If I'd known what I know now, I would have fought to my last breath.' She spoke the final sentence quietly and with utter conviction. 'It would have been better if he'd killed me.'

What do you say to her, he wondered desperately, in her honesty and her agony, when all the expert claptrap runs out? How would *you* handle it, pretty Pol of the too-easy answers: sympathetically? Please, Mr Trick Cyclist, what do you tell the patient whose personal solution is very final indeed? You have to do *something*, sunshine, because she's fading like the day itself into a permanent twilight of true madness.

She sat, pale and motionless, her eyes empty of everything except a distant, despairing plea. Suddenly, his mind was winging back across the years. In Sara's place, he conjured the image of poor plain Rosie, his first and only love. In a moment of purest insight, he perceived a fundamental truth: the two were one. Cripples both, physical and emotional, in need of simple human warmth. Show me I'm normal, they begged in unison, tell me I'm just like any other girl – worthy of a special place in someone's affections.

He moved quickly to her, standing behind her, resting a gentle hand on each of her cold and fragile shoulders.

'I'm here, Sara,' he told her softly, 'for as long as you want. You can come home anytime now.'

She tilted her head, drying a wet cheek against his hand. The floodgates burst; he had physically to support her while the sobs and incoherent words came tumbling and stumbling out.

'Oh, God,' she cried. 'I don't even know you!'

And as he held her, murmuring her name into the dying light, a mean, detached voice in his brain whispered, Beddoes, my son, what've you let yourself in for?

CHAPTER THIRTEEN

FEATURELESS DAYS became weeks, the clocks went back, and winter advanced under a barrage of freezing fog. Mayhem on the motorway and the *Crimewatch* leads dwindling. According to Evans, the old order had endured; the Monday meetings were little more than perfunctory exchanges of bald facts. Wilson himself had gone to ground in the big office, emerging fraught and harassed at infrequent intervals and snapping at anyone who crossed his path. Meantime, Evans delegated a rash of shoplifting to his junior partner and kept the details of Mission Improbable to himself. Which left Beddoes traipsing the supermarkets, soothing irate greengrocers, and feeling thoroughly disenchanted.

Occasionally, they managed a semblance of earlier, easier days: as when, late one morning, Beddoes returned buoyant from a triumph at the shooting range.

Scowling over his typewriter, sniffing the air like a supercilious bloodhound, Evans complained, 'Darro, you smell like the OK Corral!'

'Dead-eye Dick,' said Beddoes smugly. 'Never know when it'll come in 'andy.'

'Bloody cowboy! Overdoing it, you are, on and off the range.'

'Oh yeah?' Beddoes retorted. ''Oo says?'

'The whole damn nick, that's who. After live targets, I hear, you're setting your sights on a Parrot.'

'Do leave off. Just good friends, me 'n' Pol, pooling our resources.'

Evans nodded. 'Oh sure. Old as the hills, this one, mind; but you know what they say?'

Beddoes had a fair idea, but once in a while it paid to indulge a whim. 'OK, Blodwyn, I'll buy it.'

Grinning slyly, Evans said, 'Too much banging makes you deaf.'

Standing no more than a yard away, Beddoes lifted a hand and cupped it round his ear. 'Pardon?'

More often, though, beset by petty crime and conflicting priorities, they rubbed along uneasily. Or, as Evans put it later the same day, 'Like Darby and Joan in the divorce court.'

Responding instinctively, his mind on Sara Holroyd, Beddoes muttered, 'Wouldn't know; never been there, myself.' And regretted it at once.

Evans' head came up, the pale eyes drilled into him. 'Watch your tongue, boyo!'

Mostly, the Inspector was an equable soul, careless of officialdom and willing to take a ribbing. When he *did* get mean, it was best to keep your head down; like now.

'Ah, give over, only joking. I'm sorry, OK?'

The anglepoise lamp cast deep shadows, thinning Evans' face. He looked strained and very angry.

'Bit late for sorry! No medals for *your* record in that department, lately.'

'Ow d'you mean?' demanded Beddoes, stung.

'If Pol and Gloria ever compare notes, the fur will fly. Messing on your own doorstep, you ought to know better.'

Gloria was the Super's secretary, a girl for whom Beddoes still had a soft spot. Well, a *hard* spot. Whereas Pol was casual, in the line of duty. He sighed, appealing for clemency. 'Women! What can you do?'

But Evans was not to be deflected. 'Another thing. You're seeing too much of the Holroyd piece. Bad enough having Wilson on my back without you doing a restless Romeo.'

Quite suddenly, Beddoes had had a gutful. Furiously, tapping the Holroyd file with a forefinger, he snapped, 'Yeah, well, I'm working; what's your excuse?'

And hard though Evans glowered, he couldn't cap *that*!

'Not boring you, am I?' Wilson murmured sarcastically. 'Keeping you from anything important?'

'Wait all day if I have to,' retorted Evans. The tiff with Beddoes had spurred him to impulsive action; a showdown on the Mortimer affair. He'd barged into the dim, Star Wars atmosphere of the big office and planted himself unceremoniously at the desk. For several minutes, giving his celebrated impression of the deranged computer buff, Wilson had ignored him. Now, pushing the print-out to one side and squinting owlishly, the Superintendent enquired, 'A general insurrection, Evans, or merely bad manners?'

'Neither, really. Call it a top-level conference, shall we?'

'Summoned unilaterally, of course.' A machine began to beep stridently, and Wilson silenced it with a practised short-fingered jab. 'In which case,' he added, 'I assume there have been new developments.' Else why waste my time? the tone implied.

'Funny you should say that. I'm here because there aren't any.'

In the upward greenish glow of the VDU, Wilson's face looked stark and bloodless; ill disposed to argument. Peevishly, he said, 'Nil returns are not required, inspector. My instructions were perfectly clear – deploy the uniforms and wait. We *are* discussing the rapist?'

'Sparring, I'd call it; but that was the idea, yes.'

'Very well, I can spare you five minutes.'

'It'll take longer, mind.'

Wilson lost his temper, sitting straight and clipping off the words. 'Your intrusion is impertinent, your manner offensive. You've already been cautioned for insubordination; next time it'll go on record. If you have something to say, say it. Otherwise, get out!'

Evans nodded grimly. Just the reaction he'd expected.

'Right. It's a month now and no reports, no sightings, no leads from the door-to-door boys.' He paused, getting the right amount of needle to his voice. 'Unless you've got someone else on it. Spying on the spy, I mean.'

'That is a disgusting suggestion!' Wilson actually recoiled, an expression of genuine outrage.

'Oh, sure. Had to be asked, though. Look, Mortimer's been confined to barracks. We've had muggings, even murders, but no more rapes. Fair play, what's the obvious conclusion?'

Set quite a store by friendship, the Super, not prepared to give an inch. 'Good God, it's Harry Mortimer you're accusing! Say the word "arrest" and he'll have a silk round here with a slander writ for the National Debt! And what do we have against him? Supposition and a vague physical description. He's playing knight errant, man; the moment he names his partner, we're the biggest fools in Christendom!' The intercom buzzed and he slapped the switch down instantly. 'Not now, Gloria, I'm busy!'

Evans smiled grimly. So much for sparing five minutes. 'Come *on*, sir,' he insisted. 'Cloak and dagger's getting us nowhere. No evidence, you're saying; course not, we haven't looked! Standard procedure, it's all I'm asking – the chance to check his background.'

Wilson sat motionless, his hands flat on the desk top, his gaze focused on the weather outside. Looming night clouds and a thin drizzle, not the most cheerful of omens.

Quiet but insistent, Evans turned the screw. 'What happens if you're wrong, sir? All this time, and nothing on record?' No response, not a flicker; and Evans lost patience. '*Jesi mawr*, he's *your* mate!'

At last, Wilson awoke to the implication, rising and starting a ritual circuit of the office. From across the room, in a voice which had Evans craning to hear, he murmured, 'I'm not wrong, inspector, but I take the point. If he has nothing to hide, he has nothing to fear.' Though he sounded neither convinced nor convincing, this aphorism seemed to restore him. Moving more freely, speaking more crisply, he said, 'Very well, do your digging, but the ground rules stand. Nothing on paper, and no private initiatives.'

As much as could be expected, probably. Better than brawling in the barracks, too. 'Agreed, sir. Where should I start?'

Briefly, Wilson's face clouded over again; the answer came reluctantly, very much against the grain. 'Perhaps you'd better talk to his wife.'

He set out early next morning; roadworks in town, red lights solidly against him, rain coming down in stair-rods and the heater on the blink. Motorway visibility was barely fifty yards, fast-lane loonies bounced main beams off his mirrors, and the coaches swept past like ocean greyhounds. Nice day for a drive, bach. Why don't you keep your big mouth shut?

As he edged southwards, the deluge eased and the overcast gradually lifted. Five miles beyond Bolney, the Downs loomed out of the mist, green and sleek under a watery sun. Milder, too; getting near the coast. His spirits rose – could've been worse, after all.

Unfamiliar country, this, rolling hills and scattered sheep. At first sight, it might've been the Valleys. The illusion vanished as he moved away from the main road. A gentler and more luxuriant clime: tidy fields and neat hedgerows, everything more *kempt*, somehow. Every hamlet had its green; even in autumn, you could imagine the soothing echo of willow on leather, the ripples of genteel applause, the taste of real ale and the scent of summer meadows. The soft Southern underbelly, then, any resemblance purely superficial. Unemployment, old chap? Never heard of it.

He came, eventually, to a simple, understated sign – 'Uplands' – and turned between weathered pillars under a stand of beeches. The drive wound gently upwards between shaved lawns and ordered mounds of fallen leaves. Overhead, a flock of rooks wheeled and bickered; the air smelled of woodsmoke and the farmyard. At the crest, to his right, beyond a gravelled entrance and surrounded by mature horse-chestnuts, the Big House. Well, what else could you call it?

Genuine Tudor, he reckoned, but with all mod cons; solid yet elegant, broad windows and a handsome portico. Smoke rose lazily from one of several chimneys, and the low sun played lovingly on the polished chrome of a vintage Daimler.

Evans parked and approached with due deference. Landed gentry, he thought whimsically, they'd probably keep a butler in full livery. But despite vigorous and protracted hammering, the door remained firmly shut. A long way to come for nothing; better take a shufty round the garden. Thus occupied, passing an open door at the back, he spied movement in the distance: someone feeding chickens. As he drew near, the figure took form: a tall plain woman in a milkmaid's kerchief, a threadbare duffle and Home Store wellies. A churl, no doubt. She hadn't seen him, so he cleared his throat tactfully.

She whirled abruptly, scattering seed and hens. 'My goodness, you startled me!'

'Aye, sorry about that. Couldn't get an answer, see.'

She squinted up at him, framing her explanation. 'Well, now. Riley and Smith are burning leaves, George is up in the top field, Arthur and Mary have the 'flu, and the Spencers are off for the day. They work in the house.' She flicked out another handful of feed, provoking an outburst of peck and cackle. 'Stupid birds!' she muttered. Shrewd dark eyes, BBC English, and an air of subtle authority which totally belied her unprepossessing appearance.

'You'd be the lady of the house? Mrs Clare Mortimer?'

'For my sins. Who are you?' Not rude, really, just your actual aristocrat's directness.

'Evans, ma'am, Police Inspector.' He fumbled for his card and she waved it away.

'Don't bother. Oh dear, has Spencer been drinking again?' Then, seeing his perplexity, she added, 'Silly of me. They don't send inspectors for that, do they?' She cocked her head, shading her eyes and studying him curiously. 'I haven't seen *you* before; you must be new.'

He allowed himself a small grin. 'Hardly; but not local, either. Nothing official, mind; just a few questions, if I may.'

She emptied her bucket and kicked her way through the ensuing flutter; sunshine and red feathers.

'That,' she declared firmly, 'would depend on the questions.'

'Very general, really; about your husband.'

The smallest check in her stride, quickly retrieved; and a smile which took years off her face. 'Good heavens, don't tell me Harry's cooked the books!'

'Of course not, ma'am. Call it a little chat, shall we?'

She held the gate for him, latching it carefully. 'Foxes,' she explained, 'play hell with the fowls, given the chance.' He fell into step beside her, enjoying the mild air and the croon of a distant woodpigeon. 'I'll answer, as best I can, while I do the rounds. No tea in the drawing-room, I'm afraid. It's a working day.' She produced another candid, level stare. 'Ever ridden a tractor, inspector? Good-oh, a new experience!'

She led him across the yard, apologising for the mud. '*Such* a pity the police don't wear boots any more!' With much skill and no little strength, she shunted an elderly tractor around, hitched it to a hay-filled trailer, and brought the whole contraption to a shuddering halt beside him. 'All aboard,' she cried, adjusting a pair of earmuffles. 'Sorry, I don't carry spares.' And they were off.

She's conned you lovely, bach, he bellowed to himself, above the awful racket; blue blood's revenge, this. Her mouth worked joyfully and he thought she was laughing at him; then he realised she was singing at the top of her voice. Nearly two miles, it was, he checked it on the clock, through rolling sunlit pasture. Very pleasant, if it wasn't for the noise; he wondered if he'd ever hear anything again. Should've sat on the straw, stupid.

In a sheltered hollow under a broad, moulting oak, she turned him loose, killed the engine and hopped nimbly down. In the sudden, thunderous silence, she tossed him a smile and a pitchfork.

'Since you're here, you might as well help. Just spread it around, the stock won't mind.'

At this rate, he'd end up knackered as well as deaf; there had to be easier ways of gathering intelligence.

As they toiled, shoulder to shoulder, his hearing cleared and birdsong filtered through. Presently, a small herd of cows lumbered into view, lowing gently.

'Friesians,' he muttered, half to himself. 'Nice animals.'

Wielding her fork expertly, she shot him an approving glance. 'Of course, you're Welsh. The rural kind, one presumes, rather than mining.'

'Matter of fact,' he grunted, straining to match her work rate, 'my da was a rent collector.'

She snorted in amusement. 'So was mine, inspector, so was mine!'

She rammed her pitchfork into the ground and propped herself against the trailer. Breathing hard, dabbing perspiration from her face and exuding defiance, she said, 'Any minute now you're going to ask about Harry's women.'

'Am I, ma'am?'

She waited, hands on hips, till he met her eye. 'You might as well hear it from me. You'll find out anyway, won't you?'

'Oh, I expect so,' he agreed comfortably.

Exertion and sunshine had heightened her colour, the cattle had gathered around her. She made her statement blithely, to a chorus of meadowsweet breath and soft, incurious eyes.

'I don't expect to shock you, inspector. It's all the rage in the city, I believe.' She smiled, grave and unashamed. 'I'm gay, you see; my preference is for women.'

A priceless opportunity, and he took his revenge gladly. 'So is mine, ma'am, so is mine.'

Briefly, she stood transfixed, her expression totally blank; then she was laughing, great, full-throated peals which echoed from the hills and startled the browsing herd.

'*Splendid*, inspector. I *did* deserve that! One becomes so provincial out here in the sticks.' Recovering fast, sobering by the second, she asked, 'What's poor Hal been up to? A paternity summons, perhaps?'

Evans chose his words fastidiously. 'There's a woman involved, I won't deny it. A question of credibility, really.'

She nodded slowly, pushing a stray wisp of hair from her open, equine face. 'I see; you've come for a reference.' She paused, frowning narrowly. Her turn for measured phrases. 'In a marriage like ours, inspector, there has to be a certain licence – on both sides. So far, we've managed rather well; maximum enjoyment, minimal embarrassment. Harry has been very discreet. In his way, he's an honest, upright man. One day, he'll be a doting father.' A fleeting sidelong glance heavily laced with mischief. 'The answer to your unspoken question is – easier and sooner than you think.'

It was hard not to like her; but things had become altogether too light-hearted. Coldly and concisely, he detailed the danger. Unless Harry would reveal his current partner and establish his alibi, he could be in for serious trouble.

'May I ask what kind of trouble, inspector?'

Evans shrugged, very noncommittal. 'You can ask.'

She turned away brusquely, attacking the hay like a woman

possessed until the trailer was bare and the animals had begun to wander off. 'There,' she said. 'That ought to do it.' Then, retying her kerchief and speaking to the golden middle distance, she explained, 'Harry's a throwback, inspector, a latter-day fugitive from Camelot. Gentlemen observe the *code*, you see. If he won't tell you, he certainly won't tell me.'

'Wild horses,' Evans murmured, and her eyebrows soared. 'Said that, did he? There you are, then.'

She was getting set to leave. The ground, Evans reckoned, was as ready as it ever would be. Very casually, he laid out his question, the one he'd come so far to ask.

'I've got the message,' he assured her. 'Short-term bedmates, nothing lasting, tacit agreement all round. Very civilised, I'm sure. Just wondering, I was, whether there might be someone a bit special. Thing is, you'd *know* something like that; a clever woman like you.'

'Oh yes,' she said at once, 'I would.' Another of her minute hesitations; then, 'It's time we were heading back, the work's not half done.' She lifted her face to him, innocent and regretful. 'I really don't think I can help you any more.'

He declined her invitation to the cab, preferring to brave the unseasonably mild elements. He rode the trailer, gripping the chill metal sides, his hands smarting from the rough pitchfork handle. She took it very gently; from time to time, he caught her eyeing him enigmatically in the driving mirror.

Back in the yard, she bustled about mixing feed and chattering inconsequentially. She was guarded now; her marvellous spontaneity seemed muted and restrained. He followed grimly, carrying buckets and ruining his shoes, certain she had something more to give.

As the sun slipped lower and the shadows drew out, she herded him firmly to his car. She was name-dropping, listing Harry's childhood friends; maybe they could assist?

'Nigel Carter – you know, the textile magnate; the Todd girls – no, wait a minute, they're in New Zealand now. Billy Ponsonby, just down the road; Gina Howard ...' She paused, apparently struck by a random thought. 'Yes, Gina, they were virtually weaned together. Come to think of it, inspector, you might even have met. She married a policeman, you see; a very bright chap, he's done rather well for himself.'

She had stopped the Daimler, peering up at him expectantly. The mellow light softened her angular features and made her look quite handsome. 'Richard Wilson, he's called. Do you know him at all?'

Funny lot, the toffs, mused Evans as he headed north into gathering twilight. Queer, some might say, especially of Clare; but that was too simple, taking no account of her courage and humour, or of the fierce loyalty she had shown to an errant husband. It's all about upper-class codes, bach. One day, maybe, you'll crack them.

Throughout the long homeward haul, he was haunted by her final, guileless, ingenuous expression, the one which sat so ill on her spare and honest face; and by a dark inkling of what he might have to do next.

CHAPTER FOURTEEN

ALL CATS are grey in the dark; you might say the same for birds under hairdriers. The good, the bad and the lovely sitting like zombies, lobotomised by curlers, coffee and the banshee wail of the latest chartbuster. It's a bleedin' ritual, thought Beddoes, feigning absorption in a teenage fashion magazine, the weekly ordeal by fire and decibel: praise the Lord Harry I was born with a dong.

'Take her to a stylist,' Pol the oracle had counselled. 'A hairdo will work wonders for morale. Mmm, nice! Don't stop.'

'Easier said than done,' he'd objected, gently exploring the inner slope of a silken thigh. 'She's off public engagements, know what I mean?'

'Have to come on stronger, won't you? put it to her forcefully. Oh *yes* – like *that*!'

Afterwards, as they slid into sated sleep, she murmured, 'Tony ... Tony Orlando.'

''Ere,' he protested, miffed, 'it's me, Roy Beddoes, remember?'

'The *hair*dresser, stupid!'

Practical soul, our Pol; kept her mind on the job, so to speak.

But Sara had proved far less susceptible.

'Out of the question,' she'd said flatly the following morning, over the inevitable brew-up. 'I've had my fill of pitying stares and loaded conversation.'

'Leave it out! Just another paying customer; they won't know you from Adam. Well, Eve, anyhow.'

She sat forlorn and isolated in the false winter brightness, captive to the mean little room and her own insecurity. Somehow, he had to jolt her out of both.

'Why be a martyr?' he demanded. 'An accident, mind you, not an act of divine punishment.'

She shook her cropped head, her lips thin and bloodless. 'I've told you before. You don't know what you're asking.'

He leaned across the table, holding her gaze, laying down the law. 'You were bright and beautiful, Sara. Something really special. You gonna let an evil, screwed-up wreck destroy you? Survive, you said. Well, you 'aven't, and that means 'e wins after all!' He paused, breathing fast, and added harshly, 'Jesus, I'd like to lay 'ands on 'im!'

Briefly, he sensed an involuntary stirring, an echo of his own vehemence; but her eventual response came cool and sceptical.

'Steady on, sergeant. Policemen shouldn't get involved.' She was sipping tea, delicate as a cat, her composure apparently restored. Only a flicker deep in her eyes betrayed the inner pain. 'You'll never understand,' she said quietly. 'You're making things worse.'

Somewhere in the bowels of the building, a vacuum cleaner rumbled. She ignored it, passive and resigned.

Only one thing for it, my son: cruel to be kind. Drawing himself up, shoving the empty cup aside, he snapped, 'All right, girl, I'll tell you straight – you're not coming out with me looking like *that*!'

She rose abruptly, pale and aloof. She'd show him the door now, no doubt. For once, Pol had got it wrong and he'd come on *too* strong. But she merely drifted to the window, contemplating God knows what outside. She was wearing a sweater and skirt; the wintry backlight threw her figure into sharp relief. A tiny waist, trim hips, nice legs – a good girl going inexorably into decline. Well, he'd done his best. Back to Gloria and one-night stands.

She turned slowly, her expression tentative and vulnerable. 'Are you really that keen on my company?' A tone of genuine wonder, as if the very idea were beyond belief.

He nodded emphatically. 'Catch on quick, don't you.' He thought there might be a smile somewhere inside, struggling to break free. 'Another thing,' he said sternly, squinting up at her silhouette, 'the name's Roy. High time you started using it.'

She moved a step closer, searching his face. It wasn't hard to imagine the doubts she felt, she hadn't been too lucky lately. Spineless Charles, clumsy Rodney, and a nutter with a knife. To say nothing of third degree at the hands of an overzealous copper; enough to put her off men for life. In a small and apprehensive voice, she asked, 'What do you want me to do?'

Concealing his surprise and elation, he told her, 'I'll collect you, I'll wait while it's done and run you 'ome. Just be ready, is all.' He grinned, striking an official pose. 'Police sources suggest a Mr Tony Orlando.'

Her eyebrows arched upward in appreciation. 'You're well informed. He's the best, they say; but pricey.'

Lulled by success, Beddoes blundered unwisely on. 'Tell you what, I'll go 'alves. Dutch treat, OK?'

'You most certainly will not!'

A spark of green fire, the confined space suddenly ablaze with the force of her will. An intriguing glimpse of the girl she had once been: stunning. But it didn't last long. Her eyes widened, her hands came up to her mouth as though to recall the words. 'I'm sorry, I simply can't allow it.'

She returned to her chair, subdued but decisive. 'I'm beholden enough already'.

'Gordon Bennet, girl, I 'aven't been coming 'ere for the scenery!'

She avoided his eye, carting the tea things away and sloshing about at the sink. Presently, after another oblique and hesitant scrutiny from the kitchen doorway, she enquired, 'When is the big event to happen?'

He was tempted to say tomorrow. With Evans poncing about like 007 and Wilson skulking in the belfry, no one would be any the wiser. But Beddoes was a professional at heart; too much of the firm's time had already been spent on private enterprise, and this bit had to be done right.

''Ow would Tuesday suit? I'm due a day off about then.'

At last the smile appeared, faint and shaky, but worth the wait. He was halfway back to the nick before he could wipe the daft smirk from his own besotted face ...

143

She was being done now, the scissors snicking busily about her ears. The man himself fawned over her, chattering brightly. He didn't seem to be getting far – her small face remained set and serious. She hardly looked ecstatic; but then, neither did anyone else. Beddoes retired into the magazine and the romantic exploits of a TV soap-opera queen. Busy lady, it seemed. The air was sharp with ammonia, blue-coated attendants glided to and fro, noise and warmth overcame him. Open-eyed, he dozed.

'Roy?' She stood before him, her whole body vibrant in appeal. The rest of the room faded away; they might have been alone on a desert island.

You had to hand it to him; Tony Orlando knew his stuff. A sleek and golden skullcap which brought out the fineness of her features and the subtle tawny flecks in her eyes. She looked like the young Audrey Hepburn, only blonde.

'Terrific,' he breathed, meaning it, and she coloured prettily, regaining a semblance of long-lost pride.

On the way home, she asked the critical question. 'Where are you taking me, in my crowning glory?' Her hand strayed upwards, touching the lustrous hair in a kind of wonder.

He'd given this a fair bit of thought. Not too many places of entertainment these days which didn't depend on sex or romance in some guise; any of them might re-open the scars. Chancing his arm, banking on the novelty, he said, 'Reckon we'll 'ave a bit of a flutter, down the stadium. You know, greyhounds.'

Shifting gear for the junction ahead, watching from the corner of his eye, he caught her unguarded reaction: shock and disappointment. Quietly, reproachfully, she murmured, 'But I've already *gone* to the dogs.' Her shoulders were trembling, and he cursed himself for a mindless oaf. It was a connotation that simply hadn't occurred to him. Then, as the sound and a hint of her perfume filtered through, he realised she was actually laughing.

'It's a marvellous idea,' she admitted, and the unexpected closeness sustained them throughout the short journey. Outside the flat, she blew him a kiss, climbing the stairs with a freedom he'd never seen before. From the top, cheerfully, she called, 'See you at six on Tuesday.'

Keep your fingers crossed, sunshine; maybe it's going to work.

The hopeful mood sustained him through a hostile interview with a couple of shoplifting suspects. Black, sullen and sixteen years old, they sported Rasta dreadlocks and a man-sized grudge against the world.

'We was down the youth club, marn, ask any de guys.'

'Leave it out! The stuff was nicked at different times, on different days.'

'We got alibis *any time*, jus' you try'n' prove it!'

Beddoes took names and addresses, knowing it would be a waste of effort. Ghetto folk stick together, my son, you'll have to nick 'em red-handed. Well, pink-palmed, anyhow ...

The weather had turned ugly, half a November gale driving the rain along between bursts of frigid sunshine. Evans travelled slowly, approaching a confrontation he didn't need but couldn't avoid. Clare Mortimer's artful revelation and the logic of the investigation left him no choice. He had personal reservations, too, unformed and unwholesome doubts about the validity of *Crimewatch* leads which only Mrs Wilson could allay – or not, as the case may be. Fair enough, he allowed, but how d'you go about grilling the Super's wife behind his back? Bloody cautiously, bach, that's how. He wiped condensation from the windscreen and cased the locality.

Funny old business, mind, wealth. Though the Wilsons occupied a villa the average punter would kill for, Gina would be bound to see it as a comedown. Pining, she'd be, for the social peaks where she rightfully belonged. Doubtless, she would despise the upwardly mobile among whom she was forced to languish. In this light, Clare's explanation assumed added force. The familiar triangle took shape, forged of boredom and proximity; husband the last to know, as usual. Cool head, boyo, you're doing a Beddoes – jumping the gun.

He parked some distance away and shouldered into the storm. No need to alert the neighbours – yet. The front lawn lay trim and tidy, the beds dug back for the winter. The porch, though, had been built for style, not shelter; the wind sliced in like a scalpel. She was in no hurry to answer, either. Waiting, lifting his collar and rubbing his hands, he froze anyway.

Eventually, the door eased open a crack. Through it came the muted throb of music and a distinct whiff of feminine musk. Her lovely face was flushed, she seemed slightly breathless and he fancied he glimpsed bare toes. The rest of her remained carefully hidden. For one wild moment, he thought he might've caught them at it – suburban orgies, the well-bred housewife's choice. If so, she put a bold front on it.

'*Not* today thank you,' she sang. Then, studying him more closely, 'Wait a minute, I *know* you.'

'Aye, we've met.'

'Of course, one of Richard's nice inspectors. *Do* forgive me, I've forgotten your name.' Wasn't worth remembering, her tone implied.

'Evans, ma'am.'

'Well, Evans, he's not here.'

She was playing Mrs God, and his hackles rose. 'I know. That's why I came.'

A spoilt beauty, this one, hated to be crossed. Haughty and incredulous, she snapped, 'Whatever do you mean?'

'Thought we'd have a little chat. Unofficial, mind, just you and me.'

'I can't imagine what we'd find to *chat* about!' She made to close the door, and he eased his weight against it.

'You'd be surprised.'

'Indeed I would! It's not convenient, you're being *very* presumptuous. You'd better leave, before I call Richard.'

'Please yourself. Only, I went to quite a lot of trouble so he wouldn't know. It's about a mutual friend, see. Harry Mortimer.'

· There might have been a hint of anxiety, quickly suppressed.

'You're behaving as though I'm *guilty*, Evans; as though I have something to hide.' She made it sound preposterous. Well, probably it was.

146

Doggedly, he muttered, 'Guilty, no. As for the second bit – who knows?'

The rain came on again, heavy and insistent. She'd still made no move from the door, and icy droplets were trickling down his neck. Her head high, her eyes bright with mockery and challenge, she demanded, 'What am I supposed to have done, robbed a bank?'

Standing like an unsuccessful brush salesman, sick of her petulance and superiority, he lost his rag. Time for shock tactics, and to hell with the consequences. Coldly, he made his accusation. 'I'd say you've been fornicating; obviously.'

But, in the event, the shock was his. She made a curious, almost comic moué of regret, glanced quickly up and down the windswept street, and adopted a conspirator's whisper. 'Not *too* obviously, I hope. You'd better come in.'

In the hallway, he had an instant to weigh her up. She *was* barefoot, and sporting a black leotard which covered her like paint, leaving little to the imagination. Beddoes had it right – a lot of woman.

The faraway music quieted, and a disembodied voice urged, '*Swing* to the right and up and stretch, and *swing* to the left and down and relax.'

She flashed him a condescending smile and explained, 'Inconvenient, as I said. My daily dozen, you see. A girl has to keep in shape these days.' She strode away, leggy and limber, very fetching indeed. Casually, over her shoulder, she invited, 'Do make yourself at home.'

Smart lady, fair play, seizing the opportunity to get her act together. Still, he'd broken through. From now on, he'd let her make the pace.

As he expected, she took her time, and he used it to suss the place out. Plush, you'd have to call it. Real Persian rugs, silk and hand-stitched; on the floor, mind, for anyone to walk on. The curtains had the sheen and drape of sheer quality, the leather suite alone would cost a bomb. Made in Abergorky, he reckoned; nice to see Valleys' produce coming upmarket. Gina Howard's dowry must have been generous – a Super's salary would never run to this. Dodgy, though, living on the wife's birthright. A mixed marriage, Evans' mam would've

147

called it; and by no means the first to crack under the strain.

She returned in a waft of perfume and a jade-green housecoat; all assets properly concealed, only the hauteur showing.

'Perhaps, inspector, you'd be good enough to explain this impertinence!'

Bulky and awkward in his wet mackintosh, out of his element and conscious of the banality, he took refuge in officialdom. 'Routine enquiries, ma'am. About Mortimer, I mean.'

'Don't be absurd. Harry's as honest as the day! You'll be telling me next that *he's* robbed a bank!' Whatever his failings, Mortimer clearly knew how to win female loyalty. Like Clare before her, Gina came headlong to his defence.

'Nothing to do with money, mind; a question of his whereabouts on a certain night.'

'Indeed? And where do you *think* he was?'

'I was hoping you'd tell me, after what you said outside.'

'I'll tell you *nothing*, inspector, until I know what Harry is supposed to have done.'

The footstamping put him in mind of a circus pony – a pretty, pampered performer. A dicey moment, though. One thing to weigh possibilities in the privacy of the nick, quite another to cry rape before a hostile witness.

She must have sensed his discomfort. Suddenly, her lovely face twisted in disgust. 'You've been moonlighting, Evans. Creeping around here with your dirty raincoat and your little notebook! No wonder you don't want Richard to know!'

'Hey, steady on!'

'What must I pay for your silence, then – filthy lucre or my fair white body?'

Her contempt flayed him, pushing him even further on to the defensive. 'You've got me wrong, ma'am. Only the facts I'm after.'

'A blow by blow account, you mean! I *refuse* to indulge your prurient curiosity!'

Rain struck the window like shrapnel, startling him. She ignored it, standing svelte and erect, her indignation as heavy as musk; yet *still* not ringing true. The holier-than-thou attitude provoked him to retaliation. All right, lady, we'll play it *your* way.

'Come on, Mrs Wilson, we both know Mortimer's been here while the Super's away.'

'Of *course* he has; he's my oldest and dearest friend!' She paraded the rich room, raking him with baleful eyes and a barbed tongue. 'It's company, while Richard's playing cops and robbers with grubby little men like you!'

'And what do *you* two play: Trivial Pursuit?'

'It's none of your business!'

'Ah, but it *is*. Harry's gone all chivalrous and gallant, refusing to name his lady. And Richard's protecting him, out of misguided loyalty. Is that what you want, then, *both* your men in disgrace?'

'You're despicable, Evans!' She halted in the middle of the fancy carpet, eyeing him sullenly under long lashes; preserving face to the bitter end. 'Making something sordid out of a perfectly innocent relationship!'

Sensing weakness, he found exactly the right question. 'Innocent, is it? *So why has it stopped?*'

'Why indeed?' she whispered, suddenly pale and distraught.

He watched her poise and resistance drain away. She sank on to the chesterfield, her hair falling like a fine gold curtain across her face.

'It was going to be a grand affair,' she snuffled piteously. 'Something to move mountains. *I* wouldn't be another of Harry's little playthings, dear me no!' The tears welled and spilled out. She gazed up, fearful and beseeching. 'It's been over a month. Not a word, not even a phone call. God, I've been such a *fool*!'

The heart of it at last, the old, sad story. He let up a bit, more from satisfaction than sympathy. As the shower lifted and the sun stole in, her answers came rapid and ready, the breathless urgency of overdue confession.

She remembered the night well, she'd telephoned Mortimer to cancel a squash game. 'Richard was working late *again*,' she explained, with a hint of her former spirit. Harry had arrived 'to console me'. He'd left soon after eleven. It wasn't the first time, but it had been the last.

Somewhere deep in Evans' brain, connections were beginning to slot together. He ignored them, watching her every move as he asked his final, crucial question. 'How about the Super, then? Got wind of it at all, has he?'

She stared at him, appalled. The pale light made tight hollows under her cheekbones; she looked colder and older and somehow resurrected. Bloody codes again; clearly, he'd voiced the unmentionable, and given her back a strange notion of superiority.

'*I* haven't told him, and never will. Neither would Clare, for that matter.' She didn't even mention decent old Harry.

Heavily, Evans said, 'Need telling, would he, a senior CID man?'

She sighed, sharp and resentful, forced to face it and not liking it a bit. 'I may have been . . . *cooler* than usual; but know? Certainly not!'

Which meant one more interview – the most delicate and distasteful of them all.

For months after Eirwen his ex-wife had left, Evans had found the police flat unbearable: a constant reminder of someone he'd once loved. As memories faded, he'd shaped it to his own wants, and the pain eased. It wasn't much to look at – a couple of tatty armchairs, a bit of plain Wilton and curtains to match, a sofa he never used and a telly he seldom watched. Mostly, it was a retreat, shabby and comfortable as an old suit, within which he could abandon the enforcer's role and be Huw Evans, the man.

Contrary to popular belief, he was not entirely celibate. A Welsh art teacher, widowed untimely, occasionally shared his bed. Very casual, mind, nothing more than friendship, a common upbringing and warm mutual release. Less frequently, he'd even entertained one of Lil's younger helpmates for recreational purposes. At first such lapses had pricked his Non-conformist conscience. Later, he learned to rationalise them. You can't fight nature, bach. Bigger men have tried and lost. And if you've enjoyed it, why worry about the hereafter?

Sometimes he still mourned the passing of a more permanent relationship: mostly, though, he didn't. Take the current case, for instance. Not much of an advert for matrimony. A loyal lesbian and a noble philanderer, joined by financial necessity

150

and obliged to further the line; a spoilt beauty and an over-educated cuckold. Mix 'em up and what do you get? Bloody disaster. In the end, he thought glumly, there is only one factor common to all marriages: deceit.

He shook his head in irritation. Breaking his own rules, he was, bringing the office home. He got up and browsed among his LPs. The modern stereo was his sole indulgence; the grand choral pieces soothed his professional cares and reminded him of home. Beethoven's Ninth, he decided, and a dirty great Scotch: a combination which never failed. He settled into the armchair, relaxed and cosy, swirling the drink idly and wait-ing for the cure to take hold.

For once, the music left him unmoved. The case absorbed him, drawing him ever deeper into its subtle complexities. Deceit, he thought, is like an onion. You have to peel the skins back one by one, never mind the smell and the tears it induces. Well, he'd done that. At the heart of this onion lay a simple and sordid intrigue. Gina and Harry were lovers, he sang in a cracked baritone, creating an ugly dissonance with the open-ing of the second movement. Lordy, oh how they did love. And sensible Clare put a stop to it, the first chance she got. Harry lives to mate another day, lovely Gina mends her errant ways, and trusting Richard bumbles on in blissful ignorance.

He stretched his battered slippers closer to the gas fire and took a steady pull at his whisky. Balderdash, old boy, as Harry would say, too simple by half. Why the coyness and secrecy, why the cloak and dagger approach, and senior coppers using the tradesman's entrance? The music had stopped, he'd flip the record later, when he'd figured things out and could give the choral movement his full attention. Meanwhile, down to basics. When faced with inexplicable actions, consider *motives*.

Mortimer's were obvious enough – sexual opportunism, the chance for a frolic with the long-fancied lady, another notch on the old six-shooter. As for his code of silence, well, that went all the way back to Lancelot, its originator and most famous defaulter. Clare, too, could be readily understood. Plain Jane and naturally inclined in the opposite direction, she would nevertheless defend her man to the last drop of blue blood; thereby neatly safeguarding her own interests into the bargain. Even Gina might be excused, given a fair measure of charity. Neglected, see, and cut off from her wealthy playmates: a pushover. Afraid that her charms might be fading, struck with remorse when they proved as potent as ever. A messy situation, no doubt, but hardly novel.

Which left Richard Wilson, with his curious insistence on kid gloves and his apparent determination to pooh-pooh the idea of Harry the rapist. A college boy, mind, a computer whizzkid. Could he really be as blind as he pretended? Living with one, playing squash with the other, he *must* have had his suspicions. Here, then, lay the real mystery; this and Evans's own deep-rooted scepticism about the morality and motives of *Crimewatch* informers. The solution remained as elusive as ever. Leave it there, boyo; enough for one night, let the subconscious have a dabble.

He finished his drink and turned the record over. Now, at last, the harmonies freed him, bearing him back across time and distance to earlier, easier days. Rugby on the rec, sunshine on the mountain, and the compelling power of voices raised in song ...

He woke much later to a stiff neck, silence, and the sudden clarity of thought which sometimes follows shallow sleep. There *was* a darker mystery he hadn't even considered, and it revolved around a single, hitherto unasked question – *Who shopped Mortimer?* Because, clearly, whoever it was had lied; further deceit, more unfathomable motives.

He felt dreadful, his eyes gritty, his mouth foul; but his mind was racing. Memories fused, the scattered pieces of the puzzle formed a disturbing pattern. He recalled a speech heard at Smythe's send-off, and two casual comments made to Beddoes at separate times since. *'Falling about, we were'*; and later, *'Down to the leprechauns, is it?'*

Slowly, a possible solution emerged, Machiavellian in its implications. At the same time, it provided the rationale he'd always known must exist for his own intuitive mistrust of publicly solicited information. It should've been a moment of triumph, but he couldn't see it that way. Get your head down, bach, there'll be hell to pay in the morning.

CHAPTER FIFTEEN

SHE STOOD by his side on the floodlit terracing, her white-mittened hands pressed to her mouth, her eyes shining in anticipation. A fleecy-lined hood framed her face, and the cold had brought a becoming blush to her cheeks. She would've looked like this five years ago, lovely and pure, untouched by anything evil, a life to live and a world to inherit. Watching her covertly in pride and pity, Beddoes ached inside for what might have been.

The bell jangled, the hare trundled forwards, and the crowd gave out a collective buzz of excitement and release: 'They're off!' The traps clashed open and the dogs sprang free, tails aloft, quarters bunching, forepaws stretched and scrabbling at the compacted cinders.

'Go, Delilah, oh come *on*!' Sara was literally hopping as her fancy, a brindle bitch and a rank outsider, shadowed the leaders through the long first bend.

Beddoes, following the wise money and an evens favourite, murmured, 'She 'asn't got a prayer, lovely. Won't stay the distance.'

But Delilah had other ideas, running out of her skin and making a nonsense of the form. In the home straight, she shifted gear and left them for dead, crossing the line five lengths clear and slobbering over the stalled hare a good ten seconds before the nearest challenger arrived. The handlers fussed and blanketed her. She came prancing back, paws high, tongue steaming and lolling out of a winner's grin as wide as the Mall.

Sara stared, transfixed by astonishment and delight.

'Oh Roy,' she breathed incredulously, 'I've never won a penny in my life!'

He tore his tickets to confetti and pulled a rueful grin. 'I know just how you feel. C'mon then, let's pick up the readies.'

Queuing at the Tote window, her breath pluming upwards, she clung to his arm and admitted, 'I didn't know it could be this much fun!'

'Garn, you never said that when you were losin'.'

A mock-reproachful sideways glance, and just a hint of flirtation. Good to see her loosening up.

'Don't tease,' she chided. 'I haven't enjoyed myself like this since before ...' The shadows were creeping into her eyes again. Lamely, she finished, 'For a long time, anyway.'

'Broadens the education, doesn't it,' he said comfortably, glossing over the lapse. 'The problem with students is, too much book learnin'.'

Her smile had turned misty and regretful. 'Ex-students.'

The queue stirred and shuffled forwards, and he drew her on. 'Don't be daft, girl, you're going back. What else is there?'

'Let's not discuss it,' she pleaded. 'No arguments tonight, OK?'

She collected her winnings and turned to him, determinedly bright once more. 'I think we should celebrate. How does a good meal sound?'

'Terrific,' he said at once, anxious to preserve the mood. 'I know an Italian place up west, do you the works for a tenner.'

They were angling towards the car park, threading little knots of homeward-bound punters. The glare was fading behind, and he couldn't see her expression. She sounded very wary, though.

'I was thinking of a take-away.' He sensed rather than saw her helpless shrug. 'I'm not up to people just yet.'

He stopped, throwing out an arm which encompassed the whole stadium. 'Talk sense, Sara, what about all this lot? 'Ere, aren't *I* people, then?'

And now she did face him and the light; grave and troubled. 'No, Roy, you most certainly are not. Come back to the flat.'

In another time and place, an invitation to stir the blood; and

not to be refused, whatever the circumstances. 'On one condition – we split the bill fifty-fifty.'

'I told you before, I don't like to be beholden.'

'Yeah. Remember what *I* said?'

She was quicksilver, changing from one minute to the next.
A real smile this time, warm and reminiscent. 'As it happens, I
do. Very well, you can wash up.'

'Lady, you're on!'

They stopped off at a corner pizza bar. Back home, she
prepared salad and scolded him roundly when he offered the
plonk he'd bought on the sly. At night, the place took on an air
of cosy intimacy; didn't seem so bare, somehow.

Afterwards, shoulder to shoulder in the tiny kitchen, he
washed and she dried. Watch it, my son, you're getting
domesticated. Liking it, too.

The wine mellowed her. For the first time, she talked freely:
parental strife, the failings of Charles Thompson, and
Romance languages. On the latter, she spoke with authority
and a kind of contained passion. The Timms bird had a point:
a natural, and a crying waste if she let it all go. She sat in the one
easy chair, her legs curled beneath her, and bare toes peeping
under corded jeans. Her face was intent and vital, she had re-
entered the land of the living. Mostly, he sat and listened,
content to chart the landfalls on her voyage of recovery, and
getting back to an even keel himself.

It had to end, of course. At a quarter to one, he rose and
stretched.

'Past the witchin' hour, Cinders, I gotta go. Work in the
morning.'

He collected his coat and ambled to the door. Carefully
casual, he suggested, 'We must do it again some time.'

'Roy? Wait.' She came towards him, her green eyes soft and
luminous. 'I – I want to thank you properly.' She was very
close, face tilted up, lips moist and slightly parted. Irresistible,
but he held himself in, just.

'Take it steady, girl. We didn't ought to rush it.'

'*Please*, Roy!'

Ready as she'd ever be, mind you, offering herself with a
kind of poignant abandon. He'd been chasing for weeks, he

155

could hardly refuse her now. Cautiously, conscious of the appalling risk, he took her into his arms and kissed her. She closed her eyes and her hands moved lightly on his shoulders. Briefly, she melted, her breasts nuzzling his chest, her thighs yielding wide and warm. It was happening just as he'd always expected, the first eager contact of willing bodies.

He sensed the precise moment of rejection. At his own strong and involuntary stirring, she tore herself away, lurching backwards wide-eyed and ashen, her hand scrubbing fiercely at her lips. You blew it, sunshine; too much, too soon. Bowed and shaking, her arms crossed protectively, she hugged herself like an injured child. He reacted out of instinct, a desperate bid to salvage friendship from the wreck.

'My fault, Sara, I got carried away. You're really something, know what I mean?' The wrong lines, it seemed.

Coldly, her voice laden with defeat and self-disgust, she muttered, 'It's nothing to do with you. It's me.'

'Early days,' he consoled her gently, moving forward again, and she hissed, 'Don't touch me!'

She stood at bay in a room grown once more small and demeaning. He hesitated, letting his hands fall to his sides. 'On second thoughts, I'll stay. To talk it over, like.'

She shook her head, weary but decided, and lamplight made a gleaming mockery of Tony Orlando's now worthless masterpiece. More than ever she reminded him of Rosie; a lonely sorrow she didn't deserve and couldn't cure.

'There's nothing for you here, Roy. There never will be.'

'Never's a long time, girl. It's not for you to say.'

She drew herself up, fragile and bereft, dredging words from some frozen inner well of dutiful politeness. That's what was left, in the end: politeness.

'Thank you, Roy. Thank you for everything you tried to do.'

The utter finality chilled his soul. All the way home, he berated himself for a bungling, ham-fisted, *male* fool.

'Lawd, is that Phoebe? Coo-ee, it's me, Ivy; over *'ere*, dearie!'

Late dawn in the park, the mist lurking like a footpad, and Ivy Dawkins walking the dog. She waited, huffing through

Steptoe mitts on to frozen fingers, while her friend trudged bulky and indistinct down the muddy path.

'Blimey, Ive,' she began, in a great looming cloud of condensation, 'whatchoo doin' out? Oughta be 'ome in your bed, with your arfritis an' all.'

Ivy nodded vigorously, and they lumbered on together. ''Obson's choice, Phoebe. Rover's gotta 'ave 'is walkies, see. My Bert – Gawd rest 'is soul – done it every morning for nine years. It's *crool*, though, at my age, in this muck.'

Phoebe wagged her muffled head doubtfully as they breasted the next pocket of writhing damp. 'Sounds barmy to me. I mean, I *'ave* to get up, cleanin' the office.' She glanced over her shoulder, shivering. 'I *'ate* this bleedin' place, gives me the willies; but it saves one 'eck of a walk an' the ole pins ain't what they useter be.'

Ivy loitered, casting about for Rover. Vague snuffling sounds came faintly from the gloom off to their left. 'Strikes me *you're* the potty one, ducks, flogging yourself to death for peanuts.'

Phoebe shrugged, fatigued but philosophical. 'Pension don't go far these days, dearie, an' my Arfer's an 'ard man.'

Ivy checked and nudged her sharply in the ribs. ''Oos a lucky girl then – 'ard man's good to find!'

'Do leave off, Ive, you're a proper caution!'

They laboured on, squelching and giggling like the schoolmates they'd once been, until Ivy halted, remembering.

'Ro-o-over! Drat it, where *is* the flamin' animal? Bane of me life, 'e is.'

Phoebe hovered a pace or two ahead, dwarfed by the blurred outline of a massive, leafless beech. 'Big dog, is 'e?'

'Huge, ducks, believe you me. My Bert didn't care for poodles and such. Yapdogs, 'e called 'em. Ro-o-over!' She listened, furious, to the rooting noises, now much further behind. 'Bleedin' useless pooch,' she grumbled, more than half to herself. 'Why can't 'e do 'is business closer to 'ome?'

'Watcha say, dearie?' asked Phoebe, sidling near and making her jump.

''Ere, do us a favour, creepin' up like that. Scared me 'alf to death, you did!'

Phoebe's turn for sly nudges. 'Garn, you were hopin' I was one of them there rapists, fumblin' about in the fog.'

They giggled some more, and Ivy continued, 'Eats like an 'orse, Rover does. Chops, liver, scrag end, anythin' 'e can get 'is gnashers round. Only meat, mind you, none of your ole tinned stuff.'

Phoebe was restless, shuffling her feet. An icy droplet quivered on the blueing tip of her nose. ''Ow can you stand it, Ive? Me, I'd 'ave 'im put down. Had a good innings, like.'

'Oh, I *couldn't*!' Ivy protested, genuinely shocked. 'Livin' reminder, 'e is. My Bert'd turn in 'is grave. Anyhow, 'e's a nice ole thing, good as gold, usually. Can't think what's got into 'im today. '*Ere*, Rover, come on boy!' She glanced sideways, noticing for the first time Phoebe's haggard cheeks and the rheum in the faded blue eyes. Oughta be home by the fire. Gettin' on, poor ole duck, and perished with it. Well, aren't we all? 'Run along with yer, girl, I'll soon catch up.' And as Phoebe nodded gratefully, she turned and hobbled back into the swirling murk, still hollering for the blasted dog.

Briefly, as the mist closed around her and the trees loomed strange and gaunt and silent, Phoebe's phantom rapist came back to hurry her stride. She caught herself listening for stealthy footfalls, craning to see beyond the shifting blankness ahead. She grinned suddenly, secure in old age and plainness. Have to be in a bad way, wouldn't he, to settle for a leathery piece like me!

Fear and the fog lifted. Rover came loping towards her, his tail going fit to bust. He was carrying something in his mouth, and he looked as pleased as punch.

'Where you bin, yer daft ole beggar? Watcha got there, then? Show Mummsie, there's a good boy. Come on, drop it.' The dog frisked about, teasing her; then obeyed. The thing lay in the mud, pale and curled and wet with slobber, for all the world like a lifeless upturned crab. She bent over it, puzzled; funny kind of meat. Slowly, with a growing sense of horror, she made out the needles of bone, the folded fingers, the scarlet blobs of nail polish. The bile rose to her throat. Somehow, she fumbled the lead into Rover's collar and dragged him away. Gawd almighty, Phoebe, she wailed, why did you leave me alone? Behind her, the severed hand lay gleaming, cold and white and bloodless ...

When Evans arrived, shortly before nine, the entire nick was agog with the news. Warner, who should've left long ago, had usurped the desk and was holding forth to a gaggle of grinning beatmen.

'It's 'alf-eight, see, and young 'Opkins is doing point duty down the park. Bleedin' bedlam, it is, what with the fog and every man and 'is brother tootin' their 'orns. All of a sudden, 'ere comes this ole dear hauling a dirty great pooch. Straight into the traffic and not so much as a by-your-leave. She's out of 'er tiny mind; course she is, 'avin' made 'er gruesome discovery, like. Gibberin', right? Officer do your duty, know what I mean?'

An artist, Warner. Watching from the doorway, Evans could've heard a fly's fart.

'Good lad, 'Opkins,' continued Warner approvingly. 'Keeps his head in a crisis. Holdin' the buses back, stiff upper lip, and givin' 'er 'is best PR smile over 'is shoulder. "Don't take on, Ma," says he, "I'll see you right. That's our job, like, givin' the public a *hand*."'

Good thing Wilson wasn't around, mused Evans, joining the general mirth. Callous, he'd call it, having no experience of laughter as a totem against the horrors of the job.

He shouldered in and the men dispersed, sobering quickly in his presence. As they left, Warner put him in the picture. 'Super's out there now. Watchin' brief, 'e reckoned. Dead chuffed, he was.'

Aye, he would be, Evans thought. Plenty of mileage in dismemberment. Pretty soon the media vultures would gather, telly cameras in the van. An opportunist, Wilson; two could play at that game, mind.

'Beddoes in?' he asked.

'Not yet.'

'He'll take charge, then, till I get back. Having a stroll, I am; in the park.'

The sky had lightened, the fog was lifting rapidly, and you

could see the spot from a long way off. An enclosure of hessian screens, a uniform standing sentry at each corner, a waiting ambulance, and the inevitable gathering of curious bystanders. Ghouls, they were, oozing out of the woodwork at the first whiff of tragedy. No sign of the press, yet, but Wilson was obviously ready. Handsome and suave in a dark-collared sheepskin, he stood somewhat apart with an air of chilly expectation.

'Morning, Evans,' he grunted. 'Come to join the circus?'

'Not today, thanks,' retorted Evans, mindful of Gina's greeting. 'Fancy a word with the ringmaster, I do.'

Cocking his head, letting the thump of pickaxe and the scrape of shovels make his point, Wilson said, 'Hardly the time and place.'

'Off the record, you said, for your ears only.' Evans spread his hands, indicating the emptiness around. 'Where better?' He lowered his voice. 'Mortimer's clean. I know where he was that night.' A swift sideways glance of appraisal and what might have been relief.

'Excellent; just as I always predicted.' He took a step towards the screens. 'Digging's going well; I wonder what they'll find?'

Evans stood his ground, refusing to be diverted. 'A bit public, this, on account of who he was with. Fancy a stroll, just the two of us?'

Wilson stroked his moustache warily. 'Is my journey really necessary?'

'Essential,' said Evans.

He trudged away from the hurly-burly, aware of Wilson's tension at his side. The air smelled faintly rural, and a solitary blackbird spoke. Feeling his way, Evans was, hadn't played Hunt the Super before; making up rules as he went along.

'Harry the Hooded Hitman: a non-starter, really, *you* knew all along. Someone you trusted, I mean. Question is, who fingered him and why?'

'That's two questions.'

A typically pedantic protest; Evans ploughed on. 'A liar, anyhow. An Irishman, Beddoes reckons, who claimed to have overheard Harry say she wasn't wearing a bra. Nice touch –

something only Chummy would know. And anyone who read the case file.'

Beside him, Wilson tackled the slope effortlessly. A squash player, see: fit. Whereas Evans found the going hard. 'Another thing,' he puffed. 'Supergrass knew Mortimer well. The clubs he used, the womanising, his daft old-fashioned code. A friend, *I'd* say.' He paused, allowing the puzzlement into his voice. 'What kind of friend, I wonder, to finger him on the one night when he doesn't care to account for his movements?'

Still no response, and he threw his own answer down like a challenge. 'A friend who hates his guts!'

Birches swayed on the hilltop, stark and metallic against the clearing sky. Beneath them, Evans recovered his breath and resumed the oblique attack.

'Clare Mortimer put me straight, gave me a hint of *motive*. The rest came from much closer to home.'

Wilson glanced up sharply. 'I think I've heard about enough!'

'Have you, sir? Put it in writing, shall I? Another little parable?'

'Hope it's an improvement on the last!'

'Aye, well *you* be the judge.'

Evans patrolled a patch of greenery bounded by dead bracken. Wilson stood motionless, his dark hair ruffled, his expression unreadable.

'Once there was a senior copper, having a spot of domestic bother; call it a certain coolness.' Seeing Wilson's sudden pallor, Evans added quickly, 'Fair-minded bloke, hears both sides of the story. Suspicious, then, but fighting it, because it could be down to someone he trusts. Someone like Harry.'

'For God's sake!'

'A *copper*, mind,' said Evans relentlessly. 'He makes enquiries, draws the obvious conclusion, and cons one of his inspectors into delivering the warning – *I can make things very sticky, Harry, so stay away from her!* How am I doing?'

Wilson's handsome features writhed in a curious blend of pain and patronage. 'Mere conjecture, devoid of both intellectual rigour and evidential support.'

161

'Close to home, remember? Mortimer's alibi came first-hand.'

'You questioned my *wife*?'

'I followed it through, just as you said. And if you're wanting evidence, try the Reverend Paisley.'

'*Who*?'

'You did him once, at Smythe's party.'

'So I did. How very careless.'

For some reason, this revelation amused him. He stood easier under fleeting, watery sunshine, an unrepentant culprit in a fancy topcoat; and Evans' smouldering outrage finally took flame. 'You phoned Beddoes and did the Irish Crime-watcher act. Gave me a song and dance about "making up lost ground" and sent *me* to do the job; to tell Harry and Gina they'd been rumbled. *Careless?* It's bloody near criminal!'

'Spare me the melodrama, inspector; as if I'm some Holly-wood gangster! Warning him off, indeed!'

Wilson edged downhill, the dead foliage crackling under his feet. 'It was a simple test,' he admitted, and you could *feel* the weight of his reluctance. 'Of *course* I knew Harry's code – an essential part of the plan. If his loyalty had shifted, if he'd owned up and asked Clare for a divorce ... But he didn't. His friendship is no loss, and now we *all* know where we stand.' He rounded on Evans, his voice echoing harshly among the trees. 'Gina had a narrow escape from an unprincipled oppor-tunist! I will not even hear it suggested that *she* has betrayed!'

As the sun retreated behind grey clouds and a rising breeze scoured his cheeks, Evans felt a pang of sympathy; having been this way about a woman himself, once or twice. Wilful blindness, it was, and Gina could do no wrong. Then anger and a policeman's priorities erupted. 'I don't give a damn for *opportunists*! There's a real villain at large, and we've been chasing shadows. That's the trouble with *Crimewatch*, see; you get the odd liar on the line.'

Wilson raised his collar and strode out, flushed and subdued. 'Deception,' he muttered sheepishly. 'It *was* the hardest part.'

'Oh, aye? How about Harry, then, an innocent bystander?'

They were heading towards the screens, where a blue light revolved slowly on the roof of the waiting ambulance. The sight seemed to revive Wilson; a bigger case, and the media already assembled.

'Harry broke a trust,' he insisted, 'and got no less than he deserved: a nasty fright. As it happens, no great harm was done.'

'Oh sure; for the moment. But Chummy's still loose!'

The brown-clad shoulders rose and fell dismissively. 'I'm sure you can broaden the Holroyd enquiry. Meanwhile, we appear to have a murder on our hands.' A pale echo of Warner's joke. Evans, still appalled, didn't bother to respond.

'Speaking of the Holroyd case,' Wilson continued, quite the senior officer again, 'I hear Sergeant Beddoes isn't pulling his weight. Have a word, would you? Ginger him up a bit.'

'*As it happens*,' growled Evans, '*he's* got woman trouble, too.'

CHAPTER SIXTEEN

TWILIGHT AT noon and the birds struck dumb. She *knew* the horror which lurked beyond the shadowed doorway; blind fear invoked the courage to glance behind.

The night beast came, hairy and hunched and low to the ground. Mad green orbs, glistening fangs, and a breath of ancient corruption. Nearing her, it reared, its great sex throbbing. The outline shimmered and shifted and became Roy Beddoes, lustful and sneering. 'Come on, lovely, let's fuck.' She whirled from his fiery, taloned embrace, plunging heedless into freezing gloom and slamming the door in his face.

A cavern, dank and fetid, and the familiar ice block curtained in mist. Frantic, she clawed and scrabbled at the clammy smoothness while her own harsh breathing echoed and mocked. She had to see, she had to know. At her touch, the surface seemed to flex and quiver. Faint and faraway, cracked and vengeful, her mother spoke.

'You have sinned, Sara. There will be no happiness in your lifetime.'

Deep in the chilled centre, a motionless image, wizened and pinched and draped in widow's weeds. Vision cleared slowly, and the image peered out. Once more, Sara Holroyd gazed in horror upon her own face, bleak and cruel and not yet even middle-aged ...

She woke in tearful silence. Nothing to scream at now, the nightmare had become a mere extension of reality. Wide-eyed yet sightless, she curled herself inwards, running her hands over her own useless, unresponsive body. *'There's nothing for you here,'* she had told him. Or for anyone else, ever, she thought, smiling mirthlessly in the bitter dark. Poor, sad little lady, you settled for sex without love; which saint will offer you love without sex? And anyway, who wants a saint?

Wait, a weak voice of reason cried, as she writhed in the sweat-soaked sheets, maybe Roy was right: the wrong place, the wrong man, and much too soon after ... After. Charles might thaw her, he of the lovely hands. Don't be naive, you'll never see him again. Rodney, then. Briefly, he'd struck a spark which promised more than just healthy animal coupling. She squirmed in despair, clinging hopelessly to the pillow. That was long ago, a different girl in another life.

From the lamplit street outside and below, familiar sounds intruded. The muted hum of an electric cart, the clink of crated milkbottles. Just like the TV ad – everybody needs bottle. And in the end, *that* was what the faceless one had stolen. Bottle. Because she'd *wanted* Roy Beddoes, last night. In his arms, fleetingly, the physical yearning had been almost a sickness. Be strong and gentle, Roy, make me whole again. Then, unbidden, an alien and irresistible chasteness had thrust him away, leaving her frigid and stranded and evermore untouchable.

The milkman passed on, whistling. A deadly fatigue overcame her. She ached for sleep, the welcome velvety oblivion of those first few days when the drug had saved her sanity.

The capsules. She had them still, somewhere in the kitchen; but were there enough? No effort, no mess, just a comfortable slide into nothingness, never to dream or wake again. Then, perhaps, she might be remembered fondly, as Roy had seen her: bright and beautiful, full of promise. Better by far than the terrible emptiness of her mother's existence.

She moved like a ghost, cat-eyed and sure-footed, heedless of the pre-dawn chill. A glimmer of light slid through a chink in the curtains, and she counted the glistening pellets into her hand. Fourteen. She closed her eyes, picturing the bold red lettering on the label: 'It is dangerous to exceed the stated dose.' What a curious word. It is dangerous to visit pubs at night, to walk home alone. It is dangerous to *live*.

She ran the tap, working out the arithmetic. Two pills a swallow, seven swallows to a glass. More than sufficient, she reckoned. Briefly she shuffled stock phrases in her mind, composing a farewell note. I tried my best, it's too much to bear, I'm sorry. But she *wasn't* sorry; and anyway, the act itself would say all.

Seven short sips. The water was cool, soothing her throat, and the capsules slithered down soft and painless. She tidied the bed and found a fresh nightgown; her best. Then, composed and peaceful, she waited for it to begin. Consciousness dwindled, and with it, an ironic afterthought. You never did finish the Saint-Exupéry; couldn't even get *that* right ...

Beneath the screens, the diggers had opened a gaping trench. Shirt-sleeved and sweating despite the cold, they laboured on, the earth piling round them raw and stony. 'Nothing 'ere,' growled one, 'and we're 'alfway to Melbourne already.' Evans shot him a warning glare, but Wilson merely nodded and turned on his heel. Outside, he frowned with distaste at the restless crowd and elbowed clean through the clamour of pressmen and the intermittent glare of the flashbulbs.

'Anything for us, Mr Wilson?'

'Come on, sir, give us a break!'

'No comment,' he snapped, terse and tight-lipped, and ignored their entreaties all the way to the car. Unlike him, rejecting the limelight; other things on his mind, probably. He maintained his silence throughout the drive to the nick, sitting aloof and abstracted, his upturned collar masking most of his face.

The day sergeant at the desk, a new man, made an urgent bid for attention. 'Inspector Evans? Message from PC Parrot, sir.'

Evans bent an ear. Wilson, still absent in all but body, hovered like a guest who'd forgotten his room number.

The sergeant sighed, bearing the world on his shoulders. 'One of them days, sir, what with unattached 'ands and now this business.'

'Sure. So what's the message?'

The sergeant produced a scrap of paper and read, slow and expressionless. 'Sara Holroyd. Some rugger type found 'er, it says 'ere. Gone to see how she was doing.' He glanced up, earnest and indignant. 'She'd been raped, I heard.'

166

'Aye. I know.'

The sergeant wagged his head. 'What are the quacks doin', I wonder, flashin' Valium round like Beechams? She OD'd, see. Not expected to survive.'

Evans swallowed hard, passing a weary hand over his eyes. Have to walk soft around young Roy for a while.

'Right,' he muttered, swinging heavily away, conscious anew of the drab paintwork and the penetrating cold.

''Ang about, sir. Only a medical bulletin, that was. Pol's news came later, over the blower. Went down the hospital, she did.' He produced a second flimsy, clearing his throat importantly. 'Immediate for Beddoes. Holroyd pumped out and rallying strongly. Statement expected soon.' The first good news of the day, and Evans let out a breathy sigh of relief.

'Told Roy, have you?'

'How could I?' the sergeant asked querulously. 'Already gone, 'adn't 'e? That's why I'm telling *you*.'

'Gone? Gone where?'

The sergeant shrugged helplessly. 'Like a wild man 'e was, waving the bulletin in me face, wantin' to know when it came in. An hour ago, says I. Off he trots, rabbiting on about an address in the transcripts. Next thing, 'e goes tearing past at a dead run. Chaos, like I said.'

'Darro, boyo,' hissed Evans, conscious of Wilson's slow retreat down the corridor, '*where did he go?*'

'Ah,' said the sergeant, '*he* left a message, too. Tell the Inspector, he 'ollers, I'm paying me respects to Harry.'

Cat among the pigeons, thought Evans grimly. Aloud, he snapped, 'You took your bloody time, mun. When was this?'

Ponderously, the sergeant hauled back his cuff and studied his watch. 'Five minutes, more or less.'

Evans whirled.

'Sir?' he called, 'Superintendent Wilson?' Wilson meandered on, taking no notice. Evans caught him up at the first corner. 'Nasty development, sir. You'll have to come with me. I'll explain in the car.

Wilson blinked at him, vague and detached as a sleepwalker. 'Surely you can handle it alone?'

'We're wasting time, mind. Your mate's in serious trouble.'
And mine, too.

'My *mate*, inspector?'

'Mortimer.'

Wilson stared, bitter and incredulous. 'You *still* think he's my *mate*?'

'*Jesi mawr*!' Evans beseeched him, 'I'll go on my knees if you want!'

The tone, rather than the words, seemed to get through.

'Oh well. If it's that important.'

The driver looked familiar; the lad who'd collected him on the night of the rape. Evans rattled off Mortimer's address and added, 'Lights, sirens, the lot. Let's see you shift this thing.'

'Right, sir,' he chirped, grinning, 'and you'd better belt up.'

Saucy young sod. To the roar of the engine and the scent of scorched rubber, bracing himself for every corner, Evans briefed the Super.

'Roy took the call, remember?' he finished tautly. '*Your* call, I mean. Unlike you and me, though, he doesn't know the girl's recovering and Mortimer's in the clear.'

Wilson remained abstracted and unconcerned, so he said it plain. 'Seen a lot of her, he has. Got himself involved. They'll be having a showdown, I'm thinking; and Roy's a strong boy.'

Wilson swore distractedly as centrifugal force flung him sideways. Seizing the front seat for purchase, he demanded, 'Why drag me into some petty personal squabble?'

Already this morning, Evans had endured a switchback of emotions, an abdication of authority, and a classic administrative balls-up. This was simply too much to bear, and his normally phlegmatic temperament erupted. 'Oh, aye? Bloody marvellous, that is, coming from you!'

'Hold tight,' cried the driver jauntily, and heaved the wheel over and back. The tyres screeched, and they were hurled forward against the belts. The rear end snaked violently, and the cliff-like side of a double-decker bus slid by, impossibly close. 'Red light,' the boy confided, cool as you please, 'no problem.'

The force of Evans' outburst and the nearness of disaster seemed to revive the Superintendent. His eyes cleared and he dredged up a quirky smile.

'Touché, inspector, I take your point.' Then, to the hunched figure in front, he snapped, 'For goodness sake step on it, man!'

Confident of Wilson's full attention at last, Evans explained, 'Be walking soft, Roy will; sneaking up on it, like. With luck we could still head him off.' He craned forward, tapping the boy's shoulder. 'Kill the siren, take us in nice and quiet.'

It proved an irrelevant precaution; Mortimer's front door already hung ajar. Fearful of what he'd find, Evans was out and sprinting before the car skidded to a rest. He took the steps three at a time, bursting into the hallway and bellowing at the top of his voice 'Go steady, Roy; you've got the wrong man!'

In the wintry greyness of late morning, the once-elegant drawing-room was a bombsite: rumpled carpets, upturned chairs, and the lamp standard leaning drunkenly. Grunts of effort and a gasp of agony. Mortimer's bulk hung spread-eagled across the back of the sofa, one leg folded under, the other extended and twitching spasmodically. Beddoes stood braced behind him, his left hand buried in the thick hair, his elbow locked to take the strain. He was picking his spot, cold and implacable, his eyes bright with a craftsman's concentration. As Evans watched, mesmerised, his right arm arced upwards, bladed and straight-fingered, primed and poised for the fatal septum strike to the base of Mortimer's nose.

'For Christ's sake, Roy,' Evans pleaded, 'he never laid eyes on her!'

Beddoes didn't even blink.

'Leave it out, uncle: *I saw him.* Stay put!' Andle you first, if I 'ave to.'

'You'll have to then,' promised Evans, and started forwards again.

'Sergeant Beddoes! Release that man at once! What in God's name d'you think you're doing?'

Wilson, crisp and sharp as a whiplash, the voice of absolute authority. It stopped Beddoes cold, drawing him to upright attention and instant obedience. I'll be damned, thought Evans, in a moment of light-headed wonder, so *that's* what superintendents are for.

Unrestrained, Mortimer had jack-knifed on to the cushioned seating, both hands clutching his groin. The sweat flowed in buckets and he moaned, soft and eerie. Wilson gazed down at him with about as much pity as an undertaker. Darro, what a bloody shambles.

Moving to Wilson's side, conscious of the crunch of glass underfoot, Evans murmured, 'Take Beddoes next door, sir. Leave Mortimer to me.' The Super, it seemed, had done his bit for the day, and apathy was setting in once more. Urgently, Evans insisted, 'Got an idea, see; unless you want to do it yourself.'

Wilson aimed a glance of loathing at the figure on the sofa, shaking his head hurriedly. 'No, no, you carry on.' And to Beddoes, still rigid and motionless, 'Come along, sergeant, pull yourself together.'

With a furious glare for Mortimer and a muttered 'fuckin' animal', Beddoes allowed himself to be led away.

Evans set about the chores, straightening rugs, putting the furniture to rights, fastidiously gathering the scattered shards of light bulb. The room held a curious aura, something heavy and tense. Suddenly, he placed it: a lingering whiff of combat, like an empty boxing booth or the police gym after judo. Tension and old jockstraps. Be nice to open a window, for a cleansing blast of winter. Popular move, that, bet 'is nibs gives a ransom for central heating.

By this time, Mortimer had swivelled round and placed his feet gingerly on the carpet. In his doubles, deathly pale, he managed to stand.

Evans advanced solicitously. 'Getting over it, are we?'

'Hands off!' Mortimer snarled. 'Keep your damn distance. Bloody bobbies! I want to be sick, d'you mind?'

He lurched off through the debris. Presently, retching sounds carried from the nearby bathroom, followed by the gush of a cistern and the hiss of running hot and cold. Evans continued reparations, glad of the respite. There had to be some leverage somewhere in the situation, a chance to exploit

Wilson's revelations and bail Beddoes out. Don't be hasty, bach, bide your time.

Mortimer re-emerged, canted forwards from the waist and grunting at each step. He hobbled to the bar, poured himself a triple brandy and downed it at a swallow. Some of his colour returned and, with it, a kind of angry bravado.

'Make yourself scarce, inspector. Be ready for the rematch soon.' Clutching a restored chair for support, his dark eyes hard and belligerent, he explained, 'Did my share in the Guards, d'you see; unarmed combat.'

'I'll risk it,' Evans informed him. Then, wooden and toneless, 'Be laying an official complaint, will you?'

Sweating again, Mortimer cast an ironic glance over his violated territory. Somewhat less than immaculate, mind, despite the housework. 'In like Attila, not so much as name and number, and a hoof in the crutch for starters. Complaint, old boy? I'll have him drummed out!'

'Oh, sure,' Evans agreed, adopting the traditional stance. Legs straddled, hands behind the back, taking root for the duration. 'Impulsive, he was, no question. Been looking out for the girl, the one who was raped. She took an overdose last night. Rough time for him, see; extenuating circumstances.'

Mortimer snorted, wincing. 'Balderdash. The man's certifiable!'

Tough, mind. You could see the effort it cost him to stay upright. Mildly, adding insult to injury and gauging the effect, Evans continued, 'Thing is, he figured *you* for the culprit, not knowing any better. Pity you didn't level with me earlier, sir. Would've saved us all a lot of grief.'

From the next room, the muffled rumble of voices; the other side of the story, probably. Mortimer ignored it, sullen and subdued, wondering how much they knew. Let him stew a while.

'It's a fair defence, I'd say. Standing orders, take no chances with an armed and dangerous suspect.'

'Suspect?' Mortimer echoed incredulously. 'Common assault on an innocent civilian. Said so yourself, man!'

'Aye, so I did. No one's calling you a criminal, see; but *innocent* – now there's a fine word. Been talking to Gina, I have. Well, listening, anyhow.' A mortal blow. Grey, he was, and sick as a pig. 'All right, are you? Fancy another noggin? Please yourself then.' Nasty, to rub it in. Beddoes had a lot to answer for. 'Some would say you had it coming, see, for putting horns on a mate. How *is* the squash, these days?'

Flushed and crippled, seemingly close to mental and physical rout, Mortimer mounted an improbably spirited counterattack.

'When muscle fails, try blackmail, eh?' He tilted his empty glass in mock salute. 'The men in blue: *Sieg heil!*' Flawed, maybe, and oversexed, but a hero just the same. One of those who'd never crack. You had to admire him, even as you stood toe to toe.

'Be your age, sir. Who needs blackmail? Damaged while resisting arrest; minimum necessary force, your honour. It's all we need to say, the three of us.'

'Don't set much store by numbers, old boy. Take on the lot of you any time, in or out of court.'

He would, too, damaged or not. Switch to plan B, boyo. 'You're reading me wrong, Mr Mortimer. Perjury's not my style. Nor the others, either.' He jerked his thumb in the direction of the next room. 'I've given you Beddoes' line, you only have to refute it. In public, though, and Wilson there to defend the troops.'

Mortimer was watching him narrowly, catching the drift at last.

'Up to it, are you? Naming the lady, I mean?'

A flicker deep in the pain-dulled eyes. Not surrender, exactly, more the recognition of a stand he could no longer defend.

Sensing the advantage, Evans risked his last trump. 'You never have, fair play. You're a man of honour, Mr Mortimer. Let it go, will you, for revenge on a misguided copper?'

Honour was the word that mattered, you could see him clutch it like a lifeline in the storm. He'd said it before, actually: '*Nothing wrong with nobility.*'

'So what'll I tell the Super, sir?'

As if on cue, the front door opened and closed. Second meeting adjourned. If Mortimer heard, he gave no sign.

172

Visibly struggling against another wave of nausea, he mumbled, 'Just bugger off, d'you mind?'

'With or without the complaint?'

Mortimer met his eye, defiant to the last. 'What complaint?'

Evans was on his way at once, giddy with release and anxious to hide it; but Mortimer had a query of his own. 'Richard's *witting*, is he?'

He was owed a truth, and Evans supplied one. 'Not to be certain. If I was you, though, I'd look for a new squash partner.'

The car idled, the exhaust puttering and steaming quietly. Beddoes and Wilson perched like bookends on either side of the rear seat, and the driver sat straight and silent, gazing full ahead. Evans climbed in and told him, 'Home, James, but gently.' Nobody smiled. An atmosphere to chill the blood, the funereal hush of the tomb.

As Evans settled, Wilson leaned across. Pitching his voice too low for the driver, he breathed, 'I want no conversation. As of now, Beddoes is suspended; there'll be an enquiry, of course.'

'Hold on,' protested Evans. 'There's things you ought to know.'

'Not in front of the children! In the office, later, *if* you please!'

The unlikely assurance again, out of the blue; a direct order you simply couldn't challenge. Evans shrugged and watched the traffic while the boy brought them in as though piloting a hearse.

A stocky silhouette against the pale grey of the window, Evans pored over the initial path-lab report. Wilson had skimmed through it, passing it on at once in order to buy himself much needed breathing space. Slumped at his desk, he watched the big Welshman absorb it, effortlessly recalling the words to the front of his own mind. 'A neat amputation, performed by someone having surgical experience and a working knowledge of anatomy. Analysis suggests the hand belonged to a white female aged about twenty-five.

173

Fingerprints taken and checked against central records. Positive identification. Subject, Laura Brown, unmarried, of no fixed abode. Four previous convictions. Occupation, prostitute.' Academic training and an eidetic memory conferred some advantages; Evans was still reading.

Wilson sighed, staving off emotional numbness and an overwhelming sense of lassitude. Earlier, the news would have galvanised him; an important case, a chance to shine in his new role, the possibility of nationwide coverage. Since then, events had moved with bewildering speed beyond his ability to influence. Evans' astonishing insight, the exposure of his own guilty secret, and Beddoes' appalling lapse into temporary insanity. At present, the sergeant awaited judgement, consigned to the basement and effective house arrest. A decision he must soon defend, and from a position of self-imposed professional vulnerability. Wearily, as Evans advanced and tossed the document into 'pending', he girded for battle yet again.

'Interesting, sir. A lucky break, the fingerprints. First things first, though: Beddoes.' He stood there solid and aggressive, his acute blue eyes denying any prospect of evasion.

'Very well, inspector, what is it I should know?'

'Mortimer, sir; waived the complaint. Bygones, see.' He shrugged loose and easy. 'The honourable course, he said. Or maybe it was me.'

'No threats, I trust?'

'Now how could I *threaten*?' Evans wondered, all innocence, 'and him holding every card? Let's say I explained the – delicacy – of the situation.' Another of his unlikely strengths. Despite the seemingly casual Welsh phraseology, he chose his words with precision: maximum impact, minimum fuss. Verbal parsimony, as a respected former tutor would have it.

Nodding grimly, running a thumb down the curve of his moustache, Wilson said, 'Very pretty. You struck a bargain, I presume.'

'*Yes*,' said Evans simply. 'Someone had to, see.'

Wilson saw all right. Dirt under the carpet, close ranks, police solidarity in the face of danger and the public interest. His distaste must have shown.

Quite gently, Evans asked, 'Considered the alternative,

174

have you?' He was browsing slowly at the bookshelves – he had the common man's reverence for the printed word. Hardly a weakness, in him. 'The enquiry, I mean,' he was saying, 'all our dirty washing on the public clothesline.'

With a significant effort, Wilson summoned a remnant of anger. 'Beddoes's conduct was a disgrace! He must be disciplined – *pour encourager les autres.*'

Evans grinned wolfishly, a sardonic gleam in his eye. Don't try to baffle me with language, his attitude said quite clearly. 'Oh sure. He will be.'

He turned, raising a large hand, telling off points on his fingers. Wintry light from behind glinted on his thinning ginger hair. 'One. Beddoes was kept in the dark; private and off the record, you said. Looks bad, that, in a nick where communication's the name of the game. Two, we'd need to say how Mortimer came under suspicion; how he was cleared, also. Three, innocent bystanders, those like your wife who only read the papers. *Technically* innocent, mind.'

Insufferable, coming from anyone else; but he kept it cool and rational, and somehow made it stick. Maybe it's because he's older, Wilson mused abstractedly; as if reading the thought, Evans took the visitor's chair and what remained of the initiative. 'I've *been* there, sir; humiliated by a woman, and in public, too. Only one thing to do with mistakes; learn the lessons. Mortimer has, Beddoes will, and so will *she*, I promise.'

Finally, he'd ventured on to personal ground, well beyond the pale. Provoked to the limit of endurance, Wilson snapped, 'Quite the philosopher, Evans! How does it feel, being a saint?'

Very deliberately, Evans got up and strolled to the window. Consciously or otherwise, he could not more clearly have expressed the shifting balance of command. Someone should write a thesis, thought Wilson, on the symbolism of dominance: that used to be *my* territory.

Propped against the wall, his profile sharply defined, Evans gazed out over the shivering city. From the corridor, faint but unmistakable, someone whistled a carol. Evans cocked his head.

'Season of good cheer; lovely. A saint? Well no, not exactly. For once, though, it's only me who's not *involved*.' He paused, seemingly transfixed by whatever he saw below. Casually, as though asking the time, he said, 'Deal with Beddoes, shall I? Read the Riot Act, slap his wrists, let him off with a caution?'

It's a technique, Wilson realised suddenly, the way he gets things done. Steady, unrelentless pressure, a single purpose and a single goal; something they don't teach, in college.

'You seem to be running things,' he retorted. 'Do as you please.' He intended sarcasm. Even in his own ears, it sounded like capitulation.

'Just for now, then,' Evans conceded, very seriously. 'Know my limitations, I do.'

CHAPTER SEVENTEEN

CONDEMNED, BEREAVED, and solitary, Beddoes had stalked the basement with the patience of an unavenged ghost. Outside, Wilson's uniformed minder would be going spare, still waiting for the white flag. Don't hold your breath, sunshine, Alf Beddoes' boy won't squeal. The name and the train of thought awoke remembrance. Sick of today's ruin and the void which was tomorrow, his mind sought relief in the past; and found instead an image of the damned ...

Sprawled and mangy, filling the fouled enclosure, the tiger raised a listless snarl. As bolder urchins jeered and taunted, Roy flinched and turned away.

"'Ere, wotcha blubbin' for? 'E's all locked up, 'e can't hurt you.'

Sunshine glinting on stout metal bars, Alf's calloused fist clamped firmly round his own, and the reek of cat enough to make anyone weep. 'Leave off, Dad, 'oo's blubbin'? 'E don't 'alf pong, though.' But he *was* crying, somewhere inside, sensing the tragedy even at this tender age. Wildness tamed and broken, the stripy lustre tarnished, a terrible beauty caged and mocked and trailing in the dust. Gazing deep into the great tawny eyes, he saw neither pride nor the hunter's fierceness; only the dull and aimless anger of lifelong captivity ...

It happened pretty fast, inside. At first, denied freedom and maddened by grief, you lashed out at anything in sight. Soon, deprived of knowledge and human contact, you began to feel the guilt. Finally, your dignity destroyed, you slumped in the nearest corner breathing impotent rage at your tormentors.

177

No shortage of *them*, either. Wilson, shell-shocked and aghast, laying down the law like he'd invented it himself. Rich, smug Mortimer, curly-haired and stocky, your actual convent peeper to the life. The wrong man, said Evans; but then Evans, too, had crossed the floor, running private errands for the Super and treating his oppos like dirt. In the end, none of them mattered a tinker's curse: for Sara was dead.

The loss was upon him, immediate and insupportable in the gloom. Worse than Rosie by far, because Sara had never had the choice. Suicide, and down to you, my son. You hustled her, made her jump before her wings had healed; it's only right you should fall with her. One thing, though, he promised himself grimly, tidying the papers on his desk: someday, somehow, *someone must pay*.

The door opened and Evans came in, smug as Sunday and grinning fit to bust.

The last straw, and Beddoes reacted fiercely. 'Turns you on, does it, a juicy suicide? Have a good laugh then, don't mind me.'

Evans checked, holding up a placatory hand. 'Steady, boyo, I'm on your side, remember?'

'Bleedin' funny way of showing it!'

'*Duw, duw,*' breathed Evans, in a kind of awed remorse. 'You been in here an hour and don't even know. She's recovering, see, the Holroyd girl.'

'If you're having me on ...'

'Give us credit, mun! Wouldn't joke about a thing like that.'

Not exactly a miracle, but it would do for now. No guarantees, of course, more a rebirth of hope. Let Wilson do his worst; there might still be things to value, some time in the future.

Evans was eyeing him cautiously, the way you might watch an untrustworthy dog. 'You could've killed him, Roy. What got into you, then?'

'*Nothing* got into me, mate, not a single word. In the dark, I was – still am, for that matter. Harry was the man, no one ever said different, and the description fitted perfect.'

Evans settled behind his own desk. 'Well, identification's one thing, but karate – *Jesi mawr!*'

'Hark 'oo's bleedin' talkin'. Hadn't been for you, we'd have gone public from the start. Wilson does his turn, Chummy slings his hook and Sara would still be taking French lessons!'

Evans's eyes were hard and narrow. Had a rough morning himself, no doubt.

'I'm making allowances, Roy. Leave it there, now.'

Beddoes got up and paced, choppy and agitated. 'Only talked Wilson out of *Crimewatch*, didn't you? Truth is, you're leery of hi-tech – beyond your little Welsh ken! You're primitive, uncle; Stone Age bleeding Evans. I wouldn't care, except the girl got hurt.'

Evans shook his head decisively. 'Took him for the peeper, didn't you? Mortimer, I mean. *I saw him*, you said, remember? Thinking of that day at the convent, weren't you? *That's* why you went for Sara in the charge room, and why you had to make amends.' He sighed, suddenly saddened and aged. 'There's something in what you say, I expect, nobody's blameless. Hindsight, though, and nothing to be changed. Even so, you should have come clean from the start.'

'Warned me once, did Sara,' Beddoes confessed. 'Don't get involved, she said. *Involved*, what a laugh. Good job Wilson stopped the slaughter.'

Four o'clock and the day dying. The boilers came on, and the radiators thrummed asthmatically. Beddoes ignored them, finally recognising the implications. 'Jesus,' he muttered. 'A civvy, a toff, and innocent with it. What does that make me, uncle?'

'*Lucky*, boyo. After due consideration, and in the circumstances, Mr Mortimer accepts your humble apology. No charges, case dismissed. It's what I was coming to say.'

''Ang about, it can't be that simple!'

Evans turned his palms up, too innocent by far; and the penny dropped.

'I get it. Wise monkeys, deaf, dumb and blind. *Sorry, sir, what assault? Must've blinked and missed it*. Give over, Wilson would never go along.'

'Darro, mun, the Super sent me himself!' Evans sat upright, explaining as if to the feeble-minded. 'We're not denying the facts, and no one's proud of them, either. A compromise, then; why make waves?'

'I'll tell you why,' said Beddoes, fitting the plastic cover over his typewriter. 'It was a cock-up, beginning to end, and most of it down to me. Not all, though; Wilson and Mortimer did their bit. OK, pander to the Brass if you must. *I'd* rather walk a beat.'

'Watch your tongue, boyo! I've sweated blood for you; a hard bargain, see.'

'Yeah, well, next time don't bother. When I'm up for sale, I'll let you know.'

In the sudden hush, you could feel the rumble of Evans' anger. He came to his feet, his pale eyes smouldering. 'Sit down, Roy,' he snapped. 'Time you heard about birds and bees. I've had a bellyful today: a gelded mogul, college-boy scruples, a handless whore and a witless deskman. And now you playing the prima donna! Listen, you want to be pure and noble, join the Sally Army!' The outburst steadied him; he continued with more force and less fury. 'We're not saints, Roy. Bargains and barter come with the badge. You can't win 'em all, either. A time to fight, a time to run, a time to sit down and talk turkey. A time for every purpose ... Said something funny, did I?'

'Heard the sermon before, mate.'

Evans glowered, looming large and close to flashpoint again. 'All right, bach, there's no teaching those as won't learn. Fancy a spell in Traffic, do you?'

Beddoes shrugged, genuinely indifferent. 'Better than kissing arses and wondering when them upstairs'll forgive and forget.'

From somewhere down the corridor, the sound of marching boots and muffled conversation. Change of shift, he'd be doing it himself, soon. Evans listened, his big head tilted, until it was quiet again. Then, glaring downwards in icy disdain, he said, 'Do as you please, then. Order the violins, shall I, and the hair shirt? Easier than staying on, no question. You don't rebound, see, from something like this. More a slow scramble back to the bottom rung. It's taken me a year, you may've noticed. Go ahead, you, be a martyr. Work to do on the case, mind, but I can find another errand boy.'

It didn't sound too rosy, put this way. Cautiously, Beddoes enquired, ''Ow d'you mean, work?'

Evans gazed heavenwards in exaggerated appeal. 'Dear God, I'd be better off alone! All this time we've been chasing shadows and he's out there laughing! A rapist or worse, just waiting for the next one to get careless. I *want* him, Roy; how about you?' In the end, he'd got there; goaded and rummaged and worried until he found the one weak spot, the one argument which yet might hold sway. In Beddoes' mind, his own recent vow re-echoed; *someone must pay.* As he hesitated, Evans pressed on, savage and relentless. 'Capable, are you? Make up your mind, then. For two pins I'd be up there telling Wilson the bloody deal's off!'

'What the hell,' said Beddoes. 'I never looked good in blue.'

She stirred, her senses probing outwards as keen as a blind man's fingers. Cool coarse sheets, a tang of antiseptic, and the reverent hush of convalescence. Hospital, then, not heaven; failed again. But her mind still echoed to her own heartfelt cry against the encroaching dark – dear God, not yet! Nothing, she realised wryly, endears you more to life than the nearness of leaving it.

Amid the kaleidoscope of drugged and formless thoughts, a vague awareness: she wasn't alone. Somewhere nearby, a solid and reassuring presence, someone she knew and trusted. She opened her eyes cautiously.

He was sitting near the window, his battered profile washed by evening light, his expression tense and concerned. There was an air of permanence about him, as though nothing in the world mattered more than this watchful, patient vigil. Rodney.

She shifted and sighed, and he grinned down at her.

'Greetings, princess. Welcome back. You promised a rain-check, remember?'

He seemed utterly normal, and so obviously delighted. A wave of reaction and gratitude swept through her; she couldn't contain the tears. 'Oh, Rodney, I feel such a fool!'

He moved to her side, enveloping her hand in a massive, gentle fist. The bed groaned warningly under his weight. 'We all have our moments, old thing. No harm done.' Then, sheepish and deprecating, he filled in some of the gaps. 'Popped by on my way to a niner. Couldn't raise you and lost my head.' A conspirator's glance, a shrug like an earthquake. 'Booted the door down, I'm afraid. The landlady had kittens. Changed her tune when we found you.'

He paused, avoiding her eye, embarrassed at the open compliment. 'Sleeping beauty. Anyway, frantic phone calls, the blood wagon baying, stomach pumps to the fore. Just in time, luckily.' She nodded, dabbing her eyes with a corner of the sheet, and he went on, 'Should've come earlier, princess. Thing is, I didn't know what to say.' He was shouldering the burden, trying to ease her guilt.

'It wasn't your fault,' she whispered, 'but thanks, anyway.'

He stared sightlessly ahead, picking at the blanket with his free hand. 'The police were there. An accident, I told them, but I couldn't get rid of the pill box. Sorry.'

She pictured the scene. Rodney, large and truculent, taking them on regardless. Taking *her* part, too; something no one else had done for a very long time. He was, she acknowledged, a man who stood by those he cared for; and who rated the truth, whatever the cost. Quietly, she confessed, 'Not an accident, Rodney. A mistake, though, I'm just beginning to realise.'

He had released her hand, and was gazing outwards at the advancing twilight. Softly, he recited:

> 'Do not go gentle unto that good night,
> Rage, rage against the dying of the light.'

'Oh, yes,' she breathed. 'How did you know?'

'Not me, Sara. Guy called Dylan Thomas. Lost the Muse and drank himself to death.' He paused, and added meaningfully, 'Helluva poet, helluva waste.' He turned towards her, his eyes bright and anxious. 'Won't be making any more mistakes, will you?'

Close to tears once more, she shook her head and changed the subject, trying for brightness and a level head. 'How on earth did you get in, anyway?'

Another of his clumsy, confiding grins.

'One of the interns plays scrum half for the Seconds. Owed me a favour. Hope he heals better than he passes.'

There was an obscure rugby pun here, and she managed an uncomprehending smile which broke the spell and led them into idle gossip. College tattle, who was cramming, who was dating, and the latest drunken party. In the cool, clinical room, as the day faded, they shared a few moments of near-intimacy before a nurse came to shoo him out.

'See you soon, princess,' he promised; and she knew he would.

His absence left her empty and apprehensive: coming to altered terms with life. He'd mentioned the police, and she had an idea that suicide was still a crime. In which case, she'd be needing Roy's help again. Funny he hadn't looked in, perhaps he hadn't been told. Right on cue, the ward sister appeared at the door.

'A policeman to see you, Miss Holroyd.' She sounded cross. 'Nothing to worry about, just a few minutes, I promise.'

Sara considered brushing her hair, repairing the tear tracks with warpaint and eyeliner. Roy had seen her looking worse, though, and she wasn't feeling overly energetic.

'Show him in,' she said; quite gaily, all things considered.

Evans' trials weren't ended, not by a long chalk. On the point of surrender, Beddoes had turned stubborn again, making for the door purposefully.

'Where're you off now?'

'Visiting time, uncle. Amends, remember?'

Evans had sighed, mustering reserves for yet another rear-guard action. 'Give it a rest, mun. Doped to the eyeballs, she'll be, wondering if it's Christmas or breakfast time. Besides, you're not fit.'

They were off then, hammer and tongs, until Evans's overtaxed patience finally expired. 'For Chrissake, Roy,

183

we've been at it since sparrow's. Bugger off home. Find yourself a bird and a bottle, loosen up a bit.'

'When I want your advice, I'll ask.'

'Advice be damned; that's a bloody order!'

Reluctant and graceless, Beddoes eventually saw sense.

Leaden-footed and stunned with weariness, Evans had followed him out as far as Warner: fresh on the desk and busting for a chinwag.

'Evening, inspector. Heard the latest?' Eyeing Beddoes scornfully, he added, 'Run along, sonny, this is grown-ups' talk.' Heard about the fracas, then.

'Bleedin' geriatrics, you mean,' Beddoes retorted. 'Talk's all there is, at your age.' He flashed them a swift two fingers and sauntered out.

Warner hunched forward confidingly, a glance in either direction to be sure he wasn't overheard. The corridors were deserted. Outside, flakes of sleet fluttered in the lamplight like dirty moths. 'This Brown female's bin missing a week. Word is, Central found more of the bits. Wilson was on the blower an age; McKay's keepin' mum.'

Evans nodded dully. Station gossip, probably, not to be taken seriously. But Warner was well launched, stocking up on company for the lonely midnight watch ahead. Assured of privacy, smoothing his wispy grey hair, he warmed to the theme. He grinned, his milky old eyes bright with reminiscence.

'Takes me back, it does. Remember the last one we 'ad? Chunks of meat all round the Manor and the press boys doin' their nuts. Higgins the Hacker; a rare ole carve-up.'

Evans leant on the desk, letting it all wash over him. 'Before my time, I expect.'

'Would be, come to think. A Tartar, that Higgins. Shoulda seen 'is pad, down the docks. An abattoir, believe me.' He rambled on, lingering gleefully over the gory details. 'Seven, 'e butchered, before we nailed 'im, and 'alf the Force there to see 'im away when they topped 'im. Can't be done these days, more's the pity. Reckon we're in for the action replay, do yer?'

Evans shrugged, his mind on better things; Treorchy Male

184

Voice and a tidy dollop of firewater. 'Hard to say. Early days, see.'

Warner sat straighter, suddenly very definite. ''E won't stop, now. They never do.' Brief, apologetic pause. 'Bin readin' the file in the small hours. Passes the time, like.' He waved a casual hand at the dim and empty interior. 'Quiet as the grave, some nights. Gives a man a chance to think.'

Evans sighed inwardly. The Sherlock syndrome; every uniform caught it. If you weren't careful, they'd sell you theories by the gross. Sheer conjecture, most of them, useless as udders on a bull.

'Incidents and locations,' Warner was saying importantly, 'bring out the pattern, they do. He puts the wind up Lily Mendoza, whips the drawers off the Holroyd piece, and goes the bank on Laura Brown.'

Somewhere beneath layers of fatigue and lethargy, Evans' instincts quickened, sniffing out the inconsistency. 'You're dreaming. Holroyd's a student, mind.'

Warner smiled airily. 'A nutter, see. Yer actual latter-day Ripper. In 'is book, they'd all be ladies of the night.'

'You don't want to listen to Lil. Paranoid, she is.'

'So she should be. High-risk occupation, in this day'n'age. Anyhow, there's more. Nature boy, this one, the greenbelt groper.'

Evans sniffed scornfully, his interest waning. Beddoes was right, old Jack should be out to pasture. 'Don't be simple. Done in the street, Holroyd was.' Warner was almost purring with satisfaction.

'Building site, it says 'ere. Know what's behind the scaffolding, do yer? The park, mate, that's what. Locations, then. Mark my words, 'e's out there with blood in 'is eye and a cleaver in 'is 'and, measuring some tart like the Sunday roast. Shades of the past: Son of Higgins.'

They had a quiet chuckle, and the phone rang. In the hiatus, Evans made good his escape.

Sitting in the car, haunted by Warner's macabre visions, he realised the long day had yet to end. That's what you get, he thought disgustedly, when the CID chase shadows: uniforms showing the way. It *might* all be eyewash, the fevered

185

delusion of a senile deskman; but he had to be sure. Blearily, fighting sleep every foot of the way, he steered a familiar course through evening traffic and swirling sleet.

And headlong into the lissom but unyielding resistance of a West Indian ward sister.

'I don't care who you are,' she snapped. 'It's after visiting hours.' She nodded for emphasis, and the fluorescent light glinted on the gold of her spectacles. 'Doctor's orders,' she declared, like one pronouncing an act of God, 'the poor child's mentally and physically exhausted.'

Makes two of us, thought Evans, and responded in kind. 'Official business, mind. I could have you for obstruction.'

Her pretty mouth set in a hard thin line. 'Perhaps you'd care to threaten Dr Pearson. He's *white*!'

Duw, duw, all this and a racial hassle, too. 'Listen, lady,' he told her grimly, 'I'm Welsh. Don't give me any crap about minorities; you've got us outnumbered.'

She seemed about ready to plant him one, he actually heard the crackle of starch as she drew herself up. In the nick of time, she saw the joke; a flashing smile and a touch of the Rastas. 'Marn, it so tough fo' de exiles, Jamaica side. All right,' she said, in a disconcerting switch back to Roedean, 'you can have five minutes, and *I'll* keep time.'

She led him along the stark aseptic corridors, her trim rump wagging pertly, her rubber soles squeaking. The quiet and the smell depressed him: cancer and carbolic. She made him wait at the door while she murmured something reassuring, then ushered him in like an experienced butler.

It was a small, standard, functional room: stainless steel and white paint. Something obvious missing, though, and it took him a moment to grasp. No flowers. She really was a loner, then; poor dab.

Half sitting, propped against the pillows, she looked blanched and rather lovely in a fragile sort of way. He could've sworn he saw a welcoming smile fade as he walked in, as though she'd been expecting someone else. She knew him, though, no question.

'Come to arrest me, inspector?' She wanted to sound jaunty

and flip, but he caught the underlying anxiety and tried to put her at ease.

'For what, girl? Careless, you were, not criminal.'

She relaxed perceptibly, and the Sister, unobtrusive but watchful, gave him an approving nod. Aye, he thought, so much for the good news. Carefully, gently, coming to the point by degrees, he explained. New developments, a possible line of enquiry, the need for more first-hand information.

'I want to trawl your memory, see, for whatever we missed first time round.'

She wouldn't look at him; her smile went out like a light, and her fingers wrestled nervously in her lap.

'It's hard, I know, especially just now. Any little detail might help, though; about *him*, I mean.'

She seemed to shrink visibly, as though the faceless horror had actually appeared before her. 'No,' she whispered, 'I can't.'

'Two minutes,' warned the Sister implacably, and Evans said, 'Come on, Sara! He came close to you; what do you remember?'

The sister stirred angrily and Sara spoke, forestalling her. 'The smell – he smelt *awful*. There was something about his speech, too.' Her eyes were wide in pain and remembrance, and vivid green against the whiteness of face and pillow.

'An impediment?' prompted Evans. 'A lisp?'

'No, no!' She sounded scornful and impatient at the interruption. She was really trying now, perhaps sensing his own suppressed urgency. Even the sister hung on her words.

'He spoke like a foreigner. The phraseology, not the accent.' A language scholar, mind, an expert witness. 'European, I think, but not one I know. Eastern.' The technical problem seemed to soothe her, lifting her briefly out of emotional decline.

'Behind the Curtain?' asked Evans, and she shook her head.

'Of course not! *Any* fool could tell that.' And suddenly he'd lost her, the tenuous link of shared puzzlement severed. Her mind was in retreat again, her expression closed and resentful.

'I don't know. Leave me alone.' The demand had a sullen ring, reminding him of her reaction to Beddoes, that night.

187

Something to hide, then? She shot an imploring glance at the sister, who reacted briskly.

'That's enough, inspector. Your time's up.'

'Use your head, woman!' Evans snarled, frustrated beyond bearing. 'Want to be safe on the streets at night, do you?'

The sister came to her feet, the outrage pushing her briefly back into dialect. 'You better go, marn, 'fore I call the doctor.'

'Oh sure. Soon as I've done my job.'

'And what d'you think *I'm* doing?'

Their faces were only inches apart; he could smell the spicy heat of her anger.

Sara stopped them; the still small voice of resignation. 'He's right, sister. There's something he has to be told.' She was sitting stiffly, wild-eyed and skittish as a startled filly.

'Something you forgot?' he asked, and she made a tiny gesture of negation.

'I've been trying not to remember.' Bitter, she sounded, and with every reason. Harshly, seeing God knows what torment in the stark white wall, she whispered, 'After he'd ... finished ... he ran the tip of the knife around my breast. So cold, so utterly inhuman; as if I were no more than a – *carcase*!'

With Warner's prediction fresh in his mind, Evans felt the small hairs rise on his neck. The sister had taken his arm, literally dragging him away.

'Anything else, girl?' he called from the doorway.

She had collapsed against the pillow, the tears falling like rain. 'You know it all now,' she hissed. 'I hope you're satisfied!'

But of course he wasn't. Later he'd taken himself to the pub, seeking release and normality; a game of darts, a couple of pints, some undemanding chat about sport and the latest political scandal. The respite proved temporary, the cure incomplete. Back in his bed, to the hiss of passing traffic on slushy roads and the bay of a neighbourhood mongrel, he waited in vain for much-needed sleep; and his fevered brain rehashed the whole affair.

There were no *reasons* to assume the link between a groping, a rape, and a severed hand; only coincidences. A common physical description, a restricted sphere of operations, a penchant for sadism and mock butchery. Probably three other guys. On the other hand, history had a tendency to repeat itself – Son of Higgins. In his present state, frayed and apprehensive, alone in the silent dark, it was easy to accept Warner's premise. A maniac loose, prowling the shadowed park and returning to some ghastly devil's kitchen. Gleaming knives, human fricassee, and blood to the elbows. Cool head, bach, you'll be calling him Dracula next.

Motive, you have to go back to it. Rape is aggression, says Beddoes via Parrot and the boffins. If so, why should the aggressor *stop* at rape? Why not go to the logical extreme? That's what nutters do, mind. He writhed in his bed, punching humps in the pillow and cursing the persistent yapping of the dog.

First off, there had been a fatal lapse in communication. Beddoes hushing up the convent caper, secretly courting the victim, and roughing up the wrong man out of sheer ignorance; Wilson playing Hide and Seek with infidelity, setting the hunt along a false trail, and confiding in machines instead of colleagues; and Mortimer hiding guilt beneath a mantle of outmoded gallantry.

Then there was the time factor: precious weeks surrendered to muggers and shoplifters; uniforms committed to the pursuit of fruitless *Crimewatch* leads; the delicate unravelling of upper-class manners and mores; and senior officers bickering over process and priority while the telltale clues lay buried and unheeded. The investigation had lurched blindly from one crisis to the next – a sorry saga of conflict, compromise and witless, fumbling incompetence.

Confined to isolation and the midnight watch, distanced from the clash of emotions and personalities, Warner had perceived the pattern and pointed the way. Spurred by gory remembrance, trusting to a copper's instinct and the written record, the grizzled desk man had provided the first real breakthrough. It was a classic of armchair detection, and one which he, Evans, should long ago have undertaken himself. The Basement Bungler, *duw duw*.

No use crying over spilt blood, mind. Only one way to clear

the slate. Pick up the pieces, regroup the forces, and nail the *real* culprit bloody smartish. Because somewhere out there, Chummy would be licking his chops and sharpening the steel.

I'll have you, boyo, Evans promised this private ogre, before you feed again. Because, from the very centre of the mess, he had perceived a way out. A uniform's theory, a wild leap in the dark. To confirm or discard it, he could deploy the range of techniques, ancient and modern. Wilson's computers, Beddoes' way with the fairer sex, even the despised media. Plus a healthy portion of traditional legwork. With luck, two crippled coppers would be rehabilitated; might even manage to keep Chummy off the park.

He turned over, settling and relaxing at last. The dog had fallen silent; let in or gone hoarse. Tomorrow, home ground once more: some of your actual police work.

CHAPTER EIGHTEEN

By MORNING, winter and sanity had returned. Snow clouds gathered outside, chivvied by an arctic wind; while Beddoes wandered the office, bloodshot and woebegone and ripe for the second vow.

'Sara OK?' he asked anxiously.

Evans made comforting noises, omitting any reference to the latest relapse. White lies; a lot of them about, mind.

Hoisting the skirts of his topcoat, warming his backside at the radiator, Beddoes admitted, 'Bin thinking, uncle.' He inclined his chin, running a bleary eye over the comfortless room. 'No place like 'ome.'

'Grows on you, fair play,' agreed Evans, 'like dandruff. Glad to hear it, though. Got a little job for you.' He peered doubtfully into Beddoes' face. 'Handle it, can you?'

'Dunno, I'm due down the Youth Club later, checking Rasta alibis. One of them young holy rollers runs it – reckons we're persecuting the underprivileged ethnic minority. He's covering up, I reckon, he's got the eyes – earnest but shifty, know what I mean?' Beddoes' broad gesture tailed away. 'Besides, I had a heavy night.'

Evans kept a hipflask for the cold and minor crises. Wordless, he uncorked it and passed it across. In the enclosed space, the fruity bouquet reminded him of Christmas pud.

Beddoes flinched, averting his head. 'Whaddya trying to do, finish me off?'

'Hair of the dog, boyo. Do you the power.'

Beddoes shrugged and took a swallow. His eyes filled and widened, and a slow shudder travelled the length of his wiry frame. 'Right,' he gasped, blinking and quoting a bewhiskered punchline, 'where's this virgin I've gotta fight?'

Evans smiled grimly. 'Funny you should say that. It's Lily Mendoza, see. Anything she remembers about the guy who groped her. Have a word, will you?'

You could actually see the hunter in him wake, shrugging off the booze and rising to full alert.

'Oh, yeah? Connection there, you reckon?'

'Could be,' murmured Evans warily, and watched Beddoes' eagerness turn to anger.

''Ere we go again, workin' in the dark! Christ, mate, look what 'appened last time!'

The phone rang; saved by the bell. Beddoes took it, coming to attention, his expression swept clean of irritation.

'Yes, sir,' he said woodenly, 'right away.' And to Evans, 'His nibs desires the pleasure of your company. Immediate, he says.'

'Oh sure. Listen, tread soft around old Lil. A handful, she is; eats lads like you for breakfast.'

Beddoes curled a lip disdainfully. 'I'll manage. Since you're about it, give our beloved leader a cuddle from the teaboy.'

Armistice over, then; nice while it lasted.

The atmosphere upstairs was no more cheery. Breaking his own traditions, Wilson had the fluorescents going full tilt and his pet machines kennelled under plastic. He leant on the bookshelf, a tome open and balanced on his free hand. Of the window and the besieged city beyond it, he seemed wholly oblivious. There was ceremony in the air; farewell to all this.

'Evans. Sit or browse, as you please. I won't detain you.'

'Take the view, I will. After the basement, it makes a change.' He paused briefly, waiting to be put in his place. The window was the Super's country, enter at your own risk. No response; he ambled across and gazed down. Far below, dwarf-like figures merged and scurried, hunched against the cold.

'Speaking of change,' murmured Wilson, absorbed in his reading, 'you'll soon be reporting to the new man.' His head came up, steady and defiant. 'I'm resigning.' A shock, naturally, but hardly a surprise. He stood there, suave as ever in spotless linen and a bespoke suit, his handsome brow furrowed with determination. The flavour of the month, it seemed, doomed nobility.

'Allowed to ask why, am I?'

Wilson replaced one book and selected another. He handled them fondly, like old and trusted friends. Amazing, thought Evans; he values these more than a room at the top.

'*These* are some of the reasons,' Wilson explained calmly, underlining the point and indicating the laden shelves. 'I'm ill at ease at the sharp end of enforcement. My talents and ambitions lie elsewhere; in academia.' His glance had slid involuntarily to the portrait of his wife, causing Evans to doubt him; about ambitions, anyway.

'Fortunately,' he was saying, 'I'm shortlisted for a post at my former university. Between you and me, I expect to get it.' He smiled, confident and expansive. For the first time, Evans was conscious of his personal charm. 'It will be pleasant to go back to open minds, where change can occasionally be negotiated.'

You had to have charm, mind, to carry off a statement like that; there's plenty who'd take it as an insult. Watch the weather, bach, it's why you're here. Almost purple, it was now, and down to the rooftops.

'Pity, though,' said Evans, following the erratic flight of the snowflakes and getting in a dig of his own, 'all that learning wasted. Could use the talents, too.' He shifted, nodding at the muzzled gadgetry. 'Save us some legwork, those things.'

Wilson patrolled his library, immune to the barbed appeal. Might as well talk to youself. 'Got a theory about the rapist,' he continued doggedly. 'Thought we might hammer it round a bit.'

Brought him out, that did, with raised eyebrows and the familiar patronising smile. 'Come, inspector, let's not play games. The case merely reinforces my decision. I abused position and power, put personal interests above those of the force.'

'Aye, well you wouldn't be the first,' breathed Evans. 'Nor the last, either!'

Wilson faced him squarely, a man willing to shoulder the burden. 'It was dereliction, plain and simple, and complicity in the barter which followed. I'm not concerned with the morality of others; I have no choice.'

'Know what?' demanded Evans, deliberately provocative. 'You're getting to sound more like Harry by the minute!'

Momentarily, the comparison stung him; you could see the anger pinch his lips and narrow his eyes. He shoved the book away, apparently primed for confrontation. Then, for no reason, he relaxed, his even features creasing in a frown of genuine disbelief. 'We haven't agreed on a single issue; you should be first to bid me Godspeed. Why are we debating *this*, of all things?'

Evans allowed himself a thin smile. *Because you might yet earn your salt, boyo.* Aloud he suggested, 'Wanted a devil's advocate, didn't you?'

But as usual, Wilson had no time for jokes. He came to the window, solemnly fingering his moustache. Nothing out there to lighten his gloom; snow by the cartload. 'For advocate, read judge. I've forfeited the right to command.'

They were standing together, gazing sightless and mutually confounded at the swirling blizzard.

Softly, Evans mused, 'Suppose I said – if it wasn't for you, we'd be worse off. *Your* authority stopped Beddoes. No way I could've swung it.'

'And my machinations provoked him in the first place.'

From the corridor, a measured approaching tread. A uniform, you could tell by the plod.

Evans laid an edged palm under his nose. 'In it to here, I am. Unofficial enquiries, rooting about in private affairs. How would I shop you, then, and my own neck on the block?'

The footsteps halted; there was a timid rap at the door. Unhearing or uncaring, Wilson addressed the blankness outside. 'Such touching loyalty. Misplaced, I fear; and of course, you can blackmail me whenever you choose.'

'Blackmail, is it?' echoed Evans, very angry indeed. 'Thanks a million! Best if you go, after all. So who's the replacement?'

The knock came again, louder and more insistent. Wilson slid him a sidelong glance, curiously triumphant. 'Come in,' he called, and made for his desk, leaving Evans snowbound by the window.

The boy who entered was tall, even for a copper. Stooped in the doorway, his cropped hair almost touching the lintel, he looked awkward and gangling and no more than eighteen.

'Sorry for the interruption, guv,' he mumbled, forcing a sickly grin. 'Volunteered, I did.' Too green to step back, more likely. His frightened eyes darted between them. Hard to blame him, really. Could probably sense the aggro ten yards off. 'Immediate, it says 'ere,' he continued, brandishing a quarto-sized flimsy. In his massive, unsteady hand, it seemed no bigger than a bus ticket.

'Out with it, man,' urged Wilson, quite gentle, fair play. The boy ducked his head and read, halting and toneless. 'For Inspector Evans, from the desk, immediate.' He flushed, conscious of the senseless repetition. 'Sorry, I already said that. Female corpse reported, 09.43 eastern corner of the park. Believed young, as yet unidentified.' He stumbled over the last word, and Evans caught his breath. 'Mew – mutilated.'

Evans found himself actually shaking; a fever compounded of rage and defeat. Up here in the snug, bandying words with an impotent genius, and Chummy amok and unmolested. On his toes, coiled for action, he gave Wilson a furious glare. 'Coming, are you?'

The Superintendent watched from his chair, steady and aloof. 'You have my complete confidence.' He waved a languid hand at his beloved books. 'Besides, I'm busy.'

There was a word for it, mind, and on the tip of his tongue. It would keep, though. Already moving, Evans snapped, 'Aye, I've noticed. I'll be back, then. Unfinished business.' And to the messenger, 'What're you waiting for, Christmas?'

The snowfall had eased; it was a mercifully short and miserably familiar pilgrimage. The driver wittered about City's new goalie till Evans squashed him, tart and obscene. Thenceforth, they passed in sullen silence through grey and salted sludge.

The escort met him, two big grim uniforms muffled for the chill. Their wordless greenish pallor said it all. He trudged behind, his boots creaking in frigid footprints. The unlikely glare hurt his eyes, and his stomach churned in sick anticipation. Imagination, probably, but he fancied he could smell a death on the air.

The onlookers had already gathered, hunched and hooded, patient as vultures at the icy feast. He elbowed them aside roughly and they fell away, muttering, before his blazing contempt. At their focus, a sodden blue blanket, fringed by trodden and pinkly gleaming snow.

'Some teenager found it, goin' to school', the shorter uniform confided. 'In shock, she is, Gawd 'elp 'er.' He nodded towards a lank and immaculate figure, apart from the crowd. 'PS reckons it happened before the storm. On account of the colour; diluted blood, that is.' He stopped and peered upwards, his face raw, his eyes narrow and haunted. 'Ready, are yer? Not squeamish, I 'ope?'

'She's feelin' a bit cut up, see,' added his partner. 'Not expecting company.'

Evans rounded on him, prepared to let rip. The lean and craggy type, acting very casual. You had to watch the tough ones. If they couldn't laugh, they'd end up screaming. Summoning the vestige of a smile, Evans murmured, 'Very droll, I'm sure.'

The shroud slid back reluctantly; he actually heard the faint crackle of disturbed ice, and the hiss of indrawn breath beside him. Had to be nasty, mind, for the hard men to waver second time around. He swallowed and glanced down.

A sharp nose pointing skywards, dull wide eyes filmed with melting snow, the mouth slack and agape. Nothing special. Not pretty, not ugly, just another dead and empty face.

Below it lay the stuff of nightmares. Her body was a scarlet chasm, cloven from belly to larynx, as if by some rabid primeval force. You could see it all: a wealth of human frailty exposed to the pitiless light. Shards of bone, spongy grey lung, and fat translucent worms of entrail coiling free. Her sexual organs had been devastated, the entire pubic mound peeled away and swaying in the wind like an obscene scalp. The stench appalled him, the sickly sweet corruption of the charnel house.

'Cover her,' he ordered, scarcely recognising his own voice. 'For God's sake leave her decent!' Fancy, he thought, being fifteen and female and stumbling on that. You'd never rest easy again. *And we could've stopped him.*

He turned away, bowed by the waste and the needlessness. The gale, too, was dying, the flakes fell broad and feathery. Aye, cover her, then, but she won't go away. One more senseless horror for the small hours when sleep's gone walkabout; the worst he'd ever seen.

'Frenzy,' decreed the Police Surgeon, sucking a cold pipe and affecting professional nonchalance. He picked his way disdainfully, seeking in vain to protect rich and unsuitable shoes. Even at this hour, arrogance and a whiff of booze drifted in his wake. 'In my opinion, he was interrupted.'

Evans halted, utterly incredulous. 'He hadn't *finished*, you mean?'

The doctor snorted, savage and derisive. 'Call yourself an observer? You didn't look closely, man!'

'Close enough.'

'Hmph. Ought to be hardened, by now. There was partial dislocation at the hip and shoulder. A prelude to amputation, I'd say.'

Evans nodded dully, incapable of surprise. Desk Sergeant Warner, you just won this week's lucky dip.

'Amazing,' the surgeon continued. Under the fine tracery of broken veins, he was looking a mite peaky himself. 'Big job, opening the thorax. Best part of an hour, given a competent team and all mod cons.' He jerked his head towards the silent group of watchers left behind. 'Your man must've managed inside ten minutes.'

'Frenzy,' Evans muttered. 'Said so yourself, mun.'

'I was speaking of the nether regions. The initial incisions were made earlier; a feat of awesome strength.' He flailed his arms, gawky as an icebound stork. 'No precision, of course; sheer butchery.'

Evans shrugged wearily. 'What d'you expect? A nutter, see.'

They had reached the gates. Their separate cars stood waiting, the windscreens edged in white. The doctor rose to his full height, applying correction to an errant intern. 'Kindly refrain from pejoratives! We don't use such terms for the mentally afflicted.'

'You don't have to catch 'em, either.'

Unbelievable, really; raving mania abroad, and a Super still jealous of protocol. Evans had marched clean through the building and into the big office.

Wilson, standing at ease by the window, expressed his displeasure with heavy irony. 'Forgive me, inspector, for usurping the dominant position. Doubtless it will soon be yours. For the moment, I remain in charge; I believe it's customary to knock?'

'Remiss, was I?' snapped Evans. 'Pity.' He waved a hand at the misted glass. 'Last night, somewhere out there, theory became fact. Berserk, he is; it's no time for amenities.'

But Wilson had already tired of the view. He quartered the room unhurriedly, fetching up beside the shrouded consoles. 'I shall miss *this*, of course. Back to scrambling for access with a bunch of greedy dons.'

'Jesus,' breathed Evans, his voice quaking, 'you're not even listening!'

'Comfort yourself, inspector. McKay will be avid for news.'

After the park, Evans had counted himself immune to shock; mistakenly. The name stopped him dead in his tracks. '*Who* d'you say?'

Wilson offered his most infuriating smile. 'I've informed the Assistant Commissioner. "Pursue your vocation," he said. Most understanding.'

Dull old fart, thought Evans bitterly, gone soft with gin and deskwork.

'Superintendent McKay, he agreed, will assume dual responsibility pending a permanent appointment.'

A vicious revenge; delivered into the mercies of a sworn professional enemy. He who laughs loudest, *duw duw*. 'Spare a thought, then, while you dally in quad. Swabbing the shithouse, I'll be.'

Wilson's eyes crinkled fastidiously. 'Spare me the crudity,

man. In due course, McKay will learn your undoubted virtues.'

Aye, and there'll be a Second Coming, one day. From the distant unseen river, a foghorn blared. Showdown, and nothing left to lose. Goaded by long-denied fury and the stark images of Chummy's handiwork, Evans bestrode the office and spoke his mind.

'A girl got killed last night. No; slaughtered. If you hadn't meddled, she could still be walking about. Wash your hands, will you, and back to the books? A cop out, *I* call it.' Wilson opened his mouth in protest, and Evans shouted him down. 'I've earned my say, mind! On a goose chase, I was, the Super's tame bloodhound. Personal, you said, and no records. Chummy must've loved it; miles of rope and nowhere near the hanging.'

The phone rang and Wilson watched it, his face pinched and drawn and not too handsome any more.

'Leave it be,' Evans ordered, 'I'm not finished yet.' Wilson held still, whether from obedience or inertia, it was hard to tell. 'There's someone out there wants catching, that much we agree; and you *owe* me, boyo, *personal*. Stay put, then; keep McKay off my back. After, we'll call it quits.'

The clamour ceased. Into loud and abrupt quiet, Wilson murmured, 'Why, Evans, you're a crusader!'

'Look, this isn't one of your bloody intellectual *games*. He's slipped the leash, see, with his knife and his lust and no pity whatsoever. Now, I've got a theory. You want to hear it or what?'

For some reason, Wilson seemed to be rallying. Hoisting his chin in challenge, he retorted, 'You behave as though I have no choice.'

In Evans's mind, briefly, the office confines faded. He was out in the wind, the scent of death at his nostrils and a vision of depravity laid out before him. It's a battleground, he realised, and the body count is rising. He *had* the weapon; in this extremity, he would use it without the slightest compunction. Calmly and deliberately, looking Wilson straight in the eye, he said, 'One call, mind, is all it takes. A cosy chat with the AC about the whole rotten deal. We'll see how keen he is on vocations *then*! If it's blackmail you want, you'll have it.'

Wilson was watching him in a kind of appalled awe. 'I really believe you would. You never give up, do you?' He shuddered slightly, like a dog emerging from water. Ease of movement deserted him; awkwardly, he rounded the desk and slumped in his chair. 'Very well, let's hear this famous theory.'

Lunchtime had passed unnoticed in the clash of wills. Already evening had come. The picture window was a flawed mirror reflecting the tube lights and the occasional distorted gestures of the two figures at the desk.

Aftermath, a sense of unusual closeness and shared purpose; and Evans improvising on a theme of Warner. 'A progression, I'm saying,' he concluded. 'A guy who started by peeping and made it all the way over the top. Out of hand, now, see; ravenous.'

Resilient, mind, Wilson, on the mend already and getting that supercilious look. 'Sounds far-fetched to me. Take the Brown woman, for instance; haven't even found the body yet.'

'Might be better if we don't,' Evans muttered, haunted anew by the morning's carnage. Then, seeing the objection for what it was – habitual nitpicking – he went on, 'It's not complete, but it's the best we can manage for now.' He allowed his gaze to dwell on the masked rows of hardware. 'Time's of the essence, no telling who's next on the list. Give those machines a workout, then. All sexual incidents in the area *before* the Holroyd rape; all female corpses *since*. Plug in the common factors – location, use of a knife, time, physical description – and see if there's a match. Do that, could you?'

Yet again, you could see him listen, consider – and yield. The right decision, going back to college. You couldn't run a nick if you let subordinates answer back; you can't command others till you're easy with yourself. A shame, really; a worry, too. Because how the hell was a man like Wilson ever going to ward off McKay?

Pink-nosed Rudolf and merry Santa hovered overhead, outlined in shining neon. Miraculously, the weather had relented. Sightseers thronged the pavements, the shops were open late, and a two-way tailback clogged all six lanes of the highway. Lighting-up, and the city possessed of the festive spirit. Beside her, his sharp features etched in the glow of many colours, Roy Beddoes squirmed impatiently and eased the car forwards another couple of feet.

'Sorry, Sara, forgot about this lot. Gonna be a long old haul.'

Too many apologies, she thought peevishly. She felt dreadful; returning physically spent and emotionally drained, to a cold and empty flat while the world and his brother blew money they couldn't afford on junk they didn't need in the name of a deity they no longer acknowledged. If only ... She checked herself firmly. Such a lost, futile phrase, if only. 'It's not your fault. Just don't give me any "tidings of comfort and joy".'

Earlier, he'd somehow flirted his way past the sister, appearing at her bedside in a lather of concern and a snow-covered trenchcoat.

'Why?' she'd demanded tearfully. 'Why *Evans*? It wouldn't have been so bad, telling you. I've done it before, after all.' He didn't understand. Once more she'd been compelled to explain, re-entering an area of memory she'd tried so hard to seal off.

He went very quiet, as though containing some deep and private rage. When she finished, he nodded tightly and mumbled, 'Sorry, lovely, copper's code. Ours is not to reason why.' Then, winning back a lot of lost ground, he added gently, 'I came as quick as I could.'

A semblance of their former warmth rekindled. Under its seductive influence, she allowed herself to be persuaded.

'You can't stay here,' he'd protested, waving a disparaging hand at the clinical austerity. 'It's like a bleedin' morgue! Sorry, again.'

He left her alone to dress, and the apprehension flooded in. She *was* recovering; her promise to Rodney stood – no more mistakes. Which meant a return to college. A daunting prospect, even without a possible entanglement with the despised Fuzz. It would have been so much simpler if Rodney, rather than Roy, had been here to welcome her back. Because

Rodney, too, had staked a claim and, in his own coltish way, might prove equally persistent ...

The car cruised forward, gathering speed.

'Break-out,' he announced, smiling; but he spoke too soon. Within minutes, they were once more stranded among swirls of exhaust fumes and a posse of whey-faced urchins bawling raucous carols. Twice, he lowered the window and paid the ransom. The third time, he growled, 'Enough's enough. Scarper, or I'll do you for unlicensed trading.' He gave her an exasperated grin. 'Christmas!'

She could find no answering humour, still trying to think herself clear. Both men, she realised, would always be part of something she had to forget. Maybe she should look for someone entirely new. Come *on*, my girl, where does an erstwhile rape victim go for the honey?

They made it, eventually, to the flat, where she hadn't the heart to turn him away. Then, over the inevitable orgy of tea, he set out to lift her morale. He'd been working all morning, a tricky interview with a professional bawd.

'Forty-five in the shade,' he said admiringly, 'and still a sight for sore eyes. Tough as old boots, mind you. Only thing she offered I was bound to refuse. Couldn't afford it, neither.'

He rambled on, chuckling, and she listened readily enough. It could be like this most nights, she knew; she had only to give the nod. Companionship and tales of duty; but what happened when the lights went out? Had violation, Valium and despair left her anything to give in return?

He went home quite early, carefully avoiding physical contact. Alone again, washing crockery to familiar night noises and the plumbed-in gurgle of somebody running a bath, she steeled herself for the renewed onslaught of doubt and depression.

Time passed, and she made a simple solemn vow; never to look back. Ahead lay her beloved languages, and not one but *two* very presentable suitors. You have a choice, my girl. A week ago, you didn't even have a life. The knowledge held a promise of peace, bearing her, for the first time in weeks, into hopeful and undrugged slumber.

CHAPTER NINETEEN

DAYBREAK, AND media jackals baying at the kill. TV-am led the pack; freaked-out pop stars slagging off the Old Bill. Oh sure, thought Evans in disgust, and they ought to hear *me* sing the Beatles. The BBC was worse, mind: a moist-eyed social worker begging enforcement to consider the disturbed. I'll bloody disturb him, all right.

An overnight thaw had set in, sudden but stealthy. Bound for the nick through wicked traffic and seeping rain, Evans kept an eye on the hoardings. 'The Ripper rules,' they proclaimed, in blurred and soggy print. 'Crazed axeman haunts a city of fear!' The Super would have his limelight, then; too late, too bright, and not the kind he'd fancy at all.

Beddoes was already in, sullen as the weather and spoiling for the return bout. 'Jesus, you've got a bleedin' nerve! Give 'er a break, you say; and what 'appens? Soon as I turn me back, you're down there raking the whole thing over!' Didn't know any better, fair play, he was due a bit of licence.

Hauling off his raincoat and making for his desk, Evans explained, 'Warner had a brainstorm, after you'd gone. Urgent, see, no time for by your leave.' He was looking down, leafing through his in-tray. He could *hear* the scorn and disbelief, though.

'Warner? Wilson, more likely. Thick as thieves, you two.' Another false but not wholly unreasonable charge.

Mildly, Evans enquired, 'Seen the papers, have you?'

'Muggings in the park? 'Ow could I miss, they're calling it World War Three.'

Evans had found an early incident report, fully illustrated.

203

Selecting a glossy and handing it across, he murmured, 'Mug-gings, is it?'

Beddoes gave it a cursory glance, levelling an accusatory finger to press the attack. His jaw sagged, the argument died at birth, and he took a long, hard second look. 'Gordon Bennet,' he breathed in awe, 'they got it right for once! That's a very hungry boy, uncle.' He swallowed noisily, dismissing the picture and the horror it provoked, and came wading in once more. 'OK, it's ugly; but what's it got to do with Sara? We're talking rape, or maybe you forgot.'

'It's you who's forgetting; the mask and the knife.' Evans allowed a childish nursery-rhyme singsong into his voice. 'Peeper, groper, raper, butcher. Could be one and the same, see.'

'Oh, yeah? 'Oo says?'

'I do for one, Warner for another. Even the Super's half convinced. It's where we're going now; upstairs.'

Beddoes fashioned a truly savage sneer. 'An invite for the lackey at last. Take me to our leader, all will be revealed?'

'I doubt it, boyo,' said Evans. 'I doubt it very much.'

Wilson's greeting underlined the point.

'Morning, sergeant,' he grunted, cool and disdainful. 'Wel-come aboard.' Made you feel about as welcome as herpes in a whorehouse. No discrimination, mind; treating *everyone* like dirt. 'Ah, Evans. Your quaint little programme is ready to run. Central Records on line, all systems go.' Taking the mickey, he was, and none too subtle, either. 'I'm assuming,' he con-tinued, maddeningly smooth and sarky, 'that the Evans theory of progression presupposes a known offender. Otherwise, of course, the link to Records is superfluous.' He frowned, clearly annoyed at his own intellectual sloppiness. 'The words "theory" and "assumption" hardly apply. At best, you have an hypothesis, based more on faith than reason.'

Aye, go ahead and smile, thought Evans, it's funny what faith can do.

But for the first hour, the big office remained a potential battlefield. Beddoes and the Super, Evans realised, were essen-tially two of a kind. The same sharpness of mind and feature, the same concern for appearance. From different classes, though, which only added to the air of mutual distrust. Perhaps mindful of his lethal abilities, Wilson gave Beddoes a wide berth; while the younger man seemed outfaced by Wilson's rank and familiarity with the alchemy of hi-tech. Somehow, they rubbed along together, a trio without a single note of harmony.

As the morning drew out, drab and unrelenting, Evans acknowledged reluctant thrall to the Super's sheer expertise. He sat erect but relaxed at the consoles, his fingers playing nimbly over the keys, his regular profile severe in the upward greenish glow. He made it seem effortless and a little uncanny; whenever he so decreed, the machines brought forth another suspect. Briefly, the pressures of the case and the drizzle outside ceased to exist: the world turned on Wilson, and the pleasures of watching a virtuoso at work.

Husbanding reams of white print-out, Beddoes proved more pragmatic. 'Superintendent? Permission to speak, sir.'

'What is it?' Wilson sounded disgruntled; didn't care for interruptions.

'Some of these are doing time. There oughta be a way to weed 'em out.' And as Wilson hesitated, he added, 'Can't be any of *them*, can it?'

The Super peered at the steamed-up window as if seeking some reference to reality. 'Of course,' he breathed. 'Why didn't *I* think of that?' And turned the charm on Beddoes, full beam. 'Well done, Sergeant. Two heads are better than one.'

Ta very much, thought Evans, pointedly excluded.

By mid-day, they'd achieved a tenuous rapport and a list of sixteen possibles. The sky was somewhat clearer, though Wilson's disposition remained stormy.

'Disgraceful,' he growled. 'The data's obsolete. Physical matches don't mean a thing.'

'Should've done it on birth dates,' chirped Beddoes, winning a second mention in despatches.

Darro, mused Evans in disgust, and he accused *me* of toadying to the Brass.

It was Beddoes, too, who engineered the next breakthrough. They'd whittled the numbers to four: bookmaker, stevedore, gardener and chef. 'Records have photos, right,' he declared, his brown eyes glinting with discovery. 'So you find a witness, spread out your piccies and Bob's yer uncle.'

'Talk sense, mun,' snapped Evans, rising sharply and unwisely to the bait. 'He wears a mask, remember. Going to grill the departed, then? Send for the Ouija board, shall we?'

Beddoes grinned slyly, savouring the reply. 'Start small, you said, uncle. Chances are 'e was done for spying on snoggers or feeling little girls' bottoms. *Someone's* seen 'im, I'll lay odds.' He turned to Wilson, lapsing easily into the jargon. ''Ow about it, sir? A search on pinchers and peepers, limited timeframe, key words from the description.'

Wilson beamed benevolence upon him, patting the console affectionately. 'You're a natural, sergeant, you really ought to get yourself one of these.'

So Evans was relegated to paperwork, dogsbodying yet again; while Beddoes and the Super huddled and whispered like companionable matrons over their newest offspring. Boring, mind, once the novelty palled. He almost missed it the first time round. Struck by a single unlikely word, he retrieved a print-out from the growing pile of discards and checked it through again.

'Ticklebum,' he muttered dazedly, and Beddoes called, 'Yer wot?'

He read them the description first: a big man with dark curly hair who talked funny. The date was right, too, just long enough before the convent alarm and the groping of Lily Mendoza. Then, softly, he added, 'He asked the kiddie to play Ticklebum. A Sunday, it was: *in the park.*'

Wilson bemoaned their neglect of locations; but Beddoes sat bolt upright, absently stroking the calloused cutting edge of his right hand. 'Chummy,' he murmured, and his air of absolute certainty infected them all.

Even so, as the rain hammered on to the window and Evans badgered Records for immediate pictures over the phone, Wilson demanded another search including the key word 'park'. From behind the desk, the bakelite receiver slick in his hand, Evans watched the flickering screen. 'Searching,' it announced. Then, 'Philippa Elliot, aged nine' and an address. After what seemed hours, a discreet beep and a terse 'Search ends'.

'I'll get over to Records,' said Beddoes, studying his watch and twitching with impatience. 'Be at the house when she gets home from school.'

You could see Wilson waver, caught between habitual caution and the impetus of the paperchase.

'Let him go, sir,' urged Evans. 'There's not many girls'll refuse him.'

Wilson nodded reluctantly. 'Very well, sergeant, I suppose you've earned it. In the interests of elimination, of course; don't jump to conclusions.' And to Evans, severely, 'The least *you* can do is alert the parents.'

'Oh sure,' agreed Evans, dialling again. 'It was them who reported it, though.'

By which time, Beddoes was long away.

Truce, in the dying of the day. A day which had seen, for the first time, co-ordinated effort towards a single common end. Perhaps, after all, the Super had a point. Courtesy of hi-tech, they'd condensed a week of legwork into a few short hours; the shape of cases to come. No wonder Wilson looked content – he had the right, fair play.

Or did he? The illusion of camaraderie faded in the light of cold harsh facts. For weeks, while Harry courted disaster and Wilson wooed the media, Records had held the answer: we only needed to ask the right questions. In the end, it had taken wanton slaughter and the threat of a replacement to start the engines rolling. Amazing what mayhem and the shadow of McKay could achieve.

He must have voiced the last thought aloud. Wilson was watching him sourly, his face haggard in the gloom.

'You never forget, do you?'

'Not if I can help it, sir.'

Your actual custom-built semi; personalised frontage, leaded glass, and furnishings straight out of *House and Garden*. Pippa Elliot was pert and precocious and a good deal more self-possessed than her parents, who hovered nervously near by. Tossing her pigtailed head, the child demanded, 'Are you a *real* detective?'

'Of course. Want to see my card?'

She assessed him carefully, the bold and blue-eyed candour of youth. 'You're not as handsome as Dempsey,' she decided, naming a current TV idol. 'And American cops have *badges*. Are you good with a gun?'

'The best,' he admitted shamelessly. 'I never miss, prone or standing.'

Mrs Elliot caught his eye and blushed furiously; not as prim as she looked, then. But persistent Pippa had no time for adult innuendo.

'What about unarmed combat?'

Ignoring her father's disapproving glare, Beddoes let her examine the business edges of his hands. 'There you are. Got any firewood 'ere wants choppin'?'

'Gosh,' she breathed, suddenly respectful, 'that *is* tough!'

His credentials established, Beddoes launched his patter. A funny old business; vaudeville in an architect's lounge, sepia hunting prints and the wintry skyline for a backdrop, and an audience of three.

'We're going to play Let's Remember,' he began. 'It's a Sunday, end of summer, and you've been for the paper, right?'

'The *Telegraph*,' she said at once, nodding briskly. 'It was very heavy.'

'Good. On the way back, you stopped for a swing.'

She turned imploringly to her mother. 'I *said* I was sorry!'

'It's all right, darling.'

'Course it is,' agreed Beddoes comfortably. 'That's what Sundays are for. Carry on from there, then.'

Her lovely eyes narrowed suspiciously. 'You already know!'

'Only on paper. It's not the same. Come *on*, Pippa.'

'A man came to watch,' she said. She lifted a hand to her mouth and gave him an arch glance. 'I was showing off. I'm *much* more grown up now.'

'I'll say,' he murmured, and shipped a dirty look from her mother.

'I dropped the change. I had to crawl around for the pennies.' Briefly she'd transported them from December to

August. A childish bottom innocently displayed in the sunshine, and the avid man, watching.

'What did he look like, Pippa?'

She repeated the description casually, almost word for word. Then, mischievously, 'He looked like the baddies on telly. Daddy calls them dagos.'

'Pippa, *really*!' her mother admonished, while the architect writhed in embarrassment, his gaze rooted to the Chinese carpet underfoot.

Beddoes moved on quickly before she lost the thread. 'A new game, now,' he announced, shuffling the photos like playing cards. 'Spot the Dago.'

Pippa hugged herself in delight. 'Oh *goody*! An identification parade.' She preened like a duchess, proud of the big words; then studied the pictures importantly. And unsuccessfully. All too soon, her voice flat and disappointed, she asked, 'Haven't you got any more?'

'That's enough,' said her father. 'I won't have her pressured like this!'

She turned on him, the crocodile tears swimming in her great blue eyes. 'Daddy, don't be mean, it's a *super* game!'

Not much doubt about who ruled this household, and Beddoes took full advantage. 'Run 'em through once more, should we?'

And this time, after a few moments, the pleasure on her small upturned face lightened the drab afternoon. '*Here* he is! Daddy, it's really him!'

Beddoes took the picture from her, conscious of Wilson's warning and keeping his own excitement under iron control. 'You're sure, now, are you?'

'His face is whiter,' she explained, 'and his hair looks different. But it's him all right.' And, sensing his lingering doubt, she added fiercely, 'He gave me toffee eclairs and made the birds stop singing. I'll *never* forget him.'

He glanced at the photograph. Prison pallor and a basin haircut; enough to put anyone off. Chummy, my son, thy days are numbered.

As he rose to leave, grimly satisfied, Pippa asked breathlessly, 'Did I have a narrow escape? Is he really *bad*?'

Moved by her fragile purity, aware of bated parental breath, he gave them his Kojak impression: 'Why should you care, baby? Somebody loves ya.'

'Golly,' she breathed admiringly. 'You're not going to *shoot* him, are you?'

'What, and put poor old Dempsey on the dole?' he said, and bowed out, to relieved laughter.

Back in Wilson's eyrie, having done some fast homework on the way, he tossed the photograph on to the desk and made the most of his big moment.

'He's thirty; five eleven and fourteen stone in his socks. Son of a naturalised Greek and a renegade Romanian nurse. Done for indecent assault on a minor, six months suspended. A while back, that was; no recent form.'

Wilson was watching him narrowly, upright and severe at the desk. Standing at ease near the window, Evans seemed to be contemplating the featureless night sky outside. Undivided attention, all the same. You could feel it, despite a certain coolness in the atmosphere.

'Gentlemen,' continued Beddoes, with a showman's flourish, 'I give you Stavros Pavilides, assistant chef; formerly known to you as Chummy.'

'Pippa said that, did she?' Evans might have been asking the time.

'Stone blind certain, uncle. He silences birds, she says.'

'A nine-year-old,' observed Wilson scathingly, 'is hardly the most reliable source.'

'She's ten,' Beddoes retorted, 'and smart as a whip.'

'Come, sergeant, you surely don't propose to put her on the stand?'

Gotta catch *him* first, thought Beddoes; aloud, he said, 'We've got the record, the location, the description, and a witness. What more d'you want?'

'Corroboration, boyo, that's what. It's there, too, staring you in the eye, if only you'd stop bickering and look.' Evans hadn't moved a muscle. His face, reflected from the darkened plate glass, seemed mild and utterly at peace.

Beddoes, who'd seen him like this before, said nothing; but

Wilson extended a heavily sarcastic challenge. 'Perhaps, inspector, you'd be good enough to enlighten those of us who lack your gift of second sight.'

Evans shifted momentarily, a single, almost pitying over-the-shoulder glance for his handsome superior. Hullo, Beddoes thought, ole Huw's about to lower the boom.

'Butty of mine, back home,' Evans began reflectively, addressing no one in particular, 'used to love cooking. Pansy, the dull ones called him.' He grinned at the absurdity. 'Played front row for Newport, after; some pansy.'

'Fascinating,' snapped Wilson, fingering his moustache, 'but this is scarcely the time and place for sporting reminiscence.'

'Took a course in catering,' Evans continued, quite un-ruffled, 'and came up to the Smoke. We'd have a pint together, sometimes. Just one, mind. An early riser, he was. Assistant chef, see.'

'For heaven's sake,' snarled Wilson, and Evans swung to face him with a wolfish grin.

'Smithfield, he used to go, long before the dawn. Choosing carcases and humping them to the van. That's where he got the brawn, they say in Newport; for the rugby, I mean.' He was ignoring the Superintendent now, looking straight at Beddoes, his eyes alight with triumph. 'Know what he did with the meat, Roy, when he got back to the hotel?'

'Jesus,' whispered Beddoes, seeing the light at last. 'He butchered it!'

'He's boarded a 53A,' said a disembodied voice, weakened by distance and distorted by static. 'Should be with you in fifteen minutes.'

'What did I tell you, uncle?' crowed Beddoes, a dim outline huddled over the steering wheel. ''E's in the bag!'

Eight-twenty on a wet winter evening. Pavilides, just off duty, was heading for home. They'd parked opposite his seedy basement flat an hour ago. The air inside the car reeked of tension and the staleness of confined bodies.

In the wake of Evans' revelation, Wilson's doubts had subsided. Time was of the essence, he'd conceded, and deployed the men they needed. Leaving, his former arrogance fully restored, he'd even managed a vestige of dry humour.

'I expect to confront our bloodthirsty friend first thing tomorrow.' He smiled tightly at Beddoes. 'In mint condition, if you please; unperforated.'

Across the way, the single street light cast a weak and fitful glow; thin oily rain drifted through it like tracer. Out of sight round the back, a vanload of uniforms stood by, ready to seal off the noisome alleyway. A nice neighbourhood and a nice night. Waiting for Chummy, duw, duw.

'What if he cuts loose?' Evans had demanded. 'Taken by wanderlust halfway home?'

'No way,' retorted Beddoes, utterly confident. 'I got a guy at point, two to shadow, and the mobile crew on instant call. Besides, he's a small-hours man.'

Meanwhile, they sat here, poised to plug the trap the moment he set foot inside. Neat, fair play, as near to foolproof as you could expect, on stake-out. Functioning again, Beddoes, the ultimate pavement artist. Knew the streets like the back of his hand. So far, he'd manoeuvred his surveillance like a chess master, predicting Chummy's movements to the second.

Even so, Evans fretted, his mind brimming with scarlet images of what Chummy could achieve, given a patch of darkness and a few minutes' hacking time. He fidgeted, conscious of the crackle of the radio and Beddoes' barely concealed fury.

A couple passed, arguing blearily beneath an unseasonable pink umbrella. Up ahead, a mongrel slunk across the road, tail and ears bedraggled and dripping. Then, for an age, nothing stirred. The mean and rainswept street might have been the last place on earth.

'He's off the bus, sir,' reported a new voice, much clearer and louder. 'Heading your way.'

'Roger, Shadow Two,' murmured Beddoes. 'Keep him in sight, over.' He swatted condensation and stared intently at the wing mirror. ''Ere 'e comes, spot on schedule.'

Evans had half turned, easing an arm round the seat and

squinting out of the bespattered rear window. 'Black as sin, mind, and still a furlong away. You're guessing.'

'The peeper's walk, uncle. Know it a mile off.'

'Delivery,' announced the intercom. 'He's all yours, sarge.'

'Cheers, Briggsy,' replied Beddoes, his microphone discipline forgotten in the heat of the moment. 'Pull right back, don't scare the game.' He was already gripping the door handle, his slim body coiled like a spring.

'Easy,' warned Evans. 'Let him get feet under the table.'

'Just testin', OK.' Then, 'Jesus, what the hell's goin' on?'

The surge of an approaching engine. Headlamps blazed into their faces and then, abruptly, went out. Peering through the windscreen, his night vision ravaged, Evans made out white paintwork and the familiar blue light. Police. Stunned, he watched two uniforms get out and amble unhurriedly to the basement doorway. They hunched there like giant bats, their oilskins wide and slick and sinister.

'Bastards,' snarled Beddoes, in outrage. 'They're from bleeding Central!'

Evans twisted in his seat, fearful of their quarry's reaction. In a moment of improbable clarity, Chummy stood trapped and spotlit; square and bulky and only one lamp post away. His head came forward, questing and suspicious, the quivering point of the keyed-up gundog. The rap of the knocker rang sharp and distinct; official, anyone could tell. Instantly, he whirled and was gone, a big silent shadow fleeing in the rain.

And Beddoes with him. The driver's door hung open, the courtesy light shining on vacated leather already smeared with wet. Evans had the wit to seize the dangling hand mike and sound a breathless alarm. 'He's heading back, Briggs. Hold him, for Christ's sake!' Then he, too, was out and running, the drizzle driving straight into his eyes.

Hopeless, from the start; a blind sprint over an unfamiliar course, stumbling on uneven pavements and swerving round abandoned dustbins. At the first corner, a huddled sprawl, down and doubled and groaning like a sick cow. Briggs, probably. No time to check. Up ahead, Beddoes's coat tails trailed and fluttered under harder orange light. He was flagging, though, and Evans overhauled him quite quickly.

'Which way, boyo?'

Beddoes staggered to a halt, canted forward at the waist, his face wet and contorted, his mouth stretched with the effort of breathing. 'Search me, uncle, I'm knackered.' And wild with it, the kind of vacant rage he'd shown whilst manhandling Mortimer.

'You'd best look out for your oppo,' Evans advised. 'I'll have words with the competition.'

He trudged through the rain, brooding on failure, the prospect of carnage to come, and the mystery of Central's intervention.

'Routine,' said the talkative one, lowering his window a crack and eyeing Evans guardedly. 'Pilfering at the hotel, cutlery and stuff. We're checking on staff, see.' He nodded at the darkened flat. 'His turn tonight, but he's out.' His gaze flickered, a hint of contained mockery. 'You're soaked, inspector. You ought to come in from the wet.' His mate sniggered, and he stabbed a gloved finger at Evans' car.

'Interrupted something, did we?'

'Bugger off, I would,' Evans told him, 'before Sergeant Beddoes gets back. Tamping mad, he is.'

'The judo man?' asked the driver, starting the engine. 'Right then. See you around.' And left hurriedly, in a hiss of waterlogged tyres and a small rainbow of spray.

Moments later, Beddoes delivered a shaken but undamaged surveillance man.

'Never saw him coming, guv. Went right over me, didn't he, like a bleeding train!'

'Wait in the car,' Beddoes ordered. 'Keep an eye on the road.' And strode purposefully across the rain-slick tarmac.

There was a splintering crash, a yawning hole where the door had been, and a single glistening footprint to mask his inward passage.

'A bit dodgy, sir,' Briggs mumbled, as light seeped up from the basement. 'Without a warrant, I mean.'

'Nasty bump, you had,' Evans consoled him. 'You're not seeing too clear, right? Call Warner, now. The bird's flown, put out a general alert. And never mind the *warrant*!'

Leaving the crackle of static behind, Evans made his own

illegal entry, picking his way down the mouldering stairway through a waft of mildewed air. Prepared for anything, he was; anything except the clinical tidiness of what should have been the living-room. He paused in the doorway, taking impressions and watching Beddoes prowl.

It was much too bright, for a start. White emulsion, pale grey tiles, and four big fluorescent tubes which threw everything into stark relief.

'Working light,' breathed Beddoes, reading his mind. 'All the better to slice you by, my dear.'

'You're guessing, Roy. Don't force it.'

'Oh yeah? Have a gander up here, then.'

Beddoes was pointing at one of the anatomical charts which hung from the walls. Old-fashioned, it was, technicolor muscles and no sex organs. As he sidled forwards, Evans' hackles lifted to a faint, familiar scent – the sinister essence of disinfectant and decay. Leaning closer, following Beddoes' finger, he made out the tell-tale grey lines. Ruled in fine pencil, they angled across the shoulders, the elbows, the wrists; across *every* major joint.

'Could be coincidence, mind: bought 'em from a medical student.'

'Jesus, uncle, you're hard to convince!' But Beddoes' dark eyes glittered with discovery and rage. Turning, he eased the drawer out of the table and planted it on the scrubbed marble top. 'How about *that* little lot?'

They lay in their varnished pinewood beds, honed and curved and deadly; a set of butchers' knives. The wink of vicious steel was bad enough. Worse, far worse, was the vacant outline at the far end of the row. Suppressing a shudder, Evans pictured the weapon that would nestle snugly into it; a stub-handled, broad-bladed cleaver. 'You made your point; get your skates on!'

'Leave it out, you'll never catch him tonight.'

Evans nodded, weary and appalled. 'Course not. We can get back to the nick, though. Make sure Warner's beatmen bottle him up.'

Back in the car, the enclosed space smelled of wet clothing and failure. Beddoes drove with controlled fury, and Briggs huddled on the rear seat, nursing tender ribs and injured pride.

'Guess what?' asked Beddoes presently. 'Chummy's a thief, too. Arcade Hotel, it said on those handles.'

'I know. A little bird from Central told me.' Evans squinted against the diffused glare of oncoming headlights. 'On the run, see, armed and twice as dangerous.'

'Lock up your daughters,' growled Briggs, 'if they'll let you.'

Beddoes spoke slyly, for Evans' ears alone. 'Think I'll pop round to Sara's place. Offer a bit of comfort and security.'

Still putting the bird first, even in this extremity; dull young bugger.

Later, from behind his desk, Warner prescribed tea and bedrest for Briggs, a knowing grin and an early release for Beddoes; and a welcome dose of common sense for overtaxed inspectors.

'Look, Huw, we've doubled the foot patrols in the park. We're watching his pad and the hotel, and it's raining cats and dogs. For once, young Roy's got it right. Secure known targets and let Chummy make the next move.'

'It's the *unknown* targets that worry me.'

Warner shook his head, waving his hand at the dim, quiet corridors. 'We also serve, mate, who only sit and wait. Get your head down; no way you can be responsible for all of them.'

And though he eventually took this advice, Evans slept badly; dreams of oozing blood and riven corpses, and the hysterical tones of tomorrow's headlines.

CHAPTER TWENTY

'THEY'RE FITTING you up, Huw,' cautioned Warner, loitering with intent in the frost-bound car park early next morning. Off-duty, mind, but muffled and furtive as the KGB. 'Media's bin 'ere since sparrers; got wind of the cock-up last night.' Evans winced, and he added hastily, 'Their words, not mine.'

'They're right,' grunted Evans shortly, and Warner puffed steam in sympathy. 'Wilson saw 'em off,' he continued approvingly. 'Half an hour's talk and told 'em nothing. Didn't fancy it, though. You could watch him simmer.' Rime crunched under his boots as he edged closer. 'Next thing, McKay's on the hot line, rabbiting for hours. Mark my words; 'e wants you out.'

Raising his voice above the passing rumble of a red double-decker, Evans snapped, 'Don't be daft, mun, it's *our* case!'

Alarmed, Warner lifted a blue-veined finger to his lips, glancing uneasily round the frigid and deserted tarmac. 'Do us a favour, keep it down; you 'aven't 'eard the worst.' His eyes were wide and apprehensive, and Evans braced for Chummy's latest atrocity. 'Central found the Brown bird. Well, 'alf of her, anyway. Floating down the docks; like a zeppelin, they say. McKay's claiming jurisdiction, see.' He grinned slyly, unable even in this extremity to resist a ghoulish pun. 'Wants a slice of the action.'

'Oh, aye,' snarled Evans, somewhat relieved but wholly unamused. 'We'll see about that!'

Warner cowered, mournful as a house dog unjustly rebuked. ''Ere, steady! Only the messenger, me.'

Shamed, Evans touched his bony shoulder briefly and offered amends.

'Nod's as good as a wink, Jack. Thanks; I appreciate it.' And the desk man hobbled away, perished but much pleased, to his delayed and well-earned rest.

Thus forearmed, Evans entered the operational post-mortem determined to seize the initiative; the best form of defence. As it happened, Beddoes had beaten him to the punch.

'They were off-limits,' he declared, occupying centre stage in the big office and parading his indignation past Wilson's nose. 'They had no right!'

Showing the strain, Wilson was; red-eyed, unshaven, and a bit ragged at the edges. He regarded Beddoes coldly, the closeness of yesterday quite forgotten. 'Spare me the excuses, sergeant. You took unwarranted risks. Why not pick him up at the hotel?'

'Home ground, mind,' Evans pointed out, meandering to the window, 'and the odd cleaver lying about. Hate the sight of blood, I do. 'Specially mine.'

But Wilson, unmoved by banter, had Beddoes squarely in his sights. Ignoring the interruption, tapping the desk for emphasis, he went on, 'McKay's people were pursuing a legitimate lead, unaware of your so-called plans. An unfortunate coincidence, no more. Speaking of rights, sergeant, you have none here; I'll thank you to keep a civil tongue.'

'A bit harsh, sir,' Evans objected, noting the change of subject and mindful of Warner's misgiving. 'Seeing as you invited him. Look, it's the timing that bothers me; they barged in at the critical moment. Coincidence, you say. There's some would call it sabotage.'

In the sudden silence, he heard the jangle of a distant telephone and Wilson's harsh intake of breath.

'Just what are you implying, inspector?'

A boat in the river caught Evans' attention; muscling into the current and cutting a creamy bow wave across the icy-grey waters. Another uphill struggle. 'Could be gossip,' he began, 'only I heard there's been a lot of chat with Central. Top level, not for general consumption. Well, after last night, you have to wonder.'

He turned to face them, conscious of Beddoes' speculative stare and Wilson's unhealthy pallor: he took it for anger, but the Superintendent's initial response seemed pretty restrained, considering.

'McKay and I have certain – arrangements – to discuss. They do not include current cases. As long as I'm in command here, this manor will be run as I see fit.'

Clever stuff, thought Evans, in grudging admiration. Clearly, Beddoes had detected no hint of the impending replacement; and Warner's charge had been brushed aside.

Gathering force and volume, Wilson continued, 'You had your chance, and wasted it. Now we'll do it my way: publicly. Photographs and descriptions are being printed and distributed in time for the evening editions. By nightfall, friend Pavilides will find precious few places to hide.' He smiled, thin and triumphant. 'I shall also make a brief televised appeal.'

'Jesus,' muttered Beddoes, his voice laden with despair. 'Panic on the streets and the switchboard blowing fuses!'

Whereas Evans was actually grinning at this, the ultimate irony; Wilson the image on camera, looking like an unmade bed.

'Perhaps you'd care to share your amusement, inspector.'

'Better shave first, sir. Right now, you'd pass for Tricky Nixon; and we all know what happened to him!'

'My God, you two take chances!' Wilson came to his feet, eyes blazing, nostrils flaring, lips white with fury. Central had leaked the story. 'I've spent half the morning keeping your fiasco hidden from the press, and what do I get? Insinuations of everything from incompetence to conspiracy; non-compliance with direct instructions, and finally, a witless, tasteless *joke*!' He whirled on Evans, thrusting out a stiff, trembling hand. 'You! Get away from that window! When I speak, you *look* at me!' Tiny droplets of saliva sprayed out with the force of his delivery; briefly he seemed on the verge of total apoplexy. As Evans obeyed, astonished, he achieved some measure of control. Holding himself upright and rigid, bringing his voice to an almost normal level, he said, 'In future, you will observe your rightful positions; as *subordinates*. If either of

219

you so much as queries an order, I'll have him back on the beat so fast his feet won't touch the ground. Now, go and do as you're damn well told!'

For a while, the basement echoed to the stutter of Beddoes's typewriter and the gurgles of the aged radiator. Evans stared glumly at the blank sheet in his own machine. Nothing to say, really; with Chummy still loose, Wilson couldn't be challenged. He would leave any minute, his strategy vindicated, his authority intact. Which meant, in effect, surrendering the case to McKay, and a return to the salt mines of petty crime. *With Chummy still loose.* In spite of the fug, Evans shivered; remembering an even grimmer basement, and a row of glittering blades.

'What's up, uncle?' asked Beddoes, apparently recovered. 'Looking a bit peaky.'

'Edgy, I am. Frightened, you might say.'

Beddoes paused, the white-out brush hovering mid-correction. 'You, scared? Leave it out!'

'Funny thing about murderers,' mused Evans. 'There's always a reason, see. Money, sex, or just the heat of the moment. Sometimes you end up feeling grateful, understanding what moved them. There but for the grace ...' He hesitated, studying the mouldy wall, getting his thoughts in order. 'Weakness, it is. Can't resist the impulse, like the rest of us.' He looked up into Beddoes's dark and quizzical gaze. 'How often have *you* said it, I wonder; next time he does that, I'll kill him?'

'Often enough.' Beddoes was suddenly bowed and busy; embarrassed, maybe.

'This one's different,' said Evans, stating a grim fact. 'A raw urge, naked steel, and the strength of ten. You haven't seen what he can do ... I can't find his weakness, there aren't any reasons. Unpredictable, then, and lucky with it. That's why I'm scared, boyo; *I don't know how to stop him.*'

Beddoes was shuffling paper between his palms, aligning the edges of his report. 'Don't worry, mate, you heard 'is nibs. Down to Joe Public, now.'

'Oh, sure! The worm turns, Chummy gets religion, and we all live happy ever after. Joe Public? He'll knock 'em over like ninepins!'

Beddoes shrugged, indifferent. ''E's bound to lay low, till the heat's off, anyhow. Meanwhile, I got unfinished business.' He winked, knowing and familiar. 'An ill wind, 'im being loose. An excuse to hold Sara's hand, tonight.'

Duw, Evans thought, the confidence of youth; I hope to God you're right.

For a while it seemed he might be. Time passed without further alarms, and Evans breathed easier, immersed in the drudgery of his own overdue paperwork.

The call came at exactly 12.16; Evans noted the time as a matter of rote.

Beddoes took it, his usual laid-back style. 'CID 'ere; speak.' He listened wide-eyed, his body stiffening to military attention. More officiousness, no doubt; Wilson alone could invoke such respect.

Evans laboured on, ignoring Beddoes' sparse and breathless responses. He finished a paragraph and glanced up, aware of an abrupt and quivering silence. Beddoes sat like a waxen image, the telephone held at arm's length. Catching Evans' eye, he set the receiver down gingerly, as if it might explode on impact.

'That was Chummy,' he muttered, 'and you're right. He's bonkers; clean round the bleeding twist.' His voice rose, awed and incredulous. 'Only wants fifty grand, a fuelled-up Jumbo, and a police escort to Heathrow.'

'Checking out, is he?' Evans grinned. 'From the Ritz, I presume.'

'Funnily enough,' said Beddoes, without a trace of humour, 'he didn't divulge his whereabouts.' He was the colour of putty, and a muscle twitched at the hinge of his jaw. Going a bit far, mind, for a laugh. 'Meeting's set for dockland at six, in a derelict warehouse. Know it well, I do; a bleeding warren. Fancies the ride in a squad car, 'e says, and the readies in dirty oncers.'

'Ransom, is it?' Evans enquired, determined to play along. 'What's he selling, the Crown Jewels?'

221

Beddoes raised a hand and passed it wearily across his eyes. 'No such luck, uncle. 'E's got Sara.'

Stunned, his mind reeling with the implications, Evans mumbled, 'How the hell did he manage that?'

'Never mind *how*. He did!' Beddoes stabbed an unsteady finger at the silent phone. 'A real toff, Chummy; allowed us a private word. Remember Delilah, she said, and please do as he asks.' He shuddered, his face contorted with pain. 'Improving, she was, yesterday: never 'eard anyone say *please* like that before.' He was stowing papers, clearing his desk. 'She 'ad a winner, down the dogs. Delilah, fifteen to one. Wonder where 'is nibs'll find fifty grand?'

'Talk sense, Roy. You don't bargain with nutters!'

''Oo doesn't?' He was on his feet, pale and purposeful and heading for the door. 'Speak for yourself, mate!'

He had to be stopped; nothing to gain and lives at stake. Time for some home truths, then.

'Wilson'll put her name in lights, mind. Papers, TV, the whole bloody circus. Fancy it, would she, instant celebrity?' And, as Beddoes wavered, he drew in the bottom line. 'Don't hold your breath for the money; there isn't any. Sit down, Roy. You're *persona non grata*, upstairs.'

Bereft and ashen in the doorway, Beddoes extended both hands in clawed and terrible supplication. 'I've 'ad a gutsful of this place. For Christ's sake, let's get some air!'

'Anything you say,' agreed Evans, following him out and leaving pages scattered all over the desk.

Lover's Leap; every greenbelt has one. Trusting to instinct, Evans had driven straight here. In summer, the place would be thick with foliage and discarded contraceptives. Today, the trees stood stark and desolate, and the rising breeze smelled of winter and emptiness.

They trooped, single file, up a treacherous footpath, ice and dead leaves crackling underfoot. There was a bench at the crest, its weathered timbers heavily scarred; hearts, flowers, and obscene graffiti. In mutual and unspoken accord, they squatted at either end, overlooking the frozen park. Not exactly the mountain Evans would've liked,

222

but high and quiet and as private as you could hope to get.

Since leaving the office, they had exchanged neither word nor glance. God alone knew what Beddoes was thinking, but Evans's brain had been going full tilt. Softly, looking straight ahead, he made his proposition.

'He'll break cover before the pick-up, to suss things out and watch us grovel. All we have to do is beat him to it. Soon as it's dark, we find a bolthole and wait. You and me, I mean.'

Huddled like a tortoise in his bulky trenchcoat, Beddoes gazed vacantly at a toff on horseback, far below.

'No risks, this time,' Evans continued. 'Saturation coverage and marksmen standing by.'

'My,' muttered Beddoes, in mock admiration. 'Shooters, yet. Didn't know you cared.'

Evans let it pass, making allowances. 'We're talking ambush, mind. Up to it, are you?'

Beddoes faced him squarely, hot-eyed and lustful. 'Just try me, uncle. If 'is nibs'll let you, that is.'

Evans shifted his weight on the harsh, unyielding wood. 'An anonymous tip, we'll call it. Wilson'll love it; proves his point. Chummy's holed up in dockland, exact location given. A straightforward raid, then; no complications.'

The toff had spurred his mount to a gallop. The hoofbeats reached them clearly, but delayed. 'Frigging cowboys,' said Beddoes, apparently dismissing both the horseman and the plan.

'What the Brass don't know won't hurt them,' Evans pointed out. 'There's only us witting: about Sara.'

Beddoes hauled his collar up, his eyes as bitter as the wind. 'Good of you to remember 'er. She'll be thrilled.'

Evans got up and took a turn around the bench, trying to tramp some feeling into his feet. Down there, Chummy had acted out his ghastly rituals. Not all of his victims, though, were female and dead.

'They sent me to a lecture, once,' he mused. 'An Israeli hardknock posing as a cop. "There's no such thing as hostages," he reckoned. "Only terrorists and innocents. We deal with terrorists; the innocent we trust to God."'

'Terrific,' snarled Beddoes, viciously guying the Valleys

singsong. 'Medals for the lads, see, and Sara in the bosom of the Lord. Quote me no Yiddish psychopaths, mate. That's my bird out there!'

Admitting it at last, then, at the worst possible moment. A killer trapped in the dark, not only crazed but desperate. A time for cool heads, steady hands, and no personal involvement whatsoever.

'Take you off it, shall I?' asked Evans, not unkindly. 'You don't send a surgeon to operate on kin.'

Beddoes came to his feet, his body arced and beseeching. 'Jesus, Huw, you can't!'

'I've shown you the choice, boyo. Make it.'

He turned and stumbled like a sleepwalker to the exposed and vacant hilltop. For minutes, he stood silent and motionless, his hair ruffled, his coat flapping against his legs. It was, Evans realised, precisely the test Wilson had faced and failed. As a copper, anyhow. The simplest, cruellest choice of all: which comes first, love or duty?

He'd made it himself, long ago. Sometimes, in an empty flat and a solitary bed, he still paid the price. Ponder it well, bach, up there on your lonely Golgotha. No one'll blame you for staying home tonight.

Presently he turned and trudged back. The damp tracks on his cheeks might have been caused by the stinging wind.

'All right, I'm in. She's probably dead, anyhow.'

'Aye, didn't like to say it, myself.' Evans hesitated, studying him carefully. He looked older, somehow; mature. Not surprising really. 'No vendettas, mind. Remember what happened to Harry. I want you cold, Roy.'

'Uncle,' said Beddoes heavily, 'I've never bin colder in my life.'

Wrong again; night and the Arctic had arrived together. Cowering in the lee of the warehouse, Beddoes reckoned you could hear the chatter of teeth a mile off. Evans, bulky and shadowed at his side, was flexing gloved fingers to make sure they were still there.

A war of attrition, this afternoon, waged against official and civvy alike. At first, Wilson had parried their combined assault, wondering caustically if they could be trusted out after dark. Patiently, Evans wore him down, stressing the urgency and painting Chummy's unlovely portrait in flowing crimson. Then he made an obscure reference to timing and reputation; and the Super's resistance crumbled.

'Oh very well, have your childish game! This time, when he runs, he'll have half the city baying at his heels.'

Odd, the sudden capitulation, especially after his outburst this morning. Have to get ole Huw pissed one night and ask how he'd swung it.

Later, they pored over site plans. Beddoes had scrounged them, ironically enough, from a deaf and elderly Jew.

'Dummies yet; you think we're all tailors? What are you, m'boy, a racist? Fine groceries, I dealt in, till the Pakis ruined business. Cheap, the people want; so cheap they deserve. Quality, pah, who affords?' Beddoes explained, and he wagged his tasseled head in sorrow. 'A criminal? So take the papers, go with a blessing. Clear the streets for law-abiding citizens, already.'

The tatty yellowed drawings proved a Godsend; archaic blueprints for a modern campaign. Chummy, they reasoned, would wait on an upper storey overlooking the pick-up point: an exposed concrete apron to the rear of the building. Nice touch: from above, even at night, uniforms would be as conspicuous as moles in snow. Meanwhile, Chummy had a choice of exits: the original foyer, a loading bay halfway along the ground floor, and the fire escape down to the apron itself.

'That's it, then, boyo,' Evans declared, marking the spot with a blunt forefinger and raising a puff of mildewed dust. 'Sooner or later he'll end up here.'

'Under the ladder,' said Beddoes. 'Unlucky.'

'Unlucky for some.'

They'd come in on their bellies at twilight, worming like commandos through weeds and garbage to the cover of the western wall. Evans wasn't built for stealth; language to make a deacon blush. Since then, it had been a long cold wait, fraught with discomfort and doubt.

Chummy was bonkers, all right; bloodlust and delusions of

grandeur. Not exactly stupid, though, and, like Evans said, lucky. What if this was a cunning decoy: the nick and his brother pulled in here, and no one patrolling the park? Forget it, my son; doesn't bear thinking about.

An image of Sara rose, unbidden, in his mind: flushed and golden and shining with pleasure. 'Oh Roy, I never knew it could be this much fun.' And never will be again. He swallowed hard, grieving in the darkness, remembering Evans' final command. 'No chop suey tonight, mind. I want him alive.' Yeah, me too, thought Beddoes; long enough to say where she is. *And in how many pieces*. He shivered, not from the cold.

'Hear it, do you?' breathed Evans, and he shook his head. Felt it, though; a small tremor through the frame that wedged against his shoulder; a cautious footfall, high overhead. He craned out and peered upwards, the wind clawing his face and blurring his vision. Another stealthy movement, and a frozen metallic creak. No doubting it; someone was coming down. Dimly, in a sliver of icy moon, he made out a blocky figure two landings above.

Light flared and he ducked in, dazzled.

'Hold still!' Evans ordered, hoarse and hot in his ear. 'No way he can spot us.' And the oval pool moved away, sparkling and spreading on the empty, frosted apron; then shrinking again, as Chummy continued his wary descent.

Stillness, abrupt and complete; only the sigh of the wind and the restless shift of the beam. The voice came loud and shocking, the stilted tones of discovery exposing a fatal flaw in their plans.

'Step out, please. You are beneath the staircase. Of course, I cannot see; but your breath shines like smoke.'

'Do it,' hissed Evans, 'but opposite sides, see. One torch, he's got; can't cover the both of us.'

A fleeting instant to envy the presence of mind, and Beddoes was sprinting clear, conscious of Evans's grunt of effort as he broke the other way.

Brilliance pinned Evans in mid-stride, his pale face upturned and blinded. The cold a memory, Beddoes used the precious half-second to widen the gap.

'Be still!' ordered the voice, lifted sharply in rage and panic. 'Stop, or I throw her down!'

Beddoes halted, the wildest of hopes rising in his breast. *Sara?*

Suddenly, the beam lurched upwards, probing high and wild into the freezing night. From above came the noise of scuffles, the thump of bone on flesh, and an unmistakably female gasp of pain.

Evans called from the shadows, the Welsh strong and exultant, 'Hold on, girl, I'm coming!' His metal heels crashed on the iron stairway, ringing like gunshot and striking small bright sparks; the torch went out.

In a moment of freakish visual accommodation, Beddoes watched it happen; a stark and deadly ballet beneath the wintered moon. Silhouetted on the second landing, beast and beauty whirled and broke and merged again, as the third shadow climbed towards them. Briefly, the small figure seemed to rise and float, her slim white hands scrabbling at the safety rail. He heard her thin cry of surprise and fear; then she was falling, spread-eagled and headlong, towards the icy concrete twenty feet below ...

CHAPTER TWENTY-ONE

'DEAR BOY,' the scented media type had breathed, standing too close and blandly dropping the Commissioner's given name. 'Where on *earth* has foul Archie been hiding you? Such polish, such panache; I shall *insist* he makes you official spokesman!'

On the point of quitting foul Archie's command, Wilson had managed a modest smile and a hasty withdrawal; by which time the man was swigging rosé and damning the Fascist Fuzz. So much for show-biz hyperbole.

Dawdling homewards under a barrage of fairy lights, Wilson recognised the irony of his position. Extravagant as it was, the promise had struck a chord. If last night's gambit had succeeded, he, Richard Wilson, could rightfully have claimed a lion's share of the credit. His sticky start retrieved, he could retake control, silence the doubters, and settle to the task of enforcement.

He eased to a halt behind a coachload of unruly children and bent forward to adjust the heater. Looking up, he faced a rear window full of grinning urchins and grubby-fingered V-signs. He averted his eyes, forsook the illusion, and came to terms with reality.

Whatever happened tonight, the hunt for Pavilides would read like most history: a depressing catalogue of human error and opportunities lost. And if the raid should end in bloodshed – as well it might – the inevitable enquiry would advance the reputation of absolutely no one. *Wilson's First Case*, he mused wryly, setting the handbrake; or, *The Pitfalls of Policing*.

The traffic had come to a standstill; late-night shoppers, he presumed. Around him, in-car stereos issued treacly pop, and the reek of diesel rode the vicious wind. Typical, he thought; the Superintendent stranded and impotent while Evans prowls the frigid night and calls every tune. Admit it, Wilson – you're not cut out for the job.

Here on the streets, you needed a certain singleness of mind, the capacity to see things in black and white. If this meant invading privacy, defying orders, negotiating bargains, and riding roughshod over victim and colleague alike, then so be it. The end – the nicking of Chummy – justified any and every means. The creed according to Evans, and very effective, no doubt; but one to which Richard Wilson could never subscribe.

Cocooned in metal, alone in the crowd, he arrived at the heart of the problem. For him, the crucial question would always be *why*, not who. Let the Evanses of this world scheme and connive and bring the guilty to book. Only then could the real work begin. For unless someone, somewhere, discovered what made Chummy tick, there would always be shadows in the park and blood in the gutters.

He smiled involuntarily, at ease with himself for the first time in weeks. The experiment had failed; but sooner or later, the Force must come to terms with preventive diagnosis and the march of technology. Meanwhile, sadder but wiser, he would offer his talents where they would be appreciated, valued, and *used*.

The blare of a horn awoke him. Up ahead, the coach was rapidly dwindling. He waved an apologetic hand at the angry face in his rearview mirror and accelerated through the thinning column of sightseers. The lurid decorations petered out. He was nearing the suburbs; and the prospect of breaking the news to Gina.

Domestic relations remained delicate. Mortimer's name was never mentioned, but his phantom presence loomed over every discussion, poised to intrude and embarrass. Only in bed and darkness did Gina break free; as if proving something to them both, she offered a blazing sexuality reminiscent of their earliest courtship. He took this for amends, confirmation that whatever she'd sought from Harry, he himself could better provide.

Even so, his decision would raise a new issue. However she felt about policemen in general, Gina had always gloried in his steadily rising status. In her world, clearly, success was the only acceptable substitute for wealth. Or so he believed; and prepared his arguments accordingly.

He parked the car and hurried through the iron cold, sparing a thought for the men out on patrol, and bracing himself for Gina's expected outburst.

There were fresh carnations in the hall, deep red and subtly perfumed. She greeted him as from a long absence, a lingering embrace which left him flushed and breathless. She led him in, promising a *special* dinner.

'A new recipe from *Vogue*: I'm sure you'll *adore* it.'

She moved ahead, graceful and insinuating, the royal blue housecoat whispering invitation at every stride. His resolve faltered; he hated to sour her pleasures.

The meal *was* delicious – veal escalopes in a creamy sauce. Over the lemon soufflé, she boasted of a new-found prudence.

'I've been *so* clever, this month. The credit account's minute; only petrol, and some wine on special offer.' Her smile was eager and guileless, seeking his approval; but this was dangerous ground. He didn't care for reminders of the restraint he foisted on her, and her sweetness was beginning to cloy.

'Gina,' he said firmly, 'there's something we have to discuss; something important.'

'In a moment, dear. Just let me clear up.'

She floated in and out of the kitchen, and he prepared drinks. Presently she came and curled on the sofa, fair and exotic against the muted grain of the leather. 'Now: what's so important? What's making you such a *bear*?'

Tersely, he outlined his intention and his reasons. The intellectual ones, of course. The details of the Pavilides case would merely distress her, and reference to Harry must be avoided at all costs. She sat, composed and intent, the firelight glowing in her eyes and revealing a glimpse of smoothly rounded thigh. From time to time, she cast him little smiles of encouragement.

He finished somewhat lamely, confounded by her passivity.

She sipped her vermouth, eyeing him mischievously over the rim of the glass.

'Cheers, darling, I'm *so* pleased for you.'

'But,' he muttered dazedly, 'you seemed so keen on getting ahead. You know, promotion and all that.'

'Only for your sake.' She made one of her comic moues. 'You can't imagine I've *enjoyed* it, Richard; those awful, downtrodden little wives?'

'Never again, I promise. We'll be able to do things together.'

She clasped her hands in delight; there was no doubting her sincerity. 'How super! No more night duty, no more weekends in the office.' She paused, suddenly thoughtful, swirling the shrunken ice cubes in her empty glass. 'I was getting bored with the same old routine. Finance and agriculture are such *limited* topics. It'll be so nice to meet interesting people and hear some conversation, for a change.' As near as she would ever come to officially removing the Mortimers from her visiting list.

She managed this sort of thing so well, he thought, in a welcome resurgence of tenderness. Beneath the impulsive, frothy surface, she was a good deal shrewder and tougher than either of them usually acknowledged. She was grinning at him now, a lovely schoolgirl granted a favourite treat. A moment to savour, vindicating everything he'd been forced to do. No sacrifice was too great, simply to see her like this: joyful, absurdly young, and utterly irresistible.

He put his glass down and gave her a meaningful glance. 'I'm for an early night; coming?'

She stood and stretched voluptuously, arching her body against the flimsy material. '*What* a good idea!'

Later, in the aftermath of passion and on the very edge of sleep, he allowed himself to believe that the worst was past; and made his first completely unguarded statement. 'You know, this house is much too big for two.'

He felt the sudden tightening of her body, sensed her alarm in the musky dark. Then she was laughing, warm and throaty, running a playful hand across his belly. 'Don't rush me, Richard. We need a *lot* more practice!'

* * *

Evans saw her fall, her cropped hair glinting silver in the moon. Saw the dread of dying in her pale contorted face; heard the updraught crackle in the billows of her coat; actually felt the cleave of icy blackness before her wide and strangely languid plunge. He gazed down, sick and shaking, his jaw clenched for the devastation to come.

And watched Roy Beddoes step across her path; arms cradled, knees flexed, fearless as a full back under the high ball. Sheer lunacy, mind; greater love hath no man ... Impact, plump and meaty. The explosive whoomph of colliding bodies, a cry of pain fading and blending into the steady moan of the wind. They lay together, sprawled and indistinguishable, a single silent blemish on the concrete's pallid gleam.

In sudden stillness, Evans registered the quiver of metal underfoot, and Chummy's unimpeded upward sprint. Carry on, you, he thought, gazing bitterly at the careless stars; I'll be back when I've picked up the pieces. He moved heavily to the head of the landing, hunched against frost and disaster. And stood rooted by the sound of truly dedicated cursing.

'Roy?' he called in utter disbelief. '*All right*, are you?'

He couldn't fathom the windswept reply; something about her coat and a parachute. Then, clear and bitter and echoing with disgust, 'Ricked me sodding ankle! I'm grounded!'

'How about Sara?'

In the tense pause, Evans thought he heard sobs.

'Roughed up a bit, and the sky dive didn't help. She'll live, though. 'Ere, you going to stand there all day, nattering?'

'Not bloody likely!'

Evans whirled and started to climb. The gods were smiling; hustle, boyo, before they change their minds. He hadn't gone two steps when Beddoes spoke again, sharp and urgent in the icy air.

'Hang about, uncle. Take my shooter!' Dull young bugger, bent on war at night.

'Keep it,' he snapped. 'If I'm not back in twenty minutes, send for the cavalry.' And took the stairs two at a time, never mind the noise. Let Chummy feel hunted, for once.

On the top storey, exposure and prudence cooled his blood. The door hung ajar; inside, only darkness, silence and a nutter with a knife. His nerve faltered as the warnings rang in his mind. '*A feat of awesome strength.*' '*... straight over me, like a train.*' A killing breeze in his face, the scent of death in the air, a welter of guts at his feet. Briefly, he was back in the park, gazing in horror at the Mark of the Beast. He took a deep breath and went in anyway, clutching his fear like a talisman. When you're scared, you're careful.

He slid through the doorway, steeled for the lurking shadow and the hissing blade. No reaction, no sound save the pounding of his own heart. The air hung mild and lifeless, reeking of spices and rancid meat; like certain curry houses he could name. Slowly, his eyes accommodated, bringing a sense of space and distance. The faintest of glimmers, off to his left; a line of small high windows, cobwebbed and begrimed, letting in a vestige of moonlight. Just enough to accentuate the sinister corners, the patches of impenetrable darkness where a desperate man might wait; and strike.

Evans had been inching forward, placing his feet carefully on the gritty floor. He stopped abruptly, the small hairs rising on his nape. The sound came again, a fleeting rustle full of stealth and menace. In the heart of the gloom, at the very edge of vision, fiery pinpoints moved and flickered. A patter, a slither of scaly tails, and an outburst of furious squeaking.

Years ago, in the slums of dockland, Evans had seen a baby die of gangrene. Consigned to an attic while its mother humped all-comers, the child had attracted the savage attentions of the neighbourhood vermin. The wounds had been ignored and neglected. Late one night in a speeding ambulance, he had watched the young life wither away. The cries were unforgettable, the stench indescribable. He had had a profound hatred of rats ever since. Swallowing hard, cringing from the image of febrile fur and flat yellow teeth, he moved steadily on. What do you expect in a place like this; butterflies?

In the stomach, maybe. Through the next doorway, an identical room, the mixture as before. Like Beddoes said, a warren; what price the ferret who stumbles on a rabid wolf? The light hit him squarely, sudden and blood red. He reeled, blind and defenceless, seeking the shadows he had so recently shunned. Instantly, complete blackness enveloped him. True insanity, this, the kind that taunts before it destroys ... The glare came again, mocking his feeble efforts at concealment. And with it, the shuddering relief of understanding. The decorations, see, the flashing neon messengers of yuletide cheer. Chummy, rats, and a Merry Christmas to all our readers. Lovely. He shielded his eyes and studied his watch. Ten seconds on, half a minute off. Nice to know, mind; you could plan your moves in advance. Aye, and so could Chummy.

Yet another door, closed this time. Beyond it lay the heart of the building. The glow came faint and far behind, the only way out was onwards. And now he heard more distinct movement, a larger stirring very close at hand. He could actually *feel* the presence lurking behind the thin screen of mouldering wood: something coiled and taut and malevolent and as frightened as he himself. More than he expected, then; a warning.

He thrust forward, the adrenalin surging in his blood, his shoulders locked and quivering. A rending creak, a violent scrabble, a rising, maniacal howl. He braced himself, his eyes desperately seeking the unseen enemy, his arms raised to deflect the inevitable attack. Something brushed his shins and he leapt aside, suppressing an involuntary cry. Half turning, hopelessly off-balance, he watched his assailant weave and circle, hunched and hackled and threatening. And slink off, with a final baleful green-eyed glare and a lash of threadbare tail. And good hunting to *you*, Tom Cat.

In the next backlit intermission, he leaned against the wall, weak with semi-hysterical laughter. Evans the Enforcement, reduced to gibbering terror by an underfed moggy. Not funny, really. He was wringing with sweat, and his trousers chafed scratchily at the inside of his thighs. Leave him to the uniforms, boyo. In two minutes flat you could be outside, whole and healthy and drinking cold clean air.

Yet there remained a stubborn core within him which bridled at defeat. You have to haul him out, bach, see him in the aftermath of capture; just one more wrecked and hapless piece of sub-human flotsam. If you don't, he'll haunt you to the grave. The Monster of the Park, evil and all-powerful, who faced you down and saw you off and sent you crying for your mam.

So he quartered the last three rooms in intermittent orange brightness, walking soft and watching his back and fighting his phobia every inch of the way. In mortal dread, flinching at empty shadows and at each fresh scurry of ratsteps; but he did it. And came at last to the internal staircase which spiralled into the inky bowels of the building, where even neon nonsense couldn't reach.

There, Huw Evans' night of madness ended; not in fury and spilt blood, but rather in the belated dawn of reason. Quite simply, it was enough. He'd already been where no lone man should ever have to go. Gone and suffered and survived, for duty, with no one looking over his shoulder. Nothing left to prove, see; the trap was set. Now, he only had to walk out, slow and careful, and summon floodlights and reinforcements. Softly, leaning above the silent blackness, he called, 'It's over Chummy. See you in court.' And began his weary journey back into the cold.

Soon, he'd have to move. His ribs felt stoved in, his ankle hurt like hell, and cold was stealing upwards into the very marrow of his bones. He was shattered, frozen, and pining for action; the useless pistol raked at his left buttock, adding injury to insult. There *were* compensations, though.

Miraculously, a trace of her perfume had lingered, subtle yet heady in the moonlight. Her hair lay silky against his cheek, and her slender body nestled to him as if by right of long and familiar possession. Sure, she was distraught, trembling with fright and unlikely deliverance; but, as long as she needed to stay here and hold him, he'd tolerate a bit of discomfort. There had to be worse ways of spending an evening.

It couldn't last, naturally. The skyline blazed red; then darkness returned like a shroud. As the wind bored in and she quieted under his gentling hand, he read the yellow after-image printed on his brain: 'Burton's Beer, for Xmas Cheer.' Her response was lost in the tramp of approaching boots. Once more, he squinted into harsh torchlight. This time, the voice was familiar.

235

'Sar'nt Beddoes, I presume,' said Warner heavily. 'Snogging on duty, as usual.'

'Knock it off, yer daft ole berk! Can't you see I got casualties?'

'Saw lights,' Warner explained, with elaborate courtesy, 'and 'eard a kerfuffle. Sorry for the interruption, I'm sure.' The beam swung upward and his torch sharpened. 'Where's Huw?'

Beddoes told him, sitting and entrusting a reluctant Sara to a brace of hovering uniforms. 'Take it steady, lovely,' he advised. 'Be with you in a jiff.'

Warner had extinguished the torch and was staring, awed, at the dim and sinister warehouse.

'In *there*, with the Ripper? He's off 'is blooming head!'

'Yeah. It's bin one of those nights. 'Ere, help us up.'

Warner thrust his hands deep into his pockets and sniffed contemptuously. 'You're crippled, mate. Fat lot of use *you'll* be.'

Beddoes had removed his tie and was fumbling, numb-fingered, to improvise support for the damaged joint. Testing the knot, gritting his teeth against the spasm of pain, he grunted, ''E's *my* oppo. I'll bleedin' crawl, if I 'ave to.'

In the newest neon flare, Warner's expression softened, giving him the look of a wistful, jaundiced gnome. 'Fair enough. One of the best, old Huw. Wish I was ten years younger.'

'Jesus,' breathed Beddoes, upright and hobbling, 'you'll 'ave me in tears in a minute.' And more soberly, 'Best page the snipers, in case we need some fire power.'

'Will do. Mind 'ow you go, then.'

He did that, right enough. Beneath the makeshift strapping, his ankle felt about as solid as blancmange; outraged nerve ends throbbed at every step. Slowly, dripping sweat into this most frigid night, he laboured up three flights while the goddamn awful lights flashed on and off.

On the wind-torn upper landing an alleycat minced past, lean and arched and mangy. 'Ang about, Thomas, there's a super-rat at large. And plenty more besides. Sidling ever deeper into the fetid gloom, Beddoes saw the distant redness bloom in scores of tiny eyes and sensed a furtive rustling at his heels. He blundered forward, lame and unnerved, until the noise of his own passage brought him up short. *You're crossing badlands, sunshine, for Chrissake get a grip!*

He eased the gun from his hip pocket, relishing its cool and deadly weight. A whiff of cordite soothed him; nothing like a shooter to keep a bogeyman at bay. He was moving easier, the pain dwindling in the fever of the hunt and the nearness of lurking danger. Two rooms checked, three to go. Any moment, he'd be bumping into Huw. Or Chummy.

A waft of foul air, a stirring in the blackness ahead. He waited, taut and breathless, while the presence drifted closer, alien and blocky and silent as the grave. As he levelled the pistol, his finger curling gently on the trigger, his dry lips framed the challenge he dared not voice: friend or foe?

A festive message gave the answer. Filtering inwards, faint and pink, it shone on thinning sandy hair and threw the unmistakable outline into sharp relief. Evans, no less, unscathed and more than halfway home. Slack with release, blinking sweat and fatigue away, Beddoes shouldered arms and let him come. Your complete professional, Evans; poised and delicate as a wraith despite his bulk, soundless as the shadow he cast behind.

Shadow? *But the light was at his back!* The second silhouette reared above him, and neon flickered deadly on naked upflung steel. Shock took Beddoes like high voltage, raking his spine and rippling across his scalp. He stood, dumbstruck, while Chummy's face rose broad and full as a grinning orange moon. A wet wide mouth, a hungry glare, a leer of fiendish glee awash with the tint of blood. It was a vision of savagery beyond human ken, striking terror to the depths of Beddoes' soul. And the cleaver swung downwards in a great wide glittering arc.

Freed, too late, from paralysis, the pain a distant memory, Beddoes slipped instinctively into the marksman's crouch. Still unwitting, Evans loomed large and square in his sights, blocking off the target.

'Down, uncle,' he bellowed, drowning the song of the

blade. As Evans reacted, dipping into an oddly graceful curtsey, he aimed high and fired twice.

The reports erupted as one, echoing and re-echoing, mingling with a shriek of agony and the distinctive thud of fallen bodies. The muzzle flash blinded him; the red light went out.

Flattened to the wall, the gun thrust forward to repel boarders, he held his ground and charted a death in the darkness. A choked gurgle, a fading tattoo of heels, a final hideous rattle of breath. The silence reeked of blood and gunsmoke and his own harsh animal fear. Then, in utter revulsion, he heard the advance of the rats. Eager pattering, an excited squeak, a groundswell of small movement which seemed to pervade the entire building. Unseen scavengers avid for the feast; terrific.

Brightness, sudden and lurid. This time the redness was for real. It leaked from the mounded bodies, oozing over rotted boards and dripping thickly somewhere far below. He edged closer, the bile souring his tongue, the pistol trained but unsteady in his hand.

They sprawled together, peaceful and close as sleeping lovers. Chummy's head lay tilted back; his throat was a single yawning wound. That was the second shot, Beddoes thought; what happened to the first? He knelt, tense and awkward, the ankle aching fiercely once more. Gingerly, fearfully, he laid a hand on the stickiness which coated the whole of Evans' broad and motionless back. No response, not the smallest flicker of life.

A return of the dark, and Beddoes teetered on the verge. Inspector Evans, CID, dead in the line of duty. Cut down by a mate he trusted and a weapon he'd always despised. I didn't mean it, honest; what else could I do? As he rocked in anguish, hugging himself like a stricken child, his mind turned to the funeral, and Evans' own earthy remarks on the subject. 'Grey, it is, boyo; always. Mist on the mountain and a hush in the streets. Chapel heaving, and all with doctor's papers. Men only, see, best suits, beer and mothballs. Out in the rain, slow and stately, bare heads while you pass. Hymns and white lies at the graveside and into the boozer after to see you off tidy. The only way to go, mind.'

Only he wouldn't, thought Beddoes, bitter but steadying.

They'd give him the works, pipes and drums and a medal, probably. The Brass mouthing off to squads of bored beatmen who'd hardly known his name. Just two of your actual mourners: Roy Beddoes, Esq., and that randy little schoolmarm he thought no one knew about. And maybe Warner. What was it he'd said? '*One of the best.*' Amen. Jesus, uncle, I'm sorry.

The next fleeting glimmer, and the full horror of the scene sunk home. No way you can leave him there, my son, the uniforms'll be here soon. The media, too. He'd have to be moved, then, distanced from Chummy and other vermin; laid out decent, eyes closed and hands crossed, given a bit of dignity.

Beddoes hauled himself upright. Gently lifting a limp wrist, he leaned back and pulled. A big man, Huw, and he wouldn't budge easy. Setting his teeth for the pain, snarling at the watching circle of rats, he threw his weight against the solid, lifeless resistance. As sweat mingled with tears and the light died once more, he heard a gritty slither of heavy movement; and a weak Welsh voice complaining –

'The *other* shoulder, stupid; whose side are you on, anyway?'

CHAPTER TWENTY-TWO

'HE JUST walked in,' Sara said flatly, 'asked the university for my address and came straight here.'

'Jesus,' breathed Beddoes. 'They *told* him?'

'He said he was researching drop-outs.' She smiled, resigned and ironic. 'He knew the magic password, you see. Research.'

With Wilson going, Christmas coming, Evans off sick and the media getting restive, Beddoes was feeling a bit stretched; not much patience for witless intellectuals. 'Glad they're not *my* friends!'

'You mustn't blame them,' she murmured. 'I let him in myself.' Softly, appalled at herself, she added, 'Can you imagine? The man who raped me, and I didn't even recognise him!'

Appalled, maybe, but bearing up. He was skiving, looking to offer comfort and a shoulder to cry on; she didn't seem to need them. In some strange way, the latest outrage had tempered her. She used words like 'raped' and 'drop-out' casually, as if speaking of somebody else.

Taking liberties and an offhand tone, he told her, 'It was weeks back, he was wearing a mask. What d'you expect?'

'Not much, these days,' she admitted; but a ghost of the smile still lingered. Perched at the window, her litheness accentuated by a tight white seater, tapered jeans and unlikely winter brightness, she looked very tasty indeed. And remarkably composed, with it. There was a new maturity about her, a sense of battles won and fears dismissed. As she spoke of her ordeal, only an occasional tremor of voice and eye betrayed her.

'He wanted to talk and I let him. I was very frightened, at first. Babbling, I suppose.' She gave him a curiously beseeching sidelong glance. 'I didn't mean to tell him; I couldn't keep it back. That's why he insisted on calling you. You'd be sure to come, he said, as soon as he mentioned Delilah. Clever of him.'

'Cunning, you mean. A nutter, remember?'

'I'm not likely to forget.' She was staring fixedly into December sunshine, beset by ugly memories. 'He was going abroad; he needed my help for a while.' She faced him for the first time, letting him see the depths of her green-eyed anguish. 'Don't you understand, Roy? I realised he couldn't hurt me any more!'

'Yeah, sure. Till he chucked you off the fire escape.'

She shook her head, an impatient flurry of gold. 'Evans seemed so close, in the torchlight. I panicked and tried to run. Everything was confused; in the end, I think he tried to save me!'

A likely story. Only thing *he* wanted to save was his own bacon. Aloud, seeking to steady her, he said, 'It's down to the wind, believe me. The wind, and that sockin' great coat of yours. Floatin', you were, like a feather.' He shook his head and forced a grin. 'Talk about nine lives! Relax, lovely, you're booked to die in bed.'

She ignored both the joke and the hidden innuendo, clinging stubbornly to her own distorted perception. 'He was hunted and desperate, he only wanted to get away. He didn't mean any harm!'

Remembering the face of fiendish pleasure and the vicious hum of steel, Beddoes set her straight, once and for all. 'He was a monster, Sara, best off six foot under.'

She sat silent and withdrawn, in a state of almost wilful detachment. He reached for her and she shrank away, her face gaunt with distaste.

'It's what you wanted, isn't it, from the very start. His death brought home like a trophy – look, girl, I've avenged you. Don't touch me, Roy! There's blood on your hands, too.'

Hard to stomach, this, and it didn't ring quite true. She

241

wouldn't meet his eye, didn't believe it herself, really. Casting about for explanations, he noted subtle changes in her once-spotless little garret. Sunshine glinting on layers of dust and the odd book lying open; an end to exile and obsessive cleanliness. She was giving the college attitudes an airing before she went back – pity the poor loony and down with the Fuzz. Over the top, then, and who could blame her?

'Hey,' he said gently. 'It's me, Roy Beddoes, I'm on *your* side.'

She rose and began to pace. Despite the confinement and her apparent distress, she moved with a fluid, feline grace; easy on the eye. 'I'll always be grateful, Roy. I owe you ... a life. Whatever you want; you only have to ask.'

'But?' He was leaning back, watching her over his shoulder.

She stood like a lovely spotlit statue, her hands held up in supplication. 'You killed a man; you haven't shown a moment's remorse.'

'Too bleeding true; couldn't 'ave 'appened to a nicer guy. For Chrissake, girl, I'm a copper!'

'Yes. That's exactly what I mean.'

She was overdoing it, he reckoned. There was something familiar in her posture, something which took him back to another crowded cubicle and that first, fateful interrogation; *something to hide*. His gaze fell on the mantelpiece and the clue he should have noticed much, much sooner. Jesus, sunshine, call yourself a detective?

A solitary Christmas card, large and lavish, To Someone Very Special; the signature stood out bold and clear. The *real* reason, at last, and one he understood only too well. He climbed to his feet, managing a rueful, twisted smile. 'You should've told me, lovely. Rodders rules, OK?'

She swung to face him, her green eyes dark with sadness and a pride she couldn't quite conceal.

'I can't be *sure*, honestly. He makes me feel *secure*. I'd never have to watch him and wonder. He wasn't involved, you see; he's not – tainted.' She had never looked more appealing, a vision in blue and white and the warmth just waiting to bloom. Not for him, though.

'Yeah. When you put it like that ...' He shrugged helplessly:

what could you say? She came to him quickly, cool arms round his neck, a chaste and grateful peck.

'I'm so sorry, Roy.'

Maybe. But there was no mistaking the finality of the gesture. Well, at least she was back among the living; vibrant, you might say. Lucky Rodney.

'Me too, girl,' he muttered. 'Take care of yourself.' And left her, bearing a consolation prize he could do without, a tantalising glimpse of what might have been.

Rosie revisited, he thought, making for the nick under a faultless sky. You pick 'em up, heal their hurts, and they toddle off with heartfelt thanks and the boy next door. He'd been green, then. Now, according to Sara, he was past it. He'd have to test the premise on Pol. And Gloria. Let's face facts, you're not cut out for responsibility. In a day or two, you'll be calling it a narrow escape. Well, a month or two, then.

Waiting glumly for the lights to change, he wagged his head in disgust. You've lost your touch, my son; should've known the score from the start. She never even offered a cuppa ...

Evans had been back in harness barely an hour when the Super stuck his head round the door.

'I'm heading for the park. Care to join me?'

'Not particularly. Work to do, see.' He *ought* to see; files halfway to the ceiling.

'You're looking a trifle wan. The exercise will do you good.'

Evans glanced up, annoyed at his persistence. Dressed for the great outdoors, Wilson was, elegant as ever in hound's-tooth check and cavalry twills. 'It's my last day,' he explained. 'I thought we might clear the air.' A definite note of appeal, and the sun was shining; though you'd never tell, from here.

'What the hell,' growled Evans. 'Anything's better than typing, 'specially with one hand.'

Outside, unseasonable mildness and the Christmas spirit had mellowed the city; beneath their bowlers, even the pinstripe brigade could be seen to smile. Meanwhile, Wilson drove quickly and decisively, anticipating the gaps and using the gears like an expert. Relaxed, too. Throughout the short, bright journey, he kept up a stream of trivial shop talk; the Who's Who of police squash and plans for Warner's retirement party. Bandaged and bad-tempered, disinclined to join the general merriment, Evans sat tight and said little.

The park playground echoed to the sounds of Saturday; giggle and whoop, tears and tantrums, the creak of rusty swings and the rhythmic chant of the skippers. As they passed, a cherubic picaninny hailed them from the skyward end of the see-saw.

'*What* did he say?' spluttered Wilson, deeply shocked.

'Plucking donkeys, I think, sir.'

The Superintendent shot him a warning glare. 'No need to spare my blushes, man; I know a racial insult when I hear one. Donkeys, indeed!'

Not as naive as he seemed, then. Don't underestimate him, bach.

He swung off the path and struck out briskly across country. The bracken had died back and turned russet, and silver birches rose like lances against the hard blue sky. Very rural, really; a whiff of horses and the flight of birds. And Wilson, tall and tailored, your actual squire keeping a bene-volent eye on the ancestral acres. Struggling painfully in his wake, conscious of the date and the space between them, Evans felt a bit like the Wenceslas page.

As if reading the thought, Wilson slowed, squinting con-cernedly into the low sun. 'Sorry, I was forgetting. How *is* the shoulder, anyway?'

'Sore.'

'Of course. But only a flesh wound, I'm told. You were lucky.'

'Being alive, you mean, or getting shot?'

Wilson glowered, clearly disconcerted by the implications and stumped for an answer. For a while, they moved in uneasy silence.

They reached a copse of leafless saplings, a saucer-shaped hollow where last night's frost still crinkled the greenery underfoot. It was quiet and remote, not a soul in sight; the nick might have been eons away.

Wilson faced him, handsome and disdainful. 'There's something I wanted to say, before I leave. During this affair, you have challenged my authority, presumed on my private life, and run roughshod over established procedure. For you, doubtless, the end has justified the means. To that extent only, you were right and I was wrong. And much joy may it bring you.'

A bitter, back-handed compliment; yet, as the breeze eddied and a distant woodpigeon mourned, Evans felt the need for a grudging concession of his own. 'Know the one about making omelettes, do you? Rather break the *bad* eggs, I would. The machines helped, fair play. Without them, we'd still be clutching straws and counting the dead.' He cleared his throat, stirring the green and white slush with his toe. 'Said it before, remember? A shame to waste all that talent on *theory*.'

'Thank you,' said Wilson sarcastically, 'but I can do without charity from a *practitioner* like you!' He was climbing out of the hollow, his austere gaze seemingly focused on some private vision. 'So much we've been missing, so much to enjoy. Music, the theatre, a normal social life.'

Well, thought Evans, *one* of the Wilsons misses them. But the Super rambled on, as if to the most intimate of companions. 'We're thinking of starting a family – something I've always wanted.'

So *that* was it: covering the marital cracks with Paddington Bear wallpaper. Hopeless, really. When you can't get on together, kids'll only drive you further apart. And when the missus is a spoiled beauty with a roving eye ... In the end, Gina and a forgiving nature had undone him. Putting her above duty, he'd been unable to earn respect and simply wasn't nasty enough to command it.

Perhaps Wilson sensed the scepticism; maybe the glint of high-rise on the skyline brought him back. His brown eyes hardened, and hauteur returned to his tone. 'Pity Pavilides died. *What* a story he might have told!'

'Oh, sure. And a few more gory chapters. Handy for your thesis, but a bit rough on the victims.'

Wilson halted, colour and long-suppressed resentment darkening his face. 'It's beyond you, isn't it, abdicating the power you covet so dearly!'

'Me, *covet*? Not bloody likely!'

'Don't give me that! Chummy was trapped, every exit covered and enough artillery for a small war. Very well, why take risks? Why should Evans, the ultimate professional, go into the dark like some raw recruit?'

He'd wondered himself, often; in the wee hours when pain clawed and sweat sprang and a linger of ratreek overwhelmed the hospital carbolic. Now, while the Super waited and a mob of rooks took noisy flight, he found the answers. 'It was *my* case, messy or not. Friend Harry and his playmates, I mean; to say nothing of Beddoes' brainstorms and *your* little Irish games.'

He saw Wilson stiffen, and a gleam of sunlight on gritted teeth. Too bad.

'Messier still, after. Pictures don't do justice to his work, believe me. He dodged *my* trap and collared the girl *I* should have been minding. *He had to be stopped*, see: despite all the cock-ups, it was down to *me*!'

The birds were dark specks in the blue. Glancing down, he knew he'd wasted his breath. Wilson was hearing excuses, not reasons. 'Admit it, man! You were after glory and *my* job!'

Paranoid, he was, on account of his wife's betrayal; unfit for active service, unsuited to duty's demands. Leave it there, then.

Awkward and alone, nursing the ache in his arm, Evans limped over a rise into sudden awareness of surroundings. Playground bustle borne on the wind; weekend kickabouts, old dears gossiping, the scent of sunshine and a girl in pink, jogging.

'Can't you *feel* it?' he appealed, as Wilson approached. 'They're *safe*, see!'

There might have been a flicker of accord in Wilson's eyes; if so, it died young. He drew himself up, condescending as ever, and delivered the last word. 'Ah yes. But for how long?' And all the way back to the car, the inexorable answer tolled in Evans' mind: till the next time, boyo.

'Doggo,' Beddoes accused him later the same day. 'You were lying doggo, to give me a nasty turn!'

'Talk sense, mun! Numb, I was, and the roof down on my head. Blood like a fountain, bullets in the dark; expect me to sit up and wave, do you? Hard lines, Chummy, have another go?' The basement was a sauna, the mildest of winter days and the radiator going full bore: typical. Evans grinned, to hide the discomfort and temper the words. 'Doggo I'd've been, mind, if I'd known who was shooting. Bloody Rambo, you were.'

'Yeah,' muttered Beddoes. 'Sorry about that.'

An unlikely meekness, but he was looking a bit hunted and hangdog. Best to change the subject, then. 'How's Sara?'

Beddoes spread his hands, rueful and unbelieving. 'Amazing. After what she's bin through, she oughta be a nervous wreck. Not a bit of it. Over the worst, back to the studies, and shedding tears for poor ole Chummy. Women!' The tone and the smile betrayed him; bright and false as a game show compere. Evans couldn't resist another sly dig.

'Into the sunset with her rugby man, eh? Always said she had taste.'

'Walk soft, uncle,' Beddoes warned, 'or I'll stick the next one right between your beady little eyes!'

'Chance'd be a fine thing, boyo. Do that and you'll be minding the shop.'

Hunted he might be, but still pretty sharp. As he loosened his collar and shoved the Holroyd file aside, you could see him sniffing out the implication. ''Is nibs *is* leaving, then. Bound for the ivory tower, I hear. Pity.'

'Didn't know you were a fan,' mused Evans.

'I wasn't. Till lately, anyhow.' Beddoes leaned forward, his dark eyes alight with admiration. 'The media was ranting, believe me. Whodunnit, what about Mr Pavilides's rights, how come the Fuzz carried shooters? Put 'em straight, did Wilson. Previous record, the photo, Pippa's evidence, and a statement from Sara. Made it sound like the Lord's Prayer. Then 'e lays out the gun and the cleaver. "These are the weapons we found," he says, cool as you please, "and you ask why we requisitioned arms? Even now, a heroic officer lies at death's door; and you ask me to condone mass murder? Shame on you, gentlemen. No wonder the Empire's crumbling." Left 'em laughing at his expense, see. They lapped it up.' He sat restored, savouring his revenge. 'Only saved our bacon, and a college boy, mind you. Education's a marvellous thing; even had *me* wondering who did what.'

Well, well, thought Evans, so Wilson came good. Exit smiling, to roars of applause, and 'We'll Keep a Welcome' ringing in his ears. Power to his elbow; got his priorities right, in the end. Aloud, to Beddoes, he said, 'Remind you, shall I, of who did what?' and tapped his bandaged shoulder gingerly.

'Jesus, don't start that again!'

About to resume hostilities, Evans paused, struck by a distant sound. As he tilted his head and flexed his damaged arm, it came again, rising sharp and staccato above the fretful burble of the pipes. The ominous crack of iron-shod boots in the corridor, drawing nearer by the second.

'Ah,' he murmured, 'methinks the laird approacheth.'

'The *who*?'

'Listen, mun!'

'Sounds like the army to me.'

'Nearly,' said Evans, grinning. 'It's the *tartan* army, see.'

The door crashed open and McKay appeared, hard as nails and no old nonsense.

'Wee-el,' he rasped, 'and whut have we here? The dregs of the Manor, no doubt.' He stood, trap-mouthed and aggressive, his hair bristling like short, stiff flames. A devout Scot to his bootstraps, he was; you could almost smell the heather and brimstone.

'Ye can wipe the smirks off your stupid wee faces for a start,' he snapped. 'I'll no' tolerate insolence, dumb or otherwise!'

Beddoes was gawping, awed by the sheer vehemence; but Evans had to smile, inside. Comforting, really, the voice of authority, 'specially when you hadn't heard it for a while. A prize bastard, McKay, but with him around, you didn't need to guess who was in charge.

He stabbed a finger at Beddoes, exuding scorn and spraying saliva. 'As for *you*, laddie, you'd best be forgetting yon pistol. You'll not be putting *my* uniforms at risk. *Further*more, you'll conduct your whoring out o' sight of my nick. I cannae abide licentiousness.'

Beddoes had gone white with fury; stroking the lethal right

hand absently, on the verge of real foolishness again. The word 'whore' had upset him: cared for young Sara more than he was letting on. No wonder he'd taken it hard, up there on that lonely hill; where, unlike Wilson, he'd chosen duty and the Force. Rough time for him, fair play, and he'd come through pretty well. Some day, he'd be a damn good copper; daft to chuck it away on account of a routine bollocking.

'Cool head, Roy,' Evans muttered. 'It's the Super talking, mind.'

McKay turned on him, his eyes as cold as the lochs of his homeland. 'Whut's this? Inspector Evans, newspaper hero and the scourge of puir green graduates? Speak when you're spoken tae, man!'

'Ah, come on, Jock. It's a team we are, now.'

Quivering with outrage, McKay rose to his full height; only a whisker above regulation, Evans reckoned.

'I'm no' forgetting the last time, Huw Evans. We've scores to settle, thee'n'me. It's *sir* tae you; today, tomorrow, and into the great hereafter! Ye come creeping round *me* with your smarmy Welsh ways and I'll have ye brewing tea and minding the alsatians! *Mean*while, you'll hold your water, keep your place, and mebbe start earning your blasted salt!'

He whirled and stamped away, slamming the door behind him. Only a bit of imagination you needed to hear the skirl of bagpipes in the sudden hush.

'Gordon Bennet,' breathed Beddoes, in a long, respectful sigh. '*That's* the new Führer?'

'Sure. He's kind to animals, they say.'

Beddoes wagged his head and mopped the sheen of sweat from his brow. For some time he said nothing, his sharp features twisted in thought. Then he stood up, abrupt and purposeful, and made for the door.

'Where're you off to, boyo?'

'Down the youth club, mate. Time to come the heavy with that God-botherer and nick a couple of light-fingered Rastas.'

'Take it steady, then, else they'll have you for discrimination.'

'Let 'em try. In the mood, me.'

'You're in for trouble, more like.'

'So what else is new?' Beddoes' narrow face twisted cruelly. 'Speakin' of trouble, Warner's got news for *you*. Billy Stone's been at it again. Clobbered a pensioner down the docks and hasn't been home for three days.'

'Darro,' breathed Evans. 'He should be inside already.'

'You'll have to winkle him out; once more, for the cameras.'

They trudged the corridors in morose silence, passing the desk and Warner's fairy-lit Christmas tree without a trace of good will. Outside, it was grey and cheerless. The icy wind brought a hint of colour to Beddoes' cheeks and a ghostly grin to his lips.

'Got an idea, uncle, before we go back to the salt mines. Bit of Christmas shopping, see – present for his nibs.'

'Know what you're after, do you?'

'Yeah. Something to go under his kilt.'

'And what might that be?'

'Obvious, innit. A jockstrap.'

Hardly a vintage Beddoes pun, but at least the boy was trying; a glimmer of humour deep in the haunted dark eyes. Best to jolly him along, then, and hope work would complete the cure. Nodding gravely, Evans murmured, 'Extra small, mind, and lined with carborundum.' And for the first time in weeks, they both had something to smile about.